Acclaim for *Jack of Diamonds*

"At last, a highly unusual diamond thriller with a great plot, strong dramatic scenes and unexpected twists. Jack reminds me of Dick Francis' likeable, vulnerable lead characters who are easy to identify with. I enjoyed learning much about diamond mining and the gems market." - *Julian Gray, author, Interrogating Ellie*

"This gripping financial crime novel includes roller-coaster diamond and stock market speculation. The interweaving of the main plot and sub plots is masterly and they all move swiftly to their conclusions. In between are fascinating ideas on the psychology of market booms and how to handle them."

- Brendan Brown senior fellow Hudson Institute, and author Bubbles in Credit and Currency.

Neil Behrmann has written extensively on diamonds for the Wall Street Journal, The Business Times, Singapore and South African, Australian, Canadian and Hong Kong publications.

Besides gem scoops and features, Neil has also written numerous articles on mining and commodities. They range from gold, platinum, silver and copper to coffee, cocoa and sugar.

Neil's major news breaking stories and investigative features for the Journal, Business Times and other publications, include several billion-dollar scandals. They include rogue traders Nick Leeson of Barings and Yasuo Hamanaka, perpetrator of the Sumitomo copper fraud. Neil has covered underhand dealings in the mining industry, energy and coffee market crises. He also investigated and wrote a ground-breaking feature on the hidden hoard of former Philippines dictator Ferdinand Marcos. Other numerous pieces include Bernie Madoff and several other major hedge fund scams. Neil is currently London correspondent and columnist of The Business Times, Singapore, a leading Asian business publication. He has been interviewed on UK, US and Japanese TV and radio on diamonds, other commodities and mining.

Examples of his articles and columns are placed on http://neil-behrmann.net

Jack of Diamonds is a stand-alone sequel to *Trader Jack- The Story of Jack Miner*. Reviewers say that the first thriller in *The Story of Jack Miner* series is a page turner. See reviews on:- https://neilbehrmann.net/trader-jackstory-jack-miner/ and on Amazon.

Neil also wrote an anti-war fantasy, *Butterfly Battle- The Story of the Great Insect War*, which was published in 1998. The children's novel received exceptional reviews which can be seen on https://neilbehrmann.net/butterfly-battle/ and Amazon. Butterfly Battle was updated and relaunched to commemorate the 200th anniversary of the Battle of Waterloo. The opening chapter starts with a computer game on the 18 June 1815 battle.

JACK

OF
DIAMONDS

NEIL BEHRMANN

Paperback edition published 2018 by New End Books Ltd, London UK

ISBN 978-0-9533843-6-5

Cover Design by Ruth Mahoney

To Joy, Amy & Anna
for their help and encouragement

In Memory of my parents, George and Anne
and my brother Tony

PART ONE

THE LEARNING CURVE

1

THE NEW ME

The autumn light was fading fast, but Oleg Melnikov had still not returned from his daily walk. Several messages were left on his mobile. There was no response. A search party rushed to the forest, but in the encroaching darkness couldn't find him. They continued early the next morning and eventually found Oleg at the bottom of a gorge. His face was blue and frosted and a gash was on his forehead. The coroner ruled accidental death.

Yelena, Oleg's wife, protested that the ravine was a fair distance from the walking path. In late October, Oleg would have been wary of slipping. Snow had begun to fall, so it was highly unlikely that he had walked to the edge of the ravine and risked injury.

When the police and coroner broached the possibility of suicide, Yelena insisted that the very idea was preposterous. Oleg was certainly not depressed and was about to go to London to visit Sasha, their daughter.

The funeral was the biggest ever in Dobrenska, a small town that housed employees of the Dobrenska Diamond Mine. Oleg, a mining engineer, began working for Dobrenska soon after the Soviet Union collapsed in 1990.

Knowledgeable, efficient and popular, he was appointed manager of the mine and held the post for 20 years.

Dobrenska, situated in the north west of Russia and some 120 kilometres south east of Arkhangelsk, can be difficult to reach during winter. Since premature autumn snow and ice delayed her flight, Sasha Melnikov was too late for the funeral. When she at last arrived in Dobrenska, Sasha began to investigate the death of her father.

Prior to the coroner's inquest, Sasha had called a doctor friend and had asked him to examine Oleg's body. When she met the doctor in Dobrenska, he told her that he had doubts about the coroner's verdict. He was unconvinced that the fall into the gorge had caused the gash on Oleg's forehead. More likely it came from a hammer or another instrument. The doctor had also noticed bruises over the carotid artery. This indicated that someone held Oleg's neck in a "blood choke", causing him to lose consciousness. The doctor surmised that the assailant then hit Oleg on the forehead. This would give the impression that the fall had killed him. It was also possible that a fellow murderer helped dump the body into the ravine.

Despite the evidence, the police's forensic team didn't mention the possibility of foul play at the inquest. Sasha insisted that the case be reopened, but the coroner refused.

* * *

I was half dreaming about the circumstances of Oleg Melnikov's death, when I came round from my operation. What Sasha had told me, was unnerving.

My face felt sore, so I gently placed my hands over my nose and mouth and found that they were covered with bandages. Then it came back to me in a fuzzy sort of way. I was recovering from surgery. I would no longer be Jack

Miner. The new me would be unrecognisable, maintained Slater Stapler, the plastic surgeon. Mr Stapler had been brief and to the point before the procedure.

"This is not my usual sort of job."

"Sorry I'm no celeb," I said, attempting to crack a joke to relax myself.

"Don't be facetious," Stapler said in an irritated tone. "My job is to reconstruct the bits and pieces of soldiers who were blown up in Afghanistan, not wasters like you."

"You know something about me?"

"I gather you were in jail and obtained early release. You're supposed to help the police."

Plastic surgeons were supposed to be charmers who schmoozed their clients, but Stapler was obviously an exception.

"Not my normal sort of thing, but Scotland Yard twisted my arm on this one," he said.

"If you are against identity change, why are you doing it?"

"My brother is in a wheel chair because of the Russian mafia."

Stapler lifted my chin. With something that looked like a felt tipped pen, he marked my face, while I looked at the mirror in trepidation.

"Your face is thin. I'm going to flesh it out a bit."

"How are you going to do that?"

"Bit flabby here," he said, pinching the side of my hip and then digging his finger into it. "I'm going to use a syringe and suck out some fat from here and then inject it into your cheeks."

"I don't want a fat face," I protested.

"Your nose and mouth are too thin. They make you look shifty."

"Really?"

"Not after I'm finished with you. I'm going to broaden your nose and give you thicker lips to fit in with a fuller face."

"I ... I'll be chubby?"

"No. Your face will be rounder."

"What about my eyes?"

Stapler's smile was chilling: "That's your best feature. Blue, sky blue. Perhaps we should blot the left one out. Place a black patch there."

"Be careful... please!"

"See you in the morning. Remember, nothing to eat and drink overnight."

And that was how I ended up in my own private ward, prior to being transferred to a military hospital.

* * *

It was several weeks before the self-inflicted wounds began to heal in a hospital filled with soldiers wounded in the Afghan war. Compared to them, I had it easy. My time in prison was five years. They faced a lifetime without legs, hands, arms or other limbs. Many of them were suffering from disfiguring burns and post-traumatic stress was the norm.

There is no way I would have done this voluntarily. It was a painful necessity, an essential part of a deal with John Primeheart, Detective Chief Superintendent of Scotland Yard, International Branch. I was in the nick for a $7 billion fraud. My time was reduced on condition that I would help ferret out evidence to prosecute the mafia. Not the Sicilians or Americans; the Russian lot.

A few days before they let me out, Dr Klugheim, my prison psychiatrist, told me the good news.

"You're leaving because the Parole Board accepted my recommendation. I told them that you had responded well to therapy."

"I don't know how to thank you, Dr Klugheim."

"Don't deviate from the straight and narrow. An occasional share tip won't go amiss."

He chuckled; during my time, he had asked for tips and now had a sizeable pension.

"I also told them that you could be useful to Scotland Yard," he said.

"The Russian crime unit?"

"You can thank Detective Sergeant Sasha Melnikov. She persuaded Primeheart after learning about your scrapes with the Russian mafia."

"That doesn't make me an expert on Russian crime."

"What about the mining and hedge fund billionaire?"

"Yevgeny Faramazov? Doesn't he now have an aura of respectability? He bought the football club I support!"

"Melnikov is convinced that he's behind the murder of her father."

Klugheim opened my file and paged through the contents.

"What happens to me now," I said, breaking the silence.

"You're going to change your identity for your own security. Your first name will still be Jack, just in case you forget yourself in an unwitting moment."

"And my surname?"

"Sniper. Jack Miner will become Jack Sniper. All day, all night. Wake, work, play, sleep."

Klugheim passed me a book and told me to copy the first paragraph.

"You can read this later. Seems your handwriting slopes forward. Now try the reverse. Keep practicing. Pre-procedure medical documents or anything else will be signed *Jack Sniper*. Your passport, bank account, credit cards will be Sniper."

"Will surgery change my looks completely?"

"Plastic surgeons don't like admitting it in public, but their techniques have advanced considerably."

"What about friends who visited me in prison?"

"They will be told that you have been relocated for your own safety. I'm afraid you cannot be in contact again."

"Not even a Christmas card?"

"Totally forbidden."

"And you, Dr Klugheim? You've been a great help."

"I'm the exception. Now that I'm retiring, we'll find a way to keep in touch."

"What about *Trader Jack*?"

"That's the story of Jack Miner. From now onwards you are Jack Sniper. You will be released tomorrow and go straight to hospital."

* * *

Luckily for me, the weeks passed swiftly and my new face began to take form. After all that time in the nick I had become used to waiting. I read a lot, including Primeheart's books on criminal investigations and Sasha's papers on Russian corruption. She also gave me information about questionable deals during the "wild east" capitalism under former Russian President Boris Yeltsin. Dr Klugheim suggested publications on psychopaths.

To be frank, I was somewhat anxious when they let me out of prison. Five years is a long time in there. You get used to a sheltered routine without any responsibility. How would I perform outside?

There was also an emotional struggle. After fighting my own corner inside, I had, on the surface, become tough, hard and somewhat bitter. Inwardly, however, I craved affection and warmth. My mother had died when I was a boy and my father when I was a teenager. Several people had helped me and became good friends. The serious downside of my new identity was that I could never see them again. I could endanger them and myself and alert Faramazov. Hopefully he and his gang would be prosecuted and be put away for years. Then I could fall in love, get married, have a family and put my past behind me.

I realised that my own problems and fears were self-indulgent, compared to the wounded. They were learning to cope with their artificial limbs and scarred bodies. After being severely damaged in the war against Taliban guerrillas, their bravery and camaraderie was exceptional. The generals had asked for more troops and this meant that growing numbers of new casualties were pouring into hospital. I shared a ward and night after night screams of soldiers woke me.

In the morning, the physically and mentally wounded put on brave faces. They had the discipline and faith to accept visits from padres, generals and politicians who wandered through the wards mouthing cheerful words of encouragement. Frantic families waited and prayed that their boys wouldn't join the growing tally of bodies that were taken out of the wards; that they would not be attending the ritual military burial; that the Prime Minister wouldn't be reading out their names perfunctorily, before answering questions in parliament.

Soldiers kept asking the name of my unit and where I had been wounded. I told them that it was a military secret and I could not discuss it.

* * *

When the wounds had healed, I was happy to see that my features were more chiselled and angular than before. I had a stronger jawline, my nose was longer and my cheek bones were higher. My mousy blonde hair was now cropped. Happily, the new Jack was more handsome than the old, but it still took me a lot of time to adjust.

Sasha Melnikov was my first and only visitor. She was wearing a dark blue suit, holding a large, matching handbag and her dark glasses reflected the sunlight. We walked to the far, quiet end of the hospital garden and Sasha took off her glasses. She was stunning. Grey blue eyes contrasted with a tanned complexion and her black glossy hair's long waves rippled down her lower back. Half smiling at my reaction, she clinically began to examine me. First my face, then my profile and finally, the back. She then took out some enlarged old photographs from her bag and compared them to me.

"What Stapler has done is really something," she said.

We had a brief walk around the garden, sat on a bench and Sasha got down to business.

"My father was trying to defend Dobrenska from a hostile takeover. Valdia, a mining and oil conglomerate, was the predator."

"And then they find him at the bottom of a canyon," I said. "You believe that Faramazov's hitmen killed him?"

"Convinced. He's a major stakeholder in Valdia."

"If Valdia won the takeover battle, why didn't they sack your father? Why murder him?"

Her wince made me feel a little guilty for being insensitive, but she swiftly steadied herself and continued. It seemed that detective work had hardened her.

"You have to understand the history. Russia was seeking foreign investment after the Soviet Union collapsed. Trekdiam, an Australian company, discovered Dobrenska's diamond deposit. Its deal with the government was to raise finance, develop the mine and produce diamonds. In return, Trekdiam would get a stake in the company and manage the mine."

"How big a stake?"

The State was Dobrenska's majority shareholder. Trekdiam, mine managers and workers owned the remaining shares."

"So the State's mining officials accepted Valdia's offer."

"At a derisory price. Trekdiam directors were furious. Oleg and the miners, too. Trekdiam decided to take action in the London High Court.

"On what grounds?"

"There was a legal window. In terms of the initial deal with the government, Trekdiam retained exploration rights within the Dobrenska area. Trekdiam claimed that Valdia's acquisition didn't cover the rights."

"Another rich diamond deposit?"

"My father's geological tests were promising. If Oleg were still alive, he would have been Trekdiam's key witness. He was going to stay with me. I had booked some shows."

"And they killed him because he knew too much," I said. "The usual stuff, corruption, bribes…"

Sasha stood up, grabbed a red dahlia nearby, tore off the petals and muttered something in Russian.

"Faramazov has top contacts in Russia's mining department and the FSB," she said.

"The Russian Federal Security Service? Are you saying that FSB agents were involved?"

"It wouldn't surprise me."

"How are you going to prove all this?"

"That's where you come in. Before we give you instructions, you will have to learn how to protect yourself; have a spell in the army, get super fit and handle arms. After that an intensive police course. You will then be an agent of my unit. It has links to Interpol."

* * *

Out of hospital at last, I began my basic training. Not with the police force, but with a Scottish infantry regiment, preparing for action in Afghanistan. The five other guys who shared our barracks were much stronger and fitter than me. We were woken at 5a.m., sometimes 3a.m. in the morning. Our bungalow had to be squeaky clean, beds made to perfection and overalls and uniforms ironed and spotless. Fortunately, I had learnt how to iron and sew in prison, so I helped my new mates, Charlie Munger, Bill "Stoney" Stoneheart and some of the other guys with these tasks. Our daily routine was square bashing for an hour or two in the morning, physical exercise, sprints, long distance running and stringent obstacle courses.

Route marching with full pack was up and down the Scottish Highlands. I tailed behind the others, but Charlie and Stoney helped me. Charlie, medium height with thick arms and an acne scarred face, had shaved off his hair. He didn't manage to finish school and tired of being unemployed had decided to join the army against the wishes of his mother. Stoney, tall, wiry and tanned had also been jobless for several years. He was brighter and more educated than Charlie and was most definitely officer material. Both had thick Glaswegian accents.

The troops cursed and sweated on route marches. It was tough work struggling with our hefty packs up the steep mountains; but at the top, magnificent open spaces and views overwhelmed me. Out in the open after being confined for five long years, the fresh air gave me a wonderful feeling of freedom. My sense of smell seemed to be greater than fellow troopers. They were puzzled during rest periods, when I lay flat on my tummy and brushed the thick

grass with my nose; smiled when I pointed at the different
shades of green on bushes and trees. Appreciating nature's
multi-layered variations, I would pick up white and yellow
daisies and follow the flight of butterflies and birds.

Sometimes, truck drivers dumped us in an unfathom-
able place after dark. We could hardly see each other at
close quarters. The task was to find our way back to the
barracks from either dense woodland, mountains or valleys.
My night sight, hearing and smell had become so acute,
that I invariably led the way.

Then there were bouts of hand to hand combat, shooting on the run with automatic assault rifles and hand guns.
Simulated targets popped up all over the place. I do not
know how I managed to hit the bulls-eye so often, but
it was lucky that I could live up to my new name. They
even placed me in elite sniper squads while the others had
machine gun and missile training.

The months of army training passed by swiftly, as
we were so active. Compared to prison when I counted
the days, the daily routine was interesting and varied. I
was lean and fit and had a ruthless instinct for survival.
It was now time to go to Hendon Police College, north
London. There I attended courses on crime and analytical
and forensic intelligence. The operational techniques and
disciplines required to charge offenders, showed me life
on the other side.

* * *

I continued to follow the army's fitness regime in Hendon and was about to leave my room for a long run, when
there was a knock on the door. John Primeheart and Sasha
Melnikov were outside.

Sasha wore a fitted purple dress that fell just above

the knee and high heeled, long leather boots. She had cut her hair and it was now a shaggy bob. Primeheart, tall and imposing, was casually dressed.

On the face of it, they were off duty, but their stern expressions warned me that they were not.

"Hello Sniper, how are you getting on?" Primeheart asked.

"Fine thanks, but I miss the other guys."

"You won't be seeing them again. They have been sent to a detachment in Afghanistan."

"Can I contact them? They must be wondering what happened to me."

"Not possible, Jack. You're ready for the next stage of your mission," Sasha said.

"You're off to South Africa to learn about your new identity," Primeheart continued, in a flat, matter of fact way.

Sasha passed me a South African passport. Jack Sniper, born in Springs, South Africa.

"You've already given me a British passport."

"Dual nationality will be useful. South Africans don't need Russian visas."

I opened the two passports and compared them. They weren't brand new. Both had been doctored with indiscernible travelling stamps.

"Springs is a small mining town, about thirty miles east of Johannesburg. You're taking over the identity of John Sniper," Sasha said. "He was killed when a gang attacked him."

"I need to know more."

"You will, when you meet his mother. She's British, but emigrated to South Africa several years ago. We want you to know everything about your previous life and where you come from."

"What about John Sniper's family? Where he was

buried? His death certificate?"

"He was cremated. His father died when he was young. His mother still lives in Springs," Sasha said. "She's become a counsellor, specialising in post-traumatic stress disorder."

"Detective Sergeant Watson Nkozi is our man in South Africa. He's been in contact with Sally Sniper," Primeheart said. "Nkozi assures us that she wants to help and will be discrete. We have contributed to her post-traumatic stress charity."

"You are the reborn Jack Sniper," Sasha said, while she scrutinised my new face yet again. "We chose the identity of the late John Sniper to give you a 'mother'--- a more realistic life history."

"Reborn? Resurrection? Me?"

"Very funny," Sasha said. "We can thank Nkozi. It was his idea that your identity should be South African."

"Why the mining town?"

"Two options. You can infiltrate Faramazov's organisation or join an investment bank as a mining analyst. Either job should help you monitor his businesses," Sasha said.

"Faramazov is active in exploration and development of African, South American and Asian gold, diamond and platinum mines," Primeheart added. "South African geologists, mining engineers and metallurgists are sought after."

"I don't know much about that stuff."

"That's another reason why you're going to South Africa. You'll have a good teacher."

"Who?"

"Fred Carrender. You told us about him when you were in jail. Remember? We've checked his credentials and integrity. He's a leading geologist and is prepared to help."

"Carrender will give you a solid background and understanding of practical geology. You can study the theory in your spare time," Sasha said. "Your biography written in prison, shows that you have a proven ability to absorb new subjects quickly."

"Fred Carrender! He knew my dad. He'll know who I am."

"No way. You're now Jack Sniper. You briefly met Carrender years ago. As far as he is aware, Jack Miner is still in prison."

"I won't be able to keep it up."

"Don't worry. You'll be fine. Just remember we have an agreement. Don't break it. You're effectively on parole," Primeheart said.

"No way I'm going back to prison. I've been reading Stanislavski. I'll get right into the head of Jack Sniper."

Primeheart looked puzzled.

"He's referring to Constantin Stanislavski, the Russian actor and director who developed method acting," Sasha said with a wry smile. "Marlon Brando was a famous exponent of the method. Daniel Day Lewis, another. The actor becomes the character. Gets inside the head, as Jack puts it."

"What if the Faramazov lot ask for my qualifications?"

"You are a graduate in geology from Witwatersrand University, Johannesburg. Detective Nkozi has contacts at the University. Jack Sniper is now on its data base. Nkozi also managed to obtain the relevant graduation certificates," Primeheart said.

"What about John Sniper's class at university? His friends? Most people in the mining business know each other. I might come across them."

"John didn't go to university and wasn't a miner. According to Nkozi, most of his friends have emigrated from South Africa. If by chance you meet them, you should be vague; indicate that you're a cousin or relative."

"Hmm… I presume Sally Sniper, will cover for me."

"Precisely. That's what mothers do."

"I guess I'll have to improvise. What about the accent?"

"Listen to the South African broad vowel sounds. Learn a bit of Afrikaans, Zulu, Xhosa and Fanagalo," Sasha said.

"You seem to think I'm a linguistic genius. What's Fanagalo?"

Sasha couldn't help but grin.

"It's a mix of languages. Miners speak Fanagalo underground. Nkozi's father was a miner, so he knows all about it."

Primeheart shook my hand in a cold, offhand way: "You'll be staying with Nkozi's family. He'll take you around Springs and will allow you to tail him and other detectives. Good luck Mr Sniper. Enjoy your trip. You'll be hearing from us in good time."

2

THE IDENTITY

Detective Sergeant Watson Nkozi met me at O.R. Tambo International Airport, midway between Johannesburg and Springs. We drove to Kwa Thema, a sprawling township on the edge of Springs, about thirty miles east of Johannesburg. Kwa Thema was created during the Apartheid era, Nkozi explained. South African blacks then had to live in separate areas, away from whites.

"The vast majority of blacks still live in Kwa Thema, Soweto and other townships in the new democratic South Africa," Watson said. "They're happy to be with their old friends and communities, but the main reason is the Apartheid of wealth. They can't afford to live elsewhere."

Watson's home was in one of the better areas of Kwa Thema, but before taking me there, he showed me a shanty town nearby. Families were living in corrugated tin shacks, without electricity and water.

"We still have extreme levels of poverty," Watson said. "South Africa is a long demographic train that struggles up a steep hill. At each stop, another coach joins on."

"The combination of a high birth rate and rising unemployment?"

"Yes, but we also have extensive illegal immigration.

Refugees are fleeing across our borders from Zimbabwe and other unstable African countries."

Watson, about fifty, with dark greying hair, rugged features and thick strong arms, insisted on carrying my luggage into his house. It had a tiny garden in front and an Alsatian bounded up to the gate.

"Don't worry, he's friendly. Just relax and pat him on the head."

"I had a dog once. Miss him," I said patting and tickling the Alsatian on the back of his ears. "What's his name?"

"Angus. Named after a Scottish friend, when I was on a course at Scotland Yard. Wait until you see him work. He has rescued me from tight spots."

The dog led the way to the door. Watson's wife, with a pretty round face and bouncy African curls, greeted me warmly.

"Hey guys come and meet Jack," Thandi shouted, after Watson introduced us. "Give Facebook a break."

Watson grinned, when the children arrived.

"Yolande and Jim, this is Jack."

Their daughter, who smiled shyly when she greeted me, seemed to be about fourteen. She had straightened her thick black hair and tied it in a loose pony tail, which rested halfway down her back. The boy, sixteen, bore a striking resemblance to his father, but towered over him.

Jim carried my suitcase into a small room with a single bed and lots of books. Noticing that the house was tiny and that there were only three bedrooms, I insisted that I stay in a hotel. If not, I could sleep on the sofa.

"Not to worry. Jim's off to a camp next week," Thandi said. "Relax. Have a shower. The flight from London is a killer."

* * **

Early next morning, Jim woke me up: "Time for a run.

Pops told me to keep you fit."

"What about Watson?"

Jim grinned. "Can't keep up with me; bit older than you."

We ran through the township passing a long line of small brick houses and a new housing development. Then towards the main road that led to Springs' town centre. Men and women were either walking, or on cycles on their way to work. Jim had to keep Angus on a lead and kept pushing me to the side of the road as there were numerous large "combi" taxis.

"Careful! They drive like maniacs," he said.

At last we managed to get away from the traffic into open dry veld. I struggled to catch my breath and keep up, so Jim stopped to let me rest.

"And I thought that I was fit!"

"It's the altitude. We're on the Highveld, about 5,000 feet above sea level. Football players have to condition themselves."

"What position do you play?"

"Midfield. Coach says I'm good enough to be professional, but Pops wants me to go to university."

We ran for another couple of miles and once again I had to stop and drink some water. We were now on a hill overlooking some sandy old clay workings. Further on I noticed some industrial sites.

"Springs had a coal mine just over a hundred years ago. It supplied the energy for Johannesburg's gold mines," Jim said. "They then discovered gold on some farms here. At one time, there were about thirteen mines around Springs."

"Springs Mines, Daggafontein, Grootvlei, Vogels," I said, recalling my gold share trading before I went to jail.

"You've heard of those mines?"

"A South African friend told me about them. I thought

there would be a lot of gold mining dumps around here."

"You'll only see remnants. When the price began to soar, gold specs were extracted from the dumps and refined into bars.

"How come the waste didn't pile up on dumps again?"

"It was a brilliant operation. They pumped the waste down the shafts of old mines. There are now large flat areas for factories and houses."

Jim had given me my first mining lesson. Very different from gold share dealing.

* * *

The next day Watson drove me to one of the suburbs in Springs, a nondescript town on the "East Rand".

"Rand is Afrikaans for reef--- the underground rock that contains gold," Watson explained. "In the 1880s, gold was discovered on a farm near Johannesburg. Geologists then found that the reef continued to the East, where we are now. Later they found gold on the "West Rand", the Western Reef. They're still mining there."

We drove to a housing enclosure in Selection Park, one of Springs' suburbs. The detached bungalows, which were in a wide circle, surrounded a small rose garden. A security guard, behind a barrier peered at me suspiciously, but after Watson showed him his police identity, we were allowed to enter the gated development.

"Crime is rife. Tsotsis don't only rob., They kill and maim," Watson said.

"Tsotsis?"

"Gangsters. They murdered my father when he was on a train. Snatched his wage packet and pushed a knife into his spine. I was only fifteen at the time and decided to join the police."

"That's awful, Watson. How did your family survive?"

"Like most poor black families. They pull together. Fathers, mothers, teenagers, go out to work and pool their money. When my father died, I had to leave school and become a gardener and caddy."

"Why don't the Tstosis just rob? Why kill and rape?"

"Jealousy, bitterness and hatred. It's a legacy of Apartheid. Whites made money and had the best salaries, homes, education, healthcare, sports facilities. Everything. Blacks were the disadvantaged underclass, who had to carry passes in white areas."

"That's understandable, but Apartheid ended years ago. South Africa is now a multi-racial democracy. The African National Congress is in power."

"Sure. Growing numbers of blacks are becoming richer and several are multi-millionaires. Many blacks have good jobs and earn good money. I'm happy with my salary and Thandi is a teacher. We have enough to educate our children and go on holiday. But for others, life is without hope. They turn to crime and we police don't have the resources to cope."

* * *

Wearing dark glasses to help me obscure myself from nosy neighbours, I pressed the security button of Mrs Sniper's home. It was surrounded by a high fence with spiked poles, not surprising, considering what had happened. John, her only child, was about to go to university, when a gang hijacked his car. John tried to stop them and was shot. He lay in a coma for weeks until Sally Sniper reluctantly agreed that he should be taken off the life support machine. Aware that her tragedy was far from rare, Mrs Sniper told the police that she would help them fight crime.

The gates opened and we walked to the house via a short pathway that was between a small garden and a swimming pool. Sally Sniper was sitting in a conservatory, filled with Proteas and other tropical flowers. In her late fifties, she had short brown, greying hair and a face lined by the sun.

Sally stood up to greet me just as I took off my dark glasses. Her face seemed to turn white and she began to wobble. Watson moved swiftly to support her and help her sit down.

"My God, you could be John's twin."

I glanced at the large photo of her late son on the mantelpiece and then a mirror nearby. Stapler hadn't shown me photos of the late John Sniper. His work was remarkable.

"I'm sorry, I did...didn't know about your tragedy," I stammered. "I only heard about it last week. I knew that I was going to be someone else, but I thought that he had died years ago."

"It's OK Jack," Sally said, recovering slowly from the shock. "Watson approached me and told me that you would be needed for an urgent job. We must fight crime. My son would have agreed."

While we were having tea, we went through her photo albums of John Sniper from babyhood to university, before he was cruelly struck down. Sally tried to hold back her tears when she turned the pages and chatted about happy memories.

"My husband died when John was a child, but it is John I keep thinking about. He was an only child, you see... The years pass by, but it's like yesterday. What a waste."

"I hope we can be friends," I murmured, embarrassed that we were using her.

* * *

Later Watson drove Sally and I around the town and then to her son's former school. At Springs Boys High, John Sniper played cricket and rugby for the first team, was a swimmer who won medals and passed with distinction in maths and science. Afterwards we drove to the centre of the town where John went to movies, clubs and the Civic Theatre. The library was near an Art Deco Fire Station that was built in the nineteen twenties. We passed the Springs Country Club and Pollack Park golf courses, where he played golf and tennis.

After taking Sally Sniper for lunch and then home, Watson drove past Springs' industrial sites that had a diamond research laboratory, glass, tools and other factories. We passed Kwa Thema and went through the small towns, Brakpan, Benoni, Boksburg and Germiston, on the way to Johannesburg.

"The towns were founded near the gold mines," Watson said. "That's ERPM, where my father worked."

He pointed towards the shaft of the goldmine, which was near Boksburg: "He used to go down early in the morning and finish late at night."

We continued westwards until we came to Johannesburg, a large sprawling City and then drove to Witwatersrand University, where I, Jack Sniper, was supposed to have been a geology student.

"What happens if I bump into friends and relatives of John Sniper?" I asked while we wondered around the campus.

"His close friends have emigrated to Australia. Sally Sniper was an only child and has no close relatives. Cousins are in England."

"There must be a risk that I'll come across them. What should I do then?"

"You'll have to play it by ear, Jack."

"What if a future colleague went to his funeral?"

"Vowels, Jack Vowels! Get into that South African accent. Sally told me that John didn't have close friends. He was a bit of a loner. I'll try and check out who went to the funeral--- just in case."

"Ag maan I'm Saath African," I said, doing my best to mimic the accent

I was now beginning to feel seriously uneasy about "Operation F", the investigation into Faramazov's global businesses. Initially it was an interesting and enjoyable experience; great to be free and travelling after being cooped up in prison. Now reality was facing me.

Watson noticed my tension and gave me a tour of the northern suburbs of Rosebank and Sandton, with their sparkling shopping centres and plush hotels. There the white and black elite were dressed fashionably, isolated from the despair of the disadvantaged. The fear of crime, however, was ever present. Private security vans roamed around and security men and women made their presence felt in every building. It was difficult to pass through residential roads without coming across a guard. Through the barriers, home after home had high fences, security gates and intricate alarm systems. This was Johannesburg, one of the violent crime capitals of the world. People went about their business, seemingly happily, but they were street wise and acutely aware that random criminal acts could happen at any moment.

3

DIAMOND SMUGGLERS

During the following weeks, I tailed Watson while he worked on several cases ranging from petty theft to burglaries and murders.

Watson was a meticulous detective but it was exceedingly difficult to find adequate evidence and witnesses to prosecute. He complained that the police force was undermanned and that many officers were corrupt.

"If we persist, we'll get them. Look for detail, detail, detail, the smallest detail, Jack. Listen for a slip in the tongue."

We went to Soweto, the city that spawned the anti-Apartheid revolution in the 1970s and later to its Baragwanath Hospital. It was Friday and unfortunate victims of Tsotsi knifings, were patched up or delivered to the mortuary, after being mugged for their weekly wages.

"The whites complain about crime, but we've had to face it for a long time," Watson said.

* * *

I had just returned from a run a few days later, when Watson shouted: "Hurry up, we have an interesting case.

Customs have detected diamonds at the airport."

Before questioning the suspect, Watson Nkosi had briefed customs officials to repack his suitcase and put the diamonds back in their hiding place. The suspect, Pacy Palatus, was an American student who had flown in from Windhoek, Namibia. Sniffer dogs had smelt a reefer of pot, which was hidden in his socks, so customs searched for hard drugs. While they were doing so, they found seemingly unopened tubes of toothpaste, shaving and sun cream in the wash bag. They placed them through the X-ray machine and noticed that they contained gems. Since Palatus had arrived from Namibia, a country rich in diamonds, they drew the obvious conclusion and called Watson. He told them to leave the tubes untouched and not to begin the interrogation.

When we arrived, Palatus was in a small customs interview room after being detained there for about two hours. Tall and thickset with brown hair, he was dressed in jeans, a plain t-shirt and trainers. Watson began the interview with a CCTV camera and recorder on, but didn't refer to the diamonds. Sam Mtetwa, an airport detective, sat next to Watson, opposite Palatus. I was in a chair nearby, observing Palatus' reactions.

"Name, address and occupation," Watson said, as Mtetwa passed him the passport and air ticket.

"Pacy Palatus. 15 Avondale Road, San Francisco. I'm a student studying anthropology at the University of California. I've been in Namibia for a month to research and meet Bushmen for my final year project."

"Pot is legal in California," Watson said as he took the reefer from Mtetwa. "You obviously know that it's unlawful here."

"I'm not a dealer, I promise you," Palatus insisted. "I just like a smoke from time to time. I clean forgot that I had left a reefer there. We had a party before I left and I packed in a hurry."

"Cannabis is called dagga in South Africa. Ours is very potent. What other drugs do you take?"

"Nothing else."

"Hmm. How long do you intend staying in South Africa?"

"A week. I have to do more research on Bushmen at Witwatersrand University's Anthropology Department. Then I'm flying to Europe to meet my girlfriend."

"Where is she?"

"In Madrid. She's studying Spanish history of art."

"So that's why you're flying with Iberia and not an American airline," Mtetwa said.

"Yes, sir."

Watson nodded at Mtetwa who left the interview room and came back with Palatus' belongings. He placed the suitcase on one side of the table.

"I know that customs officers have already carried out the search. Do you mind if we double check? Drugs are a serious problem in South Africa. We cannot be too careful."

"Sure. I have nothing to hide," Palatus said, as he fidgeted with a pen.

"Could you unlock your case and place all the items on the side of the desk?" Mtetwa asked.

Palatus began to unpack while we observed him silently. Shirts, trousers, boxers, socks, towels were neatly placed on one side. Books on the Bushmen and files with his research and writings, were piled next to them. A small package was opened and it contained wooden carved animals. Mtetwa picked up a carved knife that looked like ivory.

"Do you know that ivory is illegal? We're trying to protect the African elephant."

Palatus was startled.

"They told me it was a plastic copy. Not ivory."

"Let me see. Oh yes, very realistic. What are these?" Watson asked as he emptied a small bag.

"Just some worthless semi-precious stones. Cost me about ten dollars in a Windhoek market."

All Palatus' belongings were now on the table and Watson casually pointed at the wash bag.

"Could you empty that please."

Out came a razor, blades, a toothbrush, small scissors, an athlete's foot powder container, plasters, a small box of condoms, two large toothpaste tubes, a large tube of shaving cream, and sun and foot cream tubes.

Watson observed Palatus silently and then smiled: "I think we can let you off with a warning this time, Mr Palatus. Don't bring in pot next time. This isn't California."

Palatus, sighing with relief began putting his things back into the wash bag.

"Seems you have a lot of toothpaste, Mr Palatus. Do you think that South Africa is an outback?" Watson said with a chuckle and he leaned over casually and picked up a tube.

Palatus looked puzzled and said nothing.

Suddenly, without warning, Watson passed the tube to Mtetwa. He squeezed it hard while Watson observed Palatus' face intently. Several small stones came out and landed on the surface of the table. Palatus' expression was a combination of horror and amazement. Mtetwa squeezed all the tubes and out came more uncut diamonds. He took out a Swiss army knife, cut off the tubes' nozzles and managed to push out some more gems. Mtetwa then took photos of the stones and slashed tubes. After that, he used some tissue paper to clean off the toothpaste and cream from the diamonds. He placed the stones in a neat pile and took another photo. While this was happening Palatus, who was becoming more and more agitated, glanced at the CCTV camera and tried to control himself.

"I swear I did not know they were in my bag. I'm not a diamond smuggler."

"Who said that we were accusing you?" Watson said in a gentle, soft tone. "We were merely going to ask you how these gems were miraculously inserted into your tubes of toothpaste and creams; how they came to be in your luggage."

Palatus was breathing heavily.

"Those people at Windhoek airport must have set me up."

"Please tell us how," said Watson with exemplary patience.

"There was a large crowd of people when I arrived at the airport. When I was about to check in, I found that my passport and ticket were missing."

"Where did you put them?"

"In the pocket of my jacket. I was carrying it because it was hot."

"You were rushing through the crowd and they fell out of the pocket?"

"I guess so."

"What did you do about it?"

"I was in a panic. I sat down and went through all my pockets and hand luggage again and again. A couple who had sat down near me, noticed what I was doing and asked if they could help."

"What did they do?" Watson asked.

"They were sympathetic. The man called a security officer nearby. The officer suggested we go to the lost property office. The man and I went to the office. The woman said that she would look after my luggage. Luckily my passport and ticket were at lost property. Someone must have picked them up."

"How long was your luggage left with the woman? Surely you're aware of airport rules?" Mtetwa said.

"She was very kind and helpful. I trusted her."

"For how long was the luggage in her possession?" Mtetwa repeated.

About five to ten minutes at the most. Enough time to..."

"Plant the tubes in your suitcase. But you had to unlock it here. How did she manage to mysteriously place them in your case?" Watson asked.

"When I was looking for my passport, I unlocked the suitcase. I was so stressed that I must have forgotten to lock it again."

"Officer Mtetwa can you call Windhoek lost property? Ask them whether they have a record of his passport and ticket," Watson said.

"No problem," Mtetwa replied and he left the room.

Watson passed a bottle of water to Palatus. He was sweating, despite the air conditioning.

"Describe the couple," Watson said.

"They looked respectable and were good to me. As I said before, they were patient and helpful. The guy was lean, looked in his forties and had a Spanish accent. He was in a light brown suit. Designer."

"And the woman?"

"She was Namibian. Elegant. Had a gold necklace and diamond ring."

Silence, while Palatus drank his water and relaxed a little.

"Windhoek lost property does have a record of the passport and ticket, Mtetwa affirmed when he walked into the room. "They said that the owner claimed them about half an hour after they were handed in."

"Told you. She must have planted the tubes in my wash bag. I brush my teeth with Sensodyne toothpaste. Those tubes are Colgate. I didn't pack sun cream."

With his left hand, Mtetwa pushed the small pile of diamonds closer and examined them. Then he took out a tissue and wiped off the remaining toothpaste and shaving cream while we observed silently. The action seriously unnerved Palatus and his face began to twitch.

"I swear I'm not an illicit dealer. I would never have anything to do with conflict diamonds. I've read that diamond dealers only accept certified diamonds."

"You seem quite knowledgeable about diamonds for an anthropology student," Watson said. "Wait here, we'll decide what to do with you."

Watson, Mtetwa and I went into the observation room and watched Palatus. The diamonds were still on the table. He moved his hand towards them to pick some up, but quickly withdrew. He then shook his head and sat there looking dejected.

"What do you think they are worth?" I asked.

"They seem to be top quality gems ranging from a half to two carats," Watson said. "Difficult to say. About $100,000, maybe."

"What are certified and conflict diamonds?"

"De Beers, other diamond mining companies and gem dealers in Antwerp, Tel Aviv and Mumbai have an agreement to prevent trade in 'blood diamonds'," Mtetwa said. "The aim is to monitor diamonds that are mined in conflict areas and are sold to finance wars."

"How can dealers be sure that they are not buying blood diamonds?"

"Expert dealers can gauge where gems come from and are only allowed to trade in certified diamonds. If they believe that the diamonds are from war zones, the gems cannot have certificates," Mtetwa replied. "The system is known as the 'Kimberley Process'. It aims at ensuring that each shipment of rough diamonds is exported or imported in a secure container. The gems have numbered, government-validated certificates to ensure that they are from conflict free areas.

"Do you think Palatus had conflict diamonds in his possession?"

"I'm not sure. It is unlikely that they were stolen from De Beers' Namibian mines," Watson replied. "De Beers has very tight security. They could have come from Angola or Zimbabwe. The Namibian border is vast."

"Do you believe his story?"

"Whether they are drugs or diamonds, most suspects say that the goods were planted," Mtetwa said. "The passport claim is more unusual and could be true. Windhoek Airport confirmed his story."

"They could have stolen the passport and ticket to obtain Palatus' personal details and his destination," Watson said "They would have watched him panic, allowing them the opportunity to hide the diamonds in his luggage. By then the passport would have been placed in lost property."

"The smugglers could then have emailed his photo, details and arrival time to gang members in Madrid," Mtetwa said. "It would only be a matter of time before they snatched the diamonds from the unwitting carrier."

"Maybe it's a double bluff. The passport and ticket were deliberately lost and handed in to give credence to his story," I said.

"You're beginning to learn, Jack. Yes, that's a very real possibility," Nkozi said, as we watched Palatus sitting there in silence, waiting.

"On the other hand, if he were a diamond smuggler, would a reefer be left in his luggage? He wouldn't have been that stupid. He wouldn't have risked sniffer dogs."

"Spot on again, Jack," Watson said and smiled at Mtetwa.

"As an observer, what would you do, Jack?" Mtetwa asked.

"If you charge him and he's guilty, he's unlikely to disclose the smugglers. I would let him go. We can then tail him to see if someone makes contact."

"That's precisely what we're going to do, Jack. We can always pick him up later," Watson said.

* * *

According to the squad who tailed Pacy Palatus, he hired a car and checked into a hotel near Witwatersrand University. During the following week, he went there every day. In the evening Palatus would get in his car and go to restaurants and movies in Rosebank and Sandton. He was with some student friends from time to time, but none seemed to be criminal types.

Late one night when we were watching a football match on TV, Watson received a call.

"You damn fools, how did you manage to lose him? Where the hell is he?" Watson shouted. "He went to Hillbrow? You lost him there? How? Keep searching."

"They lost him?" I asked.

"In the worst possible place. Hillbrow is dangerous and overcrowded," Watson said. "It's a haven for drug dealers and criminals from all over Africa."

"How did they lose him?"

"Palatus was driving through Hillbrow early evening. There was a traffic jam. He managed to slip through and our detectives were caught in the snarl up. He hasn't returned to the hotel."

The next morning, Watson received another call when we were having breakfast.

"Palatus is dead. They found him in an underground parking place in his car, the exhaust going full blast. It could be suicide but they reckon it was murder."

I felt awful.

"Hell! It was my suggestion that we release him. If he had been in the nick he would have been safe."

Depressed, I walked out of the house into the garden to relax and try and lift myself and shake off the guilt.

Watson came up to me and gently placed his hand on my shoulder: "Don't worry, Jack. It was my decision. If they wanted him dead, they would have found a way. Come, we're going to take a look at the body. Another day, another Johannesburg murder."

* * *

On the way to the mortuary to examine the body, we drove to the centre of Johannesburg. On the streets and in open spaces near decaying office blocks and skyscrapers, were vendors selling fruit and vegetables, meat, clothes, electrical and other goods. Few whites were around. Those who were on the streets were dressed simply, so that they could blend in and avoid potential muggers.

Between the city centre of Johannesburg and the northern suburbs, was Hillbrow, one of the seediest places that I had ever visited. There was some regeneration, but washing lines were hanging from balconies of filthy, tatty, high rise apartments. Some windows were broken, a few shops were boarded up and streets were crowded and dirty. It was a haven for criminal cockroaches.

Detective Sergeant Frikkie du Plessis was waiting for us at the Hillbrow mortuary, the site of a former "Non-

European", blacks only hospital, during the Apartheid years. Du Plessis took us into a room where Palatus' body was lying on a table with a sheet over it. He took the cover off and shook his head.

"What a handsome boy; what a waste," du Plessis said.

An imposing figure, du Plessis was well over six foot tall. He was around forty and the broken nose and cauliflower ears indicated that he had been a rugby player or wrestler.

"His parents will be devastated. Can you imagine losing a son, Watson?" the policeman said.

"I can't think of anything worse," Watson said.

The pathologist, a young, pretty, Asian woman in a white coat, walked in and made a thorough examination from head to toe as we looked on. The face was not contorted and there were neither bullet nor knife wounds.

"The only sign of violence is this," she said, pointing to a small bruise on the neck a few centimetres below the jaw. "One of them could have pressed the carotid artery. Within a few seconds, he would have been unconscious or dead."

"You don't think that the fumes killed him?" du Plessis said.

"They would have finished him off, but he was probably dead before they put him in the car."

"Do you think they could have drugged him?" I asked. "He looks so peaceful."

"Possibly. We'll be checking his blood."

* * *

We drove from the hospital to the scene of the crime, passed the walls of "The Fort", an historic prison and then through the main streets of Hillbrow. Angus, Watson's dog and du Plessis' Alsatian were at the back of the car. After reaching a rundown building, du Plessis, drove us down a ramp into a filthy, musty underground parking lot. The area around the car had been sealed off with tape and a policeman, holding a rifle, was on guard. The dogs were let loose and they immediately went to work. They rushed to the car sniffing and then ran around the area, searching. Watson examined the inside of the car thoroughly, while du Plessis carefully searched for objects or other clues in the immediate surroundings. Angus started barking and we rushed over. In front of him was a small white badge with a black snake. Watson picked the badge up with a hanky and placed it into a small plastic bag.

"Do you think that it could belong to one of the murderers?" I asked and patted Angus.

"Perhaps. It could be an insignia for a gang or some organisation. On the other hand, it could belong to someone unconnected with the crime."

"Do you believe that Palatus met a fence and was murdered because he didn't have the gems?"

"Possibly," Watson replied. "On the other hand, the gang could have decided to get him out of the way as he could have been a witness against them. Now that he's dead, we may never know."

4

THE GEOLOGIST

I was dreaming that I was swimming with my dog, when a huge wave dragged us down. We were struggling hopelessly against the current when I woke up, sweating. It was Sunday morning and still shaky, I dressed swiftly and went outside. Watson and Thandi were having breakfast in the garden.

"Are you OK Jack? You look upset," Thandi said.

"I'm fine, just had a weird dream."

"You've seen some bad things Jack. It's not surprising that you're having nightmares. Do you want to talk about it over breakfast?"

"I'm not feeling hungry, thanks. I better send off some emails."

"When you're finished come and join us for coffee."

Most of my dreams were forgotten quickly but this one lingered in my head. To try and forget it, I focused on my work and emailed Sasha. She would now have details on the diamond smuggling and murder of Pacy Palatus.

"You need a break, Jack. Let's go and play some golf," Watson said.

"Only played once in my life and hacked the ball all

over the place."

"You can be my caddie," Watson said. "That's how I learnt golf. I would carry the clubs and after the game players taught me how to drive, chip and put. One of them gave me his old clubs."

We went off to Springs Country Club about a mile from the Town Centre. Boys rushed towards us offering to be caddies, but Watson declined. We teed off and I sliced my drive far into the rough.

"You're too close to the ball. Just relax and swing through it."

I spent most of the time looking for balls in the rough, while Watson hit balls straight down the fairway and on to the green. The aim was to play eighteen holes but since I wasted so much time hacking about, we played nine and went for a drink on the veranda of the club house.

"We've enjoyed having you around Jack. You've been a model guest and pupil," Watson said. "Primeheart told me to teach you as much about detective work as possible, but only gave me superficial information about you."

"Sorry Watson, I have to keep my past a blank."

"No problem Jack. If you ever need a sounding board, you know where I am."

"I know Watson. I appreciate it. You guys have been really good to me."

Later, after logging into my secure police emails, I spotted a brusque email from Sasha:

Sniper,

I was aware of the smuggling and alleged murder. Detective N has been in contact and has kept us informed.

He's impressed with you and says that you are a quick learner, but you still have a long way to go. Keep your mouth shut and listen. That's what you are there for. Just follow our instructions. Don't deviate from them and let N guide you.

The snake insignia on the badge may or may not be a significant clue. We will investigate to see whether certain organisations or societies issue them. We found the victim's Madrid destination interesting, as F has some ventures there. We have arranged for FC to contact you. That's the next step in your learning process. Keep working on that South African accent.

SM

Her email left me cold. I would honour my deal with her and Primeheart and help them prosecute Faramazov and his gang. As soon as that was over I would get on with my life. To hell with them. They couldn't use me forever.

* * *

Fred Carrender was waiting patiently at the entrance of the Cullinan Diamond Mine.

He looked fit and virtually unchanged from our brief encounter, some seven years previously. Now in his late sixties, Fred's ruddy, strong, sun burnt face had brown marks from lengthy periods in the veld. His hair had turned white, but despite years of back bending prospecting, he still stood upright at six foot two. Dressed to type, the geologist was wearing a khaki shirt and matching shorts. His wide brimmed brown hat was faded and bent.

Fred shook his head with a wry smile: "You're late! You think I've got nothing better to do?"

"Apologies Dr Carrender. Got lost," Watson said. "I'm Watson Nkozi and this is Jack Sniper."

Mr Stapler's skills were confirmed once again. Fred didn't recognise me. I wanted so badly to tell him who I really was; our links in the past. His relationship with my late father and close mining friends. Unfortunately, there was no way I could. It would break my cover. To him, Jack Miner was still in prison. Now Jack Sniper, the new me, was going to learn from him.

"Thanks for advising us about the smuggled diamonds. You've been a great help," Watson said. "Where do you think they came from?"

"That unlucky young guy flew in from Namibia," Fred replied. "De Beers manages the mines there. The security is very tight, so the gems are unlikely to be Namibian. I tend to agree with your theory, Watson. They could easily have been smuggled from Angola or Zimbabwe. We can't know for sure because the carrier is dead."

"Are you a consultant to the police?" I asked, not letting on that I knew he was a Kimberly Process expert who monitored conflict diamonds.

We were ambling through Cullinan, a self-contained village for miners and other employees. Streets were lined with jacaranda trees, their light blue flowers in full bloom. Nearby were a swimming pool, mining museum and a golf course.

Fred stopped to make sure that no one was close by.

"When you're semi-retired, you take what you can get," he said. "It's a constant battle to stop trade in blood diamonds. I've been hearing that growing numbers of gems are being smuggled out of Southern, Central and Western Africa. We aren't sure whether they are direct payments for armaments and mercenaries. "

"Wonder how many smuggled gems slip the net," Watson said.

Respectable diamond dealers and cutters in Antwerp, Tel Aviv, Mumbai and New York demand gem certificates," Fred said.

"If the smugglers are not selling them to dealers, who's buying them?" Watson asked.

"That's a good question. The buyers could be dictators, oligarchs or other wealthy individuals who are using diamonds as a safe haven or funk hole for their money. Others could be tax evaders or speculators who are betting on price increases."

"Russian billionaires?" I said, hoping to get specifics from Fred, but I stopped myself from asking whether he knew Faramazov.

"Why not gold? Isn't it supposed to be the ultimate safe haven?" I asked

"Diamonds weighing only a few carats can be worth a lot more than heavy bars of gold. They can be hidden easily," Fred replied

"What could the Palatus parcel fetch?" Watson asked.

"The quality is excellent. Possibly $100,000 or more," Fred replied. "It's puzzling. The variety interests me."

"Not sure I understand," Watson said.

"You would think that the ultimate buyers would be interested in the biggest and most unusual diamonds. They would have them polished and cut into exceptional gems which obtain top prices. But the ones found on the student were relatively small."

"Perhaps the smugglers don't want to draw attention. They might offer smaller stones, so that they can occasionally slip in a really big one," Watson said.

"Perhaps. Anyway, young Jack Sniper, I'm supposed to be teaching you about geology and mining, aren't I? We'll talk about gold, silver and platinum another time, but today diamonds. You're lucky that the mine manager is a good friend of mine. He's giving me a free hand."

"You don't mind if I come on the tour as well?" Watson asked.

"Of course, the fee is..." Fred said, with a broad smile.

We walked to the mine and Fred continued.

"Diamonds are crystals formed from carbon many hundreds of millions of years ago. "Deep down, about one hundred miles below the surface of the earth, extraordinary pressure and heat turned the carbon into diamonds."

"A billion or more years ago, volcanic convulsions caused dense molten rock to burst upwards. The molten magma erupted from the volcanoes and on the way to the surface created carrot-shaped 'pipes'."

"And the pipe formations with "kimberlite" rock, contained carbon crystals that became diamonds," I said.

"Exactly. Gems were formed when the magma eventually cooled down and became a solid mass. After the South African find in the 1870s, geologists spotted thousands of kimberlite deposits and eventually discovered diamonds in other African countries."

"Where else?"

"Geologists were surprised that there were major diamond deposits in 'lamproite' rock pipes in Western Australia and in Canada. Those discoveries precipitated another global search for gems."

"Diamonds are not only mined in the underground volcanic pipes," Fred continued. "Over many years, rains and floods washed the volcanic kimberlite or 'blue ground' down mountains and rivers towards the sea. Diamonds are thus imbedded in mouths of rivers, on the coast, under the sea and former river beds. In South Africa, these 'alluvial' diamonds were mined in the mouth of the Orange River in the north-western Cape; also in Namibia and Angola."

We had gone through security and were now within the borders of the Cullinan Diamond Mine.

"This mine opened in 1902. More than a hundred years later, mining still continues here," Fred said. "The mine has produced several hundred of the world's biggest gems. One of them was the Cullinan, which weighed 3,106 carats and was the largest diamond ever mined."

"What's the weight of a carat?"

"About the same as a carob seed i.e. 1/142 of an ounce, or a fifth of a gram. The Cullinan, weighing more than twenty ounces or -- 1.5 kilos-- was about as big as a large fist."

"Skilled diamond cutters turned the rough gem into the First and Second Stars of Africa and they are now part of the British Royal Family's Crown Jewels. Others included the 242-carat rough diamond that was polished and cut into the pear-shaped Taylor-Burton gem.

"Richard Burton's gift to Elizabeth Taylor?"

"He bought the gem from Harry Winston, a legendary New York dealer and it became the centre piece of her Cartier designed, diamond necklace. Some big stones have been discovered since Petra Diamonds bought Cullinan from De Beers a few years ago. The "Cullinan Heritage" a 507-carat white diamond, about the size of a chicken egg, is an example. It was sold for around $35 million, soon after it was mined.

"Those are very rare examples. Most diamonds are small," Watson said.

Fred nodded: "A good find is only 50 to 100 gems out of some 100 tons of ore. When they begin searching for diamonds they invariably start with 'open cast' mining in a wide, open pit. This is similar to digging the foundations on a building site. The hard rock is drilled and blasted with explosives. Huge hydraulic shovels then dig up the rock and dump the ore on trucks which wind their way up roads around the crater to the processing plant."

We were now in front of a vast, open crater.

"Now you can see what has happened following years of blasting and digging," Fred said. "The hole is man-made, but it looks very similar to the craters of dormant volcanoes. From nature to man, mines have created the full circle."

* * *

Fred then took us to the shaft of the underground mine.

"Extracting diamonds from a kimberlite pipe is difficult, but less complicated than gold mining," he said, as we accompanied him in the lift that took us down some 700 metres to the underground cavern of the mine. "The workings of this and other underground diamond mines are similar. If you want to mine more diamonds you need to sink shafts, usually about 300 metres apart."

"The shaft lift that is taking us down, is for miners, dynamite and other materials and for hoisting rock to the top," Fred continued. "Air is pumped down this shaft to provide oxygen for miners below. The second shaft is used to extract foul air or gasses from the mine and to pump it outside."

We reached the bottom and entered a wide tunnel which had been blasted open.

"Horizontal passageways, such as this, are about 100 to 200 metres long and lead to the kimberlite pipe," Fred said. "Kimberlite is blasted, drilled, scraped and extracted with the latest mechanised equipment."

We observed miners place rocks in buckets and attach them to a cable and winch. Following the production line, we saw kimberlite loaded on to small trucks and transported to an underground crusher. The crushed ore was placed in skips that went up the vertical shaft.

When we came out the shaft lift into the bright, sunny light, I had to shield my eyes and put on my dark glasses. Later when we were in the diamond recovery plant, we observed the crushing and screening of rocks. The kimberlite was 'washed' in a rotary pan and through several more processes, heavier rocks containing diamonds, were separated from lighter ones.

The stones passed through an X-ray beam and photo

electric high-tech equipment detected the fluorescence of gems. To make sure that none of the diamonds had been missed, stones were also placed on a greasy, downward sloping table with water running down them. Since diamonds are hydrophobic and repel water, a few gems stuck to the grease. Air jets then blew them into boxes.

The final stage was sorting by hand. The diamonds were classified by the "4Cs" colour, clarity, cut (shape) and carat (weight). They were now ready to be certified and despatched to diamond dealers and cutters in the main gem manufacturing centres, Antwerp, Tel Aviv, Mumbai, New York and Johannesburg. All that effort and work for only a handful of gems out of many tons of rock, but it was obviously profitable, as scarce diamonds are sold at good prices.

* * *

My time with Watson and his family was over and I was now in Fred's hands. Before I went off with the veteran geologist, Watson and Thandi had a farewell party and Sally Sniper joined us. We sat around a *braaivleis,* or barbecue, eating "boerewors", the South African sausage, lamb chops and "mielie pap", South African polenta. We had some beer and wine and it was a great evening. Before she left, I took Sally aside and thanked her.

"Think nothing of it, Jack. In some ways, you're similar to my son."

"I may look like him, but he's irreplaceable," I mumbled, feeling awkward.

"Of course," she said, tears welling up in her eyes.

Her response made me feel even worse, as in my confusion I had spouted the wrong words.

"Don't feel bad about it Jack," Sally said, noticing my

embarrassment. "You have a job to do and I agreed to it. I'm sure we can be good friends."

"I'm sure we will. One day you, Watson and family can come to London to visit me."

"Be careful, Jack."

"I've been trained to look after myself, Sally. If anyone contacts you and asks about me, just tell them that I'm travelling in Europe. They must believe that your son is still alive."

"How will I know where you are?"

"I'll be in contact. Watson has assured me that you will have full time security, so no need to worry about your own safety. I hope you don't mind if I call you 'mom' when I phone. I feel bad about that, but it has to be done so that they believe me."

"Don't worry about that Jack," Sally responded, pecking my cheek and giving me a warm hug. "Watson told me that you lost both your parents when you were very young."

I looked into her eyes, clasped both her hands and said nothing. How could I compare grief over the loss of my parents, to the death of her son?

* * *

Geology was very much like entomology, when you were out in the field with Fred. We had been camping for about a week in the bush near a dry riverbed and had found a large anthill. Long lines of ants were making their way towards the mound and we followed them closely. They scurried for food and then carried back the tiny morsels to the hole that led to their nest.

"Geologists can thank ants for discovering the Jwaneng mine in Botswana," Fred said as he peered at the insects through his magnifying glass. "They spotted ants carrying tiny shiny specs up from their nests and found that they were diamonds."

"The geologists explored further and found that the ants were digging about 25 metres below the surface into kimberlite rock. Kimberlite can contain water and the ant miners entered the fissures of the rock to find water and carried stones, including gems to the surface. After geologists found more and more diamonds in anthills, serious mining began and Jwaneng, the richest diamond mine in the world, now produces about 10 to 15 million carats of diamonds a year."

Unfortunately, we didn't have such luck after we dug into one of the anthills and tested the sand and rock.

"One day we'll strike," Fred said, as we struggled in the heat under our broad sun hats.

It was hot, back breaking intricate work. We would get up at sunrise and prospect for diamonds. When the sun beat down on us and the heat was unbearable, we would either go back to our tent or find some rare shade under a tree. Late in the afternoon, when it was cooler, we would continue working, until the sun began to set.

Although I had never taken a course and had only read elementary books on geology, my fortnight in the Karoo, South Africa's semi desert, gave me great insight into the subject.

Fred showed me specimens of kimberlite, the diamond bearing rocks and made me touch and hold them, to give me the feel and intuition of a potential prospect. We would wonder around dry riverbeds and look for kimberlite that had decomposed into blue or yellow clay, place it in pans and shake and sift through the ore. There were some tiny gems, but Fred didn't believe that there was sufficient evidence to develop a diamond mine.

"We need a lot more time Jack," Fred said, when we

had a drink at a bar in Barclay West, a tiny town in northern Cape, near the historic diamond rich river beds. "Have an open mind. Diamonds can be discovered in the most unexpected places."

"I've read about the discoveries, but how many failures?"

"Countless. Despite its top geologists and prospectors. De Beers searched for diamonds in Australia without success. Instead locals found a huge diamond deposit and the Argyle Mine in Western Australia became one of the world's biggest producers."

At night, with crickets chirping and jackals barking, we looked upwards into the cloudless African sky and gazed at the galaxy. There in the dim semi darkness of the quarter moon, Fred pointed towards the Orion and the myriad of stars some blue and white, others yellow. A meteorite flashed across the sky and Fred told me that one that had recently crashed to earth, contained diamonds.

Sometimes Fred would be silent and introspective, other times he would talk about his life.

"I originally became interested in prospecting when I was a boy and read Rider Haggard's *King Solomon's Mines*," said Fred. "Allan Quatermain and other characters explored the hinterland and found a lost tribe with a treasure of gems, jewels and gold." Fred had discovered a rich platinum mine when he was in his forties and had become wealthy, but his real passion was diamonds. He also loved the sea and the Kenya coast was a favourite. One day he had gone sailing with a friend in Mombasa and the boat had turned over. His friend had kept him going with jokes for about 24 hours as they hung on to a keel before being rescued. I was tempted to disclose that his friend, Bill Miner, was my late father, but my life had to remain secret. The need to tell, was so great that it was painful, but I kept quiet.

I thought of my Dad and the last time I had met Fred.

He was at the home of Ivor Ensworth, another geologist and prospector who had died when I was in prison. Then there were Stanley and Rena Slimcop who had introduced me to Ivor and also knew Fred. They had known each other in the mining and investment world. Friends, dear friends, close friends, all were dead. So much time was lost during those years in prison. If only I had not been so stupid. The more I thought about my former arrogance and my mistakes, the more depressed I became. I walked around the tent, again and again, thinking about the years that I had wasted and then joined Fred inside and ate supper in silence.

Fred noticed my gloomy expression: "Hey Jack, what's up? I've got some music that will cheer you up." He put some CDs into his portable dual radio and player. Louis Armstrong, Ella Fitzgerald, Miles Davis and other jazz numbers that my Dad loved were soon competing with the crickets and jackals in the veld. At that very moment, I felt very close to Fred.

"What about your family, Fred, don't they miss you?" I asked.

I had touched a sore point.

"My wife left me because she couldn't stand being left alone for such long times," he said with a resigned tone. "She's in Cape Town with my disabled son. I see him rarely."

"He must miss you a lot, Fred," I said, feeling a bit bad that I had asked.

Later that night, there was a sudden African storm with fearsome crashing thunder and bursts of lightning. Rain came down in a torrent, almost washing our tent away. The next day the semi desert was transformed into a kaleidoscope of exquisite blue, yellow, orange and red colours. That morning we didn't work. We just walked silently, quietly admiring the multi-coloured flowers and listened to the sounds of insects and birds.

5

MADRID CONTACT

She lived in a rundown building, so dirty that the grey blue paint on its walls had lost its colour. Sitting in a Madrid cafe, I faced the entrance of the apartment block and sipped my cappuccino. My instructions from Sasha Melnikov were to make casual contact with the girlfriend of Pacy Palatus. Sasha had investigated the background of Amity Fernandez, Pacy's girlfriend. Amity was spending a year in Madrid to complete a PHD in History of Art. Under no circumstances was Amity to know that I had been in contact with her boyfriend; that I knew he was a suspected diamond smuggler who had been murdered. Palatus' grieving parents had co-operated with the San Francisco and South African police and had given them relevant details about their son's girlfriend.

Sasha wanted to find out if Faramazov was one of the buyers of the smuggled diamonds. The badge found at the site of Pacy's murder could be significant, she said. Spanish gangsters, who wore the badge with an insignia of a snake, had previously had dealings with the Russian mafia.

A Spanish dictionary and phrase book were my companions while I waited. Hours ticked by. By the time Amity came out of the building I was so bored that I was beginning to doze. The emailed photo did not do her justice. Amity was stunning. It was not surprising that she modelled to help pay for her course. As she ambled into the cafe, I picked up a newspaper and sneaked a glance at her. She had long brown hair, which rested on her back and shoulders. Wearing jeans and a cashmere jumper, she sat in a corner nibbling a croissant, sipping her coffee and occasionally texting on her mobile. For a second or two, Amity looked up at me, but her eyes were vacant and didn't appear to register. I noticed tracings of smudged mascara below her eyelids, possibly cemented by tears.

Amity paid her bill, opened her handbag, looked in the mirror and adjusted her face. She then ambled to the Reina Sofia art museum, which was about two hundred yards away. I followed her discretely, paid the entrance fee and deftly stood behind a tourist group. They went into the same room that Amity had entered.

The tourists followed a guide who stopped in front of a huge rectangular painting of Picasso that dominated the room. The guide, speaking English in a Spanish accent, explained that the painting was *Guernica*, Picasso's masterpiece. Nazi bombers had supported the fascists in the Spanish Civil war and had destroyed the small town of Guernica. The guide, petite and pretty, explained the symbolism in the painting. The bull represented General Franco's fascists. The wounded, dying horse and weeping woman, symbolised the suffering people, who supported the legitimately elected Republican Government.

After gazing at the work and listening to the guide, while she took notes, Amity walked into a larger room near the Guernica. I followed and examined some drawings a few feet away from her. A question about the exhibition would give me an opening.

"Excuse me, it's the first time that I've been to this museum," I said, when she turned around towards me.

She glanced at me with a frown, cynically aware that I was making a move.

"You're taking notes. Maybe you can explain the symbolism of these drawings," I insisted, with a sweet, false smile.

"Why don't you follow that guide or get hold of an audio," Amity said.

"I prefer to get the feel of the place and make my own way. If you're not interested, perhaps..." I said, deliberately showing that I was disappointed.

"Isn't it evident that the room is about the Spanish Civil War?"

"I don't know much about it."

"You're in Spain. Surely you read some of the history?"

"I've just arrived ---I--- I was going to buy a guide book..."

She sighed and shook her head, making me feel a bit of an idiot.

"In the 1930s the liberal, left wing Republicans were elected. Some senior army officers, rich landowners and the Church were concerned about communists in the Republican government," Amity explained at a rapid pace. "They decided on a right-wing coup and the civil war began. General Francisco Franco became the fascist leader of the rebel army that fought the Republican forces. There were bitter battles and numerous atrocities from both sides. The fascist army, by far, was the worst culprit. By the late 1930s, Franco had won the war and became dictator of Spain."

"How come the Nazis became involved and bombed Guernica?"

"Hitler and Mussolini backed their fellow fascists. It was a useful rehearsal for the German Luftwaffe ahead of the Second World War."

Amity's fascination with the civil war absorbed her so much that she became less wary of me. I followed her as she walked around the room showing me Picasso's fascist bull and horse drawings; then the work of André Masson and Juan Miró who also used their art to expose fascism. In an adjoining room, there were posters and magazines of the 1930s demonstrating war propaganda from both the Republicans and fascists. Black and white photographs depicted the wounded and dead, destroyed towns and villages and distressed, homeless refugees.

The exhibition was so interesting that time passed quickly. I suggested that she join me in the cafeteria for lunch. Amity was reluctant at first, but after a brief moment changed her mind and accepted the invitation. Remembering that she was mourning her boyfriend, I felt a tinge of guilt that I was tailing her.

We had Spanish *tortilla* and *croquetas*, in the museum cafeteria while Amity continued to talk about the Spanish Civil War. How Britain and France stood by and refused to help the democratically elected Republican Government.

"It was less than twenty years since the horrors of World War I. The British and French governments were also concerned about the communist faction in the Republican administration," Amity said. "The only nation prepared to back the Republicans was the Soviet Union, but by the time Russian support and arms arrived, it was too late."

"Any others?"

"American, British and other anti-fascist volunteer soldiers joined the Republican army," Amity said. "George Orwell and Ernest Hemingway described the plight of the peasants and middle-class men and women, who fought against Franco."

"It was a civil war. The Republicans wouldn't have been angels," I said.

"The fascists, were by far, the main killers. They murdered civilians to force towns and villages into submission," Amity said. "Hundreds of thousands of bodies are in mass graves around Spain. Many were buried in the mountains near the tomb of Franco, about thirty miles from Madrid. Spain remained under his authoritarian yoke, until he died in 1975."

"And now?"

"Spain is a democracy and member of the European Union. There is free speech and tolerance, but people want posterity to remember the terrible injustices. Many are digging up graves to find out what happened to their parents and grandparents."

"Why are you so interested in this grim subject?"

"I'm American, but my roots are Spanish, as my grandparents managed to escape and join their cousins in Mexico. Later they immigrated to California."

"Your grandparents were refugees from Franco?"

"Both my grandfather and grandmother fought side by side for the Republicans, but when it was hopeless, they fled. I'm working on a PHD in art history, showing how Picasso, Miró, Masson, Dali and others played their part in the campaign against fascism; how the Civil War affected their work."

"Haven't other students covered that?"

"I'm looking for different angles. I'm also studying lesser known artists who were caught up in the war."

We finished our lunch in silence. Then at last, Amity turned to me.

"What about you? How long will you be in Madrid?"

"I've just completed a geology degree in South Africa and I'm travelling in Europe. After Spain, perhaps France, Holland and Belgium. When the money runs out, I'm off to London to try and get a job."

I went on describing the experiences of Jack Sniper, my new persona. When I deliberately spoke about diamonds to draw her out, she began to get upset.

"Are you OK?" I asked, somewhat remorseful about my insensitivity.

Amity's fascination with the civil war had seemingly distracted her, but she could no longer suppress her grieving and broke down.

"My friend --- my ---- my boyfriend."

"What happened?" I asked, leaning towards her.

She tensed up and pulled away from me: "His father phoned me. Told me that he was killed --- murdered. He was an anthropology student. Was on a field trip in Namibia to study Bushmen. Went to the university in Johannesburg to do some research. Should be here with me. His parents flew to Johannesburg and took the body back to San Francisco. The funeral was on Saturday and I wasn't even there."

"Take it easy," I said as she wiped her eyes with a paper napkin. "Want some more tea? I'll get some more napkins."

When I returned, she had composed herself and drank a few mouthfuls of tea.

"Have to go. Sorry. Thanks for lunch," she said and began to walk out of the cafeteria.

Irritated that I had failed to pump her for more information at her most vulnerable moment, I tried to find a way back.

"If you're feeling bad, feel free to call me," I said passing her my mobile number. "I lost my dad when I was a boy, I have some idea how it feels."

She entered the number on to her mobile. Perhaps genuine sympathy was the best way to get through to her.

* * *

The hotel that I was staying in was a dump, but at least

I wasn't paying the bill. Sasha had a budget to pay me a small retainer with limited expenses each month. The hotel was near the Gran Via, a long wide road in the centre of Madrid's shopping district. The next day I walked around aimlessly, wondering whether I should wait for Amity to contact me. I had managed to get her mobile number, but it wasn't a good idea to be pushy while she was grieving. In the meantime, I would be a tourist.

Earlier that day I had been at the exact spot where Madrid's men and women fought Napoleon's invading French troops in 1808. In the Prado Museum later, I sauntered into a room with paintings by Goya. One of his large works depicted the Madrid battle; another, the French firing squad executing the rebels. When I left the art museum, the wide-eyed terror of a man who looked directly at his executioners, hadn't left me. I shuddered, wondering how I would react if Faramazov's thugs were about to kill me.

Later that evening I left a voicemail for Amity. If she had nothing better to do, she could have dinner with me. I would be at the Plaza Mayor.

I entered the 16th century square, surrounded by Renaissance buildings. It was a sunny evening and people were eating and drinking under umbrellas, while others were watching clowns, actors and mime artists. I sat down and was reading Hemingway's *For Whom the Bell Tolls*, when my mobile rang.

"Hi Jack. I've been shopping near the Plaza. Where are you sitting?"

"Outside an ice cream parlour in the southern corner of the square. Want an iced coffee?"

"That sounds good. Will be with you in a few minutes."

Relief and joy. Yes, I knew that my job was to glean information about Pacy Palatus, but I had enjoyed Amity's company. She was beautiful and stimulating. Reminded me of the girlfriend I should have married years ago. Now I had met a girl who was also an art aficionado. The big question was how to play it? After being in prison all those years, I was desperate for a relationship. Someone to love and share stuff with. Unfortunately, the timing was wrong.

Looking at the pages, but not concentrating on the content, I felt a tap on my shoulder. Amity, in a light green dress, was smiling and much more cheerful than the previous day.

"*For Whom the Bell Tolls* is a romance. The story could have taken place in any war. You should be reading Orwell's *Homage to Catalonia*. It will give you a much fuller picture on what happened in the Civil War."

She sat down, placed a straw in the iced coffee, which was waiting for her and drank noisily.

"That tastes good. I've been feeling a bit embarrassed, Jack. I shouldn't have broken down like that."

"Forget about it. I would have done the same. It's not surprising you're still in shock. You can talk about it, anytime. I don't mind. Really!"

She smiled. I was tempted to touch her hand, but remained disciplined.

"Where should we eat?"

"There's a market nearby. Awesome food, good wine. Very popular here."

* * *

It was no wonder that the market was packed with people. It had an iron roof and glass windows covering a wide area. Stalls were filled with fruit, fish, seafood, fresh and preserved meats, bread, cakes and snacks, wine and various gifts. We bought a bottle of white wine and sat on some stools by a seafood counter and they served us prawns and delicate fish savouries. The wine made Amity more relaxed and she told me about her grandparents who fled from Spain with their young children. In America, her grandmother became a cleaner and her grandfather a security guard, even though they were highly educated, cultured and had been teachers in Spain. They had problems with the language, but they made sure that their children received a good education. Amity's mother married an American, but they were soon divorced and he went to New York. Since her mother had to go out to work, Amity was effectively brought up by her grandparents in San Francisco. Later she went to the University of California, Berkeley, where she met Pacy.

"What about you, Jack?"

"My father died when I was young, but my mother is still living in a small mining town east of Johannesburg," I said, trotting out the background of my new identity. "My father was a miner, so I decided to become a geologist; but you need luck and knowledge to make money. Either you work for a mining company for a low salary or you get a business degree."

"An MBA?"

"Not exactly, but I know a little about investment; that sort of thing. Maybe I could join a broker, if mining doesn't suit me."

Amity turned away, seemingly in an attempt to avoid someone. She was unsuccessful. A short Spanish guy, tanned, with dark hair, rushed up. He had a smug look about him and smelt strongly of cologne. He attempted to kiss Amity on both cheeks, but she adroitly avoided him.

"Hola Amity. We can't go on meeting like this," he said.

He peered at me and then picked up my book: "Ha --- Hemingway. Told only one side of the story."

Amity rolled her eyes upwards.

"I'm Carlos," he said, shaking my hand with a sweaty

palm. He looked about thirty-five and his face was pock marked with acne scars.

"This is Jack," said Amity, who was irritated by the intrusion. "We have to go now Carlos."

"How's Pacy?" Carlos asked.

Amity turned away from him and whispered: "He's dead."

"What! What happened?" Carlos mumbled, looking stunned.

Somehow his shock didn't seem genuine. I was immediately on guard and observed him closely.

"It's a long story. I don't want to talk about it," Amity said. "Come Jack, we have to go."

"Wait. Please! I'm so sorry. Pacy was a good guy. I don't want you to leave like that. Let me buy you a drink. Wine? Coffee?"

"Yes, coffee thanks," I said quickly, indicating to Amity that we should stay with him. Maybe he knew something about Pacy. I wasn't going to lose that opportunity.

Amity glared at me, but it was too late. Carlos ordered some coffee, started small talk with Amity and then asked me: "How come you're reading *For Whom the Bell Tolls?* It was published years ago. Who reads Hemingway these days? Blew his brains out."

"That doesn't mean he wasn't a great writer," I said. "He was an interesting guy; was a foreign correspondent here."

"Hemingway was biased. Told only the Republican side of the story. Franco, Franco, always the bad guy. You should know what those Republicans did, those Communists. Their crimes against the people. That's what happens in civil wars. No side is innocent."

"Carlos' grandfather was a colonel in Franco's army. He helped me with my research," Amity said, shaking her head in disapproval.

"To get both sides of the story?"

"Yes, both sides of the story," Carlos said. "If the Republicans had stayed in power, Spain would have become Communist. Under Franco, Spain became stable for many years. He encouraged tourism, the economy grew and people had jobs."

"What about his friendship with Hitler?... Guernica?"

"OK, Hitler and Mussolini supported Franco, but Spain was neutral in the Second World War."

"Documents show that Franco was a Nazi supporter. He was a friend of Hitler," Amity said.

"Besides being a supporter for the fascist cause, what do you do?" I asked, aiming to provoke Carlos into revealing more about himself.

Through his glasses, he examined me suspiciously. His expression was nasty.

I stared back with a smile on my face: "Just joking."

"I'm in business. Do this and that," Carlos replied and passed me his card.

"Carlos Maxos, Director, MSP España Mining SA. You're in mining? What sort of mining?"

"Precious metals and diamonds. We invest in new developments. Exploration companies. And you?"

"I'm just travelling for the moment. Studied geology and business studies."

"A geologist! Small world! Maybe when you're ready, you can consider us," Carlos said with a false smile. "But no politics OK!"

He laughed in a gruff manner. Amity stood up and pulled me away.

* * *

We walked in silence for a quarter of a mile or so and Amity then burst out: "I wouldn't work for him!"

"Because he tries to justify fascism?"

"He introduced Pacy to some of his friends."

"What are you implying?"

"You wouldn't understand."

"Try me. How did you meet Carlos Maxos?"

"So much is written about the Spanish Civil War, that I decided to concentrate on something different for my thesis on art and propaganda. There had to be anecdotal evidence from both sides. To do that I had to get hold of people who were in the civil war."

"They must have been ancient."

"Some were in their nineties. Fascinating people, with memories that were still clear."

"So how did Carlos come into the picture?"

"I met him by chance in Granada. He came up to me on the ramparts of the Alhambra and started chatting about the palace's history. Found that I was interested in the Civil War and offered to take me to his grandfather's apartment. Ario Doval had an excellent memory, even though he was almost 100."

"Ario Doval?"

"Carlos' grandfather on his mother's side. He hero worshiped Franco. Doval showed me some old pictures of the war in his apartment and allowed me to take photographs for my dissertation."

"Sounds like Carlos did you a good turn. Helped you get someone from the Fascist side to make your PHD objective."

"You won't believe what then happened."

"What?"

"Doval took me into a small room. It had a shrine to Hitler."

"What? I don't believe it."

"There was a huge portrait of Hitler. The room had swastikas, helmets and other Nazi memorabilia. On the walls, there were photographs of Franco with Hitler and Benito Mussolini. Carlos' grandfather boasted that he was a Major General and showed me a picture of himself as a young man. He was in one of the pictures, near Hitler and Franco."

"What did you do?"

"Tried to get away as soon as possible. Carlos was apologetic, making out that his grandfather was losing his mind. He insisted on escorting me back to the hotel. Luckily Pacy was there."

"That's how Pacy met Carlos?"

"Yes. The worst thing that could have happened."

"The worst thing?"

We had now reached the centre of Madrid and were pushing our way through crowds of shoppers in Puerta del Sol. Amity broke away briefly and walked inside several shops. Seemingly distracted, she fingered several pretty dresses and outfits without any interest in buying.

"You probably noticed that Carlos has a knack of sucking information out of people," she said when she once again walked alongside me. "Pacy told him that he was off to Namibia. Carlos became excited and told him that he had good friends and contacts there. Pacy told Carlos where he was staying. Everything."

"Didn't you tell Pacy that Carlos' grandfather was a Nazi?"

"I didn't have a chance. By then Carlos had the information he needed."

"What are you implying? It's no crime to ask someone what they're doing or where they're going," I said, with a fair idea where the conversation was heading.

"That's exactly what Pacy said, when I eventually had

the opportunity to tell him about Carlos' background. He said that I shouldn't worry; that he could look after himself. Then, then..."

Amity's eyes began to well up with tears. To comfort her, I tried to put my arm around her, but she pulled away.

"I can't understand the connection," I said, keeping my distance. "Pacy was killed in Johannesburg, not Namibia. There's random violence there. Johannesburg is one of the world's murder capitals."

"I didn't tell you this the other day. The South African cops arrested Pacy before he died. His parents told me that they found diamonds on him. He was suspected of illicit diamond smuggling. They let him out and soon afterwards he was murdered."

"Smuggling? Why do you think that Carlos had something to do with it?"

"I don't know anymore. I cannot believe that Pacy was involved in smuggling. His parents said that the police let him go. They thought that the diamonds had been planted on him. Pass me the card Carlos gave you."

I felt for the business card in my back pocket and showed it to her.

"There! He's involved in precious metals and diamonds. Am I paranoid or is it a coincidence?"

Amity suddenly began to shiver: "I don't want to go home alone."

"That's OK, maybe you can come to my hotel."

"It's not what you think."

"I know. I understand."

Soon afterwards we walked up the Gran Via and entered a side street where my hotel was situated.

"Are you sure it's OK if I stay in your room tonight?" she asked. "After meeting Carlos tonight, I don't want to be at home alone."

"No problem. It has twin beds. Make as if you're going to the toilet near the bar. As soon as I ask the concierge some questions, get into the lift and go to the second floor. I'll meet you there."

Luckily the concierge and receptionist were busy with a small bus load of tourists, allowing Amity to give them the slip.

"Wow you're very tidy," she said, when we entered my room. "Wait until you see my place."

I lent her a t-shirt, a spare toothbrush and some shorts to sleep in. When she came out of the bathroom, I could see the outline of her firm smallish breasts through my thin white cotton shirt. My shorts looked small on her and showed off her shapely hips and thighs. It was very tempting, but she had lost her boyfriend only weeks ago. This was neither the time nor the place. Amity went straight to bed and after watching some Spanish program on TV, she put off the lights.

I could hardly sleep during the night with her being so close to me. So early the next morning, while she was asleep, I went for a run in *El Parque del Buen Retiro*. My route from the entrance of Madrid's main park, was a wide gravel walkway with sculptures; then an artificial lake with semi-circular columns and finally back home. That was the best way to get rid of my frustration. Hot and sweaty, I entered the room. Amity was still sleeping, so I tip toed to the bathroom and had a shower. When I got out, she was sitting on her bed, looking at a photo and crying.

"Hey take it easy," I said, gently sitting down beside her, taking the photo of herself and Pacy and putting it on the table besides the bed. To relax her, I gently massaged her neck and back. She was very tense and cried out when I pressed down on the knots at the back of her neck and shoulders. She turned around and faced me and against my better judgement, I pecked her softly on her cheek. She pulled away and walked to the window.

"Sorry, Amity, I got carried away," I said, feeling embarrassed and went into the bathroom to change. When I came out, she was already dressed.

Later we went for a walk in the park and had croissants and coffee at a cafe overlooking the lake. The white columns and statues of lions' heads on either side were awesome, but I was focusing on the lovely Amity.

She took me to the park's "Crystal Palace" near the lake and we went inside and sat down on some antique rocking chairs.

"Are you going to be in Madrid for long?"

"I'll play it by ear. Maybe visit Toledo or something."

"That's a good idea. It's a fascinating, walled, medieval town. During the civil war, there was a siege there."

Without saying much, we walked out of the park and our hands touched by accident. My spine tingled, but it was best to control my emotions. If I didn't, Primeheart and Sasha Melnikov would stamp on me. My job was to get information.

The next day I toured Toledo, which is a short train journey from Madrid. When I was in the town, I had an idea. The Republican forces had laid siege to the fascist garrison in the town. Carlos Maxos had told Amity that his grandfather was trapped there before Franco came to the rescue. The visit to Toledo would be a good opening gambit to make contact with him again.

6

The Barcelona Drop

Sasha Melnikov gave me some rare praise when I phoned her from my hotel room. Contact with her had to be discreet as possible, so her number was not on my mobile.

"Good work, Jack. It doesn't matter whether Pacy Palatus was a smuggler or not. It seems that Carlos Maxos either employed him, or set him up. When you see Maxos, say that you're interested in a job in the future. Our Russian contact says that Faramazov has recently become involved with a Spanish mining company. You might come up with something. What about the girl?"

"She's lovely. No way is she connected with smuggling. Can't stand Maxos. Thinks that he might have something to do with her boyfriend's murder."

"Your job is to get as much information from her as you can. Don't get involved with her. If you do, you could give something away."

"Sure, Sasha," I said without much conviction.

The next day I phoned Maxos: "Hi this is Jack Sniper. Is it OK if we meet? You mentioned that there could be a job for me when I'm finished travelling."

"OK Jack. Meet me at Hotel Melia Madrid Princesa

at eight. It is on Calle de La Princesa, near the statue of Don Quixote in Plaza de España. It's a tall building. You can't miss it. I'll be in the bar."

* * *

Maxos was sitting on a red sofa in the corner of the hotel bar with two men and a woman. They were smartly dressed; the men in striped dark suits and the woman in a black fitted suit. The men, who had gold Rolex watches, weren't wearing ties. Typical city spivs, they didn't bother standing up when I came in; didn't seem to care that I was dressed casually in jeans. They were all fluent in English; embarrassing as I knew only a few Spanish words.

"Jack Sniper --- Isabella Pinot, Philippe Santos and Roman Fredrico," Maxos said, as we shook hands. "Isabella, Philippe and Roman work with me. We raise finance for mining ventures."

A simple gold pendant necklace, in the shape of a horseshoe sat neatly in the open cleavage of Isabella's suit. Dark, cold eyes of the sultry, curvaceous brunette examined me so warily, that I was unnerved.

"Carlos told us that you recently qualified as a geologist," Isabella said. "South Africa is the best possible place for mining and a good time."

Roman, wiry, small and thin with a sharp look about him, offered me a beer.

"Yes thanks," I said, well aware that they were monitoring every pronouncement and move. "I was brought up in mining. My father was a miner. We lived in Springs, a gold mining town, east of Johannesburg."

Making a pitch that would hopefully interest them, I continued: "Besides mining, I also studied business and investment."

"What experience do you have?"

"I helped a prospector search for diamonds."

They took the bait.

"Diamonds? Where? Did you find any?" Maxos asked.

"The prospector's claims are confidential. We came across some kimberlite and some ant hills. The ants were bringing up specs of gems. Could be a possibility."

"Ants? They can lead you to diamonds?" Isabella said; her expression, acute scepticism.

"Yes. After observing ants, geologists discovered Jwaneng in Botswana. I presume you know that it's the richest in the world."

Santos, tall and muscular with longish black hair was impressed: "We have some interesting prospects --- perhaps...."

Maxos gave Santos a stern glance and spat out a few words in Spanish.

"They are confidential at the moment," he said, with a false smile.

"What is MSP España," I asked.

"Maxos, Santos, Pinot--- MSP. We formed the company. Roman has just joined us."

"Managing Successful Projects --- our slogan," Isabella said.

"English, not Spanish?"

"Yes. We are a small mining finance boutique, but we're international. We have a group of investors from Spain and other countries who place money in diamond exploration," Maxos said. "Ask your prospector friend to call us."

"How do you assess developments?"

"When we find out about an interesting mine or prospect, we commission geologists and mining engineers, Santos said. "We're expanding, so we're thinking about an in-house geologist who'll assess and monitor our developments. Would that interest you?"

"I was going to apply to one of the big mining companies," I lied. "I haven't thought of an emerging exploration firm."

"Why don't you come to our office to see what we're doing?" Isabella suggested.

"That's a good idea. When can we meet?"

Maxos was wary: "We'll think about it. Where can we contact you, Jack?"

"I'll be out and about. Is it OK if I phone you?"

"How long are you staying in Madrid?"

"Not sure. Might go down south to see Granada, Cordoba and Sevilla."

* * *

That evening, I took Amity to a movie and told her that I had met Maxos and his staff.

She was angry: "Why are you getting involved with them?"

"Geology jobs are difficult to find and Maxos might be a good contact."

"Yeah, for a route to the mortuary! What's the matter with you guys, why don't you listen?"

I was itching to tell her what I was really doing, but bit my lip and said nothing.

"Don't worry, I'll be OK."

"That's what Pacy said."

"If we find out more, we could help the police find Pacy's killers. You're fluent in Spanish. The hotel concierge said that the Government's commercial department in Madrid has company records. Let's see what Maxos' business is about. If you're right, I'll keep away."

"I don't have much time. My PHD deadline is getting nearer."

"Maybe it could provide you with an unusual angle. Besides helping me, you might find companies that backed Franco during the civil war."

* * *

Early the next day I skyped Sally Sniper in Springs.

"Hi Sally, it's Jack. How are you?"

"Fine, Jack. Where are you?"

"Madrid. I told you I would keep in contact."

"It's nice of you to phone, Jack, but what's the real reason?"

"I've met some people who may be in touch. If they ask questions about me, just say I'm travelling around Spain."

"Be careful, Jack."

"Don't worry. Just give them cursory details about me. Phone Watson Nkozi. Tell him that I called; that I want another security guard near your house."

"Are they dangerous?"

"Check your security and alert your neighbours. Someone may try and get into your home and search for things. I'm thinking of you, Sally. Look out for yourself. Thanks so much for your help."

* * *

Later in the morning Amity and I went to the government office that houses records of Spanish companies. It was painstaking business using the microfiche to find the company. At last there it was. MSP España Mining SA. It had capital of 10 million euros and had been founded two years previously. The company directors were Carlos Maxos, Philippe Santos, Isabella Pinot, Gerald Gleep and Armand Gruchot. Gleep's address was Bristol, UK and

Gruchot lived in Antwerp. The main shareholders of MSP España were Bristol GemDiam Mining Corp and Gruchot Diamond Dealing AG, in Antwerp. Maxos, Santos and Pinot held the remaining 21 percent of the shares.

The accounts were over a year old, but MSP España had already borrowed 5 million euros from Spanish and Belgian banks. The main assets were stakes in Canary Diamond Mines SA and ESBR Real Estate SA, which had undisclosed properties. The Canary shareholders were MSP España and Bristol GemDiam Mining Corp. There were no other holdings in diamond exploration companies or mines, but other investments could have taken place since publication of the accounts.

After translating for me, Amity began doing her own research, going through old company records and finding armament and other business connections with the Franco regime. She was excited, so I left her there and went straight to the nearest post office, where I used a telephone booth to call Fred Carrender.

"Hi Fred, how are you? Quick question. Have you heard of Canary Diamond Mines?"

"Is it an exploration company? I'm afraid I haven't come across it. Who are the shareholders?"

"British and Spanish companies and an Antwerp diamond dealer.

"Why are you interested?"

It's a long story. Will tell you about it, when I see you. By the way, do you have any contacts in Antwerp? Someone to explain the diamond market?"

"Good idea. You'll see how they turn rough stones into polished gems. Here's the number of a good friend of mine; Josh Zunrel. Antwerp 547837."

"Thanks Fred.

Next call was to Sasha. She sighed when she heard

my voice.

"Yes Jack. Short of money again?"

"Of course, but that's not why I'm calling."

"Go on."

"I think I might have some leads, but I'm not sure. Can you ask your team to examine Companies House's records on Bristol GemDiam Mining Corp?"

"Anything else?"

"I also need information about Gruchot Diamond Dealing AG in Antwerp."

"OK. What have you found so far."

I told her about the meeting with Maxos and his associates and said I was waiting for his call.

"That's not much of a lead, but when you go to Antwerp ask about Faramazov's diamond interests."

* * *

Later that afternoon when I was back at the hotel, I phoned Sally Sniper.

"Hi Jack. You were right. I had a call from someone. Said he was an old friend. He asked where you were. I said that you were in Madrid."

"Anything else?"

"No. He just thanked me and hung up."

I phoned Watson Nkozi.

"What's up Jack?"

"I've made contact and they've already phoned Sally. I'm just making sure that I'm covered. You've taken care of the geology degree and other stuff, right?"

"No problem, Jack. I'll get copies of the degrees and other documents to you in no time. You also have your reference from Fred's geological consulting firm. You should be OK."

"Does Sally have adequate security?"

"Don't worry. There's an armed guard close by."

"Thanks Watson. Just a bit nervous, that's all."

"You'll both be OK, Jack, but be careful. Do you think these Spanish mining guys are fencing for diamond smugglers?"

"Not sure, but if they are, the cash from the diamond sales could be laundered and used to finance their mining ventures."

Soon after speaking to Watson, Carlos Maxos called me.

"Hi Jack. We've been discussing the business plan and how you could fit in. It's a bit premature at this stage, but we'll keep in contact, OK?"

"No problem, Carlos. I'm here on holiday."

* * *

That evening I received an unexpected call from Watson Nkozi: "My colleagues picked up another diamond smuggler and he talked. In a few days, a gang will drop off diamonds in Barcelona."

"Do you have any details?"

"Yes, both Interpol and the Barcelona police have been alerted."

"I'll phone Sasha. Find out what she wants me to do."

"No need, I've already spoken to her. You must get on a flight tomorrow morning. Pedro Sanchez, my Spanish colleague, will make contact with you."

When I was walking her home from a restaurant, I told Amity that I had to go to Barcelona. She was both wary and excited.

"Why didn't you mention Barcelona before, Jack?"

"I got a call from an old friend and he said that it would be crazy if I didn't visit the place."

"Maybe I should join you," Amity said. "You're still a mystery to me Jack Sniper, but it's a good opportunity to do more research. Remember I told you that Picasso and Miro were active campaigners against Franco. They lived in Barcelona and there are two museums devoted to them."

Watson and Sasha would be expecting me to go to Barcelona alone, but Amity would be more of a help than a hindrance. For a start, she could speak Spanish. It would be better than hanging around in coffee bars all alone, waiting for the call from the Spanish detective. Amity was good company.

"I can find some good flight and hotel deals," Amity said, observing me quietly.

"Sure Amity, you can be my tourist guide."

Later Amity called and told me that she had booked the flight and managed to get a half price, two room deal at the Majestic.

"It's a four-star hotel. Antoni Gaudi designed amazing houses and apartments nearby," she said.

We arrived early the next morning and checked into the Majestic Hotel with Amity choosing a room next to mine. Soon afterwards we were heading up a winding hill to *Parc de Montjuic* towards the site of the 1992 Barcelona Olympics and the Joan Miro Foundation museum. We enjoyed Miro's paintings, sculptures and huge textile creations and Amity used the library to research his Civil War work. Later we went to the Museum of Pablo Picasso in the old city. Several "blue period" paintings were gloomy works on dying, funerals and cemeteries. Amity, previously lively and excited, became depressed and withdrawn.

My mobile vibrated. It was Detective Sanchez.

His instructions were terse: "Ask a taxi to take you to *Park Güell* and meet me at the entrance. Do it now! The drop of the diamonds is about to be made at the "Stations of the Cross" in the park grounds. I'll be wearing light blue jeans, a green t-shirt and white tennis cap."

"I'm medium height and will have a white jacket on..." I said.

"I have a picture of you," Sanchez said. "Move! Get a taxi now!"

I rushed to Amity, who was on a bench. She was in a bad way, her shoulders heaving. It was likely that the paintings had brought back memories of Pacy. My problem was time and her renewed grief had come at an inconvenient moment. There was no time for patience and understanding. Sanchez was waiting for me. The job was urgent.

I put my hand on her shoulder: "Hey are you OK?"

She didn't respond.

"Take it easy, Amity," I said, passing her a bottle of water. "I'm sorry, I can't stay. I've had an urgent call from my friend. Have to go. See you at the hotel."

I felt bad for being so crass, but what could I do? Looking hurt and disgusted, she composed herself as best she could, left the museum and climbed into a taxi. I tried to stop her, but she was already on her way. After climbing into another taxi, I tried her mobile, but it was off. I couldn't go after her to apologise and comfort her. I had to get to the park as soon as possible to meet Sanchez. That was my duty. I would think of a good story and explain later.

It was late afternoon when I arrived at *Park Güell*, another creation of Gaudi. A few tourists were around, but after waiting a few minutes, there were no signs of Pedro Sanchez. Near the open black iron grilled gate with spikes and circular patterns, were two Gaudi buildings. They looked like the fantasy homes of Noddy, a character of Enid Blyton. One of them, with a weird narrow, blue and white tower, had a shop inside. Sanchez was nowhere to be seen. Possibly he had gone directly to the Stations of the Cross where the smugglers were delivering the diamonds to the fence. Unfortunately, he had called me from a line phone, so I didn't have his mobile number. He had probably avoided cell phone contact for security reasons.

I was getting worried, so I slipped into the shop and bought a map of the park. From where I was standing between the two Gaudi buildings, the Stations of the Cross was on a hill to the left. I waited for another five minutes, but time was against me. It was April and the sun was beginning to set. The park would close when the light faded.

More tourists were leaving the park than entering it. My mobile was on, but there was no message from Sanchez. I called his line number and left a message. Something was wrong. Perhaps he didn't have time to tell me that there was a change of plan; maybe he was waiting for me at the Cross. The map indicated that it was up a hill about a kilometre away from the entrance, towards the west of the park. I rushed up a flight of stairs past a colourful ceramic sculpture of a lizard. I was now in front of a building with Grecian columns. There were yet more stairs until I saw on the left, a weird long passage that went under a bridge. The passage, built of rock, was not unlike a cavern. It was getting dark as a large cloud had obscured the setting sun. I stumbled through the passage which was about two hundred metres long, wondering if I was doing the sensible thing. Outside the dark passage at last, the pathway was heading upwards to the left of the hill. My fast walk turned into a light jog and as I came to a clump of bushes and trees, there it was. The Cross on a high mound at the very top of the hill, the highest point in the park.

It was windy and the cloud moved, but instead of the sun, a full moon appeared. Through the moonlight, I could see several men climbing a narrow stony staircase towards the top of the mound. It looked quite dangerous as there were no railings. I crept closer and it became evident what was happening. Someone was being forced up there. Two men at the top, close to the Cross, gripped the man's arms and pulled him upwards while the other two pushed him from behind.

I couldn't make out whether the man was conscious or not, but in the bad light, the shirt was green and the white tennis cap was still on. Pedro Sanchez! What was I to do? Had to help him, but how? There was another clump of trees nearer the mound, so I slowly slipped off the pathway and made for cover towards the rocky slope of the hill. As I crept along, steadying myself by holding on to some larger rocks, they pushed Sanchez off the mound. It was about 15 to 20 metres high and down went poor Pedro, landing in a crumpled heap. The men, in black hoods, swiftly came down the hill and examined him. Three stepped back and the fourth hammered him on the head with a large stone. Oh my God! What could I do? Had to phone Interpol, the Barcelona police; anyone! I couldn't take them on. Wasn't sure whether he was alive, but he was badly injured for sure.

I had to remain hidden until they left, but unfortunately, just as I reached the trees close to the mound, I dislodged a rock. One of the men who was on the lookout heard the fall and spotted me. The others looked up, pointed a gun in my direction and fired. The gun obviously had a silencer as there was no sound, but there was a ping of the bullet as it hit a rock close to me.

I had no choice but to run, even though I felt a coward for deserting Sanchez. It was now fairly dark, as the cloud was obscuring the moon. The place was a maze and I took a wrong turn and ran as fast as I could down the hill. From time to time, I turned around to see whether they were getting closer. Thank heavens for the military training. It had taught me to feel my way and keep up the pace in darkness. I was still ahead of them and leapt down several wide flattish staircases. It was beginning to rain and the rocky paths were now slippery. It was a struggle to keep ahead, although the conditions were also slowing them down.

A hiding place and escape route became urgent necessities. From the map, which I had studied earlier, I recalled that there were some more viaduct type bridges with cavernous passageways underneath. I spotted one and hid there, hearing them scuff the stones on the bridge above me. At least the rocky surface in the passageway was dry, so I crept forward and then rushed for a path that went alongside a house that Gaudi had lived in. They saw me and fired several times, luckily missing me, as the "duff, duff" and "ping ping" of bullets hit the earth and surrounding rocks. At last an exit of the park was in front of me and luckily a tourist bus was about to leave. I rushed to join a queue of German tourists and managed to sneak on to the bus, just as my pursuers reached the exit.

The rain was now pouring down and it was fairly dark, so unfortunately, I couldn't identify them. Sweating profusely, I took off my soaked jacket, found a seat on the bus and immediately phoned Sanchez's line number. One of his colleagues responded. In uneven English, he told me that the police had listened to my earlier message and had rushed to the park. They had just found Pedro, but it was too late.

Later when the tourists were well on the way to the centre of the city, the furious guide kicked me off the bus. A taxi picked me up and we were soon heading for the Majestic Hotel.

The Concierge gave me a letter.

"Dear Jack,
I have decided to check out of the hotel as I don't trust

you anymore. You are well aware that I'm in mourning. Your
insensitivity at the museum shocked me.

I've booked a flight to Madrid and will be there for a few
days to finish my research. I will then fly to California and see
Pacy's parents. That's the least I can do.

Good luck for the future.

Amity

I kept phoning her on her mobile, but it was switched
off. Sanchez's colleagues came to the hotel and I gave them
a full statement. After they had left, I checked out the
hotel and settled the bill, even though we hadn't even slept
there. At the Airport, I tried to find which flight Amity
was on. Hopefully she would still be there. I felt bad about
leaving her in the lurch. I didn't want it to end like that.
The more Amity had rejected me, the more I wanted to be
with her. The years in prison had made me feel lonely and
isolated. I needed someone like Amity. The only thing left
to me, was to bombard Amity with emails and voicemails,
apologising for what I had done. Hopefully we would get
together again sometime in the future.

To top it all, I was scared, seriously scared. Even though
it was bad light when I was in Park Güell, the gang might
still recognise me. I wanted to go back to Madrid to see
Amity, but Interpol and Watson were very much against it.
It was far too dangerous to remain in Spain. Who knows
what the smugglers could have forced out of Pedro, before
they killed him?

7

ANTWERP AND AN OLD ENEMY

Just in case anyone was trailing me, I flew to Amsterdam. The day was spent walking around the canals and visiting the Van Gogh and Anne Frank museums. It was a relief to be well away from Barcelona; good to be on the road and relax. If only Amity were with me; if only we had met at another time and in different circumstances. It was frustrating to gain her trust and then blow it.

Later, I pulled myself together to stop emotions interfering with my job. I contacted Josh Zunrel, Fred Carrender's friend and took the train to Antwerp early the next morning.

The station was near the Antwerp diamond centre. Zunrel was at the entrance, waiting for me. A tall, large man with a shock of white hair and square face, Zunrel appeared to be in his mid-sixties. He greeted me warmly, but I felt out of place. He was in a smart light brown summer suit, whereas my blue open-necked shirt was creased.

Zunrel offered to help me with my suitcase.

"Good to meet you Mr Sniper, Fred told me that you were coming. I'm sure you'll enjoy Antwerp."

"I'm looking forward to learning about the market,

Mr Zunrel, Fred told me that it's fascinating."

"Call me Josh. Most of the time, dealers transact business in their offices, but when we hold international events, dealers trade in the marketplace."

The Diamond Bourse was not far from the station. It had twenty long tables, one behind the other, alongside the windows of a lengthy room. Brokers and dealers were sitting at the tables, examining diamonds and negotiating deals.

A few dealers on the tables shouted "mazel" and shook hands.

"Mazel means luck. Diamonds worth millions of dollars are transacted with a mere handshake," Josh said. "I could spend hours telling you about the history of this place. They began trading diamonds here in the fifteenth century."

After greeting colleagues who were standing on the floor near the tables, Josh continued.

"In 1940 when the Nazis invaded Belgium, my father and other diamond traders managed to escape to England. They sewed gems in the lining of their clothes and joined 3,000 refugees on Brownsea Island."

"The nature reserve near Poole?"

"My father eventually joined the British army and returned after liberation. He and the other lucky dealers sold the diamonds after the war and started again. By the 1960s Antwerp boasted 22,000 diamond cutters and several thousand dealers. Sadly, there are now only a few hundred."

"What happened?"

"Globalisation. Diamonds were discovered in Western Australia. By the early eighties, the Argyle Mine was producing millions of carats. It mined rare pink stones, but the bulk of Australian diamonds were either tiny or 'near gems'. These stones are part gem, part industrial."

"Can dealers make money from industrial diamonds?"

"They're very cheap, a tiny fraction of gem prices, but

it can be a profitable business. They're so tough that they're used for tool making, mining and oil drills. It's an important market."

"How did the Australian discovery hit Antwerp?"

"It enabled the Indian industry to compete in the near gem, low price jewellery market. It's much more cost effective to polish diamonds in Mumbai. In terms of volumes of carats, India is now the largest diamond polishing centre in the world. Mumbai has far more cutters than Antwerp, Tel Aviv, Moscow and New York."

"So how does Antwerp survive?"

"It's the largest diamond trading centre in the world. We account for about 80 percent of dealings---some $55 billion rough and polished diamonds a year. Antwerp has the skills and knowhow."

The spin amused me a little.

"Presumably the other markets have similar skills?"

"The Antwerp World Diamond Centre is the global industry's main body. The most precious diamonds are still sent to Antwerp. We have some of the world's best cutters using highly sophisticated polishing technology."

Later, I observed cutters transform small and large rough stones into exquisite polished gems. Using computers, the diamond polishers scanned, weighed, measured and studied three-dimensional diamond graphics on their screens. Josh showed me that the best diamonds ending up on rings, necklaces and other jewellery had the Four Cs – colour, cut, clarity, carat.

Issie Shloshberg, one of Josh's top polishers, examined a rough diamond from various angles.

"We have to find the exact places to cut and polish," he said. "The skill is to cut the diamond so that the gem displays the maximum light. This gives life to the diamond."

Issie decided on a 'brilliant cut'.

"Watch closely. I'm going to cut the diamond into octahedrons --- gems with eight sides."

"Brilliants include round, oval and heart shapes," he said, after he had finished the job. "Rose Cuts have flat backs and domed fronts. Other designs include 'Step and Square' and Emerald Cuts."

"What do you do with the largest diamonds?"

"A stone weighing 50 carats, can be turned into two or three diamonds."

"Intricate work! It must be pretty stressful," I said and touched a partly uncut gem.

"Careful. A slight move can damage the diamond and destroy value," Issie said. "It's a high wire, tense job. The craftsman who cut the Cullinan Diamond had doctors and nurses in attendance!"

"You can't be serious."

"He collapsed from exhaustion after he finished the job."

* * *

Josh took me to a salt beef bar where we wolfed down sandwiches and had a beer. Later, in his tiny office near the Diamond Bourse, he took out a small packet of rough diamonds from his safe.

"Kimberly Process Certificates are required to ensure that blood diamonds don't enter the market," Josh said. "Certified diamonds can easily be classified when they arrive from mines in Russia, Botswana, South Africa, Namibia, Angola, Australia, Canada and elsewhere."

"And smuggled diamonds?"

"Kimberly Process experts, such as myself, examine them. We determine whether they were stolen by artisans who find and smuggle gems. They tend to come from alluvial diggings in West and Central Africa, Venezuela ..."

"How do the diamond exchanges monitor diamonds?"

"Antwerp has a 'Diamond Office' with expert sorters and Belgian customs officers. They check imports of diamond parcels with certificates from global producers, manufacturers and dealers. They also monitor exports to other diamond markets and jewellery manufacturers."

"Where are these diamonds from and how much are they worth?" I asked, pointing at the pile of gems on the table.

"They were mined in Angola. I couldn't find any D-Flawless diamonds, so I reckon that this parcel can be traded for about $1 million. Cut and polished, about $2 million to $3 million. Jewellers sell them for about twice to three times above polished prices."

"That's some mark up. Are you saying that these rough diamonds worth $1 million, could eventually be jewels that are sold for $6 million to $9 million?"

"It's a fascinating business. De Beers and other advertising campaigns add to the mystique. De Beers contributes about $140 million to annual global marketing of almost $300 million."

"Diamonds are a Girl's Best Friend... Diamonds Are Forever?"

"Brilliant slogans created by De Beers' advertising agents in the 1950s and 1960s."

"What's a D-Flawless diamond?"

"A diamond without any flaws; clean without scratches or inclusions; the most expensive. The colour is pure and there are no blemishes in the rough stone."

"And coloured diamonds?"

"Pink and Blue are rare, so they're more expensive."

"I guess that if a mine finds those diamonds, dealers and investors go wild."

"For sure! De Beers used to be a popular share, but

the company went private. Anglo American Corp now owns 85 percent of the stock and Botswana the remaining 15 percent. Investors trade shares of smaller producers in Canada, Australia and South Africa. Alrosa, the huge Russian diamond company, was listed in 2013."

"How big is the diamond business?"

"The diamond 'pipeline'?"

"Kimberlite pipes?"

Josh laughed: "No, but maybe that's where the 'pipeline' term came from. The 'pipe' begins at the mines where newly mined rough gems are sorted and are ready to be sold. The global worth of those diamonds is around $17 billion. A large proportion of the diamonds are then sent to De Beers' Diamond Trading Company. It buys about two fifths of global production, mostly from Southern Africa and Russia. Producers such as Canada, Australia, Sierra Leone and also Russia sell directly to the markets in Antwerp, Tel Aviv, Mumbai and New York. Some diamonds are distributed to cutters in their home markets--- for example Botswana and South Africa. Once the diamonds are polished, their value rises to about $22 billion. By the time Tiffany, Zales and other jewellers sell diamond jewellery, the global market, at the end of the pipeline, is worth around $80 billion."

"How extensive is diamond smuggling?"

"Very difficult to quantify. Customs are vigilant and have highly sophisticated detection devices. But diamonds are hidden in all sorts of places; false bottoms of suitcases, toothpaste tubes, shoes, books, inner clothes linings and other places."

Later as we left the building, Josh asked me whether I liked opera.

* * *

My hotel was near Antwerp's Town House, a 16th century,

grey Renaissance building. I was by no means an opera buff, but when I was in jail, one of the prisoners introduced me to the music. Verdi's La Traviata, was in Antwerp's Royal Opera House, a short walk away from the hotel. The opera house was packed but I managed to spot Josh at the side of the entrance. He looked young for his age with his dark blue suede jacket and light grey trousers. Next to him was an attractive, slim brunette, who appeared to be in her late fifties. Elegantly dressed, her fitted black dress was the perfect backdrop for her rose gold necklace with diamond pendant. On her finger was a striking green emerald engagement ring.

"I'm Rosa, Josh's wife," she said, shaking my hand softly and smiling warmly.

"Jack Sniper," I mumbled with embarrassment. Compared to the smart, formal opera lovers, who were making their way into the theatre, I was dressed shabbily.

The music began and we settled in to enjoy the magical music of the romantic tragedy. The singers were Flemish and from Eastern Europe, but the words were in Italian and during brief intervals, Rosa explained what was going on: how Alfred fell in love with the courtesan Violeta and how his father opposed it.

"Rosa is a specialist in antique jewellery, Jack," Josh remarked, when she left us briefly during the interval. "She's also a former soprano."

"Has she been in lots of productions?"

"Nabucco, Rigoletto, Aida, Tosca. Lovely voice, but she decided that it was better to focus on the family."

When we were in the bar during the interval, I thought I recognised a tall man going into the theatre. He had his back to us. We were about to go back to our seats, when he turned around. It was Yevgeny Faramazov.

Taken aback by the sight of my adversary, I could

hardly concentrate on the final Act. The beautiful music
and voices, when Alfred was with Violeta in her dying
moments, hardly moved me. Faramazov was all I could
think of. What was he doing in Antwerp?

Later when we were leaving the theatre, I looked out
for Faramazov. He entered the foyer with a lovely woman,
clutching his arm. She wore a long dark blue, satin dress.
Her pale skin was delicate and pure and she had thick,
opulent, black hair. Faramazov's cropped hair, which used
to be lengthy and blonde, was gradually fading into sombre
grey. He had not aged well, compared to the fit, handsome
man I once knew.

A muscular, burly, middle age man with a petite blonde
woman, wearing a shimmering, turquoise dress, warmly
greeted the couple. The four of them were talking animatedly.

Josh noticed me observing Faramazov, his wife and
three smartly dressed bodyguards nearby.

"Are you OK, Jack? You look tense. Do you know them?"

"Not sure. He reminded me of someone," I lied.

"The tall guy is Yevgeny Faramazov. He's a Russian
magnate who has interests in diamond mines."

"One of the oligarchs?"

"On a smaller scale. He's not one of the multi-billion-
aires, but they tell me that he's trying to get there."

"That's Anya, his third wife," Rosa said. "She's also
Russian. She came to my shop the other day and examined
some of my Russian antique and post-modern jewellery."

"Is she in the same line as you?"

"No, just a collector. She told me that she used to be
an historian."

"Who's the guy with them?" I asked.

"Armand Gruchot. He's Swiss. Came to Antwerp a
few years ago and helps market Russian diamonds. He also
has connections in Africa and Brazil."

The next day I searched for Gruchot Diamond Dealing AG on the Internet. I contacted the office and asked if Gruchot was available. The receptionist said that he had flown to Moscow early in the morning.

That was a good enough lead for the time being. Gruchot had a stake in MSP España, Carlos Maxos' company. He was at the opera with Faramazov and probably flew to Moscow with him.

8

A Mining Boutique

Back in London a few weeks later, I was lonely, miserable and broke. My retainer from Sasha Melnikov's special unit was ridiculously low and I was sick and tired of junk food, living in dumps and walking around in tatty clothes. My experience at Antwerp's Royal Opera House was seriously embarrassing. To impress people in the city, I would have to smarten up. With only £200 left from my £1,800 a month retainer and ten days before the next tranche, that was a forlorn hope.

My musty, depressing bed sitter was near Highgate Woods. Sasha had recommended the place. She had lived in it soon after she had arrived in London. Her flat was now in Highgate village nearby, so it was convenient for her to meet me from time to time. The tiny room was in a crumbling dirty building with peeling paint on the damp walls. The overgrown garden had a decaying shed, with ivy creeping over it in a haphazard way. The room was hot and humid; the noisy fridge and stove had seen better days; the bath and toilet had yellow stains and the TV could only get terrestrial channels when it was working. As soon as I entered that grubby hole, I wanted to get out as soon as possible.

In my flight from those Dickensian lodgings, my daily routine was to run across the road into Highgate Woods. It has a circumference of about one and a half miles and is thick with undergrowth, oak, hornbeam trees and holly. Uneven, sandy pathways lead to a large green. The open space, in the centre of the woods, is a picnic ground with a football pitch in the winter and cricket field in the summer. My route was past the field and then across the road into Queens Wood. This woodland conservation area is an example of what north London was two to three hundred years ago, before rows and rows of houses were developed on common land.

From Queens Wood, the run continued across the road into Highgate Woods again. After a quarter of a mile I would leave the woods and run slowly down a slippery slope that went under a bridge to Parkland walk. The narrow sandy pathway, which was a former railway line, continued to Alexandra Park. I would then have coffee at the Grove Cafe where Ciro, the proprietor, sang Neapolitan songs. Further on, up a grassy embankment is Alexandra Palace where BBC Television first began productions in 1936. From that high vantage point, Canary Wharf's Canada Square can be seen far away in the south; closer by, in the heart of the City, the "Shard", "Gherkin", St Paul's and 'London Eye'. The view brought back memories of my former life as a City hedge fund trader.

It was time for a briefing with Sasha and John Primeheart. They well knew that my monthly stipend was inadequate. Stuff them! They had forced me to carry out a dangerous, poorly paid job that had almost killed me. From now onwards, I would work part time unless they raised my retainer.

* * *

I asked for a meeting and the next day went to New Scotland Yard near St James' station. After waiting in the foyer, a policewoman took me to a small room and a secretary brought in some weak tea and a biscuit. Waiting with nothing to read, I began to get restless and irritated. At last Sasha Melnikov arrived in a smart, light grey suit. Her hair was in a tight, no-nonsense bun that drew sharp attention to her high cheek bones and stern expression. I wondered whether she ever let go, as she was so humourless. I gave her more details on what I had found out so far, but she didn't seem impressed.

The door suddenly opened and John Primeheart entered. Cold and stony faced as usual, he questioned me more intensely than Sasha. He also didn't think that I had achieved much.

"Carlos Maxos and his colleagues may or may not have been connected to Pacy Palatus. We have no proof that they were," he said in a dry matter of fact tone. "We also know that Faramazov is in the mining business and has a stake in Russian diamond mining. Is it that surprising he was in Antwerp?"

That irritated me a little.

"According to Palatus' girlfriend, Maxos encouraged him to meet his Namibian friends. She believes that Maxos' friends planted the smuggled diamonds on Palatus. Maxos is in the diamond business and she contends that he could be a fence for smugglers."

"That's a reasonable theory, but it's only theory. You have no proof of any connection."

"Sometimes you have to go with your gut feeling," I insisted. "What about the drop in Barcelona and the murder of Pedro Sanchez? Is Gruchot's stake in Maxos' mining business and his association with Faramazov, a mere coincidence?"

Bored, disinterested and ignoring me, they were enjoying their tea and chocolate digestives.

"Fred Carrender contends that rich Russians have been buying smuggled diamonds to evade tax," I continued in desperation. "Another possibility is that the Maxos lot are fencing the gems and the laundered money finances their mining ventures. Are you so sure that my findings don't amount to much?"

Primeheart made no effort to hide his sneer.

"That's supposition. Not fact. Look where your gut feeling got you in the past… Jail."

I had enough of this: "I almost got killed in Barcelona. You despatched me to the army to learn about firearms, but I didn't have a gun."

No response; all in a day's work for them.

"Look here. If you're dissatisfied with what I've found so far, why don't you let me work in one of Faramazov's companies, be outed and end up on a slab?"

Smiles this time; them enjoying me getting worked up.

"Please. Let me work in a mining finance company. I understand investment in mining businesses. It will give me the opportunity to monitor what Faramazov is doing; offer finance and advice to one of his businesses. Then I could get some seriously good information and feed it to you."

"How do we know that you won't get up to your old tricks again, young man?" Primeheart said in his patronising way.

I decided that enough was enough: "If you think I'm that stupid, so be it. Why the hell did I have to change my identity? For bullets that almost hit me? To live in a run-down dump?

Bad idea. Primeheart launched into a rant: "Don't you think it's time you stopped feeling sorry for yourself. If you're so miserable after having a nice trip to South Africa,

Spain, Holland and Belgium, I'm happy to open the cell door for you."

"You let me out because you needed my skills and knowledge," I said. "I've done time. You don't believe me, but I wasn't the fraudster."

"A judge and jury convicted you and that's good enough for me," Primeheart said. "In the highly unlikely event you were wrongly convicted, you were neither the first nor last to get a raw deal. There are a lot of people out there who have had a much tougher time than you or I. It comes with the ticket. Already forgotten what you witnessed in that military hospital?"

"I did my best to help those soldiers get used to their prosthetics. Do you really think that I've forgotten them? Those guys were my mates."

"You seem to think that you are entitled to a free ride. Most people keep on going, trying to make an honest living. If things go wrong, they try and pick up the pieces the best they can. It's people like you, people who think they're owed a living without doing much sweat. It's people like you who cause all the trouble."

Silence in the room. I decided that I had better cool it, as I was getting nowhere. This Primeheart guy had a chip on his shoulder the size of a boulder.

"You misunderstand me, Detective Superintendent Primeheart. I want a job to pay my way, a job that will also help us nail Faramazov. It's not that I'm ungrateful, Sir. I need to mix with the right people and Faramazov isn't exactly on the poverty line."

"I've got an idea," Sasha said. "I know someone who heads a small mining boutique. They finance mining ventures around the world and know Russia. If Sniper gets a job there he could get some leads."

"OK, but we'll be watching you, young man. If you

don't come up with your part of the bargain, you know where you're going."

* * *

When Sasha escorted me out of the building, she was more agreeable than her boss.

"Be patient, Jack. Sometimes leads go nowhere, other times they link to the unexpected. Our objective is to put Faramazov behind bars for as long as possible. His Russian and international network have grown exponentially. He's now accepted as a legitimate businessman."

"Surely that implies it's going to be damn hard to prosecute him?"

"That's precisely why I persuaded Primeheart to get you early release. You have a second sense and a gut feeling. I'm backing you as you didn't waste away in prison. You wrote your own story and read a lot. Your army and police trainers were impressed. That shows that you are focused, disciplined and motivated."

I never expected praise like this, but felt uneasy. She was peering directly into my eyes in a chilling sort of way.

"I'm saying this as I want you to have confidence in yourself. Go with your instincts. Tell me what you're thinking and planning. While you were travelling, I compiled a detailed dossier on Faramazov. It will be shown to you in good time."

* * *

Later that week, I took the tube to Moorgate in the City. From the station, I crossed over "London Wall", the street alongside an ancient, grey Roman Wall. Close by were narrow, winding streets that were near Guildhall, a medieval

City hall. Before long, I was ringing the bell on a worn wooden door of a Victorian office block and then climbed rickety, creaking stairs. Three floors up, there was a small panel: JJ Emerging Mining Finance Ltd.

Sasha had given me an advance on my retainer, so I had bought a light linen suit. Feeling sufficiently smart, I knocked on the door and walked in. There was no reception desk. Instead there was a crowded small working area where casually dressed men and women, were gazing at their laptops and speaking on their phones.

"I have an appointment with Jamey Jackenhead," I said.

"He's over there," said a young woman, with short, brown, spikey hair.

Jackenhead's office was in the far corner of the room and was not much bigger than a cubicle. The door was open and he was shuffling through a filing cabinet.

"Hi I'm Jack Sniper.

No response.

"Here for an interview?"

"Apologies, clean forgot," Jackenhead said.

He was about five foot five and as I towered over him, I glimpsed at a small bald spot in the middle of a receding hairline. He looked scholarly with round, old fashioned glasses hanging absently on a string around his neck and was dressed casually in navy cotton trousers and a short sleeve cream shirt.

"Sit down and take off your tie and jacket if you wish," Jackenhead said, examining my formal attire with some amusement.

I did what he said and felt more relaxed.

"So how do you know Sasha Melnikov?" he asked, getting to the point quickly.

"Just an acquaintance. I met her through a friend."

"Great girl, Sasha, we went out together."

Sasha had warned me that Jackenhead was a romantic fantasist. She had met him in a pub and he had tried to pick her up. She had played it cool, allowing him to eventually take her phone number. A few days later she had gone to lunch with him to pick his brains on people involved in Russian mining. That was it.

"As I said on the phone, she told me that you might have a job for me. If not, it would be good if you could put me in touch with someone else."

Jackenhead sat down at his desk, cleared away papers and read my CV.

"You had work experience with Fred Carrender? Very interesting. Graduate in geology at Wits University and a post-graduate course in investment and business. What were you doing with Carrender?"

"Prospecting for diamonds. We examined ant hills and movements of ants."

"Ha, trying to find another Jwaneng. Trust Fred, the eternal optimist.

"You know Mr Carrender?"

"He's a legend. Met him at a mining conference. And you?"

"A friend put me in touch with him. He took me to Barclay West to prospect for alluvial diamonds near the Orange River. We found a few small stones, but I think the ants were doing better."

"All you need is luck, all you need is luck," sang Jackenhead in tune with the Beatles song, *All you need is Love.*

"I was in Antwerp recently and one of Mr Carrender's dealer friends gave me good information about the global diamond market," I said, thinking that Jackenhead was a bit weird.

"Tell me about it," Jackenhead said while he, glanced through some papers.

"From what he told me the diamond market has been depressed for some time, but there could well be a shortage in coming years. De Beers and other producers have slashed production, demand from China could double and Indian and East Asian markets are already strong."

Jackenhead had a hint of greed in his eyes.

"You think that diamond prices could rise?"

"Maybe, maybe not. The dealer remembered the old days when De Beers controlled about 80 percent of global diamond supplies and supported prices. These days De Beers, at the most, only accounts for two fifths of supplies. Russia, Canada, Angola, Australia and other producers are competing and selling gems at keen prices. They are also concerned about competition from synthetic gem producers.

"What's your view about synthetics?"

"Dealers say that the market is growing but consumers seeking quality, still prefer natural diamonds. The problem is that prices are volatile."

"How volatile?"

"D-Flawless diamonds peaked at around $64,000 a carat in the late 1970s, but in the past few years have fluctuated from around $10,000 to $27,000."

"Seems you know your subject," Jackenhead said. "I'm not interested in diamonds as an investment. I'm interested in the companies. Do you like the stocks?"

"To be quite frank, Mr Jackenhead, I haven't studied the companies. I want to investigate them. That's why I'm here."

"We're interested in about half a dozen listed diamond mines and several exploration companies. We help finance the companies, find partners for them and take stakes. We also use spare cash to invest in the market."

"Can I see some charts?" I asked, knowing that I now had the opportunity to show him my experience in picking stocks; the experience I had as a trader, before I went to jail.

He searched for diamond shares on the Net.

"Do you have any chart books? It gives me a better feel," I said.

"You seem to know the market. Have you invested in stocks?"

"Only on a small scale," I lied. "It helped me get through university."

Jackenhead printed about two dozen sheets of charts from the web. Share prices covered the previous twelve months. I examined them and asked for longer time scales. Diamond shares had been horrible performers in the past few years, but they had begun to rise from very depressed levels.

"Looks interesting, but I need to examine the fundamentals," I said. "Can I see some annual and interim reports, directors' earnings guidance and brokers' forecasts?"

"Go ahead. Let me introduce you to my colleagues. They'll show you the filing system."

"Does this mean you're giving me a job?"

"On a trial basis. If we both like each other after a few months, you'll get a fulltime contract. In the meantime, will £3,000 a month do? If you perform, we'll raise you. We'll pay you a bonus if you get us business and we make money. Deal?"

"Sure. Deal," I said and couldn't help but grin.

The salary was more than I expected. Hopefully Sasha would not cut my retainer, until my job was secure.

Jackenhead took me around the office and introduced me to his staff. Michael Fredenhoff was tall with thick brown hair and a sleek side fringe that framed his tanned face. Casually dressed in light trousers and a tweed jacket, he was in charge of mining in Western and Eastern Europe. Ronnie Chim, in a formal grey suit, was the Asian specialist.

Isobel Steeplefoot blushed as I approached and shyly told me that she was mainly involved in Latin America. Her brown hair was pulled back in a ponytail and she wore a plain, loose fitting navy dress that hid her figure. She had a small oval face and a pretty smile

"Isobel is a linguist," Jackenhead said. "She's fluent in Spanish and Portuguese and can converse in Russian."

He attempted to pat Isobel's back, but she deftly avoided him.

"Emerging mining companies in emerging markets," Michael said.

"Financed and advised by an emerging mining boutique," Jackenhead said, rubbing his hands.

"Jack Sniper will be our diamond analyst. If you guys come across anything interesting, pass it on to him," he said.

"When is he starting?" Ronnie asked.

"Today. Desk next to Isobel. Give him a laptop and show him where the files are. Jack's going to take a look at some of the listed stocks. Maybe he can make us some money."

"Hope so," Michael said. "It's pretty quiet at the moment. Coming for a drink later on, Jack?"

My mobile rang and I walked away from the desks as I suspected it was Sasha.

"Did you get the job?" she asked.

Yes, but I can't talk now."

"Well done. You can tell me about it over dinner."

"Where?"

"Kiplings Restaurant on North Hill. It's close to Highgate Village. See you at seven. I want to give you more insight into F"

"Sorry Michael, can we have that drink tomorrow? I'm afraid I already have an arrangement with a friend," I said.

* * *

Later that evening, I exited Highgate station, walked across Archway Road, up the hill and through a pedestrian pathway to North Hill. Kiplings, an Indian restaurant, was on the right, about a quarter of a mile from the village. Sasha was late but when she at last arrived, I noticed that she had her hair done. Naturally dark, there were highlights in it. Cut evenly, it rested neatly on the nape of her neck. Her smart light blue suit fitted her figure perfectly. She had very little make up, but still looked lovely. Sasha shook my hand firmly, her cold, false smile, a warning that I should keep my distance.

"So Jackenhead gave you a job. Good. What will you be working on?"

"Diamond shares. He liked my views about the market."

"How much are they paying you."

"I've got a month's trial. I'm getting £3000, but if I get a permanent contract, it should be around £45,000 a year, plus a performance bonus."

"Not bad. We'll keep you on the retainer for this month, but will cut it if your job becomes permanent."

"Cut it completely?"

"Yes, except for expenses, if you go on a trip for us. My unit is on a tight budget. Can't afford to throw away money."

We ordered some beers, chicken tikka, tandoori and rice. The table was in a discreet, far corner of the Restaurant. Photographs of Rudyard Kipling's family were on the wall alongside us. Later when we were enjoying iced *kulfi* for desert, Sasha took out a thick file from her briefcase.

"You have to understand Faramazov's psyche and history to penetrate any weaknesses; every single detail to protect yourself and find the evidence we need."

She sat alongside me and opened the Faramazov Dossier.

9

THE RISE AND RISE OF YEVGENY NICOLAIVICH FARAMAZOV

This is the history of Yevgeny Faramazov, according to Sasha Melnikov. She had gleaned the information and anecdotes from intensive research and her extensive Russian contacts. I cannot prove the veracity, but I personally believe that much of it is true and perhaps almost all of it. Since Faramazov is extremely rich and can hire the best spin doctors and other professional liars, he would undoubtedly deny the allegations. Propaganda and counter propaganda infiltrates Russian business, politics and the secret service from the bottom to the top. The truth lies somewhere in the middle of the slimy swamp.

Yevgeny Nicolaivich Faramazov was born into a cultured and criminal world, Sasha's Dossier began. His mother Katya, was the daughter of Yevgeny Krakanovitch, an officer who was killed in the Siege of Stalingrad during World War 11. Irina, mother of Katya and one of the freezing and starving Stalingrad civilians, died of pneumonia soon afterwards. Her teenage daughter, an only child, had to fend for herself.

Katya was strikingly beautiful with pale white skin,

jet black hair and sparkling blue eyes. A senior Defence ministry official heard about her plight and offered her an administrative job in Moscow. His real agenda was somewhat different. He seduced the virgin and she became his mistress. It wasn't long before the official's wife found out about Katya and the girl was thrown out of the love nest. The official passed her on to his friends and contacts to advance his own career. Before long Katya was a high-class hooker, servicing top members of the Communist Party.

Despite her work, Katya managed to lead her own life. She fell in love with Sergey Faramazov, a handsome, tall, muscular Ukrainian, with light strawberry blonde hair. Sergey was charming, with a sharp wit and jovial outlook. He was a welcome relief from the sleazy, unappealing married men, Katya had to entertain. They soon began living together in north Moscow. Warm and loving when sober, but a brute when drunk, Sergey was a petty criminal who plied his trade around the haunts of privileged Muscovites.

When Sergey went on a two month visit to his parents in the Ukraine, Katya fell pregnant. Sergey was furious and gave Katya a black eye when she confessed that the child might not be his. Sergey sobered up the next day and uncharacteristically felt guilty. He promised Katya that he would take responsibility and be a good father. Katya was so grateful that she agreed to be Sergey's wife. Since they needed the money, he allowed her to continue her profession with select clients.

Sergey, a bits and pieces villain who was in and out of jail, built up a pimping business with an inventory of five prostitutes, including Katya. He operated as a pick pocket in the streets surrounding the Bolshoi Theatre, Moscow's Metropol Hotel and GUM, the 19th- century shopping arcade alongside Red Square. Since privileged officials and foreigners were Sergey's targets, it was a risky business; but

Sergey, son of a magician, had considerable skill in his craft.

* * *

Yevgeny Nicolaivich Faramazov was born in 1962 during the height of the Cuban Crisis, the Dossier continued. President John F Kennedy confronted Nikita Khrushchev, Premier of the Soviet Union and Russians and Americans feared a Third World War. The birth of Yevgeny during these worrying times, concentrated Sergey's mind. It was time that he became a responsible member of criminal society. No longer would he be a mere pimp and petty thief. He would organise others. Before long Sergey became a gang leader, making a much better living out of planned robberies, extortion, prostitution and forgery.

In the meantime, it became increasingly evident that Yevgeny was a gifted child. He began to read at four years of age and understood basic mathematics at five. The genes could have come from Katya, who was highly intelligent with roots sprouting from a polished aristocratic family. Katya was a descendant of Count Nicolaivich Krakanovitch, a colonel who fought against Napoleon and was killed in the Battle of Borodino in 1812. The Krakanovitch family lost everything during the 1917 Bolshevik Revolution, but Katya's parents had passed on their knowledge and love of music and the arts.

Perhaps Yevgeny had also inherited his exceptional talents from one of the brilliant scientists, authors or diplomats, who had slept with Katya. Classy and beautiful, Katya made sure that she impressed her clients' contacts, when she had accompanied them to dinners, concerts, the opera and theatre. Katya had read the works of Pushkin and Tolstoy and was a fan of Chekov plays. She played the guitar and had a good voice. Some of her clients nicknamed her "Geisha Katya" as her service was similar to those in Tokyo or Kyoto. In classic speak, Katya was a polished courtesan, the ultimate prize for a client, who could afford her.

Katya appreciated that the boy, who was pouring over her books before he was five, required an unusual education. She asked a client, who was a professor of educational psychology, about gifted children. He gave Yevgeny some algebra problems which the little boy solved easily. Katya had learnt to hold reasonable conversations in English, French and German with diplomats and Western business-men. The professor told her to speak to Yevgeny in foreign languages. The boy was soon conversing in them, with a growing vocabulary.

There was only one problem. Yevgeny had a puny phy-sique which irritated Sergey. Instead of encouraging the boy, Sergey jeered at him if he fell in the playground and cried.

Sergey, who enjoyed testing the delights of fresh new hookers in his business, would come home drunk and sometimes hit Katya. One night she arrived home in the early hours of the morning and this time it was Sergey who was jealous. He began to shout and slap her and the commotion woke Yevgeny, who tried to protect his mother. A furious, drunk Sergey laid into the boy, leaving Yevgeny with nasty bruises.

This was one attack too many and since Yevgeny had also been hurt, Katya decided to leave. She packed up her belongings and Yevgeny's favourite games and books and sneaked out of their high-rise apartment. They were soon on the overnight train to St Petersburg, which was then called Leningrad. Their new life began in a small, but comfortable apartment in *Kuznechny Lane*, not far from the Metro station.

A few weeks later, a significant cultural event had a marked impression on the boy. It was 1971 and a museum, commemorating the 150th anniversary of Fyodor Dostoevsky's birth, opened on the corner of *Kuznechny Lane*. It was the apartment where the great writer lived and wrote the *Brothers Karamazov*. Yevgeny was fascinated with the museum and liked the curator, who found time to teach him chess. Yevgeny soon became a prolific reader of Dostoevsky's works. Flawed characters, such as the student murderer Raskolnikov, who tried to justify his awful deed in *Crime and Punishment*, fascinated him.

Yevgeny had grown to fear and hate Sergey, dreading that his father would find him and his mother. Katya and Yevgeny need not have worried. Sergey fell out with his gang over an unsuccessful attempt to hijack a shipment of gold. He was caught and sentenced to several years in prison. Shortly afterwards, a fellow gang member murdered him.

Katya worked hard to support Yevgeny and herself and plied her trade in luxurious hotels. She did her utmost to educate her son, taking him to the ballet and opera and art galleries, to acquire the polish of her illustrious ancestors. She made him appreciate that he was named after family heroes who had fought against Napoleon and Hitler. Unfortunately, time was against Katya. She was constantly competing against youth and her clientele dropped off. She and her son slipped into poverty and they had to move into a tiny one room apartment.

Yevgeny, way ahead of his class, spent most of his time at school. Bitter about the way Sergey had abused his mother and embarrassed by his puny physique, Yevgeny built himself up in the school's gymnasium. Before long he began to grow and was soon more supple and muscular than his class mates. When he had begun school, boys had bullied Yevgeny. No longer. They would now be thrashed if they tried. The difference was that Yevgeny didn't know how to stop and he was expelled after one of his foes was beaten into a bloody pulp and was left unconscious.

* * *

Katya knew that she had to deal with a serious problem as she did not want her son to follow Sergey's example and become a member of the underworld. One day, while Yevgeny was roaming the streets in a gang and using his language skills to mug unsuspecting foreigners, Katya came across a former client. They hadn't seen each other for many years. Feeling sorry for her, Andrei Prostovich took her for lunch in St Petersburg's *Nevsky Prospekt*.

A brilliant psychologist, Prostovich had risen to a high rank in the KGB. Katya asked the Soviet secret police colonel for help, telling him that her son was becoming a criminal and needed a lawful job. Prostovich met Yevgeny and despite the teenager's lack of respect, was immediately impressed. Only fourteen, Yevgeny demonstrated his talent in maths and physics and knowledge of literature and art. Even more interesting for Prostovich, Yevgeny had a photographic memory. After boasting that a Borodino colonel was his ancestor, Yevgeny quoted word for word, battle excerpts from Tolstoy's *War and Peace*. Prostovich was fascinated by the innate brilliance and culture of a boy who was fast becoming a criminal thug. He was a bachelor who had yearned for offspring, so he decided to take Yevgeny under his wing, polish him and garner his talents. Prostovitch managed to persuade Yevgeny to reform and soon regarded him as an unofficial adopted son and protégé. By this time, Katya had become Prostovitch's mistress. They lived in a plush apartment near the Hermitage, visited the art museum regularly, ambled alongside canals and palaces and enjoyed summer outings in *Peterhof Gardens*.

Prostovitch enrolled Yevgeny at a military academy to teach him discipline. The cadet finished with top honours and went to Moscow State University, where he studied nuclear physics. After Yevgeny graduated, Prostovitch used his influence to enrol him as a trainee in the KGB.

* * *

The young man began work in the grizzly KGB, "Big House" in Leningrad and then the *Lubyanka* in Moscow. Yevgeny rose rapidly through the ranks. He travelled under cover to Britain, France and the US either as a secret agent within the Soviet Union's diplomatic service, or as a journalist with TASS, the State's wire service. In doing so he built up a wide net of international contacts.

Mining, in particular, interested Yevgeny. He had learnt that Russia and South Africa were the biggest producers of strategic raw materials, such as platinum, palladium, vanadium and titanium and also mined gold and diamonds. Yevgeny thus made sure that he could attend international mining conferences and events such as the London Platinum Dinner, London Metals Week and De Beers' "Diamond Day" at Ascot races. He dined with global mining executives and became exceedingly knowledgeable about mining, marketing, trading and the distribution of metals and minerals. His salary was low, but his expenses were high. Yevgeny, tall, muscular and handsome with thick blonde hair, was most desirable. Russian, European and American women threw themselves at him. None of them matched Yevgeny's idol, Katya, who died suddenly when he was abroad.

The unexpected death of his beloved mother, threw Yevgeny Faramazov into depression and brought out the dark side of his character, the Dossier disclosed. Faramazov had become an extraordinary mix. On the one side he had the culture, education and background from his mother and his role models, Prostovitch and the curator of the Dostoevsky museum. Through them he loved literature, theatre, art and music and was popular on the social international circuit. These attributes masked the other side of his character. Sergey's criminal influence, beatings, school bullying and KGB conditioning and training had also turned Faramazov into a cold, ruthless, psychopath.

Faramazov's exceptional mind usually put him three to four steps ahead of his unfortunate quarries. As an undercover KGB officer, he would meet foreign agents, informers past their sell by date and rebellious politicians, academics and journalists. One by one they would die in mysterious circumstances. Faramazov would never sully his own hands. Instead he would issue the order in his very own, oblique way. The instruction would go down the line so that another team member would carry out the deed.

When the Soviet Union collapsed at the beginning of the nineties, Faramazov wondered what his fate would be. The KGB, however, was far too powerful to dissolve in the way its counterparties crumbled in East Germany, Hungary, Bulgaria and other former communist states. It eventually transformed into the Russian Federation's Federal Security Service, better known as the FSB. By now Faramazov was in his early thirties and had the rank of colonel.

During the next few years Boris Yeltsin, President of Russia, allowed the former communist state to become an anarchic "Wild East" capitalist system. Yeltsin, a drunk and corrupt buffoon, with a nasty element of ruthlessness, allowed two to three dozen traders and businessmen to acquire the cream of Russia's wealth, the Dossier alleged. These men, controlling oil, gas, coal, iron and steel, aluminium and other resources became billionaires with riches beyond their remotest dreams. Initially when Yeltsin was President, several of these oligarchs had some political influence. But when he was forced to resign at the beginning of 2,000, they were booted out. Instead political power was held within the network of the FSB, with tentacles reaching upwards.

* * *

"It was not surprising that the oligarchs were called robber barons who swindled Mother Russia out of her wealth," Sasha alleged, when I put down the Dossier briefly. "Well educated, hardworking Russians were bitter as they earned a pittance and slipped into poverty."

At the time, Faramazov was earning relatively little, even though he was an officer with a high rank in the FSB, the Dossier continued. Furious that the oligarchs had taken control of Russia's riches because of the despised Yeltsin regime, he joined many of his colleagues in pushing for a slice of *medovik*. It was time to make money, but in the chaotic Russian system, Faramazov appreciated that it was best and safer to remain loyal to the State.

Those officers, who were intent on improving their standard of living, had methods that could hardly be described as subtle. Some members of the FSB demanded protection money similarly to the Italian mafia. Others, such as Faramazov, were much more sophisticated. They offered advice, expertise and top political connections in return for a share in the business. Faramazov and several top FSB colleagues used their political influence to help local and foreign companies obtain licenses to develop mines and oil wells. With inside knowledge, they also traded commodities. Ruthless in their ambitions, they became known as the "Red Mafia" prepared to kill for their own ends and the State.

The Russian Government, under Putin, began to carry out a massive propaganda campaign against the oligarchs.

It started reversing the Yeltsin privatisation of strategic assets such as oil and gas reserves.

"Despite the spin against the oligarchs and imprisonment of some wealthy opponents, there was a growing realisation that the true criminals were several members of the FSB," Sasha alleged, when I sipped some water.

"They were pocketing multi billions of roubles. They abused and still abuse their positions by taking bribes and control of enterprises," Sasha claimed. "Anyone who opposes them can either land in prison on trumped up charges, or be murdered."

Faramazov shrewdly appreciated that there were limits to power, the Dossier went on. He decided against following other FSB officers, who became directors of State owned companies. Despite their large salaries and pay offs from foreign companies, he feared that such grace and favour were very much dependent on the whims of the leader. Faramazov, for all his faults, hated sycophancy, even though he had to outwardly respect the FSB hierarchy.

Despite his efforts to remain neutral, colleagues and superiors were jealous of Faramazov's charm, superior intellect and growing wealth, so he fell out of favour. A rebellious personality, he fought his superiors' efforts to impede his progress. It was either them or him and that meant there would be barrels of blood. Faramazov decided that it would be a loser's cause as any victory would be pyrrhic. Since he had already made several million dollars, he decided to leave Russia and establish a home in the UK.

* * *

I put down the Dossier, walked to the entrance of Kiplings and stretched my legs. By this time, it was late and waiters were standing around, waiting for us to leave.

"Faramazov employs the best accountants and lawyers and has registered companies in Switzerland, the Cayman and Virgin Islands," Sasha said, when I sat down again. "The vast bulk of his capital is abroad and he hardly pays any British tax."

"A tax loophole for rich foreign residents?"

"He owns the controlling shares in a Swiss bank based in Zurich. Money from his companies are mostly funnelled through that bank. Investments are in Russian, African and European mining, shipping, transport, real estate, logistics and defence."

"Quite an empire!"

Sasha slammed the palm of her left hand with her fist.

"Yes, and his latest pet project is the global diamond industry. My father stood up to him and paid the ultimate price."

I listened silently and indicated that she should lower her voice.

"You found out what Faramazov's henchmen did to people who didn't play ball with him, Jack. You even claimed that you landed in jail because of them. His fortune multiplied while you were behind bars. Some estimate that he may now be a billionaire."

"Isn't he still small fry when compared to the Russian Rich list? Some oligarchs are worth $20 billion or more."

"Faramazov has relentless ambition. He's intent on making more money to catch up to the super billionaires. He doesn't care whether he's involved in legitimate or illegal schemes. The means justify the end."

"What is that end?"

"I believe that he wants to return to Russia and enter politics."

"But that would be suicide."

"I've studied him; followed his actions and his methods. Got to know how he thinks and what he believes. Faramazov hates both the oligarchs, and key members of the FSB. He's formed a charitable foundation. It funds Russian charities and will finance his political campaign."

"A political campaign in Russia at this time? Are you serious?"

"He will promise to clean up Russian political and business corruption. He intends to redistribute oligarchs assets and wealth to the people and purge the secret service."

"That's some risk. If that proves to be correct, he can't be all bad."

"From what happened to you, Jack, I'm surprised you said that."

"I'm happy to move on with my life."

She shook her head in disgust and whispered: "A psychopath doesn't turn into an angel. Faramazov is a killer. If he believes it is necessary to win, he will kill again; not personally, but through his henchmen."

I was beginning to think that Sasha was a bit unhinged herself: "How do you know he was behind the death of your father? You told me that Oleg also backed miners' stakes in the Dobrenska mine; believed in economic and social democracy. I don't want to hurt your feelings, but how can you be certain that your father was murdered; that he didn't commit suicide, that the coroner was wrong?"

As soon as I said that, I felt terrible. I wished that I had been more diplomatic and sensitive, but Sasha handled it better than I thought.

"That's what Primeheart keeps saying," she replied, her tone softer, less strident.

"My father was murdered and Faramazov was behind it. Several of his murders have been similar. Oleg was not depressed. He had a strong will to live. He was fighting for his miners."

"Sorry... apologies for doubting you."

"Forget it. You will go to Dobrenska and verify it. You'll find out what is happening there; how Faramazov intends building a diamond empire; how it will help him finance his political campaign."

* * *

It was late and cold outside when I walked Sasha home. Her flat was part of a converted Church near Highgate High Street and opposite the Flask, a 17th century pub.

"Imagine if he came to power. How many people in Russia would die for the greater cause," Sasha said, as we crossed the street towards her apartment building.

"You seem to be predicting that his system would not be much different from the power structure in Russia today," I said. "If your findings are correct, surely Faramazov himself would be at risk? Surely the FSB would have a contract on him?"

"My assessment is my own informed opinion. Faramazov has never given any public indication that he wants to enter Russian politics. Unlike several exiled oligarchs, he has not bad mouthed the Russian regime."

"What about his donations to Russian educational charities and the poor? Considering his background, surely he's genuine?"

"Stop being so naive Jack. Sure, the charities do good, but they also further his own sinister cause. Faramazov is similar to philanthropists who serve their own egos and ambitions. He believes that the more money he gives, the more popular he'll become. His foundation also discourages the *siloviki,* from doing away with him. They fear reprisals from the people. Generosity to the poor will be a great help, when he eventually seeks power."

"*Siloviki?*"

"Former KGB and FSB politicians."

"No doubt Faramazov has many enemies. He must have extensive security!"

"Of course, Jack. He has a loyal band of bodyguards for himself, his wife, son and daughter. They are former loyal KGB and FSB agents who worship him. They live on his estate. They are with him constantly and are so subtle in their trade that only trained eyes can notice them. His houses have electric fences and alarm systems and he has bullet proof Bentleys."

"Realistically, Sasha, what chance do we have in nailing him? He has an exceptional mind and has all the backing he needs. I'm not in his league. It won't take long before he and his minders work out that I'm tailing him. He has eyes and ears everywhere."

"You're a survivor, Jack. You know what you're up against. That's half the battle."

"Great. That gives me a lot of confidence," I said with a half laugh.

"No matter how brilliant he is, Faramazov is isolated. He's surrounded by sycophants in his self-imposed prison. That means he's now out of touch with real people and real life. Bottom line his weaknesses are a chip on his shoulder from his boyhood and an obsessive desire to get his own way. Greed will be his undoing."

"Hope you're right," I said, unconvinced. "I'll need some security myself. Can I have a police dog?"

"That can be arranged. What will you do with the dog when you travel?"

"He'll go back to his trainers, until I come home. I also need to remain fit. Maybe an army refresher course?"

Sasha laughed: "Don't get paranoid Jack. We'll be looking out for you."

"Thanks Sasha. I'm sure you'll send flowers to the crematorium."

PART TWO

DIAMONDS IN THE DEEP

10

INTRIGUING GEM FINDS

The dinner with Sasha was so tiring that I was shattered the next day. Most business lunches and dinners have a light side to them. People make jokes and even flirt sometimes. With Sasha it was grinding, relentless concentration. No wonder she was on Scotland Yard's promotion path. Sasha was a workaholic, totally focussed and fanatical in her pursuit of her quarry. Yes, she headed a secret unit to hound and eventually prosecute Russian criminals, but Faramazov was her obsession.

To be quite frank, I didn't believe that Sasha had a hope in hell in booking Yevgeny Faramazov. Besides being a celebrity and chairman of a football club, he was a significant donor to Russian and international charities. His spin doctor was regularly quoted as "a friend of Yevgeny" when the media discussed the tycoon's activities. Unlike many ego maniac football chairmen, Faramazov kept out of the limelight, leaving his chief executive and manager to buy and choose players. If they failed to win sufficient games, they would be sacked.

In the meantime, I kept my head down and worked hard at JJ Emerging Mining Finance. It was going well.

My volatile diamond stock picks had suddenly surged when gem prices lurched upwards. Jamey Jackenhead, a natural trader, decided to take profits. He was generous with his staff and paid me a bonus that helped me move into a decent two bedroomed, garden flat near Highgate Woods. I was also looking forward to my new police dog, for company and protection.

I left voicemail messages, texted and emailed Amity, apologising for my behaviour in Barcelona. She was constantly on my mind as I was lonely and I had been attracted to her. Amity didn't reply, but just when I was giving up hope, she sent me an email saying that she was coming to London for a couple of weeks. I immediately responded saying that I had a spare room for her. She was welcome to stay, but if that didn't suit her, I would find her an inexpensive hotel.

The next Saturday I went to Heathrow to meet Amity, who was in skinny blue Levi's and a black top. The long overnight flight had tired her. Hair was ruffled and her makeup had begun to fade, but the natural beauty of her sensitive, vulnerable face, shone through. Kissing me warmly on both cheeks, Amity was far more relaxed than she had been in Barcelona.

On the train from Heathrow, Amity was full of enthusiasm, telling me that her Berkeley professor was impressed with her dissertation on Spanish Civil War Propaganda And Art. She was looking forward to going back to California for her PHD graduation. The journey passed so swiftly that I almost forgot to get out at Highgate Station. It was a short walk home and after Amity unpacked her things in her room and had a shower, we listened to some music. Hopefully she had at last decided to get on with a life without Pacy as she didn't mention him. Later we walked to Muswell Hill, the nearby London village and had dinner in a Thai restaurant.

Early on Sunday there was a knock on the door. A plain clothed policeman was there with a light brown and black Alsatian. I invited him in with the dog and we went into the garden.

"His name is Cobber and you couldn't get a better trained dog," the policeman said. "He'll be friendly to humans and other dogs. If another dog goes for him, he'll turn away."

Rob, the policeman, whispered the trigger words for me to send the dog into attack mode.

"Only use that command, if you and companions are in danger," Rob said.

Amity joined us in the garden and she and Cobber were instant friends. We both petted him and he licked our hands.

"People and owners of other dogs tend to be scared of Alsatians, but generally they are well behaved and highly intelligent," Rob said. "Cobber is a pussycat, unless..."

"Unless you give him the attack command," I said.

Amity was somewhat confused.

"Is he a police dog?"

Rob glanced at me, but thankfully said nothing.

"He's been trained by the police because they turn out the most obedient and safest Alsatians," I said.

"Guard dogs and pets," Amity said.

"Precisely," Rob said.

Rob had coffee with us and I told him that I had experience with a German Shepherd in South Africa, but didn't disclose that he was also a police dog. After he had left, leaving a huge bag of dog food, Amity, Cobber and I went for a run in the woods. Later we walked up to Highgate Hill and then down towards Hampstead Heath, with Cobber at our side. We had lunch at Kenwood House and sat on the lawn alongside yellow, blue, turquoise, pink and red Rhododendrons and Azaleas.

In the next few days, Amity and I grew closer. One evening, while we were relaxing in front of the TV, she snuggled up closely. We kissed and at last, after all the time waiting and hoping, we were between the bed sheets. My patience had paid off.

Unfortunately, I had to work, but I made sure that I would go in at 7.30AM and leave around 4PM so that I could join her. Amity decided to stay an extra week, would shop in the West End and visit art galleries. Afterwards we would meet and go to the theatre or a restaurant. At last, after the bleak years in prison, my love life was golden again.

* * *

A few days after Amity had moved in with me, I was at my desk, doodling and day dreaming. Jamey Jackenhead touched me on my shoulder and I came back to reality with a start.

Jamey was amused: "Working hard today Jack?"

"Was thinking. Nodded off briefly."

"You did brilliantly with those diamond stocks, I see they're still going up."

"The charts showed that they were oversold and were due for a rally. Their businesses aren't doing badly and they have interesting prospects."

"Maybe we should have held on to the shares."

"You've only sold half. Might as well keep the others and see what happens to the diamond market."

"I spoke to a broker and he thinks that there could be a diamond shortage."

"Not for a while. The Russian *Gochran* is a big seller," I said.

"The *Gochran?*"

"The Russian Treasury. My Antwerp diamond source told me that the *Gochran* can make a big difference in the market. Alrosa, the state controlled Russian diamond company, usually sells production independently or through De Beers' Diamond Trading Company. When the market is bad and demand is poor, the *Gochran* buys Alrosa's diamonds and stockpiles them. The *Gochran* waits until the market improves and then sells the diamonds to global dealers. When it does, prices tend to slip again."

"Are you saying that the flurry in diamond prices and shares won't last?"

"They're looking a bit frothy. It wouldn't surprise me if diamond prices stagnate or even fall in coming months. When the *Gochran* stops offloading diamonds in a year or so, supplies should lag behind demand. Gem prices could then rise again. Diamond companies will do well and their share prices should rise."

"What else did your Antwerp diamond dealer tell you?"

"The older mines in Southern Africa, Russia and Australia are finding it increasingly difficult to produce large quantities of quality gems. In the meantime, diamond jewellery is becoming more popular in China, India, other Asian nations and Latin America."

"So, diamond prices could eventually rise a lot further?"

"Yes. Gold has soared more than fivefold since 9/11, but diamonds are still cheap."

"Why?"

"De Beers' Diamond Trading Company, which used to control 80 percent of the market, had a highly successful cartel. It comprised African and Russian producers. It was then called the Central Selling Organisation and dubbed "The Syndicate" in the diamond world. The cartel was so powerful that it had the cash to buy surpluses of rough diamonds. These purchases underpinned prices and created the myth that they would never fall. By the 1980s and 1990s, Australia, Canada and other big producers came on stream. They began to sell their production to independent dealers, so De Beers' share of the market, shrank. De Beers' directors came to the realisation that the diamond cartel was crumbling and could no longer control the market.

"And since then prices have been exceedingly volatile," Jamey said.

"After 9/11 and during the 2008 to 2009 recession, rough diamond prices plunged. Polished diamond prices have fluctuated wildly, but are still well below their peaks of some thirty years ago.

"You've confirmed what I've been thinking, Jack. That's why I wanted to discuss my strategy."

"Let me make an educated guess. You want me to find diamond exploration companies which are on the brink of discoveries."

"Precisely. I want you to carry out a thorough search for companies prospecting for diamonds."

"Africa, Canada, Russia?"

"Not just there. I want you to look for emerging diamond companies anywhere. They can be in the most unlikely places. Who would have guessed a few years ago that there would be large diamond deposits in the icy region of northern Canada? De Beers prospected for diamonds in Australia for years without success. Eureka! Out of the blue someone found the Argyle mine in Western Australia. Patience, persistence and lateral ideas, that's what we need, Jack!"

* * *

Over the next few days I poured over JJ Emerging's own

records and googled mining and geological sites, business libraries and companies for information on diamonds. Before long we had impressive data on gem exploration.

One afternoon, Isobel Steeplefoot was searching for a warm winter holiday on the Net.

"Hey Jack, come and take a look at this," she called.

I went over to her desk and saw her reading a local newspaper report about the Canary Islands. An environmental group was protesting about a company that was searching for diamonds on a beach in Lanzarote. The coastal exploration was close to a conservation area near a dormant volcano. The environmentalists feared that the ecology would be spoilt. According to the report, a small group of geologists and workers were messing up the beach. Divers were jumping off the rocks and taking suction pipes down to the ocean floor. The gravel was being sucked from the bottom of the sea about 20 to 30 metres from the shore and pumped on to the beach. Some prospectors were sifting the sand with pans; others were digging on the beach.

The report fascinated me as Fred Carrender had not told me about diamond exploration in the Canary Islands. The islands had been ignored even though they had experienced considerable volcanic activity, hundreds of millions of years ago. Several volcanoes were still active and Lanzarote had a massive volcanic eruption in the 18th century.

Isobel and I immediately began to research the region and found that the Canaries are an archipelago of seven large and some smaller islands. From east to west, the islands are in an arc and are a popular winter tourist spot, with Lanzarote being the most northern island. They are based near the Tropic of Cancer, about 71 miles from the West African coast. This intrigued us as Sierra Leone, to the south east of the islands, was a significant diamond producer.

Timanfaya, Lanzarote's volcano, erupted around 1750 and the molten lava burst out of the crown and poured down the mountain, across fields towards the coast. Rivers were covered with magma that turned into grey black and brown red rocks, forming an extensive volcanic pipe. From the cone in the centre of the volcano to the sea, the pipe was nearly four miles long.

"The pipe is called Atlantis, as part of it is an under-water tunnel," an excited Isobel said. "Perhaps it ends at the lost city of Atlantis."

"Another Hollywood script, Isobel?"

Laughing, we continued to sift through our database. Eventually we found a geological paper that stated that "carbonatite rocks" were found in the "Canary archipelagos".

The study stated that a proposal had been made "to deep drill Canary Island volcanic rocks" to see whether there were "carbonatites, kimberlites and lamproites." That information was seriously exciting as Fred had drummed into me that diamonds could be found in either kimberlite or lamproite rocks. Some of the world's largest and most valuable gem diamond deposits had been discovered on Namibia's beaches and offshore, beneath the sea, he had said.

Diamonds ended up on the Namibian coast because of the "weathering" of kimberlite pipes, Fred had explained. Heavy winds, rains and rivers had transported kimberlite rocks, multi millions of years old, down to the coast. According to some estimates billions of carats of diamonds, most of them gems, eventually found their way to the sea. Since only the toughest diamonds could survive the battering over the years, top notch gems eventually settled there. Few people exploited these finds, until in 1970, a Texan entrepreneur began marine mining in the Atlantic Ocean, near the Namibian coast. His marine diamond operation discovered some magnificent diamonds, Fred had said.

Excited that there might be a similar find in Lanzarote, I phoned Fred. He was unavailable as he was prospecting somewhere. Before discussing the Canary exploration, with Jamey Jackenhead and colleagues, I contacted Basil Bleedon, the reporter who wrote the story. Bleedon who worked for the Lanzarote Gazette, was thrilled that his scoop and byline had been spotted on the Net. The international exposure would help him when he applied for London media jobs. When I told him that I worked for a mining finance boutique, he was impressed and was happy to talk about his story.

"Conservationists are protecting Lanzarote's volcanic landscape, caves, coves and beaches," he said. "One of them complained about damage to a beach, so the editor told me to go there,"

"What did you find?"

"A dozen workers were scraping sand and rocks on the beach and sifting gravel in pans; others were diving off rocks and boats with suction pipes."

"Who were they?"

"They weren't very friendly and obviously disliked my intrusion. They weren't prepared to disclose what they were doing and how long they had been there. When I told them that I was a reporter, they told me to get lost."

"So how did you find out that they were digging for diamonds?"

"An educated guess. *Charco de los Clicos*, a lovely beach and cove, is a few miles away. The cove is large with a green coloured lagoon alongside the beach. Tourists go there and look for 'peridots' ---- semi-precious green gemstones. They were originally in volcanic rock which the sea crushed and wore down."

"What are the stones worth?"

"Virtually nothing. Local shops and market jewellers

sell them for a few euros."

"How come you concluded that they were searching for diamonds on the other beach?"

"My uncle is a mining engineer. I called him and he said that it was possible that diamonds were there because of the volcano. His only surprise was that no-one had bothered exploring for gems, until now."

"Did the people on the beach confirm that they were prospecting for diamonds?"

"Not a chance. Why let the world know? They must be furious that my story is on the Net."

"Did you ask them who they worked for?"

"Obviously. I might have just finished university, but I'm not a total novice," Bleedon said.

"I didn't say that you were."

"I'm getting work experience and a bit of sun here. Do you have any contacts on Fleet Street?"

"I'm afraid not, but if I can help, I'll let you know. You have my number on your mobile. Please keep me in the loop. I know a bit about diamonds and am happy to help."

"What's in it for me? Can I do some freelance research for you?"

"That depends on your info. Did you find out the name of the company?"

"Conservationists told me that it was Canary Diamond Mines."

* * *

Later that day, Amity was waiting for me on the south bank of the Thames, close to the Globe Theatre. I told her my news.

"Remember when we were in Madrid, we found that Carlos Maxos had a stake in Canary Diamond Mines.

Guess what? Canary is now prospecting for diamonds in Lanzarote."

Amity tensed up.

"Anything wrong? Did you come across Maxos again?"

She was silent for a while and then blurted out: "Yes, soon after Barcelona. He phoned me when I returned to Madrid. Invited me to have a drink with him. I decided to go and find out more about Pacy."

"Did he mention anything?"

"No, but something happened. He insisted that he drop me off at my apartment and forced his way in."

"He tried to...?"

Tears welled up.

"He tried, but I managed to push my knee into his groin."

"And then?"

"He swore, pushed me against the wall and left."

"Why didn't you let me know?

"What was the point? You had left Spain."

"Did you tell the police?"

"Do you really think they would have believed me? What evidence did I have?"

"Did Maxos pester you again?"

"A few days later, I was at the food market with one of my friends. He was there with his gang...I could see that they were laughing at me."

"Sick! I would have nothing to do with him, but now they are exploring for diamonds in the Canary Islands, my boss is going to nag me. I'll have to find out what the Maxos crowd know."

"I would steer clear of them if I were you."

"It's my job, Amity. I'll have to speak to my boss about it."

We went into the Globe, stood in the pit and watched

Twelfth Night. Amity didn't seem to be enjoying the show. On the way back home, I tactlessly asked if she knew anyone who could give me background on Maxos and friends. She glared at me. That evening I tried to kiss her, but she pushed me away. Cursing Maxos, I left the bedroom, watched TV and stroked Cobber instead.

Later that night, I opened my laptop to find out more about Maxos. I searched the Net for Major General Ario Doval, grandfather of Maxos. A New York Times article stated that a judge had decided to investigate the execution and disappearance of more than a hundred thousand civilians between 1936 and 1939. The judge had to drop the Civil War enquiry. Prosecutors maintained that almost all those who could be guilty, were either dead or too old. Moreover, after the death of Franco there was an amnesty for those who had committed Civil War crimes.

The victims' families and human rights groups, protested vigorously when the judge's inquiry collapsed. I decided that pressure groups could help me find out about the Maxos and Doval families and showed the article to Amity the next day. After some persuasion, she promised to speak to her Spanish History Professor.

* * *

Jamey Jackenhead was pacing the office, when I arrived.

"Isobel told me that they're prospecting for diamonds in the Canaries. What's up?"

"We don't know if they've found any diamonds. If they did, the discovery could be uneconomic. It's still early days."

"But they're there and have been trying to keep it secret. They wouldn't be wasting their time," Jamey said. "They must know something."

He looked at a map and I showed him the Russian

geology paper that I had found.

He began to read aloud and pointed to various areas on the map.

"The Canary archipelago of volcanic islands were formed during the Cretaceous and Miocene period some 80 million years ago. Volcanoes on most of the islands are active and Lanzarote, Tenerife, La Palma and El Hierro, have had eruptions in the past five hundred years."

"Carbonatite rocks are the key to a possible diamond find," I said, pointing to a paragraph in the paper: "Carbonatites have been found in the oceanic islands of the Cape Verde and Canary archipelagos...kimberlites likewise may well exist."

"If I recall, other Russian geologists have carried out research on the islands' resources," Jamey said, and began to ruffle through his filing cabinet. "Ah, here it is. A paper from Russia's Institute of Geology."

"Do you think the Russians are involved in this venture," I said and immediately regretted my indiscretion. There was no way that I wanted Jamey to know that I was investigating Faramazov's potential involvement in Canary Diamond Mines.

"Who knows, maybe, maybe not. They've been mining diamonds in Angola and are exploring in other parts of Africa."

Jamey paged through the report: "Listen to this! It's headed, 'Diamonds in carbonatites off Fuerteventura island'. That journalist was guessing, but he's definitely on the right track."

I peered over his shoulder and wondered what Fred Carrender would say about the fascinating geological study. It stated: "At present, diamond-bearing rocks, notably kimberlites and lamproites have been found with a high content of carbonatites."

"Wow. Papers published by two independent Russian geologists contend that diamonds could be present in the Canary Islands," Jamey said.

The geologists had "conducted field research in Fuerteventura. The aim was to search for diamond-bearing rocks. They found "three diamonds and graphite-like carbon particles" when they probed for gems. The paper added that "the diamonds were tiny and were either flat or octahedral crystals".

"The diamond microcrystals are the first finding of diamonds in the Canary archipelago," the paper said.

"Bottom line diamonds have been discovered in Canaries," Jackenhead shouted.

Other staff members who overheard, crowded into his small office.

"But they're prospecting in Lanzarote, not Fuerteventura," I said.

"Fuerteventura is very close to Lanzarote so they're probably exploring both islands," Isobel said.

11

The Bristol Connection

I was in a quandary on whether to disclose to Jackenhead all that I knew. It was almost lunch time, so I slipped out of the office, phoned Sasha Melnikov and met her in a sandwich bar in Trafalgar Square. Being as discrete as possible, we crossed over to the square, sat down near the fountain and ate our sandwiches in the sunshine.

"Jackenhead wants me to get involved in Canary Diamond Mines," I said.

"And you're wondering what to tell him?"

"I guess so."

"This is what you do. Investigate the company as if you are starting from scratch. You already know that Bristol GemDiam Mining and Gruchot Diamond Dealing have stakes in MSP España, which owns Canary Diamond Mines. After you have checked to see whether there have been any changes in ownership, tell Jamey Jackenhead that you met Carlos Maxos and colleagues; that you've now discovered they're involved in Canary."

"Then what?"

"Phone Maxos and say that you're working for a mining finance boutique; that you found out about Canary

Diamond Mines on the Net, traced the shareholders and discovered that MSP España was a shareholder."

"Won't he be suspicious?"

"If he sounds wary, tell him the truth and say that you've been instructed to assess diamond exploration companies. Tell him that your boss is interested in Canary."

"What about Jackenhead? Shouldn't I warn him that Maxos might have sold smuggled diamonds to finance MSP España's operations?"

"You don't have to tell him about that. There's no evidence that Maxos had anything to do with smuggled diamonds or Pacy Palatus' murder."

"Amity Fernandez believes that he's involved."

"Her belief isn't proof. Just tell Jackenhead that you will investigate the background of Maxos and the companies; carry out thorough due diligence."

"After that?"

"If your suspicions are confirmed, tell Jackenhead not to get involved."

"And if he does?"

"That's his decision. You will have done the right thing and warned him."

So far, we hadn't discussed an important factor.

"Have you found out whether Faramazov has stakes in Bristol and Gruchot?"

"Banque Narodsky Faramon, Faramazov's Swiss Bank, controls Narodsky Diamante Bank in Antwerp. The Belgian bank is Gruchot's banker," Sasha said.

Narodsky Faramon. That brought back memories! Hellish memories. Bad stuff that I wrote about in *Trader Jack,* while I was doing time.

"How can you be sure that Narodsky Diamante is Gruchot's bank?" I said.

"I have my sources."

* * *

After Melnikov left, I was still shaking. It struck home that I was in denial about my dealings with very dangerous people. A few months previously, I had seen the body of Pacy Palatus in Johannesburg and witnessed the murder of Pedro Sanchez in Barcelona. When the smugglers had spotted me, I was almost killed.

Involved in work, I had managed to put the incidents out of my mind. Now worries were making me fret. I shuffled around Trafalgar Square, absently watching tourists take photos and then went to the National Gallery to absorb myself in paintings.

Calm again after a couple of hours, I called Jackenhead and left a message on his voicemail: "Hi Jamey, I'm off to the Spanish Chamber of Commerce to see whether they have records on Canary Diamond Mining. My friend is fluent in Spanish and she'll check Spanish publications to see who's involved in the operation."

* * *

Later in the afternoon, Amity was waiting for me at Baker Street station.

"My boss wants me to find out more about Maxos' company, Amity. Please help me."

"You know very well that I don't want to have anything to do with him. Madame Tussauds is nearby. Can't we go there?"

"Later. Please, my boss is putting pressure on me."

"OK, OK, as long as I just research. Nothing else!"

"Promise Amity."

We walked to Wigmore Street, where the Spanish

Chamber was situated and asked if we could use the library.
It didn't take long before Amity was searching through
the records. We couldn't find information on Canary Diamond Mines, but found that Bristol GemDiam Mining
had bought Gruchot's shares and had become the majority
shareholder of MSP España. Gruchot received shares in
Bristol, as payment.

I explained the deal to Amity, who was a bit confused
about the changes: "Bristol GemDiam now owns 79 percent of MSP España and Maxos and his partners hold the
remaining 21 percent of the shares. MSP España owns
Canary Diamond Mines, so Bristol, which has the majority
stake in MSP, is now the company controlling the Canary
Islands' diamond prospect. Maxos and friends effectively
own 21 percent of the mine and Gruchot has an indirect
stake in Canary, via his shares in Bristol."

"I still don't understand why they made those changes."

"London is a major financial centre and Bristol is a
British company. They probably want to use it to raise
money for Canary Diamond Mines' operations."

"I can't get my head around finance."

"Let's try and find out what they're up to," I said, as we
began to search for news reports in Spanish publications.
Amity saw stories in *El País*, a leading Spanish daily newspaper and *Cinco Días*, the financial daily. They reported that
MSP España had found a potentially interesting diamond
prospect and had begun to search for gems. More details
would be disclosed in the company's prospectus ahead of
an impending "initial public offering" i.e. listing on the
Madrid Exchange.

I also logged into UK Companies House for information on Bristol GemDiam Mining. The company confirmed
that it had purchased control of MSP España Mining, which
had "exceedingly interesting prospects". Bristol GemDiam

intended applying for a listing on AIM, London's junior stock exchange. It had appointed an investment bank, accountants and lawyers as advisors. The money from a potential listing would be used to "finance exploration and eventual exploitation of diamond resources". Details would be disclosed once the exchange and the UK regulator, approved the listing.

The main shareholders of Bristol GemDiam were chief executive Gerald Gleep and Armand Gruchot. Faramazov's Narodsky Diamante Bank also had a stake. I was nervous and satisfied at the same time; nervous because of my memories about Narodsky and chuffed with myself for confirming the Faramazov link.

I phoned Jackenhead: "Hi Jamey. I've found out that Bristol GemDiam Mining has a majority stake in MSP España, which in turn owns Canary Diamond Mines. Bristol is about to be listed."

"Well done, Jack! We can pitch for underwriter."

"I think that they already have an advisor and underwriter for the shares."

"Who have they appointed as their underwriter?"

"Baconbrass Finance. Their lawyers and accountants are...."

"Baconbrass? They haven't been around that long. They act for a Swiss bank," Jackenhead said.

"Which Swiss bank?"

"Banque Faramon Narodsky. Baconbrass Finance has connections with Russian mining and oil companies."

This was further proof that Faramazov was deeply involved and an indication that the Canary Islands diamond prospect had considerable potential.

* * *

Afterwards we wandered through Madame Tussauds, giggling at wax works of celebrities and historical figures. Later, when we had a light dinner in a restaurant nearby, Amity pounded me with questions.

"I haven't a clue what you're doing, Jack. Explain what all this high finance is about."

"Sure. Canary Diamond Mines is prospecting for gems in Lanzarote. If it finds diamonds it will be worth a lot of money."

"Go on."

"MSP España, the company that Maxos runs, needs more money to finance Canary Diamond Mines' exploration. They intend floating MSP España on the Madrid Stock Exchange to raise that cash. Fund managers and other investors will then be able to buy shares in MSP. The capital raised from the share issue will fund the development of Canary."

"Why are these different companies owning shares in each other?"

"They have done so to keep control of Canary Diamond Mines. The public - the outside investors - will own shares in MSP España, but they won't control either MSP or the mine."

"What happens when the shares are listed?"

"The shares will go up if the company finds diamonds and does well. Bristol and Maxos and partners, who own a lot of MSP's shares, will do the best. The public, the outside, "minority" shareholders, will also make money."

"And if Canary doesn't find diamonds?"

"The shares will fall. The public will lose and the owners won't do as well as they had hoped."

"Maxos and his gang won't lose?"

"Not if they're careful. The money raised from the listing will line their pockets. They'll only lose if there's a total collapse of the company."

"So, it's win, win for them?"

"Something like that."

"How does Bristol GemDiam figure in this?"

"Think of a pyramid. Bristol is the British company at the top of the pyramid. It holds shares in MSP España in the middle, which in turn controls Canary Diamond Mines at the base of the pyramid."

"That doesn't explain why Bristol is also listing its shares in London. Surely MSP España's Madrid listing is sufficient?"

"That's an interesting one. London has a long history as a mining finance centre. The biggest mining companies in the world are listed in London, including De Beers' owner, Anglo American."

"So, Bristol owns 79 per cent of MSP's shares for good reason."

"Precisely. It is the controlling shareholder at the top of the pyramid. Maxos, Santos and Pinot run MSP España, but they are not the ultimate owners. In terms of the deal they own shares in MSP and also have the option i.e. right to purchase shares in Bristol, when its shares are listed on the London exchange. Outside investors will be able to buy Bristol shares and indirectly hold a stake in both MSP and Canary Diamonds. The sale of the shares will raise money for Bristol, which it can use to finance the Canary mine or other ventures."

"And Maxos, Santos and Pinot are likely to become rich."

"If Canary Diamond Mining finds gems, they could make a fortune, but it's too soon to be sure."

"You mentioned 'underwriting' to your boss. What's that?"

"A company issues shares and thus raises capital, when it is listed on the stock exchange. The investment bank, which is the underwriter, guarantees that the company will raise all the money it needs. It does so by purchasing shares that investors don't want. If for example, Bristol issues 10 million shares and investors only buy 9 million, the underwriter must buy the remaining 1 million. The underwriter thus underwrites, i.e. ensures that the company will get all the finance it needs."

"What's in it for the underwriter?"

"The investment bank receives a fee. They generally underwrite a listing if they think it will succeed."

"Sounds pretty speculative."

"Mining exploration issues generally are, but they manage to raise money because of investors' gambling instincts."

We climbed into a taxi and went home. Cobber was excited when we hurriedly changed and went for a run in the woods. It was a happy and sad day. Amity was going to fly back home that weekend and I would miss her.

* * *

When I saw Jackenhead the next day, he was in a rotten mood.

"Hell Jack, I thought that we had a good opportunity, but we were too slow."

"What are you getting at?"

"We lost the Bristol underwriting deal. It was your job, Jack. I told you to dig into exploration possibilities. Isobel, not you, found Canary. When she did, you should have moved faster."

I smarted under the unreasonable admonishment, but decided to bite my lip and say nothing.

"I'm sure there will be other chances," I said.

"Maybe. Why don't you check land prices around Canary beaches? If they discover diamonds in Lanzarote or

Fuerteventura, there could be a rush for claims."

I phoned a few estate agents in Lanzarote, Fuerteventura and Tenerife, another island with a big volcano. They said that land prices had already climbed because a Spanish company had been buying. One of them betrayed confidences and disclosed the identity. It was ESBR Real Estate, an MSP España subsidiary.

Later in the afternoon, while I was absorbed in my job, I heard a familiar voice: "Good day Mr Sniper, since when did you become a pen pusher? Why aren't you in the veld?"

"Fred, what are you doing here? You should have let me know you were coming?"

Fred Carrender, in a worn, dark brown leather jacket, was standing at the doorway of our small office. I rushed up to him and he shook my hand warmly and slapped me on my back.

"Was just checking up on you, young man," Fred said, his face a broad grin. "Wanted to surprise you."

"Come Fred, let me introduce you. This is Isobel and Michael. The guy in the small office over there is our boss --- Jamey Jackenhead."

The others looked up from their computers and greeted him.

Jamey overheard: "Well I never! Fred Carrender. The great man. Welcome!"

Jamey, excited, virtually dragged Fred into his office, with me behind him.

"Good to see you again Mr Carrender, I've heard that the platinum deposit you discovered has become one of the biggest mines."

"Guess I was lucky," Fred said with his usual modesty.

"What are you doing in London?"

"I'm on my way to Russia; thought I would relax here for a few days."

"Russia? What are you going to be doing there?" Jackenhead asked.

"I've been commissioned to assess a potential diamond project. It's in north western Russia."

"Are Westerners allowed to invest?"

"Maybe, but State-owned mining companies hold most of the shares."

"If Westerners can participate, maybe we should take a look." I said, hoping that Jackenhead, would take the bait.

Jackenhead, still annoyed about the Canary underwriting miss wasn't hooked.

"I need you here, Jack."

"It would be good experience for him and it would give you first bite," Fred said. "From what they tell me it's a big diamond deposit."

"Why don't we have dinner tonight so we can discuss it?" Jackenhead said. "Is it OK if I bring my girlfriend along. She's Russian and could give you some contacts."

"Is it...?"

"Yes, Sasha Melnikov, Jack."

Poor Jamey. He was still under the illusion that Sasha was interested. I was a little peeved that she was going behind my back to check what I was doing.

"What about you, Jack?" Fred asked.

"His girlfriend speaks Spanish and has helped us research Canary," Jackenhead said.

"She can also join us," Fred said. "It's a lovely evening. Let's meet in Hyde Park at The Diana Memorial Fountain and stroll across to Bayswater."

* * *

London had been lucky in the past week or so. After snow and sleet in the final dreary winter months and almost continuous rain in the summer, September was filled with brilliant sunshine. It was early evening, but the days were still lengthy and the light bright. After the gloomy, cold, dark winter and mainly grey spring and summer, Londoners were lightening up. There was optimism in the air. People were walking around Hyde Park's *Serpentine*. Children were feeding swans and ducks and cormorants relaxed on poles before diving into the water for fish.

Remarkably, all of us were on time. Sasha, in a high neck black dress with a floral pattern, was striking. She had softened her look with some glittery eye shadow and pink lipstick. I kept glancing at Amity. It was evident that her grief had not entirely subsided, but she had at last acknowledged that Pacy would have wanted her to grasp life. Light had returned to her penetrating brown eyes which glistened while she laughed and chatted. Amity's long tight fitted blue dress clung to her exquisitely crafted, hour glass figure. Her high heeled, silver shoes showed off toned legs beneath the slit in her dress. Isobel was in stark contrast to Amity and Sasha. She hadn't changed out of her crumpled brown office suit and looked awkward.

As we slowly made our way around the lake, enjoying the relaxing walk, Fred explained why he was off to Russia.

"Alexei Ignatyevna has commissioned me. He used to work for Alrosa and is chief executive of the mine."

"Does the State have total control over the Russian diamond industry?" Jamey asked.

"Alrosa is Russia's biggest diamond company. It has become the largest producer in the world, alongside Botswana. Alrosa's main mines are in Mirsky, Siberia. The Russian Federation and Republic of Sakha mines, also known as Yakutia, own the majority shareholdings in Alrosa. Management and senior employees have a small stake. A few years ago, Alrosa was listed on the Moscow stock exchange. Outside investors now own a small proportion of the shares."

"I thought that some Western companies had invested directly in Russian diamond mines," Isobel said. "What happened to them?"

"They were pushed out," Sasha said, her sour expression only noticed by me.

"Alexei wants me to give him an independent assessment," Fred said.

"Where's the mine?" Jamey asked.

"Several hundred miles north west of Moscow and east of Lomonosov and St Petersburg."

"That's fairly near to Arkhangelsk. Is it the Lomonosov diamond deposit?"

"I'm afraid I can't discuss details at this stage," Fred said. "I must still assess whether the prospect is worthwhile."

"Is it near Dobrenska?" Sasha asked. She seemed cool, but I sensed that she was now on high alert.

"Not far from there. The kimberlite pipe covers a large area. The State controls most of it, but there are Russian and foreign investors who hold stakes in other claims."

"What protection for foreigners? There has been a lot of dirty business in Russian mining deals," Jamey said. "When Yeltsin privatised industries in the 1990s, Western companies invested. Several of them were thrown out and failed to recover their money."

"If that's been happening, why are you interested, Jamey?" Isobel asked. "Surely it's prudent to steer clear?"

Jamey glanced at Fred: "Do you agree with her?"

"Russia has always been problematic for foreigners, but the government is improving its policies. I've made some enquiries. The potential mine that I'm studying is owned by Alrosa. Alexei Ignatyevna told me that Alrosa wishes to sell a small stake to Western and Russian investors, in return for other prospects."

"Do you trust him?" Sasha asked.

Fred laughed: "I think Alexei is straight. He paid my fee upfront."

"Guess that you're paying for dinner, Fred?" Sasha said with a broad smile as she shuffled closer to him.

Poor Jamey. It was evident that despite the age difference there was a spark between Sasha and Fred. Knowing Sasha, she was probably intending to use Fred. Find out what Faramazov was doing in Russia. Later that evening we sat around a large round table in a Chinese restaurant in Bayswater, sharing seafood, duck and noodles. Sasha was sitting between Jamey and Fred. Despite Jamey's efforts to get her attention, she ignored him and kept her gaze on Fred, casually touching him on the shoulder. I felt sorry for Jamey, who looked desperate after boasting about Sasha in the office. I glanced at Isobel. The irony was that she really liked Jamey, but he wasn't the slightest bit interested in her.

Amity had also noticed and brought Isobel into the conversation.

"Jack told me that you're very talented; speak several languages, play the violin for an amateur orchestra and paint. How come you're working for a finance company?"

"It's a good job," Isobel said. "I've got time for my hobbies."

"Then I should work you harder, Isobel," Jamey said, relieved that he could turn his attention away from Sasha and Fred. "When is your next concert?"

"In a fortnight. You're all invited. Mozart and Vivaldi. Our soloists have won junior competitions. They're good."

"Amity is off to San Francisco and Fred will be in Russia, so I guess we can go, Jamey," I said, attempting to be a matchmaker.

"Why doesn't Jack come with me to Russia?" Fred

suggested. "He can assess the project for you, Jamey."

Sasha and I looked at each other. No doubt, she wanted me to rush through the open door, but I thought that the best ploy was to be casual.

"It would be good experience, Jamey," I said. "If the Russians want foreign backing again, we would be ahead of the others. It would give me a good feel; not only for diamonds but also other mines."

"I've got a good friend who could be an interpreter," Sasha said. "She's a journalist and knows what's going on. They will probably offer you a state tourist guide, but it's best to get someone who's independent."

"What about the Canary Islands?" Jamey asked, unsure whether his firm should get involved with Russia.

"Isobel helped me with the research. A Spanish company has been buying undeveloped coastal land in Lanzarote, Fuerteventura and Tenerife," I said. "Prices have been going up."

"Seems that they believe that there are diamonds there," Fred said.

"Do you think I should stake some claims in the Canary Islands?" Jamey asked.

"I don't know. I've never studied the Canaries," Fred said.

"OK Jack, you can go to Russia with Fred. Please make enquiries about land, Isobel. I've got a feeling there's going to be a diamond rush in the Canaries. The deal Fred, is that Jack goes to Lanzarote afterwards and you advise us. Is that OK with you?"

"Fine with me. Are you going to be paying upfront?" Fred said.

"Not a chance. You find those diamonds first," Jamey said.

* * *

Outside the restaurant, there was an embarrassing moment.

"Can I take you home, Sasha?" Jamey asked.

I felt sorry for him when Sasha shook her head in disdain.

"It's early, let's go for a drink," Isobel said.

"Why don't you go, Jamey?" Amity said.

"Good idea. It would be good to talk to Fred. I haven't seen him in a long time," I said.

Fortunately, Jamey took the hint and went into the nearest pub with Isobel. The rest of us crossed Bayswater Road and ambled into Hyde Park again. Sasha was now walking so close to Fred, that she kept brushing his elbow.

"I'll email Sonya Moldanya and ask her if she can be your interpreter and guide," she said. "Sonya's a Moscow journalist and will give you good idea on what is happening in Russia."

"As long as she doesn't write an article about me," Fred said.

"I'll tell her to be discreet," Sasha said. "But if there is a big diamond story you must agree to a scoop."

I didn't have much opportunity to talk to Fred, as Sasha overwhelmed him with a charm offensive. It was becoming increasingly obvious what was going to happen.

"Who is she?" Amity asked, as we walked hand in hand, behind them over Serpentine Bridge towards the Kensington Road entrance of Hyde Park. By now Sasha had her elbow interlocked in Fred's arm. The Royal Kensington Hotel was close by. It was time for us to part ways.

Amity had to fly off to San Francisco the next day. We arrived home and the lights were off. Silently we undressed each other. The moon was full and the dim blue white light shone on the silhouette of Amity body as she stood, back towards the garden window. I marvelled at her shape, shuffled close to her and gently placed my hands at the back of her neck and ran them over her shoulders, down her back and spine and then kissed her deeply. Our embrace lingered and she led me into the bedroom for our final night together.

12

RUSSIAN MELEE

The flight from St Petersburg to Arkhangelsk at the northern tip of Russia, took less than two hours. Sonya Moldanya was waiting for us at the airport. Sonya, with a small, round figure, was barely five foot tall. Her hair was a deep copper red that fell in hundreds of tiny ringlets upon her shoulders. Wide green eyes were a feature of her pale, pretty face.

A driver was waiting to take us to Vogdana, the diamond mine that Fred was going to examine. We side tracked the city of Arkhangelsk and drove past the River Dvina. Our hotel was opposite *Malye Karely*, an open museum of 18th century wooden peasant huts and churches. After depositing some of our luggage in the hotel's timber cottages and trying out salted herrings for lunch, we drove to the mine. It was a sunny autumn day and the 110-kilometre journey from the hotel, took us through a magical landscape of forests, streams, gorges and lakes. After a brief break at a 16th century monastery on the edge of a lake, we headed south east. Not far from the road were marshes. Water between the reeds glinted in the sun.

Sonya tensed up when a convoy of army jeeps and trucks crossed an intersection and a military policeman stopped our car. He spoke to our driver briefly and looked inside. We showed him our passports while Sonya rummaged through her handbag. She was about to hand over her identity card, when an officer shouted at the policeman and he let us through.

"Phew...If he had noticed that I'm a journalist ...," she said.

"Do they still have nuclear missile bases near Arkhangelsk?" I asked. "What about the agreement between the US and Russia?"

Sonya translated for the driver and he shook his head.

"What did he say?" Fred asked.

"Nothing," Sonya said, with a half laugh. "Welcome to Russia."

There were no further road blocks and about half an hour later we got out the car and stretched our legs. The air was fresh and chilly despite the bright sun, but we were well covered. I shivered at the prospect of being there in the depths of winter, with the temperature well below freezing point.

Alexei Ignatyevna was in the office of Vogdana Diamond Mine when we arrived. Totally bald, the chief executive of the mine was about six foot five with thick, muscular arms. The giant's tight handshake made me grimace.

"Hi Alexei, still wrestling for fun," Fred said

"It's lonely out here. Good to see you all," Alexei said and did his best to hold Sonya's hand gently.

Alexei took out a bottle of vodka, poured large tots into five glasses and gave one to our driver.

"Try this, it will get your juices going," Alexei said. He swigged the first glass and then poured the liquid into another.

"You're a bit late. Any problem getting here?"

"Just the military. A minor holdup."

"That's normal. There have been military bases around

here for a long time," Alexei said with a thoughtful frown. "Come to think of it, there has been an increase in activity in the past month."

I'm not sure whether two to three glasses of vodka affected Fred's judgement, but his work took almost a day. We walked around the mine while he took photographs, examined maps, assessments and samples of gems. Alexei spoke good English, albeit in a thick Russian accent, but had to interpret Fred's assessment for the rest of the mine's managers. I dutifully wrote down Fred's positive comments, potential revenue numbers and projections for Jackenhead.

"I believe Dobrenska is near here," I said.

"About an hour away," Alexei said. "They've got problems. Their miners are on strike."

"Aren't the authorities against strikes? Why are they taking the risk?" Sonya asked.

"The mine was taken over about 18 months ago. Workers are dissatisfied with the deal and the new management."

"What about the miners here?" I asked, thinking to myself that it would be foolhardy for Jackenhead to risk an investment in Vogdana.

"They have a good deal. Alrosa owns Vogdana and management and workers get a share of the profits. They have free housing, medical care and good pensions. When winter comes, life here is hard. We believe that they deserve good wages."

"Fred told me that your mine needs capital. What security for Western investors, if they put money in it? What's the minimum and maximum investment for a foreigner?"

"This mine is rich. Jackenhead and his clients would get up to 5 percent and a watertight agreement. You can trust Alexei. He's an old friend," Fred said.

"I looked across at Sonya and could see that she was sceptical.

"The miners' stake in Vogdana will remain the same," Alexei said. "They are paid their wages and receive 10 percent of the profits."

"Isn't Dobrenska giving their miners a similar cut?"

"It's complicated. Ask Valdia, the new owner. We aren't connected."

"Why is it complicated?"

"After Valdia took over management of the mine, the workers' share of the profits declined. There were plenty promises but nothing was forthcoming."

"Surely the new managers realise that it doesn't pay to be greedy," Fred said. "There should be enough for all."

"It's not only about greed, it's about power," Alexei said. "The Valdia managers believe that if they give in now, the workers will ask for more and more. They are making a stand. Anyway, that's their business. Vogdana miners are well paid and get generous perks, benefits and leave. They are happy here."

Before we left, Alexei poured more vodka into our glasses while Alesha, his personal assistant, passed us soup and sandwiches.

* * *

As had been pre-arranged with Sasha and Sonya, we drove to Dobrenska. On the outskirts of the town, where there was a dense forest, we checked into a "dacha". The large wooden country house had been converted into a small hotel. Fred, who had drunk far more than he could handle, staggered into his room and dropped off to sleep. This suited Sonya and I, as we intended visiting Yelena Melnikov, Sasha's mother.

"Do you think there's a good story here?" I asked Sonya, as we strolled into Dobrenska and passed a statue of Lenin.

"That's what my editor is expecting," she said. "It will be interesting to see how Valdia deals with the strike. The miners must go back to work as soon as possible. The mine must produce as much as possible in Russia's summer. Imagine the arctic winter and the difficult conditions for mining and transport."

We passed a few shops and a couple of apartment blocks made of timber and came to a street where there were small wooden houses and bungalows. Sonya went to a house with a small garden, filled with pink, yellow and blue flowers and knocked on the door. Yelena hugged her and wiped away tears.

Sonya was also emotional.

"Sasha and I were at university together. I met Yelena and Oleg when they visited her."

I left them alone and walked around the house, peering at drawings and photographs of Yelena, Oleg and their only daughter Sasha. Later when we were having tea, I observed Yelena, who was still lovely, despite a weather-beaten face. Her hair was grey and she looked about seventy, but I knew from Sasha that she was only sixty. Yelena noticed me gazing at a large portrait of Oleg on the wall. Through Sonya, my interpreter, Yelena told me that she had painted it.

After a while, Yelena began to talk about the Dobrenska miners' strike. It had been going on for days. Miners and other staff distrusted Valdia's mine managers and were still dissatisfied with the Coroner's verdict on the death of Oleg Melnikov. They had commissioned a report from an independent doctor who recommended that Oleg's body be exhumed. They alleged that the Coroner had refused, either because he feared Valdia, or was in the company's pocket.

Yelena went to her bedroom and returned with a file on Oleg. Sonya summarised and translated. Sasha had already told me that Oleg was manager of the Dobrenska mine under Trekdiam, an Australian company; that Valdia had won a hostile takeover of the mine. Trekdiam had taken legal action against Valdia and Oleg would have been the key witness.

Yelena went further. Trekdiam and the miners were minority shareholders in Dobrenska. The miners and other employees opposed the "underhand" acquisition of their shares, but Valdia won because the State was the majority owner. Yelena's sources believed that Ministry of Natural Resources' officials, who were responsible for Dobrenska, had been bribed. They had bought new cars, TV sets and laptops and had gone on expensive holidays.

Andrei Petronsky, an engineer on the mine and close friend of Oleg, had told Yelena that her husband had received death threats. There was no way that Oleg would have wandered to the edge of the gorge as it was dangerous and there were warning signs. Before he was found at the bottom of the ravine, Oleg had despatched emails and letters to Petronsky and other senior employees. He had a plan for a new rich diamond deposit and would make a proposal to Trekdiam.

Yelena, Petronsky and other friends were furious when rumours swept the town that Oleg had committed suicide. On the fateful day, Oleg had met several people. He appeared to be thoughtful, but certainly not depressed. On his final walk, he had met an associate who was walking his dog and had cheerfully played with the husky. There were certainly no indications that Oleg was about to take his life.

The conclusion was that Valdia executives were spinning lies and their nods and winks ended up in the press. Their story claimed that Oleg had taken bribes to help seal the Valdia deal and had jumped into the deep gorge, before being exposed. Yelena, Petronsky and others insisted that this was pure fiction. They demanded that Valdia furnish proof to back the allegations.

"Of course, none was forthcoming," Yelena said. "In a radio interview, a Valdia spokesman continued to insinuate that my husband had committed suicide out of guilt and shame."

"Did they interview colleagues and miners who disagreed with the allegation?" Sonya asked.

Yelena shook her head.

"That's appalling," I said

"What do you expect from the State media?" Sonya said.

* * *

The next morning, Sonya, Fred and I went to the Dobrenska Mine to find out what was going on. A fence surrounded the open cast mine and its ore crushing operations and there was a picket in front of the gate. About two hundred workers were standing there. They were peaceful, with some holding protest placards in Russian. Sonya showed them her press card and they allowed us into the mine compound. The mine union leader, Dmitri Andreyev, showed us the diggings in a shallow, but wide hole as well as the crushing and diamond sorting plant. Through Sonya, Andreyev, explained that Dobrenska was a rich mine that produced white and blue diamonds. The gems were despatched to Moscow cutters and then exported to dealers in Antwerp, Tel Aviv and New York.

Through Sonya, our interpreter, I thought I would get straight to the point: "Was Oleg Melnikov a good manager?"

"No question. Oleg was hard, but fair," Dmitri said. "If we met production targets and the diamond market was strong, he would pay bonuses. If we failed to meet objectives, he would hold meetings to find out the reasons."

"Was he popular with the miners?"

"Of course. He always acted in the workers interests. It was a great tragedy when he died; for his family and us."

"Were the miners surprised when they heard about the death?" I asked.

"We were shocked."

"What was the reaction to the suicide rumours?"

"Anger! Oleg was committed to the mine and he was fighting the takeover. Why kill himself? He was acting for us. It didn't make sense."

"The diamond market has had its ups and downs. What did he do during the bad times, when diamond trade and prices fell?" Fred asked.

"Oleg made an arrangement with the *Gochran*, the Russian Treasury. It bought the diamonds from the mine and stored them in its stockpile. We would get paid and production would continue. Later when the market improved, the Treasury would sell the diamonds in the West. If the *Gochran* obtained higher prices and more money, it would pass on a portion to the mine. Oleg would make sure that workers received a share of the profits."

"What about the present management?"

"We don't trust them. Wages haven't increased and our profit share has fallen."

"Do you think they're cooking the books?" I asked.

Sonya explained what I meant and Dmitri nodded his head: "Yes, we don't trust their figures."

"How long have you been striking?" Sonya asked in English and Russian.

"Ten days."

"Without pay? It must be very hard on your families."

"Of course. We tried to negotiate but they wouldn't listen. These managers are becoming fat on the back of the workers. We have to make our stand. The government will respond."

"Who are the owners of Valdia?" Fred asked.

Dmitri was about to answer when there was a sudden commotion at the entrance of the mine. A bus was trying to get through. Strikers had surrounded it and were banging on the windows, shouting.

"The managers are trying to ship in other miners to get production moving again," Sonya said, as we moved closer. "It could get nasty."

A busload of outside miners and workers arrived and then another. Sonya, bravely, if not foolishly, moved closer with her recorder and camera to interview miners and take pictures of the confrontation. Three army trucks suddenly appeared. Two were filled with soldiers and the other, civilians with heavy sticks and batons. Soon there was a fierce battle. Dmitri pulled back Sonya, as rocks and other missiles were flying. The striking miners threw back the thugs' missiles and confronted them. That was the go ahead for the military. Decked in riot gear, they advanced in a Roman Phalanx formation with shields in front. The battle continued with Sonya in the midst of it, despite Dmitri's attempts to pull her away.

A missile hit Sonya and blood poured from her forehead. A thug picked up the camera and crushed it with his boot, but Dmitri managed to rescue the recorder and broken camera and put them in his pocket. Noticing what had happened, I surreptitiously took photographs and videoed the attack on the workers with my smart phone. I noticed that Fred was doing the same. I then rushed into the melee to help Dmitri retrieve Sonya who had sunk onto the ground in front of the advancing military. We shouted at them to stop and let us through, but in the noisy and fierce battle, no one took any notice. At last we pulled Sonya free and dragged her to the office, where Dmitri took out some first aid kit and bandaged the wound.

"She'll need stitches," Fred said. "We must go to the hospital now."

Outside, near the entrance, the Dobrenska miners were retreating and the buses were getting through. The battle had lasted almost two hours and Valdia's managers had won. We had to take Sonya away as soon as possible. She was concussed and losing a lot of blood. Dmitri Andreyev gave me the small recorder and Sonya's broken camera, which I threw away after taking out the memory card. Dmitri negotiated with the soldiers' officer. I guessed that he had to agree to a new meeting with the victorious managers. We gently placed Sonya in a car and one of Dmitri's aides drove us to the Dobrenska hospital.

"Well Fred, are you going to recommend investment in Alexei's mine?" I said, as we waited in the hospital's casualty unit. Fred shook his head. His enthusiasm for Russia had waned.

By now nurses and doctors were working frantically, as growing numbers of injured miners were arriving. Significantly there were neither soldiers, nor thugs, so their own medical team were obviously taking care of their casualties.

Sonya's young doctor spoke fairly good English, so I managed to ask him some quick questions.

"She has concussion but she's going to be OK, if she rests for a few days," Alyosha Fedemaya, the doctor said.

Fred went over and held Sonya's hand. Conscious now, she smiled weakly.

"You're a brave, but silly girl."

"Was it necessary for the military to go in?" I asked Alyosha. "It was a pitched battle out there. The miners were protesting peacefully."

"Valdia's mine managers are former FSB agents," the doctor said in disgust. "Sometimes I wonder. Is it the work of the government itself, or the FSB? Maggots are crawling all over the place."

"Have you heard of Yevgeny Faramazov?" I asked.

Alyosha was silent and then took me to a corner and looked around so that no-one could hear: "Of course, we know who he is. He was once a high-ranking officer of the FSB. He is now a multi-millionaire. Perhaps billionaire."

"Is he involved with Valdia? He now lives in the UK."

"We have been told that Faramazov has a large stake in Valdia."

"Who else?"

"I don't know. Valdia hasn't disclosed names. The only person that has been mentioned has been Faramazov, but I can't confirm it."

"Did you know Oleg Melnikov?"

"He was a great friend of my father. A legend in Dobrenska. The mine and the town wouldn't be here without him. Oleg was a courageous pioneer. Imagine establishing a mine in the tundra at the time. He had to contend with thick snow and ice in the arctic winter and a swamp in summer. Bastards…They murdered him. If I were you, I would take this girl and get out of here as soon as possible. It's dangerous."

"Are you Sasha Melnikov's doctor friend? Was it you who examined the body in the mortuary?"

"Yes. How is she?"

"I don't know her that well," I lied. "Met her briefly, but I'm told that she's still grieving and bitter about her father."

I had wanted to spend the weekend in St Petersburg to visit the Hermitage and the Dostoevsky museum, which Faramazov had frequented in his youth. Instead we decided to take Sonya back to Moscow for her safety. Alyosha spoke to our driver, told him to pick up our things at the Dacha and take us to our hotel near *Malye Karely*. He arranged payment and I promised him that he would be refunded as soon as possible.

Later when we arrived at *Malye Karely*, we decided not to stay. Instead we hastily grabbed our baggage and headed straight to Arkhangelsk airport. Fortunately, neither the military police nor FSB interfered with us. The recorder, our cameras, smart phones and Sonya's memory card with her photos, were packed between our shirts and trousers.

As soon as we arrived in Moscow, we took dazed Sonya to her newspaper, the *Novaya Gazeta,* where a first-aider tended to her. It was left to me to tell the editor our story. The provisos were that I would be an anonymous source and that Fred would not be mentioned. While I was there, Fred toured the *Diamond Fund* in the Kremlin's Armoury. Later he told me that behind glass barriers were huge piles of rough, uncut and polished diamonds belonging to the *Gochran.*

I was exhausted after the meeting with the *Novaya Gazeta,* but decided to get a feel for Faramazov's past life. Hoping that no-one was following me, I took the Metro to the *Lubyanka* and observed the large bleak, grey, brown building of the KGB and its successor, the FSB. Then to *Universitetskaya Ploshchad*, the campus of Moscow State University, where Faramazov studied under some of the most brilliant Russian scientists of the day. Pity that he misused his talents.

The next morning, at Moscow's Domodedovo Airport, we saw our Dobrenska battle photos on *Novaya Gazetta's* front and inside pages. There were shots of poor, bleeding, Sonya on the ground and battered miners. Back at home we read *Novaya Gazeta's* English translation of Sonya's article, on its website. Sasha told me later that after Sonya's impressive scoop, the strike had become a national scandal. Valdia management had to back down and give the Dobrenska miners a better deal. Sonya wrote that several sources had mentioned Faramazov's stake in Valdia. She decided not to risk libel and mention unconfirmed allegations that he was behind the attack on the miners and Oleg's murder. Readers would draw their own conclusions.

On arrival at Heathrow Airport, I opened my laptop and went through my emails. There was a message from Jamey Jackenhead: "More travel for you, Jack. Bristol Gem-Diam is taking a group of mining analysts and journalists to Lanzarote to see the Canary Diamond Mines development."

"What's going on," I responded.

The reply was immediate: "Bristol's listing is in November. Isobel can't make it as she's going to Chile. You have a few weeks to finish current projects and prepare for the trip.

13

A Volcanic Island Development

Gerald Gleep, chief executive of Bristol GemDiam Mining Corp, was waiting for us on the terrace of the Timanfaya Palace hotel, close to Lanzarote's Playa Blanca beach.

"Call me Gerry," he said with a southern American drawl and a broad smile that displayed whitened teeth: "You're here to enjoy yourself. Tomorrow, work."

Tall and scrawny with greying straggly hair, a reddish complexion, sunken blue eyes and thin, wasted arms, Gleep was semi-formal in his white shirt and light green trousers. Alongside him in the hotel foyer were Bristol executives and Spanish and Eastern European girls, in white tops and green miniskirts. Some waitresses offered us champagne in thin long glasses, others canapés and before long the party was in full swing.

There were twenty of us who were assessing Canary Diamond Mines; seventeen analysts from investment banks, mining finance firms and funds and three members of the press. Men dominated the group, as so often happens on trips to mines. All had been flown in to spend two days with Gleep and his executives and obtain on site information about the development. The aim was to persuade analysts and the press that Canary had excellent prospects, prior to Bristol's imminent London listing.

Others at the welcoming event were leading island officials, business people and media from Lanzarote, Tenerife and neighbouring islands. The event had a dual role: to publicise Canary and Bristol and give analysts and press an enjoyable party to encourage them to write favourable reports.

My description of the miners' battle at Dobrenska Mine, had unsurprisingly discouraged Jamey Jackenhead from investing in Russia. He found the Bristol share offer far more compelling. After I briefed Sasha about the recent Dobrenska events, she became even more determined to book Faramazov. She agreed that the trip to Lanzarote could help me find out the extent of the Russian magnate's involvement in Canary.

The event, ahead of the mine tour, was around a large pool. By now the sun was beginning to set and there was a golden reddish hue over the Atlantic Ocean. All members of our party had rushed at the opportunity to spend some time in the sun. A short break on an island, about a hundred miles west of the north African coast, would be a relief from cold, rainy Britain.

Gleep, his executives and assistants networked around the analysts making small talk and jokes. As soon as a glass was half empty, an attractive waitress would fill it up. Those who had enough champagne went across to the bar and downed beers, wine, spirits or soft drinks. In the meantime, we filled our plates with a variety of appetising dishes. The mostly overweight guests were gobbling up prawns, lobster, crab, smoked salmon and Canary potatoes. Exotic deserts and cakes swiftly disappeared.

Twilight was over. Lights went on, inside and around the pool and in the distance, the dark, calm sea shimmered under a full moon. By now the party was swinging and some inebriated members of our group made a play for the waitresses.

When I finished my meal, a slim, tanned man, who looked in his early twenties, sat down next to me.

"Are you Jack Sniper? I'm Basil Bleedon. You know... The guy who tipped you off about the Canary development."

"Oh hi, thanks for your help. It's been very useful."

"Yes, it must have been. Your colleague, Isobel, also pumped me for information. This time it was on real estate agents and land prices."

"I was going to call you," I lied. "Have we paid you? If not, please send the office an invoice."

That irritated him: "You said that you would be speaking to contacts in Fleet Street about me."

"Sorry, I should have got back to you. I had to go to Russia."

"I asked you months ago."

"When I get back, I'll do something."

"Sure, like you promised before."

"They're going to shunt us around tomorrow. Presume you'll be there," I said, swiftly changing the subject.

"I won't. As you well know, I've written enough stories about Canary," Bleedon said.

"I notice that Gleep and his girls are all in green. Canary Diamond Mines and Bristol's logos are green," I said.

"Oh, you got the message. Subtle, isn't it?"

"The Conservation guys must be going mad. From what I have read in Bristol's prospectus, Canary is going to expand."

"Protesters claim that local government was prepared to compromise," Basil said with a wink and a slap on his pocket.

"I gather land prices in Lanzarote and Fuerteventura

have shot up," I said, thinking it best to ignore the allegation.

"Yeah, mostly around undeveloped beaches and the coastline."

"My boss bought some land on spec and has applied for a mining claim," I said. "Lots of guys are obviously buying for the same reason."

"That depends...."

"On whether there will be good diamond finds," Gerald Gleep said and sat down next to us. "They will require expertise and resources. That's where Bristol GemDiam comes in."

"Who's been the biggest buyer of land, Mr Gleep," Bleedon asked.

"I'm not sure. Our company and associates have bought. I can't speak for the others."

"MSP España's shares have soared by 40 per cent since they were listed last month," I said. "That's good for Bristol."

Bleedon was puzzled.

"Bristol GemDiam is the majority shareholder of MSP, which owns Canary Diamond Mines," Gleep said.

"Then Bristol has an indirect holding in Canary via its investment in MSP," Bleedon said. "Why two listings? Isn't one sufficient?"

"Good question. The Canary Islands, as you know, are part of Spain so Madrid is the obvious stock exchange for Spanish investors."

"British, French, German and North American investors can buy MSP España's shares," so why list Bristol GemDiam?"

"London has been the centre for mining finance for over a century," Gleep said. "UK, European and North American companies feel more comfortable with a London listing,"

Clearly irritated with the questions, Gleep did his best to be charming.

"You read the prospectus, didn't you? It states that Bristol will be investing in other diamond prospects as well."

"In the Canaries?"

"I'll introduce you to Percival Meltin, our finance director," Gleep said. "He'll fill you in on the details tomorrow. No more questions tonight, thank you. Enjoy yourselves."

Gleep trundled off to speak to others, and Bleedon remained with me. A loud band began to play and we just sat there listening and observing. I was feeling a bit guilty that I hadn't reciprocated after Bleedon had given me information about the mine. The promise that I would try and get him a Fleet Street job, was unrealistic as I didn't have close friends in the British press. I had an idea that would make us both feel better.

"Do you want to meet some Fleet Street guys, Basil? I'll introduce you to them. They'll give you the inside story about job prospects."

The London journalists were sitting around a table near the edge of the pool, gossiping and drinking.

"Hi I'm Jack Sniper, JJ Emerging Mining Finance. Saw you guys at the airport, but haven't had a chance to talk," I said.

They looked up, totally disinterested.

"Do you want to meet the guy who broke the story?" I said.

"Really! Is that supposed to be news?" one said.

"He scooped the story about diamonds in the Canary Islands. They were going to delay their listing, but when the news broke they brought it forward."

"Basil Bleedon, Lanzarote Gazette," Basil said, glowing with pride and beaming at me as we sat down uninvited.

"I'm David Threstwich, *Daily Telegraph*, this is Colin Campbell of *The Times* and Jane Jodensberg, *Financial Times*," Threstwich said.

"Will this mine end up with dead canaries, Basil?" Campbell asked.

Bleedon laughed ruefully at Campbell's sarcastic reference to the days when caged canaries were left in mines to test whether workers could breathe.

"No dead canaries in this mine. Bristol believes in ecology. Take a look. Green logo, green pants, green skirts."

"Let's go inside, it's getting cold," Threstwich said.

Evidently, the journalist clique wasn't too keen to socialise with us.

"The band's not too bad. Might as well enjoy our freebie," Jane said.

"We take what comes," Threstwich said. "Mining isn't your beat, Jane, why are you here?"

"Ken Marstell our mining correspondent is ill, so the editor sent me," Jane said.

We made our way to the dance floor where some analysts and fund managers were dancing with Gleep's girls.

"Do you think some of them are hookers?" Campbell asked.

"Come on, Colin! Why don't you have a go?"

Campbell took out a cigarette and sipped his cognac. He appeared to be more interested in the male waiters than the girls.

Jane who joked around and was full of fun, danced with all of us. The party went on until about midnight before we shuffled off to bed. Some of the girls had already disappeared with a few analysts and fund managers.

* * *

The hotel phone rang at 7 a.m. Groggy from Gleep's welcoming party, I decided that I had better sober up fast. The best thing to do was to have an early morning swim in the sea. It was windy and cool on the beach and the water was cold; but after swimming for half an hour, I felt a lot better and met the others at breakfast. The others were worse for wear, but despite all the drink the previous evening, they were imbibing bucks fizz.

Twenty folders were handed to us as we climbed on the bus to take a look at the development. Jane Jodensburg of the *FT* was sitting alone near the front of the bus, away from the other reporters. I asked if I could join her as I preferred her to her colleagues and found the analysts and fund managers boring. Since Jane admitted that she didn't have a clue about diamond mining, I opened my folder and went through it with her. In the file were Bristol's prospectus, a detailed geological report, some aerial photographs, operational plans and assessments and current and future estimates of capital expenditure and costs. There was also a picture of a small pile of diamonds.

The bus began an upward climb and the microphone began with an awful, high pitched squeak. In front of the bus was a tall thin woman with cropped black hair and a tanned face. Her dark brown eyes were stern and unfriendly and she had a sharp, angular face.

"My name is Marcia Vaskilov, consultant geologist to Canary Diamond Mines," she said in a heavy Russian accent, while she adjusted the speaker. "I wrote the geological report which you have in your folder."

Vaskilov banged on the microphone and spoke louder: "As your host today, I will be taking you into the Timanfaya National Park to give you a sense of the island's volcanic geology. Some of you may wonder why the large diamond companies have not prospected here before. That's not that surprising. De Beers was successful in South Africa, Botswana and Namibia but missed a significant Australian prospect. Two independent geologists found diamonds in

Canada."

"Prospecting requires foresight, creativity, faith and persistence," Vaskilov continued. "That's why I came to the Canary Islands with a colleague a couple of years ago. What we discovered, made us excited."

"When did MSP España contact you and decide to establish Canary Diamond Mines?" I asked.

Vaskilov looked at me intently.

"Seems you have done your research. From my experience, smaller companies have the courage to try their luck and have faith in geologists."

"I think she means throw the dice and pray that they're right," Campbell said.

Vaskilov overheard him: "Ah, another cynical journalist who doesn't get involved. Very easy to be sceptical and critical if you don't risk your own money. To what extent has your own life been a gamble? Relationships, work, apartments, investments?"

The bus stopped and we climbed out on to a high point of the road that overlooked an extraordinary sight. It was similar to a moonscape; dark and light reddish brown and yellowish rocks, mixed with dark black ones.

"This lunar type landscape is the lava from the last volcanic eruption in Lanzarote," Vaskilov said. "It occurred in 1820 following the previous one in 1730. Fields and farms were once under the rocks you're standing on, but when the volcano erupted, the lava poured down the mountain into the sea. We're not concerned about those eruptions; the ones before interest us. The Canary Islands are approximately 30 million years old. They were originally a submerged mountain, but it is unclear what thrust them to the surface."

The sun was shining but we struggled to listen as Vaskilov was competing with a vigorous wind.

"Geologists who have researched the formation of the islands believe that eruptions below sea created the land we're standing on," she continued. "The islands emerged in three stages. The first period came about 23 million years ago during the Myocene age. Masses of sunken rock from the earth's crust were thrust upwards. The second phase was when the mass of rock flattened out and became thinner and weaker. Magma that had accumulated beneath that crust of earth erupted. The eruption created a volcanic ridge that over time emerged out of the Ocean and became the Canary Islands archipelago.

"Is this how the Atlantis myth came about?" Jane asked, causing some to be impressed and others to jeer.

"At least the one woman amongst you men, studied classics," Vaskilov said, managing to smile at last. "Yes, you're quite correct. Plato wrote about Atlantis. The Gods punished the inhabitants. Their island city was destroyed and it sank under the sea."

"Are you guys diving to find treasure in the lost City of Atlantis," Threstwich said.

"New slogan for De Beers: 'Diamonds are a gift from the gods'," Campbell said.

"We chose Lanzarote first and we intend prospecting in Fuerteventura," Vaskilov continued, ignoring the snide reporters. "The islands were formed during the Miocene age. During those eruptions, massive pressure created carbonatites and potentially diamonds."

"How come you haven't found a kimberlite pipe?" an analyst asked. "In Africa and Russia, kimberlite pipes were from volcanic eruptions more than a billion years ago."

"Good question," Vaskilov replied. "I'm going to take you to a crater and will then explain."

"We walked up a steep incline. Some of the guys who had drunk the bucks fizz, stumbled. One guy went behind a large rock and vomited. Vaskilov looked back in disgust as she stepped up the pace. We finally reached the crater and looked down.

"This is the crater from the eruption a few centuries ago. Note the contours. They come from the red-hot lava that spurted out of the crater and flowed down the mountain to the sea. Streams of lava then solidified into the very rocks that you now see."

"Those sandy red and dark rocks are magnificent," Jane said and took some photographs.

"Now let's think about the practicalities of our operation," Vaskilov said. "The carbonatites that could yield diamonds were formed from volcanoes multi millions of years ago. To find kimberlites, we would have to drill deep holes through the solidified lava of the most recent eruptions."

She paused as we circled the crater.

"You people understand figures. Don't you think that underground exploration in this area would be uneconomic? Do you seriously believe that the Canary authorities would allow us to develop a mine in a national park?"

"South Africa's Orange River was the conduit for diamonds from the kimberlite pipes to the sea," a hedge fund manager said. "I haven't seen rivers around here."

"Correct, but over millions of years, rain, floods and winds caused kimberlite and lamproite rocks and gravel to slide down from this mountain. They ended up on Lanzarote's beaches and under the sea. We have detected some gems. We believe that we have found a potentially profitable alluvial diamond deposit."

After spending most of the morning walking around the virtual moonscape, where they once filmed *One Million Years BC* with Raquel Welch, we were taken to a restaurant near the top of Timanfaya. The volcano was most certainly not dormant. The restaurant barbecued chicken and lamb on grills over potholes that had natural heat. Later a guide poured water into a small hole and a geyser spurted steam about three metres into the air. The hungry group tucked into the food and once again wine and beer flowed.

* * *

The bus wound down the National Park road until we came to the coast. Barbed wire fencing surrounded a cliff that overlooked a beach below. The security guard at the gate allowed the bus to pass and we climbed out at the top of the cliff and could smell the sea air. The mostly inebriated London visitors slowly made their way downwards on a narrow pathway to a prefabricated office on a narrow plateau below. Further down, on the beach, a bulldozer and scraper were digging and loading rocks on to a truck.

Gleep was there to welcome us: "Did you enjoy the trip? Amazing place, isn't it? Philippe Santos, our operations manager, will take you down to the beach and explain what we're doing."

Santos, partner of Carlos Maxos. Would he remember me?

"Marcia Vaskilov will first tell you why it's highly likely that mineable diamond deposits are here," Gleep said.

"From our investigations, we believe that a river flowed into the sea here millions of years ago," Vaskilov said. "Volcanic activity caused that river to become submerged. 'Weathering' from rain and floods transported diamond bearing rocks down the river and deposited them on the beach and on the ocean floor."

"On the beaches of Namibia and its sea, most of the diamonds have proved to be quality gems," said Gleep, who had originally qualified as a geologist before becoming a banker. "The gravel and sand there are also rich in marine phosphates which are fertilisers. We believe that we not only have excellent gem prospects here, but we can also produce phosphate fertilizers. They will boost agriculture on the islands and raise exports."

"Few people realize that the world's largest and most valuable resources of gem quality diamonds are on the coast," Vaskilov said, a little irritated that Gleep had interrupted her. "Over the years erosion and stress destroyed many imperfect stones as they journeyed to the ocean. That is why beach and marine diamonds have an exceptionally high ratio of top quality gems."

Despite being groggy from the booze, the analysts and fund managers were now interested and asked to see a sample.

While he was busy with the safe's combination to take out the sample, one of the analysts piped up: "How are the shares of MSP España doing?"

"They were up 10 percent this morning. Since it was listed, the shares have risen by 50 percent," Santos said.

That remark was enough to sway the analysts. Vaskilov's informative lecture and Gleep's explanations were secondary compared to Santos' snippet. Greed and excitement were in the air. At that very moment, it seemed almost certain that the analysts' reviews of Bristol's prospectus would be favourable. From then onwards they would probably examine the development uncritically. Gleep was beaming.

Gleep opened the small package that he had taken from the safe and spread about a dozen diamonds on a white table cloth. They were mainly small with varying shapes and sizes. The group became even more excited.

Santos, who was in a wetsuit, led us down to the beach.

"After we read Marcia's geological reports on the Canary Islands we decided to meet her," Santos said, in his mild Spanish accent. "She told us about the potential of beach 'placer' and offshore diamond deposits, so we started on a small scale."

On the beach, we observed the diggings.

"We use battery drills and spades to dig into the rock and sand; then sieves and pans to wash the gravel," Santos said. "It took quite a long time, but eventually we found diamonds. An Antwerp dealer checked them and confirmed that they were quality gems."

That was obviously Armand Gruchot, Faramazov's associate. It was another indication that Faramazov was involved. The prospect was far too interesting to miss.

"As you can see our operation is becoming mechanised, but for the moment, we only have a bulldozer and extractor," Santos said. "They are removing the volcanic rock to get to the gravel bed underneath. We hope to find good quality gems there."

"We intend constructing a crushing plant nearby," Gleep said. "Up to now we have a deal with a quarry in Fuerteventura, which is only about 45 minutes away by boat. The quarry crushes the rock, which we ship from the Playa Blanca harbour a few miles away. The crushed rock and gravel is then shipped back from Fuerteventura and our small plant washes the gravel and uses grease and X-ray methods to detect and sort diamonds."

"What about the offshore mining that's mentioned in the prospectus?" Campbell asked.

"We have also been searching for diamonds underwater. My diving colleagues and I will now give you a demonstration on what we have been doing," Santos said. We're taking a camera so you'll see a film on what we're going to do underwater. Santos and two other colleagues put on their breathing apparatus and oxygen cylinders, climbed on a rock and dived into the water. One of them held a video camera and when they came out the water about an hour afterwards, Santos linked the camera to a laptop.

We crowded around the laptop, which was on a table under a parasol. The film showed the divers swim towards a suction pipe that was connected to a pump on the beach. One of them began to vacuum gravel and sand on the bottom of the ocean floor. The sediment from the bottom of the sea was pumped through the pipe on to the beach. In the meantime, Santos and the other divers searched the gaps between and under the rocks. One of the divers found a small gem and Santos passed it around. Another tiny diamond was sifted from the sediment that had been pumped on to the beach.

Gleep and Santos were exceedingly pleased that two diamonds had been found and the audience was also impressed.

"I think we are on to something," Gleep said. The next step is to first hire and then buy a dredging boat to find diamonds further out to sea. We'll use part of the finance from the listing to buy a vessel that has 'an integrated seabed crawler' to mine the ore. It must have room for a diamond processing plant on board."

"The vessel costs about $30 million and is cutting edge technology in offshore diamond mining," Santos said. "The ship we have in mind was used successfully off Namibia's south-west African coast. If the sea is calm we'll be able to go into caves and arches and look for diamonds.

"When we have about 2,000 carats we'll ask Antwerp, Tel Aviv and Mumbai diamond dealers to evaluate them," Gleep said. "We will then be able to assess potential future production and values."

"All well and good, but won't you wreck the environment?" Jane asked.

"Good question. Once the mining is completed we will carry out a reclamation process, import sand from Africa and construct a white beach" Gleep said. "They are more popular than the black volcanic beaches here.

The tipsy crowd was suitably impressed. Analysts and fund managers left for London the next morning to spread the word about the potential of the Canary diamond prospect. The Bristol GemDiam share issue was likely to be oversubscribed.

14

DIAMOND FEVER

During the early part of the 21st century, an insignificant, unremarkable discovery on a tourist island, some 70 miles from the coast of West Africa, become a cause célèbre. Dumbfounding everyone in the business, Canary Diamond Mines set in motion a rush for gems.

Of course, the latest diamond boom didn't remotely resemble the great South African diamond and gold rushes in the late nineteenth century. In the 1870s thousands of fortune hunters from Europe, America and elsewhere were so excited by the prospect of riches that they embarked on lengthy sea voyages to South Africa. After arriving in Cape Town, men and their struggling horses and mules set off with wagons and carts seven hundred miles into the hinterland. They experienced dusty, dirty and invariably dangerous conditions on the way. Once they had reached the desolate outback, they joined a throng of professional and amateur miners who frantically dug for the elusive diamond in the most primitive circumstances. Their filthy camps, with open sewers, were boiling hot in summer, freezing cold in the winter and rife with typhoid, cholera and other diseases. As time passed, miners dug deeper and deeper with some injuring or killing themselves. Eventually they created the Kimberly Big Hole, one of the wonders of the world. Some diggers were lucky, finding prize gems, others were left penniless.

The diamond fever of the 21st Century was very different, but remarkable none the less. It began on the London stock market from an unexpected quarter. On our expedition to Lanzarote to examine the Canary development, I had noticed a portly investment banker with a flushed, blotched red face. Other members of the group were casually dressed, but for some reason this character insisted on being dressed formally on all occasions. He wore a dark blue suit with light stripes. It was obvious that he had put on a lot of weight since his suit had been fitted in Savile Row. It was so tight that he sweated profusely. Indeed, I don't recall him ever being out of that particular suit, which was badly creased by the end of the trip.

The gentleman, Manfred Fokes-Mailsford, of the historic securities house, Fazeldoff, Trogan & Fokes, was always first in the queue for food. After piling up his plate, he would taste the wines on offer and help himself to a bottle. Large portions of desert, cheese and biscuits, would be washed down with a treble tot of cognac or whisky. Indeed, some of us were so fascinated with the spectacle, that our own plates were taken away before we finished eating.

One of the analysts at another investment bank noticed me gape in wonder at the extent of the gluttony. Appreciating that I was a new member of the mining analyst circle, he summarised the background of the individual in question. Most of the mining analysts had geology, mining engineering or business degrees, so that they seemingly had an understanding of mines, their accounts and business operations. Fokes-Mailsford, however, was from a somewhat different background. He was grandson of Lord Fokes, a former junior treasury minister in a one term Conservative Government, that had been voted out of office because of incompetence and minor corruption. After the Tory government fell, Lord Fokes became one of the founders of Fazeldoff, Trogan & Fokes. Following the tradition of his mildly famous family, Manfred was educated at Harrow and read Ancient History at Birmingham University. There he was nicknamed "Prince Regent" as his body and his culinary habits resembled the much-parodied prince, who eventually became King George IV. Manfred scraped through with a third-class degree. The result helped him take advantage of his privileged background and connections and enter stock broking. Fazeldoff's managing director, swiftly side-lined Manfred and he ended up selling stocks listed on AIM, London's junior stock exchange.

I would never have guessed that Manfred Fokes-Mailsford's review on the coming Bristol GemDiam Mining share issue, would be the catalyst for an extraordinary diamond boom. He sat next to me on the plane when we flew back from Lanzarote and in between tots of whisky, he struggled with his report. For the umpteenth time, I had to get up when he shifted his bulk from his seat alongside the window, into the narrow aisle.

"Sorry to disturb you, old boy," Manfred said, in his rather posh, polite accent. "Could you keep an eye on my laptop? Have to go to the toilet. Call of nature, what, what."

Manfred was away for some time and I couldn't help but notice his Bristol review. It was turgid prose, mostly lifted without any comment from an already poorly written, naturally optimistic prospectus. Manfred had cut and pasted Vaskilov's geological assessment of the Canary Islands and some marketing material on the global diamond market. By the time he returned, the plane was about to land. I handed him his laptop and we exchanged cards.

That was that.

During the next few days, the press and wire services hardly gave Bristol and Canary a mention. Jane Jodensburg told me a few weeks later that she had written a thousand-word piece for the *FT*. It had been cut down to three paragraphs and was placed as a "filler" on page 37 of the inside company pages. *The Times* and *Telegraph* financial editors decided that the story was worth a paragraph down page. In contrast, mining correspondents Campbell and Threstwich received good play for their winter sun pieces in their papers' travel supplements. Canary potatoes and black volcanic beaches appeared to be more interesting than chances of an unlikely gem discovery. In short, the Canary diamond development appeared to be doomed to obscurity.

Something else put Bristol GemDiam on the map. This was the end product of what famously became known in mining gossip as the "The Prince Regent Report". By chance I learnt how Fokes-Mailsford's analysis became a celebrated City and media story at a party of Jane Jodensburg. That report, which Fazeldoff, Trogan & Fokes distributed to clients and later, the press, helped Bristol open on London's AIM, with a bang. The listing was so oversubscribed that the company managed to double the equity issue to £100 million or 100 million shares of £1 each. The extra cash would be used to purchase dredgers which would scour the Canary Islands' coastline for gems. Bristol's shares opened at 150 pence, well over the listing price of 100 pence. Within days it touched 180 pence.

Jane and I had got on well during the Lanzarote trip. Out of the blue, she invited me to a party at her flat in Chelsea. Jane shared the apartment with Meredith Price-well, tall with straight long blonde hair and a full fringe. She had a long prominent nose, friendly blue eyes and an enticing smile. Garrulous after a few drinks, Meredith took me aside and poured her heart out. I don't know why she chose me, but perhaps she had noticed that I had sneaked glances at her earlier in the evening. I was lonely without Amity and I quite fancied Meredith. I had guessed that the feelings were mutual and happily was proved right.

Meredith told me that she had applied to Fleet Street and provincial newspapers after she had graduated, but had no luck. She ended up as an editor for the rich, famous and infamous at Fazeldoff, Trogan & Fokes and had to accept her lot. Meredith's job was to turn works of illiterate analysts, who didn't have a clue about spelling, grammar, context and organisation, into readable reports. Manfred Fokes-Mailsford was one of the worst members of this elite group of philistines, who received bonuses of anywhere between £100,000 to £500,000, when the market was buzzing. Despite her finished products, which attracted client orders and sometimes media attention, Meredith had to accept the "comparatively meagre salary of £28,000 a year, with either a miniscule bonus or no incentive at all".

"Here was I, with a degree in English Literature at Bristol University, having to rewrite the illiterates' ghastly tomes," Meredith said, while she sipped her wine. "I'm ready to go home on a Friday afternoon. But before I can escape, this ignorant, beneficiary of nepotism comes up to me and shoves his report on my desk."

"Let me guess, Manfred Fokes-Mailsford?"

"None other than the Prince Regent in all his inebriated glory. He tells me that some mining company is due for listing the next week and the deadline for the report is Monday."

"He passed it on to you just before the weekend?"

"Standard practice. The rewrite, publishing division is near the bottom of the employee hierarchy. Reports have to be out early in the week to clasp commissions from the unwitting."

"And the analysts, who can't write English are always late."

She nodded and finished her wine. I poured some more into her glass.

"Despite all our efforts to persuade them to meet their deadlines, they almost always land their garbage on our desks on Friday," Meredith continued. "Weekends are invariably our busiest time. Anyway, dear Manfred notices my glare. He apologises that he doesn't have time to edit his report in time. He's worried that sales people will stamp on him as they need the report to sell the shares ahead of listing. It's hunting season and he's already got pre-arranged commitments with Lord and Lady Whoever."

"So, you took it on."

"Had to. Otherwise Prince Nepotism could speak to the firm elders and get me fired."

"You worked on the report over the weekend?"

"Yes, but for the first time since I was in this mind-numbing job, something fascinated me. When I saw the name Bristol, it was a sign. Me at Bristol University and Bristol GemDiam Mining with its offices in Clifton; an area of the city that I loved and shared a flat."

"A sign just because your student flat was near the company's offices?"

"When I saw that the report was about diamonds, I became intrigued. I've always been interested in diamonds, even though I can only afford costume jewellery. I started reading the report and it was dreadful, probably the worst that had ever crossed my desk. Despite that, I was curious. I read the prospectus and then searched for stuff on the history of diamonds and the market on the Web and was soon absorbed. To cut a long story short, I was so taken with the topic that I spent the whole of Saturday in Kensington Library and the Victoria Albert Museum researching diamonds and jewellery. I then scanned and downloaded some amazing pictures"

"People in the City are talking about the report. Do you have a spare copy?"

"Sure. Let me get you one."

She took me into the bedroom and pecked me on the cheek. That was enough to let me in. I gently touched her long hair and kissed the nape of her neck. Within an instant we were in a sublime, deep French kiss. Meredith pulled herself away from me, went to a cupboard and showed me her work. The front cover design was a photograph of two open hands alongside each other. The left palm held a handful of multi-coloured uncut rough diamonds and the right, beautifully polished and shaped gems, ready for jewellery. On the inside pages, as background to Meredith's words, were pictures of the most famous diamonds in the world, unpolished, then cut. They included the Cullinan, Hope, Koh-i-Noor, Marie-Antoinette Blue, Taylor-Burton, Regent, Red Diamond, Jubilee and Premier Rose.

The opening sentences of the final rewritten report were: "Great diamond discoveries are as rare as these gems. At an unexpected, propitious moment, a prospector strikes it lucky. In the sun-baked Canary Islands, not far off the coast of diamond rich West Africa, such an event seems to have taken place."

The following page had Timanfaya Volcano as a background picture. Meredith's words were about the Canary Islands and a simplified description of Marcia Vaskilov's enthusiastic geological report. There were illustrations of diamonds and glorious black volcanic and white beaches alongside photographs and descriptions of Namibia's coastal diamond mines.

Meredith was such a skilful wordsmith that she didn't claim that the discovery would lead to a major mine, producing millions of carats a year. She didn't embellish the facts and the prospectus' estimated projections of Canary Diamond Mines' profit potential. Instead her re-creation of the Fokes-Mailsford's bullish, but unreadable review, was recommendation by association. She narrated the history of the Namibian diamond discovery on the west coast of Southern Africa in 1900 and the rich rewards that followed. In a separate page in her report there was a picture of Canary divers and an article on what was "happening now". Alongside it was a piece on "the future". This part of the report had a detailed photograph of a dredging vessel with a sophisticated crushing and sorting plant on deck.

The powers that be at Fazeldoff, Trogan & Fokes had obviously decided that an expensive print run of the report was worthwhile. As one of the underwriters of the Bristol GemDiam listing, the decision proved to be shrewd. Meredith's vivid illustrated descriptions and statistics won over professional and amateur investors. Convinced that diamond demand in China, India and elsewhere was "well in excess" of production, they piled into the shares. "You've got a lot of talent," I said, stroking Meredith's hand and lightly kissing her on her lips. "You should be writing for *National Geographic*. You're wasted at an investment bank."

"Do you think I should send it to the magazine and offer a feature about diamonds?"

"Why not? You have nothing to lose. At the moment, you're just a brilliant ghost writer."

Jane opened the door just as we were once again kissing passionately.

"Hey you two, stop being unsociable. Come and join us."

* * *

The following Monday the *Daily Mail*, the most widely

read tabloid of Middle England, had a two-page feature on diamonds, liberally quoting Meredith's words. Besides the colourful pictures, the writer had done his own homework. The article had a colour picture of a glorious D-Flawless, glittering oval diamond. It was white with shades of blue, perfect in colour, clarity, cut and weight. Next to it was an historic chart of D-Flawless average diamond prices from the seventies to the present. The chart had the relative performance of gold and platinum. While diamond prices were languishing, gold and platinum quotes had soared. The chart's message was clear. Diamonds were relatively undervalued and prices could be on the point of take-off.

As soon as the *Mail* article was published Bristol burst through 200 pence, double the listing price and ended the week close to 250 pence. Trade was active and contagious. Stock prices of large and small diamond companies went into orbit. Shares of Diamond Feeds, a company that milled wheat and barley, jumped by 10 per cent before the market throng realised that its business was somewhat different.

Since the author of the report was supposedly Manfred Fokes-Mailsford and Meredith Pricewell, was very much in the background, the said gentleman was soon a celebrity. Diamonds became the next "big news" story and Manfred was whisked around the radio and television studio circuit to pontificate about the Canary diamond discovery and gems market. Manfred's only knowledge about the diamond market came from Meredith's research and report. With extraordinary and praiseworthy effort, he ensured that he was sober during the day. He performed with charm, narrating anecdotes about his experience on a camel at Timanfaya and described the market's prospects with suitable platitudes. The directors of Fazeldoff, Trogan & Fokes were impressed and Manfred was shifted out of the mining department and became a member of the investment bank's public relations staff. The tabloid press tailed Manfred who attended parties and charity events with male models. Snide gossip columnists claimed that the partners were hardly accompanying him, because of his looks.

Weeks turned into months and before we knew what, a New Year was upon us. The Great Recession was past history and financial forces played a big part in spreading the diamond boom. The global central banker cabal printed money and slashed interest rates to zero. Their aim was to boost economies and employment. That policy had mixed results. Instead equities and "real assets" --- gold, silver, platinum and other commodities --- spurted upwards. There was a rush for real estate, art and anything else the well-heeled crowd fancied.

After the Fokes report was published, diamonds soon became the most popular and best performer. People rich and not so rich rushed to buy, as gems were relatively cheap, compared to gold and had become fashionable again. Sensing an opportunity, the global mining, diamond dealing and jewellery industries stepped up their advertising campaigns.

Diamonds are a girl's best friend, a number originally sung by Marilyn Monroe in the 1950s, jingled on the airwaves. Romantic ads ending with De Beers' slogan, "Diamonds Are Forever" were on billboards. Quiet during the recession, De Beers' shops in London's Old Bond Street, and 5th Avenue Manhattan, were crowded with customers. The super-rich marvelled at and bought designer jewellery, priced anywhere between $100,000 to $1 million or more. Professional and middle classes spent $5,000 to $50,000 on engagement rings, bracelets, necklaces and pendants. Tiffany was busy and its shares boomed while Zales, the chain jewellery store, had its own rush as women and men bought gifts containing small but glittering gems. Diamonds, long forgotten as an investment, became popular again and prices of D-Flawless and other quality diamonds from South Africa, Botswana, Russia, Canada, Australia, Africa and Brazil, surged. D-Flawless prices rose to more than $20,000, a carat, double the depressed levels during the recession. Rumours that they would soon beat the record of $64,000, boosted prices to $27,000 a carat the very next week.

Soaring diamond prices and the constant publicity and articles about the topic, fed a frenzy on stock markets. After twelve months, with quarterly results showing a few samples, Bristol GemDiam Mining touched £5 a share, while MSP España Mining on the Madrid Stock Exchange had risen in a similarly spectacular manner. The only regret was that De Beers was still a private company controlled by Anglo American, a large mining group. Then rumours abounded that Anglo would be spinning off De Beers and the great historic diamond company, founded in the 19th century, would be listed on the stock exchange again. Anglo's shares hit the rooftops and there was even more excitement in the air.

Thousands of fortune hunters flew to Lanzarote, Fuerteventura, Tenerife and other Canary Islands. They bid for land with the ultimate aim of making a claim for ground that possibly contained diamonds. Naturally, property prices took off and the islands struggled to cope with tourists, business people and others who examined prospects while they enjoyed the winter sun. Real estate investors, who ventured there in the hot summer, came back with painful sunburn, but were full of optimism.

I must admit that I was one of those caught up in the fever and gave tips to Jamey Jackenhead, other office colleagues and Dr Klugheim, who had retired as a prison psychiatrist. Since the market was booming, more diamond exploration companies were coming to the fore and our firm, JJ Emerging Mining Finance, was the underwriter. Jamey Jackenhead's business was doing so well, that he decided to move the office to larger premises in Mayfair. That would help the firm cultivate hedge fund managers, whose offices were nearby.

* * *

By this time Meredith and I had become lovers. She was aggrieved that Manfred had all the glory, on the back of her creation, but at least she now had a good portfolio to show the *National Geographic* and other magazines. Meredith patiently waited for a response from editors and in the meantime had to grind on, turning illiterate analysts' reports into readable, marketable copy. In appreciation, Fazeldoff, Trogan & Fokes raised Meredith's salary by £4,000 to £32,000.

Meredith wanted to leave the Chelsea apartment that she shared with Jane and move in with me. She stayed in my flat mostly over weekends, but Amity was constantly on my mind. One evening, Meredith caught me talking to Amity on Skype.

"Who's that?" Meredith shouted, rushing into my study.

I swiftly rang off: "An old friend. She lives in California."

"Is she a girlfriend?"

"Not exactly."

"What do you mean?"

I didn't answer.

"What about me? We keep trekking across London to see each other. Don't you want me to move in?"

No answer.

Meredith, frustrated by the inadequate response, started shouting and Cobber began to bark. I grabbed hold of his collar and took him into the kitchen.

"That dog's a nuisance. He shouldn't be here."

That put my back up: "I know you don't like dogs, but Cobber has been trained by the police. He's my friend and he protects me."

"Protects you from what? Are you paranoid or something? Obsessed with running in the woods and training at the gym; spending time at the firing range. That pistol in the drawer, next to your bed, under some clothes. Sometimes I wonder. Who are you, Jack? Do you have a license for the gun?"

"Yes, of course. I'm a member of a shooting range. It's a hobby; that's all. London has become a violent place. You need to know how to defend yourself."

"Really? You're not living in Johannesburg or Bogota, Jack. I know very little about you and often you seem detached. Do you want our relationship to continue or not? Your accent is mild South African, but there is a bit of Yorkshire in it as well. Were you born in Yorkshire? There's something you're holding back from me."

This was beginning to get heavy and too close to the bone, so I went over to the mantelpiece and showed her a photo of Sally Sniper and myself.

Why don't you phone my Mum in South Africa? I'll take you there sometime."

"Jack, I believe you. Relationships are about trust. Don't you trust me, Jack? Can't you tell I love you?"

I went over and kissed her to make up. We were soon on the sofa making love, probably the most passionate it had ever been; Meredith releasing her frustrations and shouting so loudly that people in the street might have stopped to listen; me getting rid of my anger and concerns that she might get behind my mask. Afterwards, we relaxed inter-twined and she kissed me.

"I love you, Jack Sniper, I really do. Please forgive me for shouting at you."

"I quite understand, Meredith, I love you too," I lied.

I didn't want to hurt Meredith's feelings, but it was Amity who I really cared for.

* * *

Caught up in the diamond boom and at last making money for myself, I had temporarily put aside my main task. I had given Sasha Melnikov snippets, but had made no progress whatsoever about the business dealings and activities of Yevgeny Faramazov.

The very next morning while I was on a run, my mobile rang: "Hello, Jack, long time no talk."

"Oh, hi Sasha, I was thinking about you. Was about to call."

"Sure, of course you were."

"I've got no further leads about Faramazov. He's gone quiet."

"We have a task for you, Jack. We hear he's in New York. He's going to be at Christie's jewellery auction, next week. He's interested in a piece of Catherine The Great."

"Fred Carrender told me that her jewels were in the *Diamond Fund* at the Kremlin."

"Obviously not all. I've got a strange feeling that the auction might lead us to something."

"I've got some leave due. Do you want me to go?"

"Yes. Book a flight to New York this weekend."

Back at the flat at 7 a.m., I opened my laptop in the kitchen, closed the door to make sure that I would not disturb the sleeping Meredith and called Amity on Skype. San Francisco was eight hours behind London and she was likely to be home at 11.

"Hi Jack, you look sweaty. Been on a run with Cobber?" Amity said.

"Yeah there he is," I said pointing the laptop camera towards the dog."

"Hi Cobbs. How's the best dog in the world?"

Cobber pricked up his ears, came to the Camcorder and then began to bark when Amity spoke to him. I stroked the dog and he stopped.

"Amity I'm off to New York this weekend. Why don't you meet me there? It would be great to see you."

"Gee, I was thinking of doing just that. There's a commemoration and exhibition of the International Brigade --- Americans who fought against Franco in the Spanish Civil War. It should be amazing. Veteran soldiers will be there."

"You could talk about your PHD thesis. They're bound to be interested in propaganda during the civil war."

"Great idea, Jack. I'll contact the exhibition organisers."

The kitchen door opened suddenly.

"Have to go Amity, will speak later," I said, turning off my laptop.

Meredith rushed in and fortunately Amity was no longer visible.

"Talking to your American girl again?" Meredith said.

I didn't reply.

"Don't bother lying. Your bloody dog woke me up. I overheard everything. You're meeting her in New York. You're a lying, cheating bastard."

Meredith paced up and down the room, tears welling up in her eyes.

"I've had just about enough of this relationship. You're not prepared to let it develop."

"If that's the way you want it," I said shrugging my shoulders as I placed a lead on to Cobber, and took him into the garden. No point in having another argument.

Meredith, who was shocked by my negative response rushed into the bathroom sobbing and had a shower. Leaving the dog in the garden, I entered the flat in an attempt to part friends. Struggling to control herself, Meredith ignored me, went into the bedroom, packed her things silently, threw her keys on the floor and left.

The next morning, I booked a ticket to New York.

15

The Auction and International Brigade

Amity had already checked into the quaint Algonquin Hotel on Sunday evening, when I arrived. It was ironic that Meredith had told me about the hotel, hoping I would take her to New York. Meredith was a fan of Dorothy Parker, who held her "Round Table" lunches at the Algonquin with other authors, playwrights and critics. The walls of the Round Table Restaurant and Blue Bar had etchings of Parker and her elite circle in the 1920s. The hotel pamphlets boasted about guests who included Simone de Beauvoir, Gertrude Stein, Sinclair Lewis and William Faulkner. Actors, past and present also stayed there.

Amity and I lived far apart, but I still yearned for a relationship. We had grown closer in London, but Amity had stressed that it would be a strong bond of friendship, nothing more. She had told me that she didn't mind if I had other girlfriends, as it would take a long time to get over Pacy. As we explored the famous hotel, I felt a bit guilty about Meredith. She would have loved to be there, but as talented as Meredith was as a writer, we were temperamentally unsuited. Meredith had a fierce temper and could be shrill when she wasn't getting her way. With Amity, I felt at peace and she had a delicate beauty, which Meredith didn't match.

Christie's, facing a courtyard in the Rockefeller Center, was near the hotel. We dawdled in the gallery looking at some paintings, when Faramazov entered with his wife. Faramazov, with short, greying, blonde hair, had lost weight since I had last seen him in Antwerp. His face was gaunt and he looked stressed. Waiting for the start of the auction, he chatted quietly with his wife, who had delicate features and long black hair. Anya was about twenty years younger, but despite the age gap she seemed to be attached to him, touching his arm from time to time. Perhaps this was third time lucky. The first wife, who I had met several years previously, had been divorced some time ago. The second marriage hadn't lasted a year.

Amity suddenly became tense. Carlos Maxos, in a light brown suede jacket, was confidently marching towards the Russian couple. He kissed Anya on both cheeks and chatted loudly. We slipped behind a large sculpture, so that we were partially obscured. During their conversation, Maxos couldn't stop himself from ogling Anya who was in a low cut yellow dress.

"Creep. That guy should kill him for looking at his wife that way."

"He's quite capable of doing that, Amity. He's a former FSB colonel."

"How do you know that? Have you met him?"

"It's a long story. He's big in mining. Has stakes in diamond mines."

"Let's go in first. I don't want Carlos to see me," Amity said.

"Don't worry, someone is joining them," I said gripping her hand.

We recognised the sultry dark brunette in a black and white check suit, immediately. It was Isabella Pinot.

We went into the large salesroom that had high ceilings. There, sitting in the fifth row was Josh Zunrel with his wife Rosa. He spotted me and called us over.

"Jack Sniper! Good to see you. I had no idea that you were interested in jewellery"

"Still learning, Josh. Thought auctions would be a good idea."

"How are you getting along Jack? Fred told me that you guys had quite a time in Russia."

"We sure did," I said and swiftly introduced Josh and Rosa to Amity.

"That's a lovely diamond brooch," Amity said.

The flower-shaped piece, pinned on Rosa's dark blue dress was exquisite.

"Maybe you'll be able to find something here," Rosa said. "Some lovely jewellery is on show."

"They're going to be expensive in this booming market," Josh said. "I wonder what the big ones are going to fetch?"

"The Catherine the Great Emerald and Diamond Brooch?"

"I hear that Yevgeny Faramazov wants it badly," Josh said. "It's one of the best pieces I've seen. The emerald weighs 65 carats. It is set within a circle of diamonds and is mounted on gold. It will go well above the reserve price."

"What about The Emperor Maximilian Diamond? Do the French and Spaniards want it?" I asked, wondering whether Isabella Pinot intended spending some of the fortune she made from the MSP España listing.

"That will also attract bidders. It weighs about 40 carats and was owned by Archduke Maximilian of Austria. He was then Emperor of Mexico in 1860. There was a revolution and the diamond was in a small pouch around his neck, when a firing squad executed him. Maximilian's widow, Princess Charlotte of Belgium, managed to retrieve the gem and sold it. Imelda Marcos, widow of deposed Philippines dictator, Ferdinand Marcos, bought it years later."

"Not surprising that a member of the Spanish mafia is probably bidding for it," Amity said.

Josh was taken aback.

"Spanish mafia? Here?"

"Carlos Maxos and Isabella Pinot. They're sitting near that Russian FSB guy," Amity said.

"Maxos has a stake in Canary Diamond Mines," Josh said.

"So what, he's still a Spanish fascist and gangster."

Josh looked quizzically at Rosa and then me.

"Amity be careful. You could be sued for libel," I said. "I've researched the background of MSP España directors. They don't have criminal records."

"That doesn't mean that he hasn't done anything wrong...He's a rap ..."

I put up my hand to stop her.

"I'm examining a sample of their diamonds tomorrow," Josh said, swiftly changing the subject.

"Can I come with you?" I asked. "I'm officially on leave, but I haven't seen the mine's latest production."

"No problem. I'm meeting the New York dealer who values them. Come to the Waldorf Astoria and have breakfast with me."

Christie's auctioneer was ready to begin.

It soon became evident that the price estimates in the catalogue were too low. The bidding was fast and furious and the fortunate sellers, received prices far above expectations. Rosa made a few bids for designer gold and diamond bracelets but was beaten. The piece that she really wanted was a cultured pearl and diamond necklace. The list price was $60,000 but she had to pay $110,000.

Faramazov's wife and Isabella managed to get some pendants and earrings. I was tempted to bid for jewellery that Amity liked, but both Rosa and Josh stopped me.

"They're going a bit nuts here," Josh said. "You'll find better value at Tiffany or De Beers' 5th Avenue shop."

The Catherine the Great Emerald and Diamond Brooch, went on the block at last and there were murmurings of excitement. The bidding on the floor, via telephones and the Net, started at $400,000. A man next to Faramazov, appeared to be working for him. He swiftly bid $1.2 million upwards, but withdrew when the price exceeded $1.5 million. The piece was eventually sold for $1.65 million. Carlos and Isabella were auspiciously active until a persistent rival beat them with a successful $1.76 million bid for the Emperor Maximilian piece. The way the market was going, prices of both pieces would easily soar in future years.

* * *

Amity, Josh, Rosa and I were just about to leave the building, when I heard a shout in a Spanish accent. Carlos Maxos rushed up to me.

"Jack Sniper? I thought it was you, but I couldn't be sure. Hola Amity."

Amity glared at him. I was worried that she would make a scene, but thankfully she bit her lip and said nothing.

"Philippe Santos said that he saw you in Lanzarote," Maxos said. "Why didn't you speak to him?"

"I was in a large group. He was busy answering questions and went diving for diamonds."

"I've been in contact with Jamey Jackenhead. He told me that you would be here."

"Really? He didn't tell me that you had spoken to him."

"Let me introduce you to my colleague and friend, Yevgeny Faramazov," Maxos said. Come and have some lunch with us. I'll tell you what Jamey and I have been discussing."

"Do you want to go shopping with us, Amity?" Rosa asked, sensing that Amity wanted out.

"I'll book Calamity Jane, if that's OK with you, Jack? It had great reviews," Amity said when I was introducing Josh to Maxos.

"Pleased to meet you Mr Zunrel," Maxos said. "Solly Sidenberg, our New York dealer, told me that you were going to examine Canary's diamonds. Please join us."

Maxos organised a large table for six at The Sea Grill. It was disquieting to be near Faramazov again. I had last seen him before I went to jail. During the pleasantries, it became clear what the lunch was all about. Maxos was making a pitch for a new project in the Canary Islands. This time it was in Fuerteventura.

"I've already spoken to Jamey Jackenhead and he's keen to be an underwriter," Maxos said.

"I'm in charge of JJ Emerging Mining Finance's diamond division. Jamey hasn't mentioned this to me," I said.

Faramazov glanced almost imperceptibly at me and continued with his meal. Maxos barely disguised his annoyance that I had intervened.

He then whispered loudly across the table to Faramazov: "It's a very interesting prospect, Yevgeny."

It was obvious that Maxos had invited Josh and I to impress Faramazov. Jackenhead had already agreed to back the Fuerteventura project and Zunrel, an established Antwerp dealer, would be examining the diamonds. Faramazov's silence showed that he knew exactly what was going on.

"I spoke to Jackenhead over the weekend," Maxos

said. "I told him that Marcia Vaskilov is confident that we'll find diamonds there. He's enthusiastic."

Isabella Pinot smiled and rattled off capital spending projections.

"Initial samples of diamonds from our Lanzarote operations are beyond our expectations," she said. "The mine will soon be profitable."

I glanced across the table to see how Faramazov was reacting. Possibly disappointed because he had lost the bid for Catherine The Great's brooch, he seemed to be irritated with Maxos' pitch. No doubt, people continually hassled him with their schemes. Faramazov also appeared to be concerned about the boredom of his wife, who kept glancing at people on another table. I guessed that they were their bodyguards, as they seemed to know her. Realising that Anya was about to leave, I decided to make small talk with her. She was polite and pleasant and was most interested when I told her that Amity was an art historian.

"I gather you're involved in diamond mining in Russia, Mr Faramazov," Zunrel said, cutting straight to the point. "They seem to have succeeded in Lanzarote. Do you think there's a chance in the other islands?"

Since I believed that Faramazov had stakes in Bristol GemDiam Mining and MSP España, I thought that he would wax lyrical about the new project. His neutral response surprised me.

"Vaskilov is a leading geologist in Russia. I respect her work and findings, but geologists are optimists by nature."

I thought that this might be a good opportunity to get some information for Sasha.

"I've met Alexei Ignatyevna, head of Vogdana Diamond Mine," I said.

"Good man. Knows the diamond business," Faramazov said.

"It's interesting that he's managed to keep his employees happy. Dobrenska isn't far from Vogdana, but I heard that the mine has been bugged by strikes and violence."

Faramazov peered at me closely, eyes cold and penetrating, making me fear that he saw right through the plastic surgery. Bad mistake. It was a silly remark. Forgot that there were CCTV cameras at Dobrenska when the riot was going on. He might well have seen me in the footage taking videos and photos. If he did know, he wasn't letting on.

"Yes, it has had its problems," he said.

"I heard that you have a stake in the mine Mr Faramazov," Zunrel said, saving me from any further stupidity.

Faramazov ignored the question.

"We're concentrating on our international interests." I hastily changed the subject.

"Who do you think is going to win the Premiership this season, Mr Faramazov? Hopefully the new players will help your club."

His laugh was hollow: "We buy players at ludicrous prices and they either fail or get injured. We have to perform a lot better than last season, we almost got relegated."

* * *

Later in the afternoon, Amity and I went for a run in Central Park. We ran past the pond and the baseball pitches towards Strawberry Hill Fields which Yoko Ono founded in memory of John Lennon. As I was running, memories flooded back and I wondered who was living in the apartment I once owned on the West Side. Then I was Jack Miner. Now as Jack Sniper, I was still failing to penetrate Yevgeny Faramazov's web.

It was a humid day and running was hard going. Hot and sweating, we had a cold shower together, but afterwards,

Amity kept me at a distance. We enjoyed the Broadway show of Calamity Jane and later, when we were walking back to the hotel, Amity confronted me about Maxos.

"Why the hell are you wasting your time with that low life? I cannot believe that you're so reckless. Why are you investing in his operations?"

"I haven't put a penny in either MSP España or Bristol GemDiam," I said. "I've invested in South African, Canadian and Australian shares."

"So why are you in discussions with him?"

"My boss, Jamey Jackenhead has money in their companies and he's making fortunes on the shares. Maxos says that our firm will be underwriting his new venture."

"What's the matter with you? Didn't you warn your boss about Maxos?

"Of course. I told him that I was wary of Maxos and Co. He would have invested a lot more if I had kept quiet."

"Good at least you've done something!"

"It hasn't done me any good at all. Bristol's stock is shooting up and Jackenhead is resenting me. He's reminded me each day that Maxos hasn't got a criminal record; that Bristol has outperformed my share recommendations by a wide margin."

"What's his problem? He's still made money, hasn't he? You can at least tell him to avoid Fuerteventura."

"If I do, he might fire me."

* * *

After breakfast at the Waldorf Astoria the next day, Josh Zunrel and I had a relaxing walk to New York's diamond district in lower Manhattan.

"There are about two thousand diamond businesses around here," Josh said when we passed diamond and jewellery signs in West 47th Street. "Solly Sidenberg is a member of the New York Diamond Dealers Club. His rooms are near the trading floor."

We pressed the security button of Sidenberg's premises. The receptionist, her hair covered in the traditional Jewish way, opened the door. Solly, behind a large white desk, was examining diamonds with his magnifying eye glass. Dressed in black with a *yarmulke*, Solly had a thick greying beard that virtually covered his face. Six foot three, with a tummy that bulged over his black shiny trousers, he almost knocked over the desk when he stood up to greet us.

"Shalom Josh, Good to see you after all this time," he said, in an accent that sounded part American and part Eastern European. "Well, well, after all these years, another diamond find."

"We'll have to wait to see what will happen," Zunrel said.

"Who's your friend? Does he want to do business? Canary has some wonderful diamonds," Solly said.

"That's up to him. Can I see the goods?"

"Goods?" I asked.

"Trade talk for diamonds," Josh replied.

Solly went to the safe and pulled out a bag of stones and then placed them on the table. There were about two dozen white, yellowish and light blue uncut diamonds in various shapes and sizes. Josh picked up a large stone that looked as if it weighed about five carats and examined it closely.

"Do you know that there are about 3,000 categories of diamonds?" Solly said. "We've got lots more here for you. Are you getting married? An engagement ring, pendant...?"

"I guess you have to be pretty skilful in valuing them," I said.

"Hmm --- Not bad, not bad at all," Josh said, as he

sorted and examined each gem in detail. "Good quality alluvial diamonds. A mix of colours. Interesting that some are green."

"That's exactly what I thought myself," Solly said. "The Canary Islands may have alluvial deposits as rich as the southern and West African coastline."

"Is that because the islands are less than 100 miles away from Africa?" I asked.

"Maybe, maybe not," Josh said. "Let's see what they produce in the future."

"Are they for sale?" I asked.

"Investors in the mine have the first option to buy. I'll let you know when I'm free to sell the remainder."

"By investors do you mean Armand Gruchot of Antwerp? I hear he has a stake in Canary Diamonds," Josh said.

"Armand could be interested. He's the main diamond assessor, but they commissioned me to carry out independent valuations," Solly said.

"Do you have shares in Bristol and MSP?" I asked.

"Who doesn't? They're going up like a rocket."

"So how can you be truly independent?"

"I am totally objective. I bought the shares as soon as I saw the diamonds. I knew that the mine would be a winner."

Zunrel was deep in thought after we left Solly.

"Do you think that diamond shares and gem prices are in a bubble?" I asked.

"I would say that the balloon is in an advanced phase of expansion," Josh said. "Sidenberg is an indicator. He usually tends to buy real estate, not shares."

"The question is how long will it last? Last week I advised my boss to start taking profits and his shares are up again," I said. "He's not terribly pleased with me. What do you think of the diamonds?"

"Pretty good quality. Excellent colour and clarity. Medium and small. They should fetch good prices."

"And the diamond market?"

"Let's go to Tiffany and Zales to see how jewellery sales are doing."

A little later we were wandering through Tiffany on 5th Avenue. The shop was almost empty. Josh spotted a floor manager, he knew.

"Not many customers today, James."

"It's been quiet for weeks," James said. "It's a two-tiered market. The very wealthy are buying large pieces, but most of our customers are resisting higher prices."

"Tiffany's stock price is soaring," I said.

"Beats me," the manager said. "The stock market has a will of its own."

"We were at Christie's auction yesterday. Prices sold well over estimates," Josh said.

"Confirms my view that it's a two-tiered market," the manager said. "Go to Zales it's even quieter there. They're cutting prices."

"What's the difference between Tiffany and Zales?" I asked.

"Tiffany tends to cater for middle to wealthier customers. Zales sells to a broader market."

"I see you have quite a few items on sale," Josh said.

We went to the counter and I noticed a white diamond ring. On impulse, I decided to buy it for Amity. The price had been cut to $4,000.

"Getting engaged, Jack?" Josh asked.

"I don't know," I said, feeling self-conscious. "Maybe, if she wants me."

* * *

The ceremony honouring veteran American survivors of

the Spanish Civil War was held in *El Museo del Barrio* on Fifth Avenue. It was moving. Half a dozen men, in their nineties, proudly received Spanish passports to honour their role in the fierce battles. Several were bent over, or in wheel chairs.

Joe Kahn, a frail veteran, stood tall and upright on a platform and made a speech.

"During the Spanish Civil War, almost forty thousand men and women from the US, Britain, Russia and other countries travelled to Spain. They joined the International Brigades to fight fascism. We're here to represent the 2,800 brave Americans."

"American volunteers fought and served in medical and transportation units," Joe continued. "We became known as the Abraham Lincoln Brigade who fought for the legitimately elected Republican Government. General Franco, backed by Hitler and Mussolini, won the war because we were outgunned and our generals and armies were disorganised."

Amity gave an excellent presentation. Her slides showed propaganda posters, publications and paintings of both the Republicans and fascists. She made the point that there were atrocities on both sides, but Franco and his fascist forces perpetrated most of the violence and genocide.

"Picasso, Miro and other great artists promoted the cause of the Republicans and the message encouraged volunteers from America and other nations to join forces and fight Franco," she said. "It's a sad blot on our history that the US authorities refused to allow American volunteers from entering Spain. Most entered the country illegally, crossing the Pyrenees from France or as stowaways on ships."

The floor was open to questions and a microphone was passed around to a woman at the back of the crowded room. I turned around. It was Isabella Pinot and next to her was Carlos Maxos.

"The speakers are biased! America, Britain and France decided not to support the Republicans for good reason," Pinot said in her Spanish accent. "Communists were the leading faction of the Republican Government. That's why Russia was only too willing to help. If Franco hadn't won, Spain would have become Communist."

"That's a simplification of history," Amity said. "The Popular Front coalition which won the elections in 1936 included moderate socialists and professionals, not just the Communists. Bottom line, the Republicans were elected democratically."

"Most of the American volunteers and journalists were Communist supporters," Maxos said.

Joe Kahn, who had been sitting with the other veterans on the podium behind Amity, slowly stood up and asked for the mike.

"What Rubbish. Are you saying that Ernest Hemingway was a Communist? I lunched with him in Barcelona during the civil war. He filed objective, unbiased reports. I'm no Communist, nor are my fellow soldiers here. We went to Spain to fight for democracy."

"You make it sound so simple," Pinot said. "The Communist faction was not democratic. The Republican government interfered with religious processions and Catholic teaching. Its economic policy was hopeless. People lost their jobs. When Franco came to power, he made Spain stable and the economy improved."

"At what cost? Hundreds of thousands of good people were killed. I don't know who you are and you are entitled to your view," another veteran said. "Thousands upon thousands of murdered people lie buried in unknown graves."

"The past is the past. Is there any point in digging all this up?" Maxos said, interjecting on Pinot's behalf.

"I've been told that there's a new species of Spanish and other European cockroaches. They are racist, bigoted, extreme right groups," Joe said. "They still worship the memory of the dictator."

Afterwards speakers and audience mingled, drinking cocktails and munching snacks. When Amity was speaking to someone else, a smiling Isabella Pinot came up to me.

"So what do you think Jack? I know you're with Amity, but you have your own mind."

"From what Amity has told me and from my own readings, the Spanish Civil War was complicated," I said tactfully. "Both sides were no angels, but Franco was by far the worst."

It was then that I noticed something that made me search my memory. On Pinot's black blouse was a brooch. Its background was white enamel with a black snake engraved on it.

Luckily Amity didn't notice me talking to Pinot, as we were behind some other members of the audience. I swiftly left Pinot and joined Joe Kahn and her. A remarkable man, He had also received a medal for bravery in World War II, according to the program.

"I know those people," Amity said to Joe turning her head towards Maxos and Pinot who were on the far side of the room. "The grandfather of that jerk was a fascist Major General who died recently. He lived in Granada and had a shrine to Hitler."

"Really? Who was he?" Joe asked.

"Ario Doval."

"Heard of him," Joe said. "People told me that he led some troops into a village. They rounded up innocent civilians, took them to the mountains and shot them."

"You seem concerned about current developments in Spain and Europe," I said.

"The extreme right represents a small minority in Spain so far, but I'm worried. Youth unemployment is very high. If the economy worsens, the cockroaches will multiply. France, Italy and some other European nations have the same problem. These extreme right, neo Nazi movements are dangerous."

* * *

Afterwards, Amity and I walked across Central Park holding hands. It was late afternoon and humid, hot New York, was at last beginning to cool down. I led her to the shade and privacy of a huge oak tree. A little nervous, I kissed her lightly on her cheek, took out the ring and showed it to her.

"Amity will you...?"

"Oh Jack, I cannot believe --- No! Sorry I can't."

"Why? We're great together. I love you," I said with an air of desperation, the desperation from all those lonely years in prison, desperation from wanting to have a family. A long, lost family; the one that had vanished when I was a boy, when both my parents died.

"It's still too soon, Jack. It's Pacy..."

"I understand, but I'm sure he would want you to be happy, Amity."

"Jack, I don't want to hurt your feelings. You're a great guy, a good friend, but I'm not ready."

"OK if that's the way you want it," I said, hurt and embarrassed that I had made a fool of myself.

As usual she read my mind: "Don't feel bad, Jack. I love you as a special friend, who I can trust. Sorry."

The reminder about Pacy, jogged my memory; the brooch that Isabella Pinot was wearing.

It was coming back to me; the car park in Hillbrow, Johannesburg; the car park where Pacy was murdered. Angus, Watson Nkosi's police dog, had found a badge with a white background and black snake. Watson had sent out enquiries about the badge. He was told that the black snake was the sign of the Black Python, an extreme right Spanish movement.

I was tempted to tell Amity, but had to keep that part of my life confidential. Detective work was secondary at that moment.

I felt desolate. Here was the loveliest girl imaginable; beautiful, intelligent and sensitive. The rejection meant that I wanted her all the more. Amity realised this, of course and that night she cuddled up to me in a friendly, platonic way, leaving me frustrated and wretched. The next morning was a little tense, but we parted good friends when we checked out of New York. I wondered whether I would ever see her again.

PART THREE

THE ERUPTION

16

CRYSTAL BUBBLE

A month later, an International Diamond Investment Conference took place at London's InterContinental Hotel in Mayfair. The conference room was packed with mining executives, pension fund managers, hedge fund executives, individual investors, bankers and global gems dealers. Diamond mining luminaries from South Africa, Russia, Botswana, Angola, Sierra Leone, Canada and Australia wandered about the conference room. Officers and geologists of Asian and South American exploration companies and gem merchants from Mumbai, Hong Kong, Shanghai, Thailand and Singapore, were also present.

Faramazov was not on the list of delegates, but I guessed that he had representatives who I hadn't met. I searched for Dobrenska and Valdia officials on the Russian list, but couldn't find them. Two good friends were present; Fred Carrender and Sonya Moldanya, who was covering the conference for the *Novaya Gazeta*. They were with Alexei Ignatyevna of Vogdana Diamond Mine. It was the first time that I had seen them since the Russian trip.

The organiser opened the conference saying that it was the most well attended diamond event that she had ever experienced. Her firm would hold more conferences in the coming year and the venues would be in New York, Antwerp, Tel Aviv, Mumbai, Moscow and Cape Town. The programme had numerous sponsors and exploration companies. At the back of the room were reports on the various diamond companies and flyers promoting the expertise of geologists, mining consultants and gem dealers. Public relations executives networked around the side rooms of the conference during coffee breaks, shaking hands and swapping business cards. There was unusual media interest with TV, radio and newspaper reporters collaring participants and questioning them about the diamond and jewellery market.

The main story was the new find in Lanzarote and the potential of new diamond exploration projects in the Canary Islands' volcanic archipelago. Speakers on the global gems market and mining prospects included executives from De Beers, Alrosa and Jwaneng. Some analysts sniggered that the large companies had failed to discover the Canary diamond reserves and it would only be a matter of time before they acquired the minnows.

The buzz that day was the Bristol GemDiam presentation of chief executive, Gerald Gleep, financial director, Percival Meltin and consultant geologist, Marcia Vaskilov. Carlos Maxos, Philippe Santos and Isabella Pinot of MSP España were also going to talk about their company. Early that morning Bristol had announced that the latest sample of diamonds had been valued at $10 million. This news raised the market temperature to sauna levels and Wordspread, Bristol's public relations firm, arranged press interviews with the company's executives.

"The gems are as good, if not better than those found on the coast of Namibia and other rich alluvial deposits," Raymond Mildew, Wordspread's chief executive, said.

Bristol, listed at £1 a share, only a year previously and

closing the previous day at £5, opened at £5.60, after the latest announcement and swiftly rose to £6. MSP España Mining was also surging on the Madrid Exchange. Bristol and España directors and management were growing richer by the second, let alone the minute and other shareholders were also beaming.

The market capitalisation of Bristol, which had initially raised £100 million, when it was listed, was now £600 million. I noticed some guys on mobiles on the side of the room shouting orders to their brokers, most buying, others taking profits. As Bristol's stock soared in a jagged upward line, investors bid up prices of other diamond shares regardless whether they were producing or exploring for gems.

At one side of the coffee room were terminals highlighting *CNBC*, *Bloomberg* and *Reuters* reports and interviews on the diamond industry.

"Much has been written about general stock market booms and busts, but mining speculation has its own special characteristics," Fred Carrender said, when we were sitting down for lunch.

I was sharing one side of a large round table with Fred, Sonya Moldanya and Alexei Ignatyevna.

"This boom is a classic example. Just over a year ago, virtually no-one was the slightest bit interested in diamonds. Gold, silver and platinum were rising, but diamond prices and shares were languishing. Then diamonds were found in the Canary Islands and suddenly everyone wants to play."

"Doesn't that happen in all markets," I asked.

"Yes, but the mining community and their brokers have a much greater gambling instinct. They are fortune hunters by heart; optimists by nature. They like the thrill of discovery, drilling the hole and hoisting out gold or gems. The energy community is the same. Hole after hole are drilled in the desert in the hope of striking oil. When they strike it lucky and the black stuff whooshes up, investors go wild. If there's a whiff of news, stockbrokers and fund managers rush to buy."

"Analysts have mining, geology, engineering and business degrees, so they must evaluate the resources properly," Alexei said.

"True, the vast majority have excellent qualifications, but if a prospect excites them, they read what they want to read, believe what they want to believe," Fred said. "During the many years I've been involved in this industry, the gullibility and wishful thinking of participants have never ceased to amaze me. The higher the qualification of the geologist, mining engineer and stock broker analyst, the greater their belief that they have exceptional insight."

"Surely not all of them?"

"A sizeable majority."

"If you can't trust them, who can you trust?" Alexei asked.

"Resource investment is speculative, so you have to be extra wary. The mining and energy industries are rife with tips, insider information, manipulation and stock ramping," Fred said. Shrewd stock manipulators spread the net. Once the fish begin to bite they feed them their shares."

"I thought that the authorities were stamping down on insider trading," Sonya said. "There have been some major prosecutions in New York and London seems to be following."

"Unless it's overt buying ahead of an announcement, it's very difficult to prove," Fred said.

"So how do they get away with it?"

"A lot of information isn't deliberately illegal. The mining community is tight knit, very much like an international family. Analysts travel to mines around the world."

"Take a simple example," Fred continued. "An analyst meets a miner in a pub who likes talking about his job.

They have a few drinks and the miner tells the stockbroker what he thinks is happening on the mine. The miner could be wrong or telling only a small part of the story, but the broker draws his own optimistic conclusions and recommends the shares."

"What about the insiders at this event?" I asked.

"Directors openly promote their companies here. If there's an important development, they make a public announcement. That's legal, but it raises the fever. The vast majority of people here are bullish about diamonds and diamond stocks. They have either bought shares or are about to buy."

"Surely there are sceptics," I said.

"Of course. But investors become irritated when they follow cautious advisors and sell prematurely. If the stocks rise even further, the pessimists lose their credibility."

"Some of the people here, must be taking profits."

"Sure. Time after time, metals and mining stocks have risen ahead of precious metals conferences and other events. If I were a serious speculator, I would buy gold, silver and platinum the week before the events, sell them during the conferences and make a tidy sum in the process."

"Did you buy diamond stocks last week?" piped up a voice near our table. "I couldn't help but overhear your conversation."

"I don't believe we've met," Fred said with a frown, annoyed that he had allowed himself to get carried away and talk loudly.

"Raymond Mildew, Wordspread. We represent Bristol GemDiam."

The spin doctor who had just sat down uninvited, had a haughty square face, a supercilious smile and carefully groomed, longish dark hair. His dark, elegant suit was tailored and he wore a green silk tie with the Bristol

GemDiam logo.

"Since you overheard my uninformed opinion, what's your view Mr Mildew?" Fred asked in a deliberately flat and uninterested tone.

"I think you should speak to Gerald Gleep yourself. I'm no expert about diamonds and mining. Here's the latest press release," Mildew said and promptly distributed the release and his business card. "If you wish I can send you the latest analysts' reports."

"What's their view?" I asked.

"About fifteen analysts follow Bristol and the current rating is 'overweight'"

Sonya was puzzled.

"Overweight?"

"They're advising their clients to buy a large quantity," I said.

"Do you have shares in the company, Mr Mildew?" Sonya asked.

"That's a rather personal question," Mildew said. "As it so happens, I don't."

"What about your wife? Your partner?"

Mildew glared at her.

"Who are you. I don't believe that we've been introduced."

"Sonya Moldanya, *Novaya Gazeta*."

"Everything's off the record, OK! There's a press conference in the Roman Room, later."

"I wasn't going to quote you. Did you say anything worth quoting?" Sonya said.

Mildew stood up in a huff and went to his client on the main table. We packed up laughing.

"Hear that! Fifteen out of fifteen broker analysts are bullish about diamonds and Bristol," Fred said. "When prices were depressed last year, there were only three or four analysts covering diamonds and they were bearish."

* * *

A celebrity politician made a speech full of platitudes on how British mining investment was creating jobs around the world. The delegates wolfed down their food and the wine flowed. Coffee was at last served.

"From my experience, beware of bankers, brokers and financial advisors who make you promises," Fred said. "If they encourage you to overtrade, you'll come a cropper."

"Sounds as if you're a disenchanted investor," Alexei said.

"To be frank, I do play the market and I've won and lost," Fred said. "Perhaps my market theories don't interest you."

"It's obviously practice, not theory. Please go on."

The three of us listened intently to the wise old prospector.

"A successful independent investor with no special information, studies the business prospects of a company and carefully decides whether to buy or sell," Fred said.

"That goes without saying," Alexi said.

"Give the same person inside information and he's likely to believe that he's much smarter than other people. So much so, that he may well ignore the most obvious risks."

"I assume you're referring to directors who follow regulations and disclose their dealings. Surely their actions indicate how their businesses are doing?" I said.

"Their businesses, yes. Share prices, no. I have known company directors who have either bought or hung on to their overvalued shares when outsiders were selling. They ended up losing."

"What's your view about the current mood in the diamond market?"

"The various temperature gauges show that the market is overheated. Justified or not prices of gem and diamond stocks could rise a lot further. It is very difficult to predict when the crystal bubble will shatter."

"It seems that the diamond boom is contagious. People have been buying all sorts of shares--- mining, tech, everything. Those who are out of the market are kicking themselves."

"Hindsight makes everyone a genius. What's better, Jack? Opportunity loss or actual loss?"

"But money in the bank is yielding virtually nothing or even zero. At least equities provide dividends and potential capital gains."

"A small capital loss can easily wipe out a dividend."

Fred stood up and stretched his long legs and led us out of the hall.

"What if you've sold your stocks and the market boom lasts much longer than expected?" Alexei asked.

"It's a matter of reverse psychology. Be thankful. Luck's been on your side. You've made a profit. Let the other guy make something."

"But your money is now in the bank and earning nothing."

"Give some to charities. Go on holiday. Savour your health."

"And the rest of the cash?"

"I 'amortise' my gains. A portion of my profits is syphoned off each year, if I need the income. Take a simple example. The share I sold for $100,000 has a dividend yield of 3 percent i.e. $3,000. The profit I made from the sale is $30,000. I can safely pocket $3,000 per year for ten years. In other words, I treat the $30,000 as income in advance."

"People find it difficult to accept that. It isn't just greed. The natural tendency is to try and make money work for you. Get some return," Alexei said. "They can always cut their losses."

"Only the most disciplined speculators cut out and many a time, they're too late."

How do you assess value in a boom, when the experts predict higher and higher prices?"

"You don't need calculus. One and one makes two, not three or four. A shrewd South African finance minister once told me: 'It takes hard work and time to make money; easy to lose it.'"

"What about latecomers who missed the bull market and want to take a chance?"

"If you're thinking that way Alexei, go and play golf or tennis, go to a movie. Listen to some music. Shares don't remain overvalued forever."

* * *

At 4.35 PM, after the London market had closed, Gerald Gleep announced that Bristol GemDiam was going to have a rights issue of 20 million shares at £5 a share

"The price is at an attractive discount to the closing market price of £6.25," he said. "The £100 million issue will finance an exciting alluvial diamond mining prospect in Fuerteventura."

"Jamey Jackenhead is sitting in the front row, shouldn't you be with him?" Fred said after Gleep mentioned that JJ Emerging Mining Finance was one of the underwriters of the issue."

"I no longer work there," I said.

"What! I thought you had a good job and the two of you got on well with each other."

I then told Fred what had happened.

"The day I returned from New York, I went straight to JJ Emerging Mining Finance's new spacious offices. They were in Curzon Street, in the heart of Mayfair's hedge fund land. As soon as I arrived, Jamey greeted me excitedly. He told me that Carlos Maxos wanted his company to raise more money for Canary Diamond Mines and that I should be in charge of the share issue. I refused on the grounds that Maxos and co-director Isabella Pinot were supporters of Black Python, a Spanish fascist movement. We had a row and Jamey fired me."

"You did the right thing, Jack," Fred said, slapping my back. "I'll speak to Alexei. Maybe you can come with me to the Canary Islands and help assess his project."

"Alexei has a claim in the Canaries?"

"Yes, in Lanzarote---- a beach to the north of Canary Diamond Mine. Vogdana Diamonds wants to expand outside Russia."

We were about to leave when I spotted Percival Meltin, a skinny tall, slouching man, dressed in a black suit. He could have been one of Charles Dickens' miserable characters. I had seen him briefly at the analyst trip in Lanzarote, but didn't have a chance to speak to him. Maybe he would give me some information on the Canary Islands. That would help me gauge the viability of Alexei's claim.

"Hello Mr Meltin, could I contact you sometime? It would be good to get more information on Canary Diamond Mines' expansion," I said.

Meltin appeared to be highly stressed about something.

"I'm very busy, but if it is urgent, here's my card," he said in a squeaky voice. "Everything is happening so quickly."

* * *

Later that evening I had dinner with Sonya Moldanya and Sasha Melnikov who was pleased that I could work full time for her again. Unfortunately, it was at the same miserly salary. I decided that I had better sell all my diamond shares to ensure that I had enough cash to keep going. I had bought my flat and could use some of the money to reduce my mortgage.

We met together in the empty upstairs part of a restaurant in Notting Hill Gate, close to Portobello Antique market. Even though I was out of work, I insisted that dinner was on me. They chatted away in Russian and I noticed Sonya glance at me and giggle.

"What are you guys talking about?" I asked.

"Girl stuff. Nothing for you to worry about," Sasha said, winking at Sonya.

"I've got an interview with Yevgeny Faramazov," Sonya said.

"Really? I thought that he avoided the press," Sasha said, looking intensely interested.

"That was my impression too. Faramazov phoned me after I was injured at the Dobrenska mine," Sonya said. "He insisted that he wasn't to blame for the violence."

"You don't believe him, do you?" Sasha said.

"I don't know. I asked him if I could interview him. He offered me a slot in his diary and that's why I'm here."

"I thought that you came for the diamond conference," I said.

Sonya finished off her wine.

"It was a good idea to combine the two,"

"I think Jack should go with you," Sasha said. "I've told you about Faramazov's reputation. He's a psychopath. It could be dangerous."

"Thanks Sasha, I knew that you would take care of my health."

"No need for sarcasm, Jack. Sonya will need your protection."

"Does Jack work with you Sasha?" Sonya asked, somewhat surprised.

"Jack has many talents, Sonya. He'll take care of you. He can even help in the interview."

"I'll do my best, Sonya. I know quite a bit about his background," I said.

"I'll get him," Sasha said, gritting her teeth.

"I know how you must feel, Sasha, but I have to be objective," Sonya said.

17

THE INTERVIEW

Yevgeny Nicolaivich Faramazov's country mansion was in Hertfordshire, about 25 miles north of London. He lived there with his wife Anya and their children. According to the tabloid press, Faramazov's first wife and two eldest children were still in Moscow. They were not terribly well off, as Faramazov left them when he was a lowly paid officer of the KGB. Later, when he had made serious money, Faramazov married a Russian model. That marriage broke up, soon after a son was born. His second wife, who I had met briefly some years ago, was a classic gold digger. She was much younger than Faramazov and ended up with millions, a large country house alongside the River Thames and a townhouse in London's Chelsea. Her most recent lover was a celebrity footballer. According to the media, she lived in grandeur but was in a legal battle with Faramazov to obtain extra maintenance for her son. There was a rumour that Faramazov wasn't the father, as when he was married to her, she had a toy boy on the side. The media couldn't confirm the story, but soon afterwards the lover had a fatal heart attack. The coroner ruled that the young man's cardiac arrest was sudden death syndrome, but Sasha suspected otherwise.

Faramazov was a classic example of those brilliant egotistical businessmen, who make the worst possible emotional investments, notably trophy, mercenary wives. Fortunately for him, he was third time lucky. According to a three-page spread in the *Daily Mail,* his third wife loved him. The tight knit family of four were very close. The boy and girl aged ten and eight went to a local private school between the two nearest towns, St Albans and Hatfield. Anya, a former university lecturer in history, had a PHD on the similarities of two unsuccessful invasions of Russia. The *First Patriotic War,* which was Napoleon's failed attempt to conquer Russia and the *Second Patriotic War,* Hitler's disastrous campaign. Both were defeated by the tenacity of their opponents and the Russian winter.

Faramazov had commissioned Anya to piece together the history of the two heroic ancestors on his mother's side; Nicolaivich Krakanovitch, a colonel, who fought against Napoleon and was killed in the Battle of Borodino in 1812 and his grandfather, Yevgeny Krakanovitch, who was in the Siege of Stalingrad, the horrific battle against the Nazis. Anya, beautiful, intelligent and cultured, looked almost identical to Faramazov's mother, from the photographs Sasha had shown me. She had developed her interest in history of art to help Faramazov build his collection. Anya was also an accomplished violinist who held concerts with top performers in their own private concert hall.

Sonya and I had found the gossip and snippets about Faramazov, when we scoured microfiches at the *Financial Times.* Jane Jodensberg, my reporter friend and room-mate of my ex-girlfriend Meredith, had used her influence to help us get access to the library. Jane had persuaded her features editor that besides the *Novaya Gazeta,* Sonya could also write an article about Faramazov for the *FT.* Sonya was thrilled as she desperately wanted to become a Russian correspondent for a major British newspaper. The feature on Faramazov would hopefully open the door to her.

Sonya had been to London only once before. To give her a feel of the history of England, I drove north on a Roman tourist trail to Verulamium Park, near St Albans. Then to Hatfield House, home of Elizabeth I, when she was a princess. Sonya, small and curvy with her pretty freckled face and longish red hair, looked good in her fitted floral dress. Her looks were neither in the same league as Amity, nor as sexy as the neurotic, possessive, Meredith. Yet she was constantly smiling and joking and I felt completely relaxed and comfortable with her.

We ambled through the garden where Elizabeth played as a child and went to the very Oak tree where courtiers told her that she would be crowned Queen of England. Considering that the Elizabethan court was known for its intrigue, it was as good a place as any to plan the interview with Faramazov. We were well aware that he was notorious in disguising the truth and was skilful in spinning the story in his favour. It would be a tough task, but we would do our utmost to draw him out with lateral, surprise questions and varied topics.

* * *

Yevgeny Faramazov's palatial home, some five miles from Hatfield House, was surrounded by a high wall with electronic wires. We approached the steel gridded gate, painted in dark khaki green. CCTV cameras could be seen on the wall and on the top of a guardhouse alongside the gate. Two burly security guards, who looked like nightclub bouncers appeared. The first one had a portable phone and called the household in a thick Russian accent; the other asked us to get out of the car. They searched us and then carefully examined the inside of the vehicle, its engine, the boot and chassis underneath. Planning to catch the flight to Moscow just before midnight, Sonya had checked out of her hotel and her suitcase and laptop were in the boot. The guard took out the case, rummaged through her clothes, opened and then closed the laptop and took out the tiny recorder in her handbag.

"What are you using this for?" he asked.

"For the interview with Mr Faramazov," Sonya said.

The guard called the house, spoke in Russian and gave it back to her.

Satisfied at last, the guard signalled to a third colleague in the guardhouse and the gates opened. We drove slowly over road bumps on a winding narrow cobbled road towards another gatehouse about 250 metres away. A large pond with ducks and swans was on one side of the road and in the distance on the other side, an artificial ski run. Closer to the house there was a paddock with several horses, a tennis court and a 20 metre, club size, swimming pool. The second security house was at an entrance of a courtyard, about 100 metres from the front door of the mansion. It had several windows and doors on either side and we passed under its archway before we reached the mansion. Faramazov's servants, gardeners and security staff, probably lived there.

The huge homestead was Georgian and no doubt an aristocratic family were the owners between the 18th and 20th centuries. Now the super-rich, the new aristocracy, resided there in feudal glory. There was a tower at the top of the house and the only thing missing, was a moat. Another security guard could be seen through the tower window and CCTV cameras were everywhere.

A butler, dressed smartly in a black suit, let us into the house. He was English and was stiff and polite. His lean, muscular physique indicated that he doubled as a bodyguard.

The hallway, with high ceilings, had knights' suits of armour with swords and shields propped up against them. Paintings on the wall appeared to be scenes from the Battle of Borodino as alongside them were portraits of Napoleon and his adversary, the one eyed Russian commander, Prince Mikhail Kutuzov. A painting of Russia's Catherine the Great was similar to the one in the Christie's catalogue at the New York auction, where I had recently encountered Faramazov. At the side of the hallway was a door leading into a large room containing about 100 chairs. It had a podium with a grand piano on it and the Butler said that it was Anya Faramazov's concert room. We were ushered into a waiting room with two plush, light blue sofas, matching arm chairs and modern art on the walls. Sonya shuffled around the room in admiration, explaining that the paintings were by Kandinsky, Jawlensky and Russian revolution artists. A small flexible camera in the corner of the ceiling followed our movements. On a table directly underneath the camera, were bottles of water, vodka, whisky and cognac with crystal glasses next to them. We were both thirsty, so I opened a bottle of sparkling water.

After about a quarter of an hour or so, Faramazov's butler returned. In silence, he ushered us into the hallway and through a passage way, alongside windows that overlooked a spacious landscaped garden. The passage led to a modern lift. We entered and it rose past two floors to the top of the house. The lift's doors opened directly into a narrow passage. The butler knocked on a door and we entered a light largish room surrounded by book cases containing numerous antiquarian books. Since they were in English, they were probably part of the house's fixtures and fittings when Faramazov bought it. I glanced around swiftly and for the first time I couldn't spot a CCTV camera. Faramazov obviously didn't want his security guards to monitor his private activities.

Faramazov, who was sitting behind a desk in a high chair, stood up and came over to us. He was casually dressed in a plain dark blue shirt with light blue trousers that were too big for him. To be sure, I was shocked at the transformation in his appearance. In New York, a month previously, he was strained and tense, but had appeared to be in fair health. Faramazov had lost a lot of weight since then and it didn't suit him. He was now too thin and his face was pale, haggard and drawn. The room smelt of stale smoke, but no packets of cigarettes could be spotted near the prolific smoker. His voice was rasping when he greeted us.

"Ah yes, Mr Sniper, Miss Moldanya told me that you were accompanying her," Faramazov said, shaking my hand lightly. "Sonya Moldanya. Good to meet you at last. Thanks for coming all this way."

He held Sonya's hand for a brief moment, looking at her intently: "I'm very glad that you have recovered from that blow to your head."

Faramazov, former KGB and FSB, Faramazov the psychopath. I could hardly believe it. He seemed to be genuinely concerned.

"I heard that you no longer work for Jackenhead of JJ Emerging Mining Finance, Mr Sniper," Faramazov said, with an intense look that made me feel uneasy.

"How do you know? Has he become one of your advisors?" I asked, somewhat concerned.

Faramazov coughed out a laugh: "No doubt you have researched me thoroughly. Do you really believe that I would not have done the same with you?"

For a brief moment, I was worried whether he had twigged on that I was really Jack Miner, but he continued: "Russia and South Africa have a lot in common. They're rich in resources and corruption."

"Thanks for offering the interview, Mr Faramazov," Sonya said, keen to get started.

He pointed towards two dark brown leather sofas that were next to the window. Far below was the garden where his children were playing with a football. They were near their mother, who was sitting alongside a table under the shelter of a sun umbrella. In the distance, were the private lake, the dry ski run, horses and cows and the high walls surrounding his estate. We sat down with the feudal Russian lord, member of the select, stupendously rich and faced him across a dark, antique coffee table.

"Do you mind if I use this?" Sonya asked and took out her recorder from her handbag.

For the first time, I detected the ruthlessness of the former KGB officer and infamous FSB colonel. The grey blue eyes that peered out of the sunken face, narrowed and scrutinised the journalist and her companion. I couldn't help but shudder.

"If you wish. The proviso is..."

"I switch it off, when you want to talk off the record."

"Precisely," Faramazov said, his insincere smile making me feel even more uncomfortable.

He picked up a book on the corner of the table. It was a biography of William Tecumseh Sherman.

From a marked page, he read what the US Civil War general said: "I hate newspapermen. They come into camp and pick up rumours and print them as facts. I regard them as spies, which, in truth, they are."

Faramazov grinned and we half laughed uneasily.

"You said that you wanted to put the record straight, when you phoned me, Mr Faramazov," Sonya said.

It was a quiet, non-confrontational interviewing method, the very opposite to the aggressive techniques of some American and British journalists and broadcasters.

"Yes, I did."

"Why don't you begin and if I may, I'll ask you questions as you go on."

"I phoned you in Moscow after your physical and mental traumas, as I was concerned that you were caught up in the Dobrenska mine violence," Faramazov began in perfect English, with a very slight Russian accent. "I also wanted to rectify what you wrote in your articles. There has been a lot of misinformation about the events surrounding the diamond mine."

Sonya stopped him and replayed what he said. Satisfied that the gadget was working, she put it on record again and Faramazov continued: "You and others in the press were correct in stating that I had a stake in Dobrenska. Where you were wrong, very wrong, was that I had control of the mine. My holding was small."

"It's important to understand Dobrenska's history. Trekdiam, an Australian mining company, was allotted Russian exploration rights at the beginning of the 1990s. Boris Yeltsin, as you know, was then President of Russia. Trekdiam discovered rich gem deposits and in partnership with the Russian government founded Dobrenska Diamond Mine to develop the new project. At the time, I was a senior official in the government's Natural Resources Department, in charge of the development. As an incentive, I was awarded a small stake in Dobrenska. Oleg Melnikov, a talented mining engineer, managed the operation. He brought the mine into full production and his work was highly satisfactory. After a few years, Dobrenska became an exceedingly profitable diamond mine."

That information confirmed what Sasha and Yelena had told me, but I was unaware that Faramazov was one of the State's mining officials.

"After Yeltsin resigned as president in 1999, the new Russian administration decided that it no longer needed a foreign partner in Dobrenska. It appointed Ivan Bigganoff, an ambitious Russian businessman, to strike a deal with Trekdiam."

"Valdia, Bigganoff's company made an offer to Trekdiam, but the Australian company refused to accept," Faramazov continued. "Valdia then conducted a successful hostile takeover of Dobrenska. It became the new manager of the mine, but the State remained the controlling shareholder. For his part in the deal, Bigganoff, was awarded a sizeable, undisclosed holding in Dobrenska."

"If it was Trekdiam which discovered the diamonds and developed Dobrenska Mine, its directors and shareholders must have been furious," I said.

"They most certainly were. The compensation was insulting and Trekdiam owned another rich diamond deposit within the Dobrenska area. Trekdiam couldn't get anywhere with the Russian justice system, but since Valdia had international interests, the Australian company decided to take action in the London High Court."

"Apparently Oleg Melnikov was going to give evidence in London on behalf of Trekdiam," Sonya said. "Unfortunately, he had a fatal accident. I contacted Valdia and their spokesman hinted that he had committed suicide."

"How convenient for Valdia," Faramazov said, opening a bottle and pouring water into his and our glasses. "It wasn't suicide. Melnikov was murdered."

This unambiguous statement took me completely by surprise. Sasha Melnikov had insisted numerous times that Faramazov was behind the murder of her father. If he was, he would surely have agreed with the coroner's accidental death verdict. Alternatively, he would have spun the same suicide spin as Valdia.

"Who do you think murdered him?" Sonya asked, deciding to get to the point swiftly.

"Could you please switch off the recorder."

Sonya leaned over and clicked the switch.

"I knew Ivan Bigganoff when we were both in the FSB. Afterwards he became very rich. He was a talented businessman who managed to buy mines and businesses at knock down prices during the chaotic, corrupt Yeltsin era. Melnikov got in his way. Melnikov was a man of principle and supported Trekdiam, which had taken good care of the miners. As you say, he was going to be a witness on Trekdiam's behalf. That would have been very embarrassing for Valdia, Bigganoff and several key Russian officials."

"So Bigganoff was behind the murder?"

"Melnikov and I got on well when we used to meet in Moscow," Faramazov said, not replying directly to the question. "He had an exceptional intellect and was very knowledgeable about diamond mining. Moreover, Melnikov was concerned about growing corruption in the Russian mining world."

Suddenly, Faramazov had a coughing fit into a clump of tissues, which he snatched from a box on the table. I thought that I could see blood on one of them, but couldn't be sure. Sonya passed him some water which he gulped down quickly. He took a minute or two to compose himself. The interview then continued.

"Apologies for that. I'm recovering from flu," he said gasping for breath. "Off the record, strictly off the record, several FSB factions are jostling for power. The aim is to find favour with the President and Prime Minister. The FSB is not only in charge of State Security. It has become an exceedingly complex organisation. Most disturbing, the security system has numerous corrupt officers who are out of control. Leaders of the factions and their sycophants have become greedy. They are demanding stakes in businesses in return for protection. Western companies that have invested in Russia have and are still encountering obstacles."

"Russia is near the top of the global corruption league, according to surveys," Sonya said.

"That's an accurate assessment. Those who fall foul of the system..." he said, slicing his finger across his neck.

"No doubt they took a course from the Sicilian professionals," I said, marvelling at the hypocrisy of this Russian Mafioso.

Faramazov noticed my sneer immediately.

"You are quite right, Mr Sniper, I'm no angel. I'm the first to admit that. But that is my history and I'm now trying to make amends through the Faramazov Foundation."

"It does good work for disadvantaged Russian children and teenagers," Sonya said. Her swift sideways glare, warning me that another tactless remark could stymie her interview.

Faramazov was unfazed. He was giving us his side of the story.

"You can switch on the recorder again," Faramazov said. "The point I'm making is that I had no involvement whatsoever in the murder of Oleg Melnikov. Nor did I have anything to do with the violence against Dobrenska's miners."

"Valdia and Bigganoff were behind them?" Sonya asked again while she scribbled furiously in her notebook.

"I don't know. You have the opportunity to investigate yourselves. Perhaps they will allow you to interview them," Faramazov said.

"My editor once told me that there are three sides to every story; your side; their side and the truth."

Faramazov smiled. It seemed evident that he was beginning to like and trust Sonya.

"The Coroner should reopen the case to determine

the truth," he said. "Whoever was behind these criminal activities wanted to discredit me. The media, the miners and Melnikov's family believe that I ordered the attack on the miners. I swear that it was not me and I have witnesses. Unfortunately, they are frightened to speak out. They are in fear of their lives. They know what happened to Oleg Melnikov."

"I heard that you were interested in eventually returning to Russia; that you want to go into politics," Sonya said.

"Please switch off the recorder. Yes, that's true, but I'm out of favour with the present regime. It would be dangerous to return now. For the time being I will have to remain in exile."

"Why are you out of favour?"

"It's a long story ---- Bigganoff and some others have seen to that."

"Until the President gets tired and drops them," Sonya said, glancing at me. "Some democracy. It's like the history of Hatfield House. Tudor kings and queens. Plotters for and against Elizabeth I. Those who fell out of favour had their heads chopped off!"

"History tends to repeat itself in strange ways," Faramazov said.

"Assume the time is right for your return, what do you propose doing?"

"Clean up the corruption, prosecute FSB criminals and end their parasitic non-productive influence on politics and business."

At that remark, I foolishly blurted out again: "You can talk Mr Faramazov. That is precisely what you did and now you're telling us that you're going to stop it?"

Sonya glared at me for potentially ruining her interview yet again, but instead of getting angry, Faramazov calmly nodded his head.

"You're quite right to think I'm a hypocrite. But don't you agree that my past makes me exceedingly knowledgeable about the FSB and all its tricks?"

"I guess the model is Joe Kennedy, the bootlegger and stock market rogue. The guy who President Roosevelt appointed as chief of the SEC to clean up the market?"

"Ha! You've also studied the 1929 crash and Great Depression, Mr Sniper? Yes, but Joe was father of Jack Kennedy, who eventually became a popular American President. Who better than a Russian equivalent? Someone who knows all the dirty tricks; someone who the corrupt would fear."

He slowly drank his water and went on: "The Russians are a great people with a remarkable history. Millions are highly skilled, talented, educated and cultured, but are poor and struggling. Pensions are miniscule. It is a disgrace what is going on. Russia needs a true democracy and transparent fair business that operates in a free open, honest market. It can be a combination of capitalism and democratic socialism; worker participation in company profits and a justice system that protects all. If that happens, Russia, rich in resources, has a great future. If not, it will degenerate into a third world mess."

I looked around at the opulence and thought about Faramazov's ambitions. If he got in a position of power would he make a difference or would he make it worse? Sonya, incredulous at the outburst, had scepticism written all over her face. Faramazov, observant as ever, noticed.

"You obviously don't believe me; all this wealth that I accumulated. Would the Russian people have faith in me? Who knows? I'm telling you what I would wish to do, if I had the opportunity. Obviously not as man at the top, but as a key player; either as a politician or advisor."

I decided to turn the interview in another direction: "Something concerns me, Mr Faramazov. You claim that you are repenting for what you have done in the past, but very recently you became involved with Spanish fascists."

"What are you talking about? I'm not associated with fascists," Faramazov said.

No doubt about it, he was genuinely surprised and angry.

"According to our information you have sizeable holdings in MSP España and Bristol GemDiam. This means that you have a large indirect stake in Canary Diamond Mines."

"I don't discuss my international business interests, but yes I do have shares in those companies."

"You were with Carlos Maxos in New York. He's a supporter of Black Python, an extreme right-wing Spanish movement."

"Are you telling me that Maxos is a member of a fascist organisation?"

"Yes, and as far as I'm aware, so are the other directors of MSP. You have also met Isabella Pinot. She was heckling courageous American veterans of the Spanish civil war, at a New York commemoration. They were being honoured with Spanish passports. A friend of mine is a Spanish civil war historian and she delivered a speech there."

"You can't be serious."

"Yes, I am! Pinot called the old veterans, Communists."

There was silence with Faramazov deep in thought. He looked stunned.

"Did you know that Carlos' grandfather was Major General Ario Doval? That he was one of Franco's favourites?"

"Of course, I didn't know," Faramazov said.

Clearly agitated, he was opening and closing his fists.

"During my friend's research for her PHD, she met Maxos' Grandfather," I said. "Doval, who recently died, had a dedicated room with a shrine to Hitler. There was a big portrait of Hitler, commemorative candles, a large Swastika, Nazi memorabilia and medals."

"A shrine to Hitler? Are you sure your friend wasn't exaggerating?"

"She took a picture on her mobile, when they weren't looking. I saw it."

"A grandson cannot be responsible for his grandfather's actions," Faramazov said.

"Agreed, but Maxos took my friend there. He obviously wasn't ashamed of his grandfather and the shrine. She carried out research on the general. According to surviving villagers he was responsible for the killing of hundreds of innocent men, women and children in a village that supported the Republican Government. They are buried in a mass grave in the mountains."

"If you are suggesting that I support fascism, Mr Sniper, you can get out of here!" Faramazov said.

He was seething and barely audible and Sonya was also angry with me.

"My grandfather was an officer in the Spanish civil war. He fought against the fascists. Britain, France and America stood back, but we Russians helped the Republican Government."

Faramazov stood up, walked over to his desk, opened a drawer, took out a pistol and a revolver and put them on his desk. Sonya, terrified, clutched me. Noticing her fear, he put up his hands and smiled and put the pistol back into the desk, opened the revolver barrel and showed us that it was empty. After rummaging in the drawer, he took out several medals and brought them and the revolver over to us and handed them to me.

"That's the revolver that my grandfather used in the Spanish Civil war. I'm named after him. See this medal awarded to Yevgeny Krakanovitch. That was for bravery in action during the civil war. This other medal was awarded posthumously to my grandmother after he was killed in the Battle of Stalingrad."

"I'm s---sorry I d---didn't wish to offend you..." I said. "I wasn't suggesting that you were a fascist, I--- I was just curious why you were involved with one."

"Mr Sniper, let me tell you something. My grandfather was a real sniper. Not someone with just a name," he said, making me wince. "He was a brilliant shot who picked off Nazi officers in Stalingrad. They captured, stripped and tortured him and dumped his body on the ice and snow. He lay in the street so that his comrades could see what happened to captured snipers. His comrades couldn't get to him as they would have been shot. Over a long agonising day and night, he eventually died from wounds and exposure and his body remained there for days."

Sonya glanced at me and shook her head at my lack of tact.

"My grandfather's wife and daughter- my mother- were left in poverty. They almost starved to death during that terrible winter when he and other courageous soldiers forced Hitler's troops to retreat."

Faramazov began raising his voice, his emotions now overtaking him.

"My mother came from a wonderful cultured family, but she had to do things that she would not normally have done. She married my father, a criminal who died in jail. I'm making no excuses for his or my past as a KGB and FSB officer, but I swear on my mother's grave that I will make amends. The Faramazov Foundation is already a major charity and my wife Anya is supervising it."

I glanced at the recorder and the red recording light was on. Faramazov had not noticed. What a story for Sonya!

"You didn't know that Maxos was a member of a neo

Nazi Spanish party?" I repeated in amazement.

"No! Maxos met my wife and I in Spain. We were retracing the steps of my grandfather, when he advised officers of the Republican Army. We were in Madrid and Maxos came up to me in a bar. He never let on that his grandfather was a Major General in Franco's army. Please join us for dinner tonight. Ask my wife, she'll tell you what happened."

"You talked about the Spanish civil war? Didn't you suspect Maxos?"

"When Anya, my wife, told him that she was researching the Russian involvement in the civil war, he told us what he knew about the history. We thought that it was a neutral, objective account. He never disclosed which side his family supported and that his grandfather was a general."

"He obviously knew who you were."

"In retrospect, I believe he did. But at the time it appeared to be coincidence, a chance meeting. After we had a few drinks, he told me that he had commissioned a top Russian geologist to examine diamond prospects in the Canary Islands; that she was confident there was a promising deposit. When he told me that it was Marcia Vaskilov, a geologist with a good reputation, I knew that the exploration had potential. I then decided to invest."

"When was that?" Sonya asked.

"Soon after Oleg Melnikov died, I knew that they didn't want me to be a shareholder of Dobrenska. Before being thrown out, I decided to walk and sold my shares. The deal was done in secret. This is the first time it has been disclosed, Sonya. When you get back to Russia, confront Bigganoff. You can also contact the Ministry of Natural Resources and ask them to comment. Whether they do or don't, it is the truth. I don't have proof that Bigganoff instigated the murder of Melnikov. But I will give you a source in the army, who will confirm that he made an arrangement with a senior officer. That officer ordered the attack on the miners. The claim that I was implicated was a lie."

Faramazov excused himself suddenly, rushed out of the room and went into the ensuite bathroom. Sonya, amazed at the revelation switched off the recorder and we sat there in silence absorbing what he said. We heard him cough again, spit out the phlegm and flush the toilet.

"Do you believe him Sonya?" I asked.

"You never know with these Russian political factions, but yes I believe that he's sincere."

"I also think he's telling the truth."

I turned around and noticed that there were several large paintings stacked against one of the bookcases."

I nudged Sonya: "Do you think he's just bought those or he's selling them?"

Before she could reply, Faramazov returned: "It's getting late. Come let's go down to the garden and have dinner."

* * *

It was late summer evening and we sat with Faramazov, Anya and their children Tanya and Misha, around a large oak table in the garden. It was a simple family meal with traditional Russian borscht as a starter and roast chicken and vegetables, the main course. But for the butler and house-keeper, the cooks and maids and bottle of 1990 Chateau de Rothschild, it could have been a family meal anywhere.

Anya, lovely in a sleeveless, printed dress, was a charming hostess and the children were boisterous and friendly.

"Do you miss Russia?" I asked.

Anya replied with a tired smile, making me feel silly for a question she must have heard umpteen times: "I love England, especially the rain."

"I'm told that you are an historian and also an authority on art, especially Russian Revolutionary art?" Sonya said, looking for an angle about the Faramazov's art collection.

"I was offered a post as lecturer in Russian history at University College London, but had to turn it down," Anya said. "We have a London townhouse in Eaton Square, but Tanya and Misha go to school near here and I want to be there for them."

"What's your view about the art market? Is it a bubble, like diamonds and precious metals?" I asked, using Sonya's technique to draw out information.

"Money is easy and interest rates are low, so prices of real estate, stocks, gold, platinum, silver, diamonds and art have risen," Faramazov said. "Are they in a bubble? It depends how you interpret a bubble, but yes prices are no longer bargains."

"You have wonderful paintings. We noticed that some were stacked up in your husband's room. Are you taking the view that this is the time to sell?"

That was tactless intrusion too far and Sonya flushed and kicked me under the table. Anya glanced at Yevgeny and I detected the signal.

She changed the subject: "I find your articles in *Novaya Gazeta* fascinating, Sonya. You are courageous to be an investigative journalist in Russia."

"Someone has to do the job."

"You must be careful ---- How many journalists have the FSB murdered?"

Bowls of fruit and ice cream arrived and the conversation reverted to small talk. As we ate and drank, I wondered whether they were really happy in their fortress. Despite all his money, Yevgeny Faramazov's health had deteriorated and Anya and her children were isolated. No doubt, they held court with their own private concerts;

frequented holiday homes and the five-star hotels of the super-rich; had a yacht moored in Monte Carlo; owned a massive art, jewellery and antique collection and lived in a home with a private lake, dry ski run and numerous servants and lackeys to serve them. And yet, something was missing. How many family and friends fawned over them to receive their largesse and favour? How many were genuine? Stanley Slimcop, my late dear friend who died soon after he had visited me in prison, had a saying: "Too little or too much money are bad things."

* * *

Later that evening, Sonya and I drove out of the fortress, noticing for the first time the family helicopter on its pad, near the house. It was twilight and it was gradually getting darker when I got lost on a country road, in the hope that we were on a short cut towards north London. There were few cars on the road, but after a while, I noticed that a Convertible Golf appeared to be tracking the same roundabout route as us.

"We're being followed, Sonya. Do you think they're Faramazov's security guards?"

"I don't know. Could be anyone," Sonya said.

"Let's test them out," I said and pushed my foot on the accelerator.

"The other car did the same and we raced along, until we reached a pub just before the open highway. There were lots of people in the garden drinking, so I decided there would be safety in numbers. We found a parking space, near the noisy throng. The car that was following us drove in and parked near us. As we rushed for the garden, the driver got out the car and came up to us. We were dumbfounded.

"Sasha why were you following us? You gave us a fright,"

Sonya said.

"I tried to reach you on your mobile, Jack, but it was switched off."

I checked it and she was right.

Sonya was now fuming.

"Why didn't you tell us that you were coming?" she asked.

"I thought you needed protection. You never know," Sasha said.

"OK, forget it. Next time flash your lights or something," I said.

"How could I? That's not a police car," Sasha said pointing at her vehicle.

"OK, what do you guys want to drink?" I said in an attempt to ease the tension.

I went inside and brought out some beers for Sonya and myself and a glass of wine for Sasha. When I came out, the two women, sitting on a bench in the corner of the garden away from the crowd, weren't speaking to each other.

"What did that the bastard Faramazov have to say for himself," Sasha said. "Sonya refuses to tell me. Obviously, he won her over."

Sonya shook her head, so I decided to say nothing.

"Let me hear what's on the recorder," Sasha said, snatching at Sonya's handbag.

Sonya pulled it back: "A journalist protects her sources. You can read the article when it is published."

"How dare you talk to me like that," Sasha said, attempting to take the handbag again.

"Stop it Sasha. She wants to write her article first."

"And what about you, Jack?"

"I respect Sonya's integrity. I was there to back her up. That's all. I would not have been there, had it not been for her."

"It was me who suggested that you accompany Sonya for her own personal safety."

"I'll tell you one thing, Sasha. I do not believe that Faramazov was responsible for the murder of your father."

Sasha went ballistic.

"Nonsense. You've fallen for his lies. He would say that wouldn't he?"

"I agree with Jack," Sonya said. "You'll read it in the *Novaya Gazeta*."

"I'll tell you something. I've heard that Faramazov is in all sorts of financial trouble," Sasha said. "He's got paintings and jewellery on the market and has been selling properties. He's over extended himself and is seriously in debt. He's using you."

"I'll check it out," Sonya said.

"There you go. A good tip for another article. The impending bankruptcy of a billionaire psychopath. Now can you tell me what happened?"

I was about to begin but Sonya glared at me and put up her hand.

"The agreement Jack, was that you would keep the interview confidential."

"Sorry Sasha, I can't tell you anything at this stage. When Sonya gives me permission, I will. An agreement is an agreement."

Sasha stood up in a rage, left her half-finished drink and began to walk off in a huff to her car.

"John Primeheart will hear about this Jack."

"Who's John Primeheart?" Sonya asked. "Does Sasha have a hold on you?"

"It's a long story. I can't talk about it. One day perhaps," I said touching her hand. "I gave you my word. I will not breach your code. Your article and information will be kept confidential."

* * *

We drove back in virtual silence, exhausted from the remarkable interview with Faramazov and the encounter
with Sasha.

"My dog needs food and a walk badly, he hasn't been
out since early this morning. Do you mind if we stop at my
apartment?" I asked, when we approached North London.

Cobber was all over me in excitement when I opened
the door of my flat. Sonya laughed and opened her arms.

The dog went to her, tail wagging and she stroked
and tickled him.

"You're pretty good with animals, Sonya," I said.

"My father is a vet and I help him in the surgery
sometimes," Sonya said. "We have a Samoyed with thick
white fur. Very much like a Husky. Cobber is a police dog.
It's to do with Sasha Jack, isn't it? Can I trust you?"

"You can Sonya. I swear you can. Faramazov's story is
dynamite. I think you might have to postpone your flight
to Moscow. It's too dangerous. Stay in London. I've got a
spare bedroom where you can work. Cobber will protect
you. Someone may try and get hold of your laptop and
recorder after the story breaks. I'll find a good hiding place."

"Thanks Jack, maybe that's a good idea."

I moved the sofa, unscrewed two floor boards and
placed the recorder and Sonya's laptop in the hiding place.
After I pushed the sofa back to its original place, we fed the
dog. It was a clear night and we took Cobber for a walk to
Muswell Hill, which was about half a mile away. Later, we
had a meal in Toffs, a fish restaurant. When we returned,
I made up her bed. Sonya then unpacked her things, had
a shower and went to bed.

Much later, when I was asleep in my bedroom, I half
dreamt that someone was creeping into my bed. A warm,
soft body was next to me.

18

CANARY MINES

Sonya's interview with Faramazov and the further allegations of Russian corruption made the front page of the *Novaya Gazeta*. Such was the interest, that excerpts of her article were carried on the international wires and Net. Faramazov's off the record comments about Bigganoff's role in alleged Russian secret service corruption, were not published. The newspaper feared libel and it was too dangerous for Sonya. The recorder, which included Faramazov's fascinating interview, was deposited in my safe custody box at the bank and I bought Sonya a new one. Her editor decided that it was safer for her to remain in London that summer. We went on many walks with the dog and spent a lot of time in Alexandra Palace and other outdoor cafes and restaurants in Hampstead Heath, Regents Park and Primrose Hill.

Sonya and I had become close. About a week after she had decided to stay at my apartment, we became lovers. Instead of being wildly passionate, sex was gently relaxing and soothing. The nicest thing about Sonya was that she let me be. Unlike Meredith, she neither nagged me, nor raised her voice. It was peaceful with her. When we were reading, or when I was watching sport on TV, it seemed as if she wasn't there. Sonya was that quiet. Cobber also became attached to her and I was glad, as I knew that the dog would guard her when I was away. She now had to be very careful.

Sonya followed up Sasha's tip off and found that Faramazov had been carried away by the international property boom. He was now over exposed in a weakening market. Several of his paintings were soon to be auctioned. Sonya contacted some estate agents in Hertfordshire and they told her that they had a well secured country mansion on their books. They didn't disclose the identity of the owner, but the property had sophisticated security, a gatehouse for servants, a swimming pool, tennis courts, a lake, ski run and helicopter pad. Yes, Faramazov was indeed in financial difficulties. Sonya wrote a draft of the article, but needed a comment from Faramazov to confirm whether he had lost some or all of his fortune. He was unavailable for comment, of course.

It was now early autumn and Sonya and I had dinner with Sasha. To placate Sasha and maintain their long friendship, Sonya gave the detective more details about the interview. Sasha was satisfied, although she disagreed with our view that Faramazov was not behind the murder of her father. Sonya and I decided that Sasha was fixated with Faramazov and was determined to get him prosecuted for past crimes.

* * *

In the meantime, exceedingly interesting developments took place in the diamond and stock markets. De Beers and Alrosa raised rough gem prices. Share prices of Bristol GemDiam, MSP España and other diamond companies soared to new heights. Remarkably Bristol, which had 120 million shares, after the rights issue, touched a peak of £22 compared with its listing price of £1, some 12 months previously. It was now valued in the market at almost £2.7 billion! Trading volume in diamond producer and exploration shares was massive. Prices sank from their heady heights, rose to their peaks and then dipped again. The bulk of trade occurred in Bristol and España shares, which had also surged to more than twenty times their original listing price. The founding directors and original investors who had held on to their shares from the time the companies were listed, had made fortunes. Since I was prejudiced against Maxos, I had not bought a single share in the two companies. I had purchased other diamond stocks and companies that had interests in the gems business, but I had sold them all, when I had left Jamey Jackenhead's firm.

It was frustrating to be out of the market as I could have made a lot more money, but when I told Sonya, she said that greed and hubris were invariably followed by nemesis. I should be thankful that I had almost paid off my mortgage and had more than sufficient money to spare. Despite Sonya's words of wisdom, I couldn't help myself when I saw the latest prices in the newspaper. I would crunch up the paper and throw it in the bin, cursing myself for my stupidity. Envious of the traders and investors who were becoming richer, I looked for holes in their bullish arguments. As an outsider, who was not caught up in the crowd's euphoria, I could at least be cool and objective. I decided that they were trading on the "greater fool theory". Shares were being bought and sold to other "fools" at higher and higher prices. More money could eventually be made from selling short excessively overvalued stocks. That would be done via futures and options on derivative exchanges. Alternatively, the shares could be borrowed from banks and sold in the hope that they could be purchased profitably at a lower price. Big relief! Had I done that a few weeks before, I would have been blown out of the market with big losses, as the shares kept going up!

The market had become increasingly volatile and had spread to precious metals shares which had also soared in the wake of surging gold, silver and platinum prices. To me, the wide price gyrations indicated that knowledge-able players were selling their shares to unsophisticated newcomers. Bristol GemDiam Mining and MSP España Mining promised rich gem reserves that were still to be mined. But their share prices were at such heights, that they were reflecting potential profits in the far distant future.

Individuals, day traders and rank amateurs, who had just discovered the diamond and stock market, joined ebullient pension, mutual and hedge fund managers who were riding the upward wave. On a trip to Hatton Garden to buy a birthday gift for Sonya, the taxi driver chatted enthusiastically about his diamond, gold and platinum shares.

When I arrived at Hatton Garden, there were queues of people outside the shops. Initially I thought that they were buying diamond and gold jewellery, but I soon found out that they were selling. The general public, not involved in the stock market asylum, were sensibly taking advantage of high prices. Diamond engagement rings and other jewellery had become so exorbitant that people were trading in heirlooms and other pieces, for cash. A jeweller told me that D-Flawless one carat diamonds had burst through their previous record of $64,000 a carat. Experts in the trade were forecasting on business TV channels that they would reach $100,000. "Prince Regent", aka Manfred Fokes-Mailsford, was the new diamond guru. Now a partner of Fazeldoff, Trogan & Fokes, Manfred pontificated on CNBC and Bloomberg that $100,000 would eventually become the base price for the D-Flawless. There would be a "brief correction in the diamond market" because of "a sizeable increase in supplies from the Canary Islands". But afterwards, D-Flawless gem prices would soar to $150,000 a carat. Other diamonds would climb in tandem.

"If share prices dipped during the 'correction', it would be an exceptional buying opportunity," Manfred said.

As soon as the City's "dial a quote gem sage" mouthed his predictions, Bristol GemDiam's shares surged to £24 and for a few seconds hit £25 before heavy selling drove it back to its earlier peak of £22. That to me was a further sign that some big holders were taking profits.

I was in an electronics shop when I saw the interview of Manfred on TV. Next to the shop was a jeweller who had some lovely silver and emerald earrings at reasonable prices. They were an ideal present for Sonya.

It was around noon and I phoned Isobel Steeplefoot on her mobile to hear about the latest gossip in the City. She was happy to hear from me and I met her nearby Hatton Garden at the Bleeding Heart Tavern, which Charles Dickens had frequented.

Isobel greeted me with a smile and surprise.

"This lunch is on me. I've just resigned from JJ Emerging. What's it like to be in the ranks of the unemployed?"

"Not bad, not bad at all. Let me show you something."

I put a small box on the table and opened it.

"Jack it's beautiful. Is it a good luck gift for me?" Isobel said with a wink.

"It's for Sonya Moldavia, a Russian journalist."

"A new girlfriend? The very one who's written some interesting stories? That's great news Jack, I'm going to commission you to find a Russian for me!"

"My rates have gone up. They're now 10 percent."

"In diamonds or gold? Better cash them in, before

prices fall!"

It was good to see Isobel. She had a great sense of humour.

"So why are you leaving Jackenhead?" I asked.

"After you went, I became worried about Jamey. He began to sail close to the wind. He's promoting highly speculative new issues."

"Diamond stocks?"

"Yep."

"I thought that you fancied him."

"We went out a few times, Jack, but I don't like guys trying it on, before I get to know them. I want relationships to develop. In any event, wherever we went, he was looking at other women."

"Seems he's desperate."

"He's a loser as far as women are concerned."

"But not in his business. He gave me opportunities to invest in several new listings. I should have bought," I said.

"Their shares have gone crazy."

"Yep, plenty rumours of new diamond finds."

"Their shares have been shooting up and then falling back again," Isobel said and glanced at other tables to see if anyone was listening.

"I noticed that as well. Happened today. Bristol jumped to £25, for a few minutes, but quickly fell back again. Trading volumes were massive, according to Bloomberg."

"Some Swiss banks are very active," Isobel said. "From what I heard, two banks are sellers and another two are buyers. When the price jumps the sellers come in and when it dips, the others are buying."

"Sounds quite an operation. I'll tell you what I think is happening," I said recalling my experience as a trader, before I went to prison. "There are big sellers out there. They're using several banks to distribute their shares. They're selling through two banks and buying through the others to confuse the market. The aim is to stop prices from collapsing."

"Are you saying that the banks that are selling, are offloading more shares than the other two are buying?"

"Precisely. The net effect is that a large investor or investors have decided to sell Bristol and MSP España for some reason. Are the rumours emanating from Switzerland?"

"I don't think so. The rumours come from Madrid. Spanish and French banks seem to be buying the shares from Swiss banks."

"Do you know who the seller is?" I asked.

"Brokers don't know. They're mystified."

* * *

Sonya loved the earrings and we celebrated her birthday with a romantic dinner and a show. Isobel had hinted that I was fickle, as only a few months before I was in love with Amity and had proposed to her. She thought that Sonya had caught me on the rebound and chided me, saying that I had better not hurt her. Isobel was wrong. Amity had rejected and hurt me. Sonya had grown on me. My love was now deep.

Meanwhile I agreed to go to Lanzarote to help Fred Carrender complete a prospecting job for Alexei Ignatyevna of Vogdana Diamond Mine. He needed a young assistant to help and bring him luck. It was October and Sonya and Isobel joined me on the trip to have a break and enjoy an autumn holiday. Isobel would be useful as she was fluent in Spanish and could act as an interpreter. I also informed Sasha Melnikov that I was going to the Canary Islands to try and find out whether Faramazov had been selling his investments there. Cobber, my police dog could be useful for my security, so I obtained a passport for him.

Sonya and I booked rooms at the Timanfaya Palace, where Fred and Alexei were staying and fortunately the dog was allowed to stay in our room. Soon after we arrived we had a swim with Cobber in Playa Blanca, near the hotel. Later we took the dog for a walk on the promenade overlooking the sea and then had a drink with Fred and Alexei next to the pool. It brought back memories. It was almost two years since Gerald Gleep of Bristol GemDiam, had hosted a welcome party for analysts, fund managers and the press, at the very same hotel.

Fred, normally jovial, was down hearted: "We've been here almost six weeks and have found zilch except these."

He took out some stones from his pocket. They were olive green peridots. The girls liked them, but we knew that they were worth less than 10 euros in the tourist market.

"How have other prospectors done?"

"There are lots of claims in Lanzarote, Fuerteventura, Gomera, Tenerife and even Gran Canaria," Fred said. "From what we have heard, they've had no luck."

"Where have you and Alexei been looking Fred?"

"On the beach and within 150 metres offshore."

"Do you want me to have a go? I'm a good swimmer and can dive for you. By the way where can I meet some prospectors?"

There's a bar in the village. The guys have been getting drunk because of their frustration, but maybe they have some ideas."

"I can't keep throwing money at this," Alexei said. "If Jack can't find anything, I'm selling my claim."

"Why don't you come out with us tonight?" Sonya said. She had noticed that Isobel seemed to like Alexei.

"Why not? What about you Fred?"

"No thanks. I'm feeling tired. I'll have an early night."

Fred didn't seem his normal energetic self that day, but it didn't faze me as he wasn't a young man any more. He never disclosed his age but I knew that he was either in his late sixties or about seventy.

* * *

Later that evening Isobel, Sonya, Alexei and I had dinner with Basil Bleedon who arrived at the restaurant in a convertible Peugeot Cabriolet. It was a vast improvement on the battered Ford that he used to drive.

"Some car Basil," I said admiring the sleek design and observing his designer sun glasses, cream chinos and white linen shirt. "Seen lots of your stories in UK papers."

"I've had some good scoops," Basil said, his smugness, insufferable.

"I thought that you were looking for a job on Fleet Street?"

"Not anymore. I'm freelancing for most of them from here. I've got good contacts; the weather is great and I'm doing OK."

"One thing that puzzles us is that Canary Diamond Mines is the only company that seems to have discovered gems around here."

"The others need to be patient," Basil said. "My sources at Canary Diamonds say that potential resources are massive."

"Really?"

"Of course. As you know Bristol bought a $30 million dredging boat to find diamonds further out to sea. They told me that it's an 'integrated seabed crawler' with cutting edge technology in offshore diamond mining. I explained that in my story the other day," Basil said.

"Other mining companies have come up with volcanic

ash, peridots and other worthless precious metals stones," Alexei said. "Their findings do not remotely meet the optimistic reports that you've been writing."

"Bristol and España shares have been amazing performers," Isobel said, as we closely observed Basil's reaction, now that he had a few drinks.

The reply explained all.

"Absolutely brilliant. Bought me an apartment and the car."

"Not terribly objective, is he?" Isobel said, after we left him and walked over to the pub that Fred had recommended. "Do you think he's on their payroll?"

"Doesn't need to be. They probably allotted him shares when they were listed and he's made a fortune. How much would you wager that he's up to his neck in Bristol and MSP paper?"

Sonya who had listened quietly, had a shrewd suggestion when we entered the pub.

"Isobel, why don't we go to the bar and let guys come up to us? Jack and Alexei can wait for us in the corner."

The ploy worked and soon they were surrounded by locals. Eventually Isobel brought back one to the table and spoke to him in Spanish. Sonya broke away from the other men and followed her.

"All the guys I spoke to confirmed what Fred and Alexei told us. Only Canary Diamond Mines has found anything worthwhile," Isobel said. "Their efforts have been a waste of time."

A short stocky guy, with closely cropped black hair, joined us and Isobel passed him a beer.

"This is Juan. He's a diver who did some work for the Canary operation and has something interesting to tell us," Isobel said.

Juan could hardly speak English but this was the gist of

Isobel's translation. He dived for diamonds during the day and found a few lovely gems between the rocks. He passed them over to the mine's foreman who was happy with his results. One week he was less successful and fell out with the foreman. He was sacked, but found work elsewhere and dived for diamonds for other prospectors. Following the exact methods of Canary Diamond Mines, he searched for gems between and under rocks and used suction pipes to pump out gravel. Results were zero, although there were some lovely, but worthless volcanic stones.

Juan was mystified, but one day he met a fisherman who had been trawling the waters near the Canary diamond development around 4 a.m. There was a lot of activity there. The fisherman went closer and noticed that there was a boat, not far off shore. It was a half moon and what they were doing at that ridiculously early hour, did not make sense. He could see a diver jump off the boat into the water, stay down for a while, climb on to the boat and dive again. People in the boat noticed the fisherman, sailed closer and warned him not to return. The threat scared him.

Later as we walked home, Sonya nudged me. Isobel and Alexei were lagging behind, laughing and enjoying each other's company. We sat on a bench overlooking the sea and the light of the full moon was on the rippling sea. Nearby Isobel and Alexei were getting close.

"You see Jack, I have another talent," Sonya said.

* * *

The next day Sonya and I jogged on the promenade with Cobber. We raced onto the beach and into the water, the dog running ahead and then swimming alongside us. When I put my arms around Sonya and kissed her, the jealous dog came alongside us, seeking attention. Afterwards we played hide and seek with Cobber. Sonya sneaked off and hid behind some boulders and I commanded Cobber to "fetch Sonya". No matter how difficult the hiding places, the dog found her and wagged his tail happily.

Later we joined Fred for breakfast, but Alexei and Isobel weren't there. They arrived together when the waiters were clearing the food away. Sonya, triumphant, winked at me.

"I've been thinking what Juan told us about the fisherman," Alexei said. "Why don't we go and take a look for ourselves."

"When?" Fred asked.

"Tonight. The moon is full, do you want to come with me, Jack?"

It was evening and in the twilight, Alexei, Cobber and I went to his mine claim. It was on a beach about half a mile from the Canary Diamond Mines' site. We waited there for several hours while I adjusted my camera. Around 2 a.m. we slowly made our way towards a cliff about two hundred yards away from the mine's operations. There were no guards there because the cliff acted as a natural barrier for the mine. Alexei had a sophisticated video camera with night vision. He peered into the camera as we looked down towards the beach and a boat offshore.

"It is difficult to see what they are doing," Alexei said. "Wish we had Fred here."

We walked back to Alexei's claim and he took the film out of the video camera.

"I think we should try and get a bit closer," I said, noticing a rubber dinghy nearby. "Let's get in and paddle there."

"There's only room for one," Alexei said, as we loosened the dinghy rope from a pole on the beach. "I'm not a very good swimmer."

"OK I'll go. Come on Cobber, you can squeeze in. Wait for me here, Alexei. If you hear someone coming, get in the car and go back to the hotel. We don't want anyone to take the camera and film."

"What about you?"

"Don't worry about me. Cobber and I can take care of ourselves."

"Be careful, OK! Don't get too close."

Lanzarote is usually a windy island, but that night the wind had died down. I pushed the dinghy into relatively becalmed waters and paddled under the moonlight about 250 metres out to sea and then about 300 metres across the bay towards the Canary Diamond Mines beach. We were soon fairly close to the offshore dredging boat; about 100 metres away, at the most. A diver was jumping off the boat, disappearing under water for a time and then returning. The diver took off his oxygen mask. Despite the dim moonlight, I could make out that it was Philippe Santos.

I was so intent on observing what was going on that I didn't notice that I had been spotted. I heard a motor and noticed that a motorised rubber dingy was being launched from the mine's beach. I picked up the paddle and rowed furiously towards another beach. The dinghy was getting nearer, but fortunately by now, we were in rocky shallow waters, so it was difficult for the guy in the dinghy to catch up to us. His engine propellers would get damaged in the rocks and he would have to row. Luckily, I had my trainers on. We jumped out and ran towards the cliffs, the man close behind us. I needed help fast, so I commanded Cobber to "Fetch Sonya". The dog looked at me quizzically but I panted out another command: "Cobber fetch Sonya now!"

The dog was off, racing in the direction of the hotel. We had been running for about twenty minutes and by this time had reached the top of a path that ended at *Los Hervideros*, a popular tourist spot. During the day, the cliffs and the frothing sea far below are magnificent, but in the inadequate moonlight, it was a nightmare. The only thing in my favour was that my pursuer found it difficult to see me and was also struggling on the sharp volcanic rocks.

I managed to follow a narrow path through a maze of rocks alongside holes, which I recalled had nothing but the sea below. It was a battle not to fall down the fairly large holes and my only hope was that my opponent would trip and tumble. I kept on stumbling, sometimes scratching my thighs and calves against the rocks. The moon came out of the clouds giving me some visibility, but the downside was that my pursuer could see me. I heard the faint sound of "ping" nearby. I turned around briefly and saw that the man had a gun, which evidently had a silencer. He shouted out something in Spanish, but I was already at the edge of a cliff that jutted over the dark water below. I remembered that there appeared to be no rocks directly below that point and thanked my lucky stars that I had been on a tour of *Los Hervideros* a few days before.

It was Hobson's choice. No way was I going to take a chance and give myself up. After backtracking a few yards to give myself momentum, I raced towards the edge and jumped. It seemed forever as I fell down, down, down, into the icy water below. Thankfully there were no rocks directly below as I sank. I recalled from the tour that there was a grotto to the right of me. I turned in that direction and swam underwater for as long as my breath would hold. Eventually I surfaced under the roof of the grotto. Hopefully I was out of sight.

Wet and freezing, I covered myself with some partially dry seaweed, in a futile effort to warm up. I tried my mobile, but it wasn't water proof and didn't work. Exhausted, I tried to sleep, but it was so cold that I kept waking up. My arm and legs were sore, so I washed the scratches on my legs with salt water and grimaced with pain. The hours ticked by and I was getting hungry by the time dawn broke. It was very tense as I feared that the tide would come in and huge waves would crash into the cave and drown me. As pre-dawn light entered the cove, I noticed that I was close to nests of seagulls or other birds. Relief. Their nests indicated that the level where I was standing, was too high for the waves, even at high tide. I was so hungry that I broke a gull egg and sucked the gooey, foul tasting liquid.

No way could I shout for help, otherwise the Canary Diamond Mine people could find me.

At last I heard a dog barking and Alexei and Sonya, calling from above. Cobber had found me because of his extra sensory powers and brilliant police training. My friends were accompanied by the Canary Island police. They called firemen, who lowered a rope with a seat and hoisted me up.

Cobber ran up to me wagging his tail and licked my face. Sonya hugged me.

Alexei shook my hand warmly, gave me a bear hug and kissed me on both my cheeks.

"I feel terrible, Jack. I left you in the lurch."

"Don't worry Alexei. There was no way you could tell what would happen."

"I waited for about an hour and then heard a car, so I followed your instructions and drove to the hotel."

"That was the right thing to do, Alexei."

"I waited in the bar next to the lobby, but you didn't arrive. About an hour later, I called the police and Sonya and about 4 a.m. we drove towards the beach," Alexei said. "The police followed us and on the way, I saw a dog running towards the headlights of our car. Sonya called and the dog stopped and ran towards us. He was exhausted. I expected you to follow, but you weren't there. The dog was barking like crazy at Sonya who was trying to pull him into the car.

"Eventually, I let him go and shouted ' fetch Jack',"

Sonya said, patting Cobber. He turned around and started running towards the beach, even though we were still about four or five miles away."

"When we got close to the tourist spot, the dog stopped and began to sniff. He then took off, ran around the rocks, picked up your scent and rushed towards the edge of the cliff," Alexei continued.

"You're a wonderful dog," Sonya said, as we both hugged Cobber, who was licking my wounds.

They thought of taking me to hospital for treatment, but instead a doctor tended to my wounds at the hotel. It was far too dangerous. We had to leave Lanzarote as soon as possible.

* * *

Fred took us to a table well away from other passengers, when we were waiting in the airport departure lounge,

"I've been thinking about what happened," he said "I've decided to change my flight to Tel Aviv."

"Why the change of plan?" Alexei asked.

"Josh Zunrel is examining gems at the Israel Diamond Exchange and I need to consult with him."

"Is Canary selling diamonds in Israel?" asked Alexei, touching Isobel's hand absently.

She responded, showing that there was chemistry there.

"Can't talk now," Fred said and he rushed to his flight.

19

BRUNEL'S BRIDGE

Back at home, Sonya and I spent the next couple of days walking in Highgate Woods, Alexandra Park and Hampstead Heath. My pistol rested in my pocket and Cobber was always with us. It was time for a meeting with Sasha and Primeheart.

"Prison is better than being a target," I said, when I was sitting in front of Primeheart in his stark Scotland Yard office. "I could have been killed in Lanzarote. And for what? You can put someone else on the case."

"Do you want to quit and sit in a cell again?" Primeheart said. "You're like the English football team. They make it to the quarter and semi-finals and blow penalty shoot outs. No guts, no staying power."

"Typical. General behind the firing line," I said, being cheeky with him for the first time. "How the hell can you compare football to this?"

"You don't know what I've done in my career," Primeheart said.

Completely out of character, he loosened his tie and undid the buttons of his shirt. There were deep scars under his Adam's Apple and on his chest. He then closed the buttons and stared at me with disdain, as I tried to hide my embarrassment.

"Well, what's your next step?" Primeheart asked.

"Sonya's working on another Faramazov story," I said. "But she won't tell me what it's about. She thinks I'll tell you."

Sasha clasped her hands tightly.

"That doesn't stop you from seeing what she's got in her laptop."

"I don't read Russian and I wouldn't do that anyway."

"Can you believe it? He's fallen in love with her," Sasha said. "He'll probably marry a journalist who's in the pocket of an arch criminal."

"She's not influencing you, is she?" Primeheart said. "Does she know about your background?"

"Sonya hasn't influenced me and she thinks I'm a South African," I said. "One day I'll tell her, but not before it's safe for both of us."

"Oh no you won't!" Primeheart said. "You're Jack Sniper now. Jack Miner is history. Don't you forget it."

"No time for emotional attachments," Sasha said. "You still have a job to do. Find out more about Faramazov's involvement with Bristol GemDiam."

"I met their financial director at a conference," I said.

"That's a good start. Say that you're an institutional investment consultant and arrange a meeting."

On the way back from Scotland Yard, I picked up an Evening Standard. The business pages had a page feature on Bristol GemDiam, its new development in Fuerteventura and pictures of diamonds that it had mined in Lanzarote. A chart of the share price showed that Bristol was by far, the best performer on the London market. After swinging in a trading range for a few weeks, the shares had once again broken through to record heights. The market capitalisation of the small mining company exceeded £3 billion. According to the article, several large mining predators were circling the company, but none confirmed the takeover rumours. Trading volumes were huge and Bristol's price was now so high that the shares would probably be split into smaller units, the article said. Instead of buying at £27 share, the public could buy ten for £2.70 each.

The Evening Standard reporter also wrote that several hedge funds and other bears had previously sold the shares short. They had hoped to repurchase the shares at a profit, if and when prices fell. Their timing was badly wrong, as the stock price had risen further. The bears had been squeezed and had lost fortunes as they had been forced to cover their short sales by buying the shares at much higher prices. Indeed, the bear squeeze played no small part in causing Bristol's stock to race to an all-time peak. That mind-boggling quote was 27 times the company's original listing price of £1. A £10,000 investment in the shares when Bristol was first floated on the stock exchange, was now worth £270,000!

I wondered who the bears were and called Isobel.

"Hi Isobel, what's going on with Bristol?"

"Hell, Jack, a few weeks ago, I was thinking of shorting the stock. Luckily Alexei advised me against it. Can you imagine how much I would have lost?"

"Do you know any of the bears?"

"No. But some Swiss hedge funds have been active."

"What about the buyers? The Evening Standard mentions takeover rumours. Which company would be stupid enough to bid for Bristol at these prices?"

"No-one, Jack. It's just a rumour."

"Have you spoken to Jackenhead?"

"Yeah, he called me. Wants me back. Offered me a stupendous salary and bonus."

"Obviously making a packet. Are you going to accept his offer?"

"No way, Jack. He's got serious diamond fever."

* * *

The next day, I left Sonya to work on her latest article and drove to Bristol on the south west coast. Cobber was on the back seat, head out of the window, enjoying the breeze. The journey from north London should have taken about three hours on the M4 motorway. Instead there were road works and stifling traffic jams, so we arrived late in the day.

I checked into Bristol's Avon Gorge Hotel that overlooked the Clifton Suspension Bridge. Percival Meltin, Bristol GemDiam's financial director, would be joining me for dinner. He had sounded wary on the phone, but he fell for my story that I was representing potential investors. Meltin was to come to the hotel and have a drink on the terrace. Afterwards we would go to a restaurant in Clifton, the upmarket Bristol area where his company was situated.

When I phoned Bristol GemDiam's office around 4.30 p.m. to confirm the meeting, the receptionist said that Meltin had left for the day. She promised me that she would tell him that I had called. By 5.30 p.m. there was no response from her, so I phoned the office again. The receptionist insisted that she had called Meltin's mobile several times, but could not connect. She refused to give me his number and also informed me that Gerald Gleep, was unavailable as he was in Tel Aviv. The company was about to announce production results and display some of its latest gem finds at the Israel Diamond Exchange.

There was nothing else to do but to wait for Meltin to come to the hotel. I regretted that I had not given him my mobile number, but after my recent experience in Lanzarote, had become cautious. Cobber needed a walk, so we went out for a short while and then waited on the hotel terrace. By 9 p.m. it was evident that Meltin had stood me up. There was only one thing to do. Go to Bristol GemDiam's office the next day and wait for him there.

Early the next morning, I went for a jog with the dog. It was misty and we ran along a pathway up an incline towards a hill that overlooked the bridge which crossed the deep Avon Gorge. We ran downhill and began to cross the bridge. Cobber suddenly stopped alongside a moveable maintenance platform that was on pulleys, on the outer rim of the bridge's railings. Irritated I pulled the dog's lead and he reluctantly followed. We continued to run across the 200-metre-long bridge towards Ashton Court, a large estate, about a kilometre away. There were lots of hills and woods there, so I took off Cobber's lead to allow him to run free. By the time we were finished, both of us were exhausted. We walked back to the bridge, which is suspended from wrought iron chains that are linked to wide brick and stone towers on each side of the gorge's cliffs. By now it was 8.30 a.m. and the mist had cleared. I tied Cobber to a post and went into the tiny museum on the side of the tower to find out about Isambard Kingdom Brunel who designed the bridge and had died before it was completed in 1864.

While I was in the museum, Cobber, unusually restless and difficult, was annoying early morning joggers with persistent barking. I rushed out, stroked his bristling neck to quieten him and we slowly continued our walk on the bridge's pedestrian pathway. While I was admiring the view of the river some 70 metres below, Cobber yanked the lead. Once again, he stopped alongside the maintenance platform, refusing to budge and sniffing at the high railings. Close to him was a button on the ground. The high horizontal thin wire barriers on the sides of the bridge had gaps of about half a foot between them. They weren't taut, so I managed to widen the gap and look down below.

A partly submerged body appeared to be in the river which was flowing in a trickle because of the low tide. It was difficult to climb over the railings on to the moveable platform and get a better view, so we back tracked to the Ashton Park bridge entrance next to the museum. The view was better from there. Far below on the other side of the river, the upper half of a body was on the muddy bank and the legs were in the water. From that distance, it was difficult to make out whether the person was male or female, but it appeared that he or she had fallen from the platform. It was still early in the morning and it seemed that I was the first to have spotted the accident. Before sounding the alarm, I took Cobber back on to the bridge to have another sniff around the platform. He went to work and stood on his hind legs. There was an ever so tiny spec of blood on one of the horizontal wires next to the platform. Rushing back to the museum to alert the bridge officials, I noticed a sign on the side of the Tower: *Samaritans Care- Talk to us anytime Night or Day on….*

"They don't call this suicide bridge for nothing!" the museum curator said. "The barriers are supposed to stop them, but somehow they manage to get through and jump."

She called the police, but I didn't wait for them. The river bank where the body was lying was near an underpass of a busy road near the bottom of the Gorge. We crossed the bridge towards the Avon Gorge Hotel, ran along a path near the edge of the cliff and found a route that lead to the river below. Cobber raced ahead and I stumbled down the narrow, steep path until we reached a busy road. Luckily a car didn't hit Cobber as he rushed across the road to the river bank. He ran down the embankment towards the body and waited for me. By the time I had reached him, the police had arrived and told me to stand clear.

The still body was flat on its back and remarkably the face was undamaged. It was Percival Meltin and the obvious question was whether he had committed suicide or had been murdered. The body was skinny, so he probably would have been too weak to lift himself to the top of the bridge's barrier and jump. More likely the murderers would have acted as workmen who were repairing the bridge. They had probably lifted him on to the platform and had pushed him.

"I was supposed to meet him last night and he didn't turn up," I said. "He's Percival Meltin and he's chief financial officer of Bristol GemDiam."

"How did you know he was down here?" the burly officer asked in a West country drawl.

"I reported the suicide. My dog alerted me when we crossed near the maintenance platform."

"Your Alsatian?"

"He's a police dog. He smelt blood."

"Ha! Another amateur detective. Lots of them around here. Four suicides a year and you think it's murder?"

"I didn't say it was murder, you did," I said, passing him my mobile. "I suggest that you phone this number."

"What number?"

"Scotland Yard. Ask for Detective Sergeant Sasha Melnikov. She will inform you who I am. I will tell you what I know, but I can't be delayed for long."

It was early afternoon when the police left me at the hotel, shaken by the untimely demise of Meltin. On the terrace two pints of lager were swiftly downed while I stroked Cobber and absently fingered the pistol in my side pocket.

My mobile rang. It was Isobel.

"Hey Jack, have you heard the news?"

"Percival Meltin. Is it already on the wires?"

Isobel sounded puzzled.

"What happened to him?"

"He's dead. Jumped, or more likely, was pushed off Brunel's Bridge. I'm here and I've just seen the body."

"What the! It must be connected."

"Connected to what?"

"Seven guys have been arrested for insider trading. According to Reuters they raided their homes in the early hours of the morning. The case revolves around Bristol GemDiam deals and false takeover rumours."

"Surprise, surprise. Bristol must be the market ramp of the century," I said, thinking of poor Meltin's body, which the forensics were now examining.

"Guess who's been arrested?"

"It's obviously not Meltin," I said, feeling a little ashamed of my gallows humour.

"Jamey Jackenhead!"

"Surely not? He may be greedy, but a criminal?"

"I don't know. It normally takes months before the Serious Fraud Office decides to prosecute."

"Who else?"

"Two Fazeldoff, Trogan & Fokes traders."

"What about Manfred Fokes-Mailsford?"

"Not him. They probably think he's too thick."

"Anyone else?"

"The usual suspects; spiv brokers and a hedge fund manager."

"Bristol's stock must have tanked."

"It's suspended, but other diamond stocks are well down."

"What about MSP España?"

"No news, so far."

On the way back in London, there were several radio

reports about Bristol GemDiam and the death of Meltin. Jackenhead and others were released without charge, all proclaiming their innocence. SFO officials said that they were collating evidence but that it would take time before alleged miscreants could be charged.

The air was escaping from the Bristol GemDiam balloon. After the Stock Exchange suspension was lifted, Bristol's shares opened at £21, more than a fifth down from their record peak of £27. Within minutes they sank to £18 and then £16. MSP España also slumped. Other diamond stocks recovered slightly, but remained well below their peaks.

Feeling sorry for Jamey, I phoned him.

"I should have listened to you, Jack. I'm in one hell of a mess. I hope that you don't think I'm an insider trader," he said, sounding tired and miserable.

"I would be surprised, Jamey, but the definition of insider trading has broadened."

"The lawyers will cost me a fortune---£600 an hour!"

"You better get out of the market, Jamey?"

"I'm waiting for a rally."

"Clear it with your lawyers. If they give you permission, sell everything. At least you'll know where you stand. With cash in the bank you can concentrate on your business and defend yourself."

"Thanks Jack. You're a good mate. Did you know that someone built up big short positions in Bristol?"

"I thought that the authorities would be monitoring that."

"It's legal and it happened before the arrests."

Jamey was referring to large purchases of put options, the right to sell Bristol shares at certain prices. If the shares continued to slump, big profits would be made on the options.

When I told Sasha all I knew, she insisted that Faramazov was behind Meltin's murder. She believed that Faramazov had sold all his shares weeks before, when there were extraordinary trading volumes. Afterwards he had sold short via the purchase of put options. I asked Primeheart what he thought and he said that there was insufficient evidence, even though Sasha's theory could be correct. The death of a company's financial director was bound to suit the bears. An intensive investigation was necessary.

What was certain, was the professionalism of the hit men, if indeed Meltin had been murdered. They had left no clues, other than the spot of blood and button on the bridge.

* * *

Out of the blue, Amity phoned me from California.

"Hi Jack, how are you? Haven't heard from you in a long while."

"I'm fine Amity."

"I hope we're still friends, Jack. How's Cobber?"

"He saved my life, but that's a long story," I said trying to sound casual, even though the sound of her voice brought back hurtful memories.

"It's good to talk to you Jack, but I'm phoning to alert you about something."

"Yes?"

"You're well aware that Maxos and his gang are making a fortune out of diamond mining. What you don't know is that they are donating large sums to Black Python. The money is being used to unify right wing Spanish extremist parties with counterparts in Italy. A united front will make them a political force."

"As strong as France's *Front Nationale*?"

"Potentially. The European Central Bank has been pumping money into weak eurozone nations. On the face of it, economies have improved, but that's a myth. The rich have grown richer and the poor, poorer. A quarter of the Spanish working population are unemployed and around 45 per cent are school leavers and other young people. That's a powder keg."

"France and the rest of Europe also have long lines of jobless. They're resenting war zone migrants from the Middle East and Africa," I said.

"That's right, Jack. The Spanish and Italian extreme right-wing parties could easily unite with Le Pen's Front National or even split into a separate group. They claim that they aren't bigots, but do people really believe that?"

"Could a French, Italian and Spanish fascist force link up with neo Nazi movements in Germany, Austria, Holland and Hungary?"

"The warning signs are there."

20

Truth Will Out

Back in London the following day, I watched the webinar of Bristol GemDiam's press conference at the Israel Diamond Exchange. Neat piles of diamonds were displayed in glass display cabinets. Photographers were particularly interested in the rare light green diamonds.

CEO Gerald Gleep read out a brief statement: *"Percival Meltin, financial director of Bristol GemDiam has died in tragic circumstances. Percival was a dedicated officer of the company. His most recent report demonstrates that Bristol GemDiam and Canary Diamond Mines are financially sound. The diamonds on display show that Canary is producing greater numbers of high quality gems. We will shortly issue an update on the company's future operations and financial strategy. The directors and staff wish to pay tribute to Percival and we pass on our sympathies to his wife Cindy and sons Ray and Sam."*

Gleep then asked his audience to observe a minute's silence. Afterwards he stressed that the "deceased had a truly exceptional financial mind", but in response to questions hinted that Meltin "had been suffering from depression for some time".

Several reporters grilled the CEO about the Serious

Fraud Office's arrests. Gleep calmly replied that he couldn't comment, but the company was fully co-operating with regulators. It was a market, not a business matter, he said.

Bargain hunters bought Bristol GemDiam shares and the price touched £20 briefly, before sinking once again.

* * *

Soon afterwards, Fred Carrender skyped me. Josh Zunrel was alongside him.

"I heard that Percival Meltin was found at the bottom of the Avon Gorge," Fred said. "That's a dramatic way to commit suicide. What's your view, Jack?"

"Sasha believes that Faramazov was behind the murder."

"I find that highly improbable," Josh said. "He's in Israel."

Josh then narrated that he had taken Fred on a tour of Jerusalem, the previous day. One of the sites that they had visited was the *Garden Tomb*, outside the walls of the old city.

"While we were walking in the garden, we spotted Yevgeny Faramazov. It was late in the day and he was sitting on a bench with his eyes closed," Josh said. "We were shocked. Faramazov can't be much more than fifty, but he looked a lot older. He was haggard, thin and frail."

"When the garden was about to close, Faramazov opened his eyes and noticed us," Fred said. He invited us to dinner at the American Colony hotel. He told us that he had been selling assets to raise cash for his charity."

"Faramazov said that he was an atheist, but his visit to Jerusalem made him question his Communist upbringing," Josh said. "He was in poor health and seeking spiritual guidance. Is it likely that murder was on his mind?"

I wondered if the meditation in the *Garden Tomb* and

enthusiasm for the Faramazov Foundation indicated that the former KGB and FSB spy, was seeking forgiveness for past sins.

"By the way, have you guys found out anything more about Canary Diamond Mines," I asked.

"Look out for an announcement tomorrow. London regulators are on the wrong track again," Fred said.

* * *

Early on Friday, I switched on *CNBC* and presenters were trying to unravel details on a broadening financial scandal. The Madrid Stock Exchange had announced that Spanish police had raided Canary Diamond Mines and had discovered irregularities at the mine. Share trading in MSP España had been suspended and soon afterwards, the London Stock Exchange had stopped trading in Bristol GemDiam.

According to a Bloomberg report, Carlos Maxos and other MSP directors were unavailable for comment. They were in South America examining prospects. There were TV clips of Gleep and staff emerging from Tel Aviv's Hilton Hotel. Flushed and confused, Gleep rasped "no comment."

I immediately skyped Fred. He and Josh were eating breakfast at the Carlton Hotel, across the way from the Hilton.

"Well Fred, what's going on? Is this about Meltin?"

"Maybe. The Spanish authorities investigated the mine in the early hours of the morning, after we told them what had happened to you in Lanzarote. We also disclosed what Josh and I had discovered."

"Discovered what?"

"Let me first continue. Using night vision binoculars and videos the police observed divers pick up bags, plunge into the sea and then come up for more. They also spotted planting of diamonds in holes on the beach. They found several small bags of diamonds on the mine's dredger. A simultaneous police operation took place in Fuerteventura and while we are talking, the police are now diving for diamonds.

Sonya, overhearing our chat, joined me.

"Does this mean that Canary Diamond Mines is some sort of hoax?" Sonya asked.

"Yes, I'm convinced that the mine has been salted," Fred said. "Canary Diamond Mine has no gem resources. Its diamonds came from other mines. They buried them on the beach and placed them between rocks and other designated offshore places. They then mined the planted diamonds and told investors that the results were excellent."

"What has that got to do with salt?"

"It is a term used for a mining scam, Sonya," Fred said with a wide grin. "In the early nineteenth century, when America was being colonised, salt was a scarce commodity. As people began to move west, they found salt springs and people who owned them made a good living selling salt. Some con artists dumped salt into fresh water wells and claimed that they had found salt water springs. Suckers wanting to get into the profitable salt business bought the property from the fraudsters."

"So how did the term evolve in mining?" Sonya asked.

"When American pioneers went west on their wagon trains, they discovered gold in Colorado, Oregon and in the Sierra Nevada mountains. There was a huge rush for claims and fraudsters 'salted' mines by placing gold dust in the earth. Some fraudsters loaded their shot guns with gold pellets and fired them into the soft rock of derelict mines. They then sold the claims to naive amateur miners. Numerous cases in America, also included the salting of diamonds in Arizona, the forerunner to Canary. There was another intriguing South African salting case."

"South Africa?"

"Yes. It took place in the 1950s. Norbert Erleigh, a businessman, who came from a wealthy mining family and was keen on horse racing, formed a partnership with Joseph Milne, an insurance salesman. They salted a gold mine in the Orange Free State, a South African province, that had rich gold mines. The shares of their company went through the roof, until the fraud was discovered. Both were jailed and fined. The most recent major salting case was all the more remarkable because of the extent of investor gullibility."

"Go on."

"In the 1990s, Bre-X, a small Canadian mine, supposedly discovered a huge gold deposit in Indonesia. The market went wild and the stock soared by so much that they had to split the shares into smaller units. By the time it peaked, the effective price was almost 300 Canadian dollars. At the market top, the worthless mine had a market capitalisation of around 6 billion Canadian dollars."

"I read about that. Fortunes were lost. Are you saying that Bristol GemDiam and MSP España Mining, could go the same way?"

"That is likely to happen."

"But if they have salted the Mine's beach and coast with diamonds, how will the police prove that all the diamonds were planted? The directors have more than sufficient money to hire top defence lawyers."

"That is what Josh and I have been doing in Israel during the past couple of weeks. We checked Canary parcels carefully. Josh and other knowledgeable diamond dealers can detect where the gems came from. For example, the Argyle Mine in Australia has pink diamonds in its samples and Alrosa, in Russia, blue. Many Southern African Alluvial diamonds have yellow tinges."

"What about the diamonds that they displayed at the press conference?"

Fred grinned.

"We've been in contact with Watson Nkozi, your detective friend and mentor. Watson had told us that there had been 'an epidemic' of gem smuggling in the past year. De Beers and mines in Angola and Botswana had to tighten security. Those measures prevented smuggling on their mines."

"But you said that the smuggling continued despite that," I said.

"Smugglers have been paid much higher prices, so they have been prepared to take the risks," Josh said.

"So where are the latest smuggled diamonds coming from?"

"Alluvial producers in Central Africa, Sierra Leone, Liberia and Venezuela. High quality gems can be found offshore. Many of the sellers were probably 'artisanal', i.e. individual or small diamond mining operators, who received better prices from fences than bigger mining companies. They also bought diamonds from Zimbabwe," Josh said.

"Watson, who now heads a counter smuggling unit, recently detained two men with a large parcel," Fred said. "A Kimberly Process expert checked out the diamonds. He maintained that the greenish colour and shapes showed that they definitely came from a diamond mine in Zimbabwe."

"Did Watson manage to find out where they were taking their diamonds?"

"Yes. Both of the carriers were on the way to Barcelona, Cadiz in Spain and Palma, in the Spanish island of Mallorca"

"The smuggled diamonds were heading for Spain and Mallorca? So that was what that drop at Barcelona was about? Where I saw them murder Pedro Sanchez. Have they found his killers?"

Sonya peered at me closely.

"Witness to a murder! What's going on Jack?"

"It's a long story, Sonya."

"Watson told me they haven't found enough evidence to prosecute Sanchez's murderers," Fred said. "Same with Pacy Palatus. For some time, Watson, myself and Josh have been trying to understand why smugglers haven't tried to sell their diamonds on the market. Now we know."

"We believe that it is highly likely that the smuggled diamonds were shipped to the Canary Islands," Josh said. "The Canary Islands are part of Spain, so there are no internal customs controls. Smugglers and money launderers sold the diamonds to fences working for Maxos, Santos and Pinot in Madrid, Barcelona, Cadiz and Mallorca. The gems were then shipped to the Canary Diamond Mines operations in Lanzarote and Fuerteventura, without being detected."

"But the diamonds must be costing them millions," Sonya said.

"Correct, Sonya, but it has been win, win for them," Fred said. "They bought the diamonds from smugglers and salted the mine. They then mined the same diamonds and sold them at a big profit in Antwerp, Tel Aviv, Mumbai and New York."

"In the meantime, they made a fortune on the stock exchange as they are major shareholders in the Spanish and UK companies that own Canary Diamond Mine," I said. "Wow! That's some scam! There's only one problem. Evidence, or lack of it thereof. How do prosecutors put them behind bars?"

"They've become greedy and careless," Josh said. "Initially they were mining diamonds smuggled from alluvial operators, so they could get away with those. But now that there is extensive security to prevent smuggling, the vast majority of their latest diamonds come from Zimbabwe. Expert dealers, seeing the green gems will detect the similarity with Zimbabwean output. Green diamonds have never been found on beaches and offshore."

"We should thus have evidence that the diamonds aren't from an alluvial mine and are very different from the original gems that were planted, mined and sold on world diamond markets," Fred said. "The latest smuggled batch that Watson detected, is already on the way to Antwerp. Kimberly Process officials and detectives will compare them with the green gems on display."

"We have done our job, now it is up to the authorities," Fred said. "We'll get together in London tomorrow."

* * *

On arrival in London, Fred called me and asked me to help him and Josh prepare a detailed statement for the Financial Conduct Authority, the UK financial regulator and the Serious Fraud Office. The three of us were to meet for lunch at Josh's favourite Italian restaurant around the corner from Hatton Garden.

In the meantime, there was another brief announcement from Bristol, written in the best spin possible: *"As we reported Percival Meltin, chief financial officer of Bristol GemDiam died in tragic circumstances. Percival was a dedicated servant of the company. His staff and our auditors are prudently conducting an internal investigation. We will shortly issue an update on the company's operational and financial affairs."*

"How convenient, they're blaming poor Meltin," I said, when I met Josh. "Have they arrested Gleep?"

"They're questioning him. It is possible that he was

so enthusiastic that he was blind to the risks and was not party to the fraud," Josh said.

"If the London market is true to form, Gleep will resign with a bonus and pension, in terms of his CEO employment contract," I said. "Same with the other Bristol directors. What about the Maxos lot?"

"They are still in South America," Josh said. Their staff said that they were in Bolivia and were going to Argentina."

"Surprise, surprise. What happens now?"

"The SFO has contacted the Spanish police and have commissioned alluvial diamond mining consultants and experts to examine Canary Diamond Mines. That could take weeks."

"What about the shareholders?"

"The shares are no longer suspended. They were trading at £8, the last time I heard."

"You're out of date, Josh. I've just checked my mobile. They're already down to £4.

"Good grief! They were £27 only a few days ago. What about MSP España's stock?"

"It has also collapsed."

"And the rest of the market?"

"Diamond shares have led mining stocks southwards and they have brought down the entire market."

"When our news is published, Bristol and España's shares will be worth toilet paper," Josh said. "What do you think will happen to the rest of the market?"

"The usual. Irrational exuberance will eventually become irrational gloom."

"Are you expecting a crash?"

"Something like that. Markets never change, only the people do. I learnt that a long time ago."

"You seem to be very experienced for a young man, Jack."

Silence. If only he knew.

Fred was late so we phoned him several times, but his mobile didn't respond. Josh and I decided to lunch without him and then walked through Hatton Garden. There were lots of sales, showing that the general public were resisting high diamond, gold and silver prices. I spotted an emerald engagement ring, offered at a 50 per cent discount. With Josh as my advisor, I went in and bought it.

"When did you decide to take the plunge, Jack," Josh said, after the jeweller wrapped it up.

"Been thinking about it for some time," I said.

"Which one? The American or the Russian?"

His jocular remark didn't amuse me. Late afternoon when I was walking out of Highgate tube station towards my car nearby, my mobile rang.

"Are you Jack Sniper?" the caller asked.

"Yes."

"I'm a nurse at Barnet Hospital. Mr Carrender asked us to call you."

"Barnet Hospital? What's happened? I've been trying to get hold of him. Has there been an accident?"

"No. Mr Carrender has had a heart attack. He was admitted at noon and is being monitored."

"Oh no! How is he?"

"His condition is stable. He wants to see you."

The journey to Barnet Hospital was at the most seven miles, but traffic was heavy and it seemed to take forever. I parked my car and rushed up to the ward. Fred's eyes were closed and his chest was wired to a heart monitor.

"He's had a severe attack, but he wants to talk to you," the nurse said. "Don't stay too long."

"Hello Jack, thanks for coming," Fred said and attempted a weak smile. "I've been in the wars..."

"Take it easy Fred."

"Strange how it happened. I had to see Yevgeny Faramazov to get some information about Canary Diamond Mines. We had lunch at his home and when I was driving home, I felt queasy and had chest pains. Luckily I saw a sign to a hospital and here I am."

"Yevgeny Faramazov? Why didn't you tell me? He's dangerous. Could have given you something. Have you had heart trouble before Fred?"

"Yes. I had a heart attack about three to four years ago."

A brief silence. Me thinking, Fred closing his eyes.

"I had to see Faramazov. Alexei Ignatyevna told me that he had been a big seller of Bristol GemDiam and MSP España shares. Faramazov has also been selling claims and properties in the Canary Islands."

"Had I known that you were going to Faramazov, I would have warned you that he was one of the original investors in the Canary Diamond Mines," I said. "He's a former FSB agent and is dangerous."

"I knew that, Jack. Alexei told me all about him."

"Faramazov didn't give you anything unusual, did he?" I asked, getting very concerned.

"No, he didn't lace my drink or poison my chicken," Fred said, managing a weak smile. "We had a meal and some wine and swapped information. He told me that someone had tipped him off; told him that the MSP España partners were fascists. That was sufficient motive to sell."

"It was me who told him about the fascists," I said. "Was he aware that they were salting the mine?"

"No. He was stunned when I explained what they were doing."

"Are you quite sure?"

"Definitely. I've come across a lot of liars in the mining business. He wasn't lying."

"You were supping with the devil, Fred. The Russian

mafia."

Fred managed to cough out a laugh.

"Don't worry Jack. When we met Faramazov in Israel, he asked me to work for him; examine some of his mining interests. In any event he is ill, very ill; probably cancer. He was coughing blood and was very thin. I don't think murder was on his mind. He seemed more concerned about his family and his charities."

"You reckon that he's atoning for his sins?"

Guess so, maybe I should too," Fred said, his smile, faint. "Whatever Yevgeny Faramazov has done in the past, he seemed pretty straight to me."

"Do you want me to do anything for you Fred?"

A nurse came in and made him more comfortable.

"He needs to rest. I think you should leave now."

"I want you to contact Josh Zunrel and tell him to make the statement about the salting," Fred said, when I was about to leave the room.

"I was with Josh in Hatton Garden. The UK and Spanish regulators have already received the report."

"Good, we've done our duty. Now let's see what happens," Fred said. "I hope you've sold all your diamond shares?"

"Lucky for me, I'm completely out of the market. It's already well down."

Fred looked weak, so I decided to stay close by. Walking around the perimeter of the hospital, I phoned Sasha and told her what had happened.

She went ballistic: "Why didn't you phone me earlier. That bastard poisoned him. They're very sophisticated. You know what happened to Litvinenko!"

She ranted on, referring to the poisoning of Alexander Litvinenko, former agent of the FSB, and some other murders involving Russians.

"The doctors said that Fred has had a heart attack.

Fred does not believe that Faramazov did anything wrong."

"Don't contradict me, you know nothing about the FSB," Sasha said. "I'm coming over to Barnet to see for myself. I want to see what Faramazov did to him."

* * *

A doctor had just completed examining Fred when I returned.

"How is he?" I asked.

"Are you family?"

"No, I'm a friend. He's divorced. He has a disabled son who is with his ex-wife in South Africa."

"Any brothers, sisters? Family in the UK?"

"No siblings. He hasn't told me about any relatives here. How serious is his condition?"

"Not good."

"Is it just his heart? Any other problems?"

"No, just a weak heart. He had a triple bypass a few years ago and now this."

The nurse came out of the ward: "He wants to see you."

The doctor nodded.

I went inside the ward, sat close to Fred and held his hand.

"Jack will you contact my ex-wife Sheila and make sure that my son, Daniel is OK?"

"Sure, Fred, I'll take care of that," I said, my eyes beginning to water.

He looked tired and on the point of falling asleep. I had to come clean and made sure that no one else was around.

"Fred my real name is Jack Miner. They changed my identity. You were a good friend of Bill, my father."

"Jack Miner? Son of Bill Miner? You don't look anything like him. He was from Yorkshire. You're South African.

Jack Miner is in jail."

"Yes, Fred that's true. I was in jail, but I've changed my identity.

Fred, as weak as he was, attempted to look at me closely and was silent for a minute or two.

"Your Dad saved my life," he said, believing me at last. "We were caught in a storm when we were sailing in Mombasa. Our boat capsized. Your Dad had a great sense of humour. He kept me going for more than 24 hours. Now it's your turn, Jack."

"Sure Fred, sure," I said, trying to hide my tears by turning around and wiping them off with the back of my hand.

I held Fred's hand and he smiled at me and appeared peaceful. The monitor bleeped. The chart on the monitor was horizontal. The doctor and nurse rushed in and pumped Fred's chest, but it was over.

I rubbed my eyes and shuffled slowly out of the emergency room.

Just as I was leaving the hospital, a police car sped up to the entrance. Sasha, in her black police uniform, rushed out.

"How is he? I must speak to him; find out what Faramazov gave him."

"He's gone," I said. "The doctors are convinced he had a heart attack. He had a triple bypass a few years ago."

Sasha was furious, but I was too upset to get into an argument.

"Think what you like Sasha. Let your forensics examine him. You always know best," I said in a broken voice.

"We'll see what Faramazov has to say about this," Sasha said, shouting through the wind.

"Fred laughed when I told him that Faramazov was dangerous. He had commissioned Fred to do some work. What was his motive? Why kill Fred?"

"Wait here," Sasha said and rushed into the hospital.

Three uniformed officers who had arrived with her, sat comfortably in their car, while I stood in the wind and rain, cold and miserable.

21

THE WILL

The weather turned for the worse, while we waited for Sasha to appear. After about a half an hour she came out of the hospital. Her expression was hard and cold; no signs of sadness, even though she once had a brief relationship with Fred.

"We're going to question Faramazov," she said.

"A police investigation?"

"You as well."

"Me? No way. Why do I have to get involved?"

"Get in your car. We need you. You've been inside his house and saw the security. You met his body guards."

"Is this a sick joke, Sasha? I've already told you what Fred said. He left Faramazov on good terms and laughed off any possibility of poison."

"We still need to investigate whether he was responsible for Carrender's death."

"Didn't the doctors tell you that Fred had a triple bypass, a few years ago? That his heart was weak? Didn't they confirm what I said?"

No response. Just a cold-blooded stare. The cops in the car had opened the window to listen to the shouting match. One of them smiled and restrained a laugh.

"They won't let me in, I've got a gun in my car. I'm not in uniform like you guys," I insisted, hoping that this would be a way out.

She shouted at the driver of the police car.

"We'll follow him. He knows the quickest route."

"I don't want to come!"

"You had better. If you don't, I'll inform Primeheart. Where's your car?"

We struggled against the strong gale and the rain towards my motor, at the far end of the car park. I took out the pistol from the cubby hole.

"You had better take this," I said, handing it to her. "They won't let me into the grounds if they find it."

"OK," she said tersely and pocketed the gun.

"Who's going to follow who? I can't drive at police speed."

"It's only about 20 miles from here. If we lose sight of each other because of the traffic, I'll call you. Make sure that your mobile is on. If we get too far ahead of you, we'll stop about 400 metres before the house. Our light will be flashing, so you won't miss us. Get going!"

She ran back towards the police car, which through the driving rain and winter darkness was hardly visible. The brightly lit hospital, a couple of hundred yards away, was a blur.

Anger turned to grief again when I began the journey towards the Faramazov mansion. After a mile or so, I didn't bother to check whether the police car was still behind me. Sasha's obsession wasn't important. On my own again, I thought of Fred and the sadness overwhelmed me. I was crying so much, that the car lights coming towards me were blurred. Long ago memories raced through my mind. My mother and father, dead. Friends, dear friends, gone.

I drove like a zombie, managing by some miracle to stop at red lights and then carry on when they turned green. My mind was trapped in the past, so much so that I clean forgot to phone Sonya that I would be late. Cars whizzed by me on the motorway, until I took the turning towards Hatfield and then the country road towards Faramazov's home.

As arranged, the police car was in a lay-by about 400 metres from the house, lights flashing. Sasha stormed out of the car.

"What took you so long? Faramazov could be gone by now!"

I didn't bother to reply.

"OK, let's proceed. You go ahead first."

"What am I going to say to them? I don't have a police card."

I will inform them that you're helping us in an investigation."

We drove slowly towards the gate and the security guards came out of their guardhouse. One of them recognised me: "Aren't you the journalist who came in the summer to meet Mr Faramazov?"

"I'm not a journalist," I said. "I was just accompanying a friend."

"The Russian journalist?"

"Yes."

The guard looked wary, but Sasha and two of the uniformed police officers came up and she flashed her police card.

"He's with us," Sasha said.

"You never told us that you were a police officer," the guard said suspiciously, in his thick Russian accent. "Can I see your identity?"

I got out and showed him my driver's license. Thankfully

the rain had stopped, but the strong wind was biting cold

"Search his car if you must. He is with us. That is all that you need to know. You have my details. Call Scotland Yard, if you wish," Sasha said.

Under the bright light of the guardhouse and gate, the guard looked her up and down unconvinced. He contacted his colleagues in the house and phoned Scotland Yard, while his partner searched my car. Eventually they let both cars through.

* * *

We drove to the front door and Sasha, myself and the three other officers went into Faramazov's house to interview him and search the premises. Sasha instructed the officers to round up staff. It was now around 9 p.m. and Faramazov came down the stairs with Anya.

"Can you please tell us what this is all about?" Faramazov asked.

His appearance shocked me. He had lost most of his hair and he was thin and pale. His movements were very slow.

"We have come here to speak to you about Dr Fred Carrender," Sasha said.

Faramazov was puzzled.

"What about him?"

"When did you last see him?"

"He was here earlier in the day. Why?"

"He died in hospital this evening."

"Oh my god! What happened?" Anya asked.

Highly embarrassed, I tried to intervene.

"The doctors said…"

Sasha pushed me aside.

"I'm Detective Sergeant Sasha Melnikov. We're here

to investigate what happened."

"You're Oleg Melnikov's daughter, aren't you?" Faramazov said as he peered at her more closely. "Where's your search warrant?"

Sneering in a strange way, she took out the document which was neatly folded in her top pocket.

Faramazov examined it closely.

"OK, I'll call my staff."

Sasha instructed her officers to look for anything suspicious.

"What's he doing here?" Faramazov said, pointing at me.

"He was with Carrender when he died."

"I have nothing to do with this," I said awkwardly and trying to avoid Anya's expression of disgust. "Detective Sergeant Melnikov insisted that I come."

Faramazov stared at me and sighed.

"OK come with me," he said, indicating to his butler and two other bodyguards, not to follow.

Sasha pushed me forward towards the lift. As we went up with Faramazov in silence, he looked at me so intently that I felt ashamed. When we came out on to his private floor, Sasha went inside his office and closed the door behind her. That was as good a sign as any that she wanted to talk to him alone, not only about Carrender, but probably about her father too.

The passage way from his office led to another room. On the walls were modern paintings of Soviet dissident artists that I had seen in the *Tretyakov* gallery in Moscow. Curious, I slowly opened the door of the room. There was a bed, where I presumed Faramazov took afternoon naps, a spatula on the bedside table and an oxygen tank and inhaler. On the dressing table were several black and white and coloured photographs of a beautiful woman, most likely his mother, Katya. Next to the photos were Faramazov as a boy and a man in a military uniform. I guessed that was Yevgeny Krakanovitch, his grandfather. On the walls were large paintings of the Battle of Borodino, where his ancestor, Nicolaivich Krakanovitch was mortally wounded and the Siege of Stalingrad where Faramazov's grandfather fell. I waited in the room for about ten minutes, paging through an English book about Napoleon's retreat from Russia. Wondering how the interview was going, I walked back towards Faramazov's office. My mobile bleeped. Sasha's name came up. I knocked on the door, opened it and was shocked at what I saw. Faramazov was slumped on his desk, a pistol lying close to his hand. Next to the window was Sasha, holding the side of her left shoulder, which was bleeding. She was on her mobile, telling her officers to come up quickly and call an ambulance.

"Sasha, what the hell...?"

No response. She seemed to be in shock. I went up to her to take a look at her shoulder, but she pushed me away. Then I rushed to the desk to take a closer look at Faramazov. Blood was seeping out of his temple and was splattered everywhere. He was dead. Another pistol was on the desk. Just as I realised that it was mine and stupidly picked it up, two of the officers rushed in and pointed their guns at me. I immediately put the gun down ever so gently on the desk and put my hands up. I had read about trigger happy police and Faramazov had already been shot.

"Sasha what happened?" I asked.

No response and just then I noticed that she had gloves on and knew what was going to happen.

"Mr Faramazov took out a pistol and this young man panicked and fired," Melnikov said, in a matter of fact tone. "He hit Faramazov who managed to fire as he was falling. Luckily, it only grazed my shoulder."

"You liar! You shot him! I wasn't even in the room," I said.

Melnikov nodded at her officers and they put my hands behind my back, handcuffed me and led me out the room. Thoughts raced through my head. Sasha had planned to avenge her father for a long time and I had fallen into her trap.

* * *

Back in a cell, some three years after being released, I walked back and forth, in a fury. Sasha had stymied the fall guy.

Caught in the act, holding my pistol; my bullet in Faramazov's temple; my finger prints. Motives, plenty. Five years in jail because Faramazov had outsmarted me; released early from prison to get him prosecuted, but lost patience and shot him. Finally, death of close friend Fred Carrender, after he had visited Faramazov.

Revenge, it was an act of revenge. With Sasha, as a key witness, they would throw the book at me. The only good thing about my predicament was that I had long experience in prison. The diary about events up to now, would make another book. All these thoughts went through my head, as I once again adjusted to the hard bunk bed, the cold cell and dirty, stained toilet.

The next morning, the procedure began in earnest and I was taken to the interview room. Sitting there behind a desk, brought back memories of Pacy Palatus. Was he guilty or not guilty? My belief was the latter. Surprise, surprise! Instead of the normal detective interview routine, Primeheart walked in. With him was one of the officers who had arrested me in Faramazov's house. He was the guy who had smiled when Sasha and I were arguing in front of the entrance of Barnet Hospital. His presence wasn't comforting.

"I'm not going to say anything without a lawyer," I said.

"You can have one later," Primeheart said without any emotion. "This interview is preliminary. It won't be used against you."

"Bit irregular, isn't it? What guarantee will I have?"

"You have our word."

"Some word! Talking about trust, where the hell is Detective Sergeant Melnikov?" I asked, noting that this was the first time I had been with Primeheart without her. "Sonya Moldanya is still waiting for me at my flat. She must be worried. I haven't had an opportunity to phone her."

"We have already contacted Moldanya. You can talk to her later. You've met Detective Bradley Smithsonian," Primeheart said.

"Yes, but this is the first time, we've been formally introduced."

"You haven't replied to my question. Where's Melnikov?" I asked. "She's the one who has accused me."

Silence for a minute or so; them waiting for me to cool down.

"We'll discuss that later. Give us your version of events."

"I already told him in so many words," I said, pointing to Smithsonian. "He ignored me when his fellow officers dragged me out of the house."

"You're drawing conclusions. We're listening to you now," Smithsonian said.

I gave them full details of the argument I had with Melnikov at the hospital, insisting I had agreed with the doctors that Fred Carrender had died of natural causes and that Faramazov was not responsible.

"Are you sure she was convinced that Faramazov caused the death of Carrender?" Primeheart asked.

"Yes Sir, I believe that he overheard my conversation

with Melnikov," I said pointing to Smithsonian, who nodded his head. "He would have heard me tell Melnikov loud and clear that I had no desire whatsoever to accompany the police and go to Faramazov's residence. Melnikov pushed me into it; threatened me that she would report to you, sir, if I failed to obey her."

"You believe that Carrender's encounter with Faramazov did not lead to Carrender's death?" Smithsonian asked.

"Yes Sir, I believe that it was a coincidence. Fred had a triple bypass a few years ago, and the doctors emphasised that he died of a heart attack."

"They could be wrong."

"I don't believe so. When Fred Carrender told me that he had visited Faramazov, I was worried he had been given a drug that had precipitated the attack. Carrender reassured me that they had got on very well. Faramazov had commissioned him to do some work for him. He also said that Faramazov was very ill. Faramazov had no motive to kill him. Fred told him about the salting of Canary Diamond Mines."

"Wasn't that a motive? Faramazov was a big investor."

"Was is the operative word. Faramazov had already sold all his shares by the time he had the meeting with Fred."

"Tell us what Carrender discussed with you before he died."

I then repeated everything that Fred had told me and they listened intently.

"Why do you think Carrender went to see Faramazov?"

"Fred wanted to find out who were selling Bristol GemDiam and MSP España shares. He knew that Faramazov had been a major shareholder. Fred was trying to get as much evidence as possible that the mine had been salted. He believed that Faramazov was the seller and had found out about the salting."

"Do you think Faramazov was aware from the beginning, that the mine wasn't producing diamonds?"

"Fred said that Faramazov was very surprised to hear about the alleged salting. He believed him."

"What about you?"

"I agreed with Fred's conclusion. Faramazov had other motives to sell the shares."

"Both Bristol and MSP published regulatory information that Faramazov had cut his initial stake in their companies, when they were listed. Did Carrender inform you that Faramazov had sold the rest of his holdings recently?"

"That's what Fred told me before he died."

"If that's what happened, surely Faramazov was aware of the salting?"

I thought quietly for a moment and then continued: "I still agree with Fred's view that Faramazov didn't know. For a start, he had great faith in Marcia Vaskilov, the geologist. She had made an important diamond discovery in Russia and had written a comprehensive study on the possibility that the Canary Islands had diamonds. He had other motives to sell."

"Such as..."

"Did Detective Melnikov tell you that Yevgeny Faramazov's grandfather had fought in the Spanish civil war against Franco's fascists?"

"No, she did not. Her files on him state that his grandfather was an officer in the Second World War and was killed by the Nazis in the Siege of Stalingrad. There was no mention of Spain," Primeheart said and glanced at Smithsonian.

"Did she tell you that I accompanied Sonya Moldanya, when she interviewed Faramazov at his home?"

"I read Moldanya's article in the *FT* and the Russian ones were translated for me, but Melnikov never mentioned that," Primeheart said, his eyes narrowing.

"When we met with Faramazov in the summer, Melnikov followed us there in her own car. Did she tell you that?"

Primeheart and Smithsonian glanced at each other again and then looked at me intently.

"Are you saying that when Moldanya and you interviewed Faramazov, Detective Sergeant Melnikov followed you into his mansion?" Smithsonian said. "The place is a fortress!"

"No, later. After the interview, we drove towards London and I noticed that a car was following us. Initially I thought it was either Faramazov's men or his enemies. It turned out to be Sasha Melnikov. I presume she didn't inform you about that either, Detective Smithsonian. Surely you, her deputy, should have been told?"

Smithsonian shuffled about, somewhat embarrassed.

"When Melnikov caught up with us, she wanted to know details about the interview, but Sonya refused. She demanded that I divulge the information, but I was not prepared to compromise Sonya's journalistic integrity. I had promised to help her protect her source, so I refused. Obviously Melnikov never informed you about that. What is this all about? I thought this interrogation was about her allegations that I had killed Faramazov."

"Later. Back to Faramazov. What do you believe was the motive to sell his shares in Bristol GemDiam and MSP España?"

"I initially thought that he was in deep financial trouble as he was over exposed to property and mining, especially diamonds; that he needed to sell his stake to pay off debts. Later, Fred Carrender and Josh Zunrel, a diamond dealer, told me that they had seen Faramazov meditating at the *Garden Tomb* in Jerusalem. He told them that he was selling assets to repay debt and to raise money for his charity, the Faramazov Foundation."

"The second reason?"

"At the interview with Sonya Moldanya, I told Faramazov that his Spanish partners were involved with fascist organisations and asked him why he was doing business with them. It was evident that he was unaware of their association with extreme right-wing groups. He was furious. He stated that he was deeply anti-fascist and the partnership would sully the memory of his grandfather who had helped the Republicans fight fascists in the Spanish Civil War. I believe that it was the main motive to get rid of his entire stake. If it was just financial, he would have kept some shares. Dr Carrender told me that he had sold the lot."

An officer walked into the room and gave Primeheart a sheet of paper. He read it briefly and showed it to Smithsonian.

"Is Sonya Moldanya in contact with Melnikov's mother?"

"Not recently."

"Take that phone and ask her to speak to Mrs Melnikov and enquire about her health."

"Why should I do that?"

"Later... Please phone her."

They put the phone on speaker tone.

"Hi Sonya, I'm sorry I haven't called you..."

"Jack, I've been worried about you. The police phoned and told me that you had been locked up."

"It's a long story. I can't talk now. Please phone Yelena Melnikov."

"What's all this about, Jack? You don't even bother to contact me for more than 24 hours and now you order me to phone Sasha's mother in Russia!"

"I'm sorry Sonya, but things happened beyond my control. Please Sonya, you have to do this for me. Please!

Trust me."

"Why are you asking? Is she OK? Has something happened to her?"

"I'm not sure. I'm a bit worried. Please phone back when you've spoken to her."

"I think you owe me an explanation," I said, after I put down the receiver.

"Detective Sergeant Melnikov has sent me a text. She has boarded a plane to Moscow because her mother is very ill," Primeheart said.

"Moscow? She must be getting an interconnecting flight to Arkhangelsk."

"Now tell us your version of the events in Faramazov's house," Smithsonian said.

"Is this part of an internal investigation about her and not just about me?"

"Tell us all you know."

I told them how Melnikov and Faramazov went into the office alone and how I wondered around looking at the paintings in the passageway and had gone into his spare bedroom. In doing so I gave them as much detail as possible.

"We know that," Smithsonian said. "Our forensic expert confirmed it."

"Remarkable what they can find these days," I said and scratched my head to see if any dandruff fell on to my shirt.

"You knocked on the office door and went in. What happened next?"

I told them what had happened in Faramazov's office, before Smithsonian's colleagues rushed in and handcuffed me.

"You shouted and swore at me and my officers, pleading your innocence. Now you're calmer, tell us what you believe happened," Smithsonian said.

"I did not kill Faramazov. I was out of the room when it

happened. It is circumstantial evidence. Detective Sergeant Melnikov had gloves on when I handed her my pistol in the Barnet Hospital car park. I recall that now. I was damned stupid because I picked up the gun in Faramazov's office. My finger prints are on it."

"How do you think he was killed?"

When Sonya Moldanya and I interviewed Faramazov, he searched for the old revolver that belonged to his grandfather. While he was doing so, he placed his pistol on the desk.

"So, he then had two guns in his desk?"

"Yes. The revolver at the time was empty."

"Did Melnikov know about this?"

"I don't recall telling her, but Sonya might have."

"Hmm--- OK, if you claim that you didn't kill him, tell us what you think happened," Primeheart said.

"I didn't hear the shots as my pistol has a silencer and Faramazov's gun must have been silent too. There are two possibilities. The first is that Melnikov asked Faramazov to clear his desk. When he took out his pistol from the top draw, she used it as a pretext to shoot him. He tried to defend himself and fired back."

"But Faramazov was regarded as a brilliant shot. How come he merely grazed her shoulder from that short range?"

"The second possibility is that after Melnikov shot him, she grabbed his pistol, held it fairly close to her shoulder and shot and grazed herself."

"Her story is that you fired the first shot. Faramazov in a knee jerk reaction, shot wildly and luckily the bullet did not wound her seriously."

"That's a lie."

"Doctors and forensic scientists agree with you. After treating Melnikov, they were of the view that the shot was from a very close range. They contend that the wound was self-inflicted."

"Phew. You believe me."

"Can you phone Moldanya again please."

"Hi Sonya," I said, with the phone on loudspeaker again.

"Yelena said that she was pleasantly surprised when Sasha phoned her. She was looking forward to her visit," Sonya said.

"How is she?"

"She was cheerful on the phone. She had a mild cold, a few weeks ago, but was better. Nothing serious. Why are you asking me about this?" Sonya asked.

"Thanks Sonya, I'm sorry but I can't talk now. They're interviewing me. It's about Faramazov's death."

"My God. What happened?"

"Sorry, Sonya, have to go."

"The health of Melnikov's mother cannot be described as bad," Smithsonian said.

He and Primeheart went out the room and came back after about ten minutes.

"Thanks Sniper, you can go now," Primeheart said.

"Is that it? I spend a night in jail. My girlfriend is frantic and that's all you say?"

"It's quite obvious that you didn't shoot him. You didn't want to go to Faramazov in the first place. You didn't believe that he was dangerous."

"No apologies! Nothing!"

"Take it easy Sniper, we had no option. You had a gun in your hand when the officers entered. What did you expect? A pat on the back?" Smithsonian said, without any hint of regret.

Primeheart tried to hide a smile.

"Melnikov is highly intelligent. She knew that as soon as the forensics were completed, that she would be in trouble.

You were a delaying ploy. I hope you had a pleasant night in the custody of Her Majesty."

"Very funny. Obviously, she's done a runner?"

"Probably. We shall see," Smithsonian said.

"What made her do it? Was she frustrated about the investigation? Did she crack up? Why avenge her father that way?"

Silence. Them just looking at me, neither agreeing nor disagreeing.

"You may be interested to know that Europol joined the Spanish and Canary Islands police in the raid of Canary Diamond Mines," Primeheart said, changing the subject again. "They have more evidence indicating that Carrender and Zunrel were right."

"Such as?"

"They found more sacks in Lanzarote and Fuerteventura hiding places. Some of them contained diamonds. They have been interviewing workers, divers and fishermen. Their initial investigations confirm that both mines were salted."

* * *

Later that afternoon, I returned home and told Sonya what had happened. She was very cool towards me, wondering why I had not called her and explained that I was going to Faramazov's place. She wanted to know why I was involved with the police and was very wary of me. First, however, she had a job to do. Using me as her source, she immediately filed the story about the death of Faramazov and an article that police, diamond dealers and the late geologist Fred Carrender had detected salting of the Canary Diamond Mines. She scooped the opposition.

The next day newspapers, TV and radio ran stories about the diamond mining fraud. Stations interviewed the head of the Canary Islands police force and Basil Bleedon, who was shaky when he was questioned about his former wildly optimistic reports. I wondered how much money he had made and lost. Bristol GemDiam's shares fell like a stone, as frantic holders tried to sell. The only buyers were the bears who had sold short at higher prices and had repurchased their shares at depressed prices, making a huge profit. At the close of trading that day, Bristol GemDiam's shares were quoted at 85 pence compared to the peak of £27 only a few weeks previously. They were now below their original listing price of £1.

Investors were now worried whether their shares would be worthless. Much would depend on the extent of debt and prices of assets, notably the sale of the offshore diamond dredging vessel and mining equipment. Little wonder that Percival Meltin was nervous and reluctant to speak to me, a few weeks before his untimely demise.

Such were the losses during the market panic, that diamond and other mining stocks were dumped. The slump in the mining sector was the catalyst for a general stock market slide. Within weeks, global equity markets were steeped in gloom.

It has never ceased to amaze me how market moods can change from euphoria to fear and then deep pessimism. A few weeks previously, the majority of pundits were blue sky bulls and market pessimists were a maligned species. As the downward spiral took hold, dial a quote bears began to dominate the airwaves, with predictions of further declines. During the bubble, popular technical analysts forecast that "market momentum" would push shares higher and higher. Now they were discussing "breaches of support" on charts that were pointing towards the floorboards.

Regardless whether they were good, mediocre or struggling companies, all shares were treated the same and sold at giveaway prices. Since I had experienced this as a trader, before I went to jail, I wondered whether it would soon be bargain time. Fred and my other old friends had taught me that crises cause considerable losses for holders of over-valued assets, but also create opportunities for those who have the cash and are brave enough to seek value and buy. I began to dip into the market and purchase shares of the top mining corporations.

Gerald Gleep and several other directors of Bristol GemDiam Mining were arrested, but the founders of MSP España, notably Maxos and Pinot, were still in South America and could not be traced. Police wanted to interview Marcia Vaskilov to find out whether she was complicit in the fraud or just a geologist who had so much faith in her Canary Island theories, that she believed her own fantasy. To me it was the latter, but we couldn't know for sure as she had disappeared. Some thought that Vaskilov was in Russia, but relatives said that they didn't know where she was. Vaskilov was single, with no direct family who were looking for her. Perhaps she had ended up like poor Meltin, but so far, no one was the wiser. The Spanish police had one success. They caught Philippe Santos and in the weeks ahead he made a deal with the police and became a witness for the prosecution in the Madrid courts. Spanish cartoonists depicted him as a "singing canary".

The media who were uncritical during the boom, reported with relish the latest financial scandal that had brought down the markets. The fraud was dubbed "Salted Canary" and Manfred Fokes-Mailsford, "Bird Brain". Investigative reporters had a field day trying to unravel other potential mining frauds. Analysts, pension and hedge fund managers who had been caught up in the euphoria, were sacked and lawyers offered services in "class actions". These legal suits enabled stricken investors to act as a group and sue everyone in sight.

Investors, of course, did not blame themselves for their greed and rank stupidity. It was the other guy's fault. From past history of booms and busts, these suckers would shun shares of mining exploration companies, for years. Genuine mining businesses would thus find it exceedingly difficult to raise capital for new projects.

* * *

The bell of my flat rang at 7am in the morning two days after the meeting with Primeheart and Smithsonian and the beginning of the stock market crash. Cobber barked furiously and I swiftly put on some shorts and a tee shirt and went to the door.

"Who's there? Do you know what time it is?" I said.

"Gregory Muskowitz. Can you please let me in. I'm Yevgeny Faramazov's solicitor."

"Wait a bit," I said and swiftly grabbed a large sharp knife in the kitchen and returned, holding Cobber tightly on his lead. When I gingerly loosened the chain and opened the door, I swiftly looked around to make sure that no-one else was with the tall, balding man in shaded glasses.

"You are Mr Sniper, right?" Muskowitz asked and stepped back from the dog. "I have something for you."

Muskowitz handed me a large brown envelope, which I decided to open in front of him. Cobber tugged on the lead and the lawyer stood back, observing him warily. The envelope contained a thick wad of documents.

"Can I come in? Please put the dog in another room."

"Don't worry about him. He's well trained. Do you want some coffee?"

We went into the kitchen and sat down at the table while the kettle was boiling.

"What's this all about?" I asked, as I placed them on the table and poured out the coffee.

"These are copies of documents which I have kept in safe custody at our bank," Muskowitz said. "Mr Faramazov wanted me to give them to Sonya Moldanya and you."

I paged through the papers, which with two exceptions, were in Russian. I called Sonya who was in the shower and began reading the opening letter from Faramazov. It was in Russian with an English translation.

"Dear Sir/Madam,

These documents should be copied and given to Ms Sonya Moldanya, London correspondent of the Novaya Gazeta and her friend Mr Jack Sniper. Rathbone & Muskowitz, my UK solicitors, must keep the original documents in safe custody. Ms Moldanya can fully report the contents in Part A of the Dossier. After she has published all her reports and commentaries in newspapers or a book, she is free to distribute the contents to other journalists, historians and students.

Part B must not be copied and MUST remain in safe custody. It must not be distributed to either Ms Moldanya or any other person. That part of the Dossier should only be released if there is any harm to my present and past wives, children, relatives, any individual mentioned in Part A as well as Ms Moldanya, Mr Sniper and their relatives and friends. Part B contains vital information about several people who have been instigators of corruption in Mother Russia. The crimes of these individuals in State Departments, notably the FSB, Police and the Department of Justice, will be exposed. The same applies to business people and other individuals who benefited or were involved in the crimes. These wrong doings against Russians and other peoples of former Soviet Bloc states, including Ukraine and Georgia, include atrocities against humanity, murder, beatings, torture, theft, kidnapping, cybercrime, fraud and protection rackets, drug running, blackmail, bribery and

other corrupt practices. Copies of the Dossier are also held in
safe keeping in Switzerland, Germany and France. The names
of these banks are confidential and hold the safe custody codes.
If anything were to happen to the partners and employees of
the firm Rathbone & Muskowitz, the contents of Part B will
also be released from these sources.

   It must be stressed that the information and detailed ac-
counts in Part B are an even greater exposure of past and present
culprits, than the contents of Part A and will be disclosed if any
harm comes to any of the above.

   Yours faithfully
   Yevgeny Nicolaivich Faramazov

By now Sonya was showered and dressed and after
introducing her to Muskowitz, she began reading Part
A of Faramazov's dossier and was shaking her head in
amazement.

   There was one more letter in English. It was to me.
   Dear Mr Sniper,

   You must find it odd that I am writing to you, but you
have done me and my family a great service. In my worst error
of business judgement, I invested in the operations of Carlos
Maxos and partners. Their association with Marcia Vaskilov,
a highly respected Russian geologist, persuaded me to believe
that there were serious diamond exploration possibilities in the
Canary Islands. Indications that diamonds would be discovered
there also encouraged me to purchase properties in the islands.

   Your information that Maxos and his colleagues were deeply
involved with Spanish fascist organisations committed to the
memory of Franco and Hitler, took me completely by surprise.
As I told you and Sonya Moldanya during her interview, my
grandfather fought against Franco and the Nazis. There is no
way that I could be associated with people committed to these
parties. As a result, I sold all my shares in MSP España and
Bristol GemDiam Mining and real estate in the Canaries. The

sale of those assets at very attractive prices and also profits from put options, enabled me to substantially improve the finances of the Faramazov Foundation and ensure the future for my family.

I carried out my own investigations and found that large amounts of money raised from Maxos' stock market listings, were used to fund right wing organisations. The intention is to unite with extreme right parties in France, Italy and other parts of Europe and become a serious political force. As the European economy is in recession and unemployment is high, membership of these political parties is growing rapidly. The Faramazov Foundation will in the future play a role in backing legitimate parties and candidates to ensure that the Far Right does not gain leeway in Spain and the rest of Europe.

This letter is also a personal apology to you for past events, following our encounter some years ago. You are, I am sure, aware of my role in those matters and I wish to compensate you with a gift of $250,000 from my estate when I die and a codicil has been added to my will. As I write this, my health has deteriorated badly. Some months ago, doctors detected lung cancer, which despite treatment has spread and my prognosis is terminal.

Dr Fred Carrender has told me that you have become financially astute. The proviso for the transfer of the $250,000 is that you must agree to advise my wife, if she wishes you to do so. Anya is already in charge of the Faramazov Foundation, which is doing a lot of good in Russia and other parts of the world. The foundation will reward you for any further services and performance, over and above the initial down payment.

I wish you well for the future

Yours sincerely

Yevgeny Nicolaivich Faramazov

"All that coughing when I interviewed him was from lung cancer?"

"Yes Sonya, the claim that he was recovering from flu

was a cover."

"Something puzzles me," Sonya said, peering straight into my eyes. "I thought that you had never met him before. Why the gift of $250,000 and apology for 'past events'?"

"I'll talk to you about that later," I said.

I was shocked that Faramazov had been aware of my true identity, despite the plastic surgery and my cultivated South African accent. The $250,000 proposed gift, provided that I advise Anya and his foundation, also stunned me

"Your paths have crossed before, haven't they?" Sonya said.

"I need to go to the office," Muskowitz said, sensing that a row was brewing.

I showed him to the door and faced an agitated Sonya.

"Who are you Jack? Why the pistol in the bedside drawer next to the bed? Why did you go with the police to search Faramazov's house? Why were you under the influence of Sasha? We have been living together for months and I don't know anything about you."

"Let's go for a walk and I'll tell you why," I said, gently touching her on her arm.

She swiftly withdrew, went to the living room, pushed the sofa to the centre of the room and placed all the documents in our hiding place under the floor board. I helped her push the sofa back and tried to hold her hand, but she recoiled from me.

"Please, Sonya. It had to be confidential. I'll try and tell you everything you want to know."

In desperation, I rushed to the bedroom and put the box with the engagement ring in my pocket, went into the garden with Cobber and waited until she had calmed down. Later we had lunch at the Grove Cafe, listened to some opera music and then walked around Alexandra Park. Despite Primeheart's instructions to the contrary, I confessed that I was really Jack Miner and had changed my identity on his and Sasha Melnikov's instructions. While we walked she listened to the story of my earlier life and about *Trader Jack,* the book I had written in prison and which I now hoped would be published.

"Who's the real Jack? Sniper or Miner?" Sonya asked shaking her head when we sat down on a bench overlooking green cricket and football fields, in the middle of Highgate woods.

"I am just me."

"Who am I to believe? The fraudulent hedge fund operator, ex-convict, amateur geologist, share analyst, detective and now writer?"

"I'm all of them, Sonya. All of them. I'm not a bad person. Really!" I said, taking out the box from my pocket and showing her the engagement ring.

She looked at me as if I was crazy, put up her hands and stood up. Cobber wagged his tail, came up and rubbed his body against her. It seemed that he was also rejecting me.

"I suppose you want me to play a part in the third phase of your life, have children and live happily ever after," Sonya said with a sarcastic half laugh.

"Yes, Sonya, I want some stability in my life. I'm no criminal, Sonya, I was set up. Sasha Melnikov and her boss gave me no alternative, but to help them bring down Faramazov."

"Spoken like a true sociopath, Jack. Always blameless; always someone else's fault," she said, taking a good look at the emerald ring. "Sasha told me that you had a few girlfriends before me. You must have a stockpile of these."

"When they let you out of jail, you crave company."

"What number is Sonya Moldanya, three, four, five? Maybe Anya Faramazov is next. You'll help her with the Foundation and you'll live in the style you're accustomed."

"I don't intend to. It's a charity, but how much of its money is tainted?"

"Oh, you're now into ethics, Jack. I'm impressed."

"Please Sonya, you've lived with me for some time. You know me."

"No Jack, I don't. I'll spend this week writing up Yevgeny's dossier. We will go to Fred's funeral, but both of us will need time away from each other."

Later, Sonya moved into the spare room. During the following week, she worked ten hours a day filing article after article exposing underhand dealings of the FSB and various individuals in the Russian Secret Service. The "Faramazov Confession" was published in the *Novaya Gazeta*. I helped edit her English and the stories were also published in the *FT*, the *Wall Street Journal* and other newspapers around the world. One of the articles covered the alleged role of Roman Bigganoff in his battle against his enemy, Yevgeny Faramazov. It included the allegation from "informed sources" that Bigganoff had issued the order to murder Oleg Melnikov. Bigganoff also instructed a rogue army commander to help thugs attack the striking Dobrenska miners. There was documentation to prove Faramazov's allegations and the letters and emails were published in the *Novaya Gazeta*.

Another piece quoted the dossier's allegations that the FSB had corrupted both government and business; that the big time Russian mafia were some enriched criminal officials within the FSB, including former members of the KGB. Faramazov also castigated the "carpet bagging" during Boris Yeltsin's regime that led to the enrichment of billionaire Russian oligarchs and the infinite gap between the super rich and the Russian people.

It was remarkable how Faramazov managed to obtain the information, but he had been a brilliant secret agent and had contacts everywhere. Money, no doubt, had also helped.

When Sonya was sleeping after an exhausting virtually non-stop writing spate, I took the Faramazov dossier to a printing firm, made copies and returned the originals to the flat. By then, Sonya had woken up and was waiting for me. There was an awful row and for someone so small, Sonya had a strong arm. She could have been a cricketer, baseball pitcher or even a javelin thrower. I ducked and weaved, but one of the cups that she threw, hit me on the shoulder and it hurt badly. There was nothing more to do but to escape to my car and drive to Scotland Yard and deliver the copy to Primeheart. He was too busy to talk to me, but promised to see me later in the week. I felt treacherous but that was the closure of my deal with him and the Force. Later when I returned to the flat, Sonya had left. Cobber with his tail right down, crept into her room, ignoring me.

22

Murder a Blessing in Disguise

The funeral was expected to be a quiet affair. It was anything but. The news that Fred Carrender had died, dismayed the global mining world. The chapel at Golders Green Crematorium was overcrowded with CEOs, geologists, mining executives and investment bankers. Alexei Ignatyevna and the board of Vogdana Diamond Mines were there and Isobel was sitting with him. I sat with Fred's former wife and son and listened to eulogy after eulogy on the famous South African geologist who had touched lives everywhere. I myself delivered an address about my time with Fred in the veld and how close I was to him. Anecdotes about ants discovering diamonds and failed prospecting, drew laughs.

Someone from the past was there. It was David Drummond from Wardle & Co, the Hampstead brokers who first dealt for me, when I was a youth. *Elgar's Violin Concerto*, Mozart's *Requiem*, John Lennon's *Imagine* and Miles Davis' *Blue* were played and my mind went back to my own Dad's funeral. It was time to go back to Yorkshire and visit a loyal friend, who had written to me while I was in prison.

When we came out from the dark chapel into the winter sunlight and the Crematorium garden, the long queue of Fred's fans went up to his former wife Sheila and Daniel, his son. I wandered about the rose garden; plants pruned and naked, ready for the summer bloom. Memorial notices were next to each flower. Near them were two sculptures of birds. Underneath them were the words: "In memory of Rena and Stanley Slimcop".

I wept, oblivious to those near me. It was as if my whole life poured out of me. Sonya looked on, but she didn't come up to me. I walked away from the bushes and went up to her, attempting to kiss her on her cheek. She withdrew and shook my hand coldly.

"Sonya, please …," I said, tears still in my eyes.

"I'm going back to Russia, Jack. My work is finished here. I need some time for myself; must research my book. The people mentioned in the Faramazov Dossier have a right to reply."

"That will be dangerous, Sonya, do you really need to interview them? How many journalists have died in Russia before time?"

"If anything happens to me Part B of the Faramazov Dossier will be released. Dates of each interview and the identity of the subject will be recorded and will be sent to Gregory Muskowitz. I've got to know him. He's now my solicitor and can be trusted."

"Have you been in touch with Anya and the children? She hasn't contacted me."

"She's keeping to herself. Told me that Faramazov's funeral is for family and close friends. She doesn't want the press there."

Isobel and Alexei came up to us.

"Why don't you two get together again?" Isobel said. "You're made for each other."

"Sonya needs some space. She's going back to Moscow," I said.

"Go back with her you idiot," Isobel said and proudly showed off an engagement ring with a large blue diamond. "We want you both at our wedding."

"Congrats Isobel!" I said smiling for the first time and kissing her and shaking Alexei's hand. "Where is the wedding going to be? Here or Russia?"

"Here," Alexei said. "We've bought a house in Surrey. I'll commute once a month to see how the mine is doing."

"Jack, I'm starting a new business and I want you to be my partner," Isobel said.

"Corporate finance?"

"Presume you read the news today; the Fazeldoff, Trogan & Fokes collapse; the impact on other firms. The door is open for a knowledgeable mining finance boutique when markets settle down."

"Sounds good, Isobel," I said cheering up a bit. "Let's have lunch next week. I'll be busy in the next few days helping sort out Fred's affairs."

"Fred would be proud of you."

"Sheila and Daniel Carrender are staying with me, before they go back to Cape Town,"

Jamey Jackenhead was at the edge of the crowd and was looking in our direction. It seemed that he was too embarrassed to come up to us."

We waved to him, showing that we did not bear him any ill will. It was not the Jamey that I had once known. The confident swagger had gone. He shuffled up to us and shook our hands limply. Our group was smartly dressed in dark suits and black dresses, but Jamey was in a dark blue sports jacket that looked worse for wear.

"Why haven't you returned my calls, Jamey?" Isobel asked. "I'm sure you'll get off with a fine at most. I can't see how you can go down as an insider trader."

"What's the definition these days? You innocently ask

a guy how the business is going and you're an insider," Jamey said.

"Are you OK?" I asked.

"After what's happened in the market? The lawyers? The regulators?"

"I heard that you were going into farming," Isobel said.

"A relative has a pig farm. Couldn't think of a better place for me."

* * *

Some weeks later, John Primeheart took me to the Reform Club for lunch. He had a steak and I chose fish and chips. For the first time since I had met him, my boss was warm and friendly. There had to be a reason.

"Are you satisfied that I've finished my job, Sir?"

"Yes Jack. It's time for closure."

"You mean I'm now completely free? No chance of going back to prison? There are still a few months," I said, half joking and half serious. You never knew with Primeheart.

We finished our coffee and I glanced around the spacious room. No-one was near us.

"Any news about Sasha Melnikov? Why wouldn't she face you guys? She probably would have been reprimanded or suspended at the most."

"I'm not so sure about that," Primeheart said. "The irony is that the shooting was a blessing in disguise. Faramazov had terminal cancer and was suffering. The pathologists said that he was riddled with tumours. It was too late for chemo and radio therapy. She gave him a quick way out."

"Melnikov was totally obsessed with the murder of her father. There was no way that she could nail Faramazov, so she flipped and took the law into her own hands."

"Yes, that's one theory," Primeheart said.

"Or perhaps another?"

"Yes, perhaps another. Did you know that Bigganoff drowned in his bath on Sunday? Had a heart attack?"

"What a coincidence."

"Yes, a typical Russian coincidence."

"It was a deal. Melnikov kills the loose cannon with political ambitions. In return, the FSB takes care of her father's real murderer."

"Perhaps."

"And all the time she was in your team, she was working for the FSB. Infiltrating Scotland Yard; the Russian flag, here, there, everywhere."

"That's your view," Primeheart said, as we walked out of the club into Pall Mall. "I couldn't possibly make that presumption."

For a brief moment we were silent, while we waited in the drizzle for a cab.

"Well Jack, you've done your time and helped us," Primeheart said. "What are you now going to do?"

"I've been offered a partnership in a mining finance boutique. Prospects are excellent and I get on well with the founder. She is currently seeking regulatory permission."

"You'll probably make a lot of money there, but is that everything?" Primeheart said. "I gather you've done well from buying mining stocks at rock bottom prices. You can also share in the Faramazov inheritance, if you help his wife."

"Who told you that?"

"I have my sources."

"Dr Klugheim?"

Primeheart smiled. I wondered whether he had also piled into the market. Whether my former prison psychiatrist had passed on my tips.

"Well Jack, do you really need the money? You're free and you've bounced back. You're Jack Sniper now and your record is clean," Primeheart said.

"I guess I have enough. You can't eat the stuff."

"Indeed, Jack. That's exactly what I'm thinking."

"What do you have in mind, Sir?"

"A detective---- I think you've got the makings of being a good detective."

"And be with you lot every day. Risking my life! No way."

"It's perfect for you. You're in the clear. You've made good money legally. You're Jack Sniper now, or perhaps you want to go back to being Jack Miner again."

Typical Primeheart. Effective blackmail. No chance for a partnership in Isobel's firm, with a criminal record.

"OK, so you want me to be *Copper Jack*. What job do you want me to do?"

"Much the same, Jack. Use your instincts and financial knowledge. The force needs people like you, but first you must do some training."

"Not more military workouts. I've had enough of those."

"No, a proper detective course. You'll enjoy it. Psychology of the criminal mind. You'll get top honours for that, won't you Jack?" Primeheart said with a snigger.

I couldn't help but smile. Miracles never cease. After all this time, he seemed to be quite human, calling me "Jack" instead of "Sniper". So casual, so friendly.

"Russian mafia again?"

"No, it's more international. Maxos and his crew are still in South America and the Spanish police are looking for them. They're also underground because Black Python is searching too. It lost a fortune on its shares in MSP España and Bristol."

"You want me to deal with such nice people!"

"Precisely Jack, precisely."

THE END

Trader Jack

The Story of Jack Miner

Jack Miner, behind bars for a multi-billion scam and prime suspect for murder, proclaims his innocence. Desperate to prove that he didn't do it, he writes his own story.

From poverty to hedge fund trader, Jack's dealings and flight from the Russian mafia rapidly take him from London to Brazil, New York and South Africa. After a cut-throat betrayal, he becomes embroiled in market turmoil, fraud and murder.

In the world of money mania, swift deals and beautiful women, is Jack just 'another villain' or an innocent target?

Trader Jack is fiction, but it illustrates how fraudsters can manipulate the markets until they spin out of control. The character of Jack Miner is a blend of teenagers who have beaten market professionals in competitions and young, reckless city traders. Financial market scenes are humorous, exciting and easy to understand.

This is a thriller with a difference. It examines important issues: from the cocaine dealers' exploitation of Latin American coffee farmers to the shady underworld of the Russian Mafia. The novel reveals the stark contrast between the poverty-stricken underclass and extensive wealth in the financial community.

Reviews are on:- https://neilbehrmann.net/trader-jack-story-jack-miner/ and on Amazon

BUTTERFLY BATTLE

THE STORY OF THE GREAT INSECT WAR

Evil Superwasps invade the butterfly paradise of Leponea.
Nature loving Kim hears the butterflies call for help. She
and her brother Robert, enter the insect world and join in
the fight for freedom.

Robert, a war games enthusiast, forms the Allied Army
of butterflies, ants and other insects. He carefully makes
plans for battle. The Allies strike, but the cunning Super-
wasp Commander, counter attacks.

As thousands of soldiers fall, Robert finds that real
war is not just a computer game.

**Full review from the prestigious School Librarian,
magazine of the UK School Librarian Association:**

This is a highly original and exciting book. It tells the
story of a war between the insects: the superwasps versus
the rest. Two pre-pubescent children, Kim and Robert,
find themselves shrunken down to insect size and drafted
in to help. We follow their adventures and the saving of
Leponea, the land of the butterflies, and meet some wonderful characters on the way: Morpho, the brave, resource-
ful daughter of the emperor of all the butterflies and her
husband, Morphan. We also meet the demonical dictator,
Wreka, leader of the Superwasps. The book is masterly in
its interweaving or the lifestyles of various insects with the
demands of a modern war story: and Robert's understanding
of military strategy which he learned from his computer
games is handled with assurance and effect. Description

is a strong point of the book, especially the battle scenes which are magnificently conveyed. They are realistic and convincing, and will allow children to begin to understand something of the horror, as well as the heroism, of all wars. The black and white drawings are sensitive, well researched and detailed, adding a great deal to the visualisation of the text.

An exciting, fast-paced book which will appeal to children between 8 and 14. **Irene Babsky**

The London Parents' Guide

Computer-mad Robert spends his time playing electronic war games. His sister loves the outdoor life and longs to help endangered species. Outside their doors, there's very real danger in the insect world - Superwasps want to take control and are killing every insect in their way. The children get drawn into the Great Insect War and Robert finds his war strategy skills are the key to survival. He also learns that wars are not just about winning. A gripping fantasy on one level, there are many deep messages within the story. My 10yr old loved it.

Book background and more reviews can be found at:- https://neilbehrmann.net/butterfly-battle/ and Amazon.